BARBARA COPPERTHWAITE

Invisib

About the Author

Barbara Copperthwaite is a journalist with 20 years experience, who has been editor of a number of national magazines in the UK. She was raised in Skegness , Lincolnshire, and now lives in Birmingham.

INVISIBLE

BARBARA COPPERTHWAITE

Invisible

Copyright 2014 by Barbara Copperthwaite

The moral right of the author has been asserted.

All characters and events in this publication, other than those clearly in the public domain, are fictitious and any resemblance to real persons, living or dead, is purely coincidental.

All rights reserved.
No part of this publication may be reproduced, stored in a retrieval system, or transmitted, in any form or by any means, without the prior permission in writing of the author, nor be otherwise circulated in any form of binding or cover other than that in which it is published and without a similar condition including this condition being imposed on the subsequent purchaser.

INVISIBLE

BARBARA COPPERTHWAITE

Invisible

For Paul, whose generous spirit changed my life

*What doesn't kill you makes you stronger;
Thanks to everyone who has made me stronger.*

INVISIBLE

BARBARA COPPERTHWAITE

Invisible

JANUARY

Tues 15
There really isn't a thing to say. A year ago I'd have tried to say something. I'd have wracked my brain to find some inane comment to make. Probably about the programme we were watching. We're both sitting here watching the news, maybe I could say something about one of the stories…another soldier killed in Afghanistan, a big company announcing job cuts, the Prime Minister visiting a school somewhere or other… Not exactly light, chatty topics. The newsreader's voice drones on, but I'm finding it hard to concentrate. I wonder if Daryl will get curious about this diary and decide to have a sneaky read. I hope not, but it wouldn't surprise me; he hates secrets, likes to know everything that's going on in my head. Just the thought of him reading this though…damn, I've crinkled the paper, my hand clenching at the corner just at the thought of what he'd say. He'd be furious. But I've got to get my thoughts out somewhere, haven't I? I can't, simply can't face talking to him about this. Not yet.
From the corner of my eye I can see Daryl glancing at his mobile, thinking I won't notice. Or maybe he just doesn't care any more whether I noticed or not, in the same way that I've stopped caring about filling the silence between us. So, is it just me he doesn't have anything to say to any more?

INVISIBLE

Are there other people out there that he actually bothers communicating with properly?

Funny how I have so much to say to myself. In my head I can't shut my internal monologue off. Is this what happens to all marriages? Slowly but surely you just run out of interesting stuff to say and slide into the mundane, and finally into total silence. Like those couples in restaurants, who are clearly only there because the woman has insisted on a romantic night out or she'll kick off, so the bloke's given in for a quiet life. And they sit there, opposite each other, one more dressed up than the other because the evening means more to them, and each making polite conversation.

'How's your food?'

'Great, very nice. The sauce is just right. How's yours? Looks nice...'

'Mmmm, lovely...'

Then silence. An awkward glance around the room, trying to find something to comment on. The waiter surreptitiously looking over, fighting a smirk at the desperate atmosphere at the table. The clink of cutlery on plates filling the pause that grows longer and longer. A throat clearing. 'It really is *very* nice food...'

So I've started this diary, just so I have somewhere I can air my thoughts. Then I realised I'd nothing to put in it but the humdrum. Still, maybe that will galvanise me to actually do something to change my life, because on the very first, pristine page I wrote a little something, a sort of mantra I suppose, to try to focus myself.

If you're not happy with something, change it; if it won't change, get rid of it.

Doubt I will though– haven't so far have I? Let's face it, the vast majority of us start off in life thinking that we're going to do something amazing with our time on this planet –

didn't Shakespeare or Oliver Wendell Holmes or someone say something about how 'nothing is so commonplace as the wish to be remarkable'. Life kind of sucks you dry of those feelings though.

Actually it's not even that dramatic, it's just that all the other stuff of life gets in the way of really living; you know, the falling in love, getting a job to pay the bills, even watching telly, it all just conspires to stop you thinking about the big picture, and before you know it you're married to a man you barely say two words to, in a house that's all right but nothing special, in a job that's…beige. Bland, nothing special or inspiring about it. That's what happened to me anyway. Sometimes I think if something exciting doesn't happen to me soon I'll go mad.

Beside me, Daryl grabs the remote and switches over without even asking me after a report about some horrible rape up in Manchester pops up on the news. Sounds like she only just got away with her life. Do I pipe up, say something to Daryl about turning over, given that I was watching that? No, of course not. I can't be bothered. How am I going to motivate myself to do the extraordinary when I can't even be bothered to speak to someone sitting right beside me?

What is it with men and remote controls anyway? Why do they feel the need to keep hold of them? He's sat there now, holding it, finger running over the buttons absently. I wonder if cavemen only had clubs because they were remote control substitutes?

Sat 19

The highlight of my weekend so far has been nipping to the supermarket for an hour or so. Daryl was too exhausted to come; he didn't arrive until the wee small hours of last night having spent most of the week driving his truck on the continent. When I got back, he was up though, watching football on telly.

'Your mates came round,' he said, eyes never leaving the match.

'Which mates?' I groaned with the effort of lifting onto the kitchen counter a bag that was threatening to burst with shopping – not that my husband seemed to notice.

'Don't remember their names. Saggy tits, crazy hair – that was one of them. Yes! Did you see that?!' This last comment was about a goal. No, I hadn't seen it. No, I wouldn't have cared even if I had. As for the 'saggy tits' comment, sadly this is about par for the course. Daryl's not great at remembering the names of any of my friends (to his mind they aren't important enough to make that kind of effort) so instead they are described as a list of mainly unattractive attributes.

There is nothing even remotely saggy about Amy's boobs, they are just really rather big. As for her hair, she has fantastic shoulder-length pre-Raphaelite-type curls. Yet my man always, always refers to her as 'saggy tits' with the sometimes added extra of 'crazy hair'. She probably came round with Hannah, aka Bossy Cow, or sometimes Lesbian-Haired School Mate (we used to go to school together, and she currently sports an Audrey Heburn-esque crop).

'Did they leave a message or anything?' I asked tentatively. He held his hand up to silence me because something interesting was presumably happening on the box. I hate it when he does that.

Giving up on a reply, I went out to the car again and fetched another bag then struggled back into the kitchen, leaning to one side at a dangerous angle to compensate for the weight.

'Jesus, sorry, I'll help you,' said Daryl, finally jumping up, a gent at last. He brought the rest of the shopping in for me, bless him, but don't think I didn't notice that it was because it was half time.

Weds 30
I'm so very, very tired of being alone. I love Daryl but I have serious doubts about his love for me. Or at least, I know he loves me but I wonder what that love actually adds up to. I have a problem trusting him, but there's absolutely no reason why I feel like that. He's never cheated on me. So maybe that's just my problem: that I'm somehow always vaguely suspicious of him. It's because he's never around. He does so many hours, driving his lorry all round the country and Europe that he's often away all week and some weekends too. Sometimes I feel like I barely see him. Maybe we've just grown apart.
He just doesn't seem very interested in me. When I speak he doesn't bother listening half the time. Even today, we were talking over dinner and he asked what I'd been up to.
'Well, work was just work, you know... But I went jogging this morning, and it's starting to go really well. I've built up to fifteen minutes non-stop, and did that twice, with just a three minute walk in between to catch my breath! And you know what? It felt good!'
'Oh don't worry, you'll get there,' he said, glued to the news on telly.
I felt like screaming, 'Yes, if you'd been listening properly you'd know I'm already getting there!!!!' He quite clearly hadn't been listening to a word I'd said, the goings on of Manchester police were far more riveting.
Maybe my jogging isn't interesting to him, but he knows how hard I've been working on it and that it means a lot to me. I've always been a lard arse and now I'm finally making

an effort to get fit. Because if I'm overweight, it'll be harder to get pregnant... not that we're trying at the moment because he doesn't feel ready.

I just feel so desperately lonely. I'm 31 years old and have spent most of my adult life alone, because Daryl is never here. His work doesn't allow him home much, he sells days off and refuses to book holiday in advance most of the time because he never knows when he'll get a last minute trucking job.

Worse though, I feel lonely sometimes when I'm with him. Like at dinner just now. Like watching telly yesterday.

I want a husband who is a partner, someone who is there for me through the tough times, who likes listening to me witter on, who wants to spend time with me, and have kids. I don't want to be alone any more.

Even if Daryl desperately wants to be with me, his job will never allow it. If I don't have children I'll blame it on him and resent him, and I don't want that to happen. For all those reasons I don't see how Daryl and I can go on.

I know we made a commitment to one another when we married but...I feel lost. And I want a child so much! My clock is ticking so loud I think the alarm's about to go off. Life is slipping away, I feel as though I'm trapped in the top bulb of a huge egg-timer and each hour is a grain of sand slipping away beneath me, each day makes my footing more treacherous. Life is escaping, my chances of having a child are dissipating, and I'm not doing anything about it!

One day soon I'll wake up old, alone, no kids, a shitty career, and a relationship where I spend 60 per cent of my time alone – in fact, no, closer to 80 per cent, or even 90 per cent of my spare time.

Would things be any better if we had a child? I don't know. I've a horrible feeling the answer is no though, because it wouldn't change the fundamental problem – the amount and quality of time we spend together.

For all those reasons I don't see what future we can have together – or at least what happy future we can have. Bugger. Am I really thinking of ending my marriage?

Thurs 31
I can't do it. I know as soon as I see his face I'll crumble because, sensible or not, I love him. Oh bloody hell.
This is just a blip. We just have to try harder.

FEBRUARY

Sun 3

I'm really bored. Daryl had said he might be able to come home and see me, but I've heard no word. It probably means he won't be coming over, but I've still made no plans, just in case – I so rarely get to see my husband these days, so I don't want to mess up any chance I have by arranging to see someone else. Not now I've decided that I need to make more effort. That *we* need to make more effort if we're to keep the marriage together.

I wonder if he even realises how close we are to the edge? I wonder if, if he did realise, he would want to pull us back from it or simply give us a nudge so that we plummet into freefall?

But I have decided freefall is not for me. It's an exhilarating theory, hurtling through life with nothing but the sound of the air rushing past to distract me, nothing to stop me or get in my way. Freedom. But the reality of freefall is that the ground is waiting below you, hard, unforgiving, and it's going to bloody hurt when you hit it. That's what life outside of marriage would be: a great theory but in practise it would be hard and horrible and I'd suddenly realise how much better off I was in it. Nope, I'm clinging on to my marriage, teetering back from the brink.

It all sounds very dramatic but practically speaking it just consists of me hanging around, waiting to spend time with Daryl. But, after lurking round the house all day like some kind of lost soul haunting the fridge (my favourite place to hover when bored. No matter how many times I peer inside it or the surrounding cupboards, I always hope there'll suddenly be something tasty and wonderful in there that I've somehow missed all the other times I've peered in. Shockingly there never is) I decided to call Amy yesterday afternoon.

It was actually good fun. Went shopping then to the pictures to see that rom com with whatsherface in it – can't remember her name but she's always in that type of thing. Then we ended up coming back here and eating pizza, listening to music and watching classic Moulin Rouge, and drinking vodka until 5am… See, not having kids does have some advantages!

So now I'm that lost soul again, lurking round the house, waiting. I don't mind so much, not really, because I'm so tired from all that drinking. I haven't had an all-nighter like that in ages! Too long really. There's not enough fun in my life.

Tomorrow I'm going to get up extra early before work and do my exercise dvd. And hope Daryl will call.

Wonder if there are any nice treats hiding in the fridge… No, stuff it; I'm off to the corner shop. Ric, the owner, is always only too happy to sell me emergency chocolate. Just going there makes me happy; he's always got such a big smile on his face, and calls all the women 'lady' and all the men 'sir'. 'Thank you, lady, have a wonderful day,' he always smiles at me, it's so sweet.

Mon 4

At 2am the phone rang. I must have sounded very unattractive, all gravelly-voice and confused from being shocked from sleep, trying to stop my heart from pounding through my chest. Still, Daryl had sounded happy to hear my voice.

INVISIBLE

'Hello gorgeous,' he exclaimed, and I'd known at once two things. One: he was in a really good mood; the kind of mood that's contagious. Honestly, when he's like that being near him is like being near the sun. And two: he wasn't going to be coming over.

My head slumped back into the pillow, too disappointed and tired to be bothered with the faff of attempting to sit up.

'Sorry Gorgeous, I've been delayed, there's no way I'll make it home,' he said. Didn't even have the decency to sound upset, Mr bloody Chipper.

Still, I swallowed down my annoyance. If I'd let it show it only would have led to an argument and him huffing something like: 'See, this is why I never normally bother phoning you. Cos when I make the effort you have a go!' And then he'd slam the phone down and switch it off, which he knows drives me mental.

So, instead I blinked my eyes several times so I'd sound more awake than I felt, and made myself smile because, well, I know it might be daft but I always think you can hear a smile. Seriously, I think it makes a difference to the way people sound.

And then I made myself say, 'It doesn't matter, babe. It would have been lovely to see you, but I know you tried your best.' For good measure, I added, 'And I really appreciate you calling me to tell me.'

I added that because I'd read an article about training puppies and about how they need praise when they do well. And the bad stuff? You ignore it rather than shout, because shouting is giving them attention; apparently, for them any attention is better than nothing. That had struck a chord with me, and made total sense. Maybe because I crave attention, any kind of attention, from Daryl. I'd rather be shouted at than ignored. Sometimes I feel like I'm disappearing, like I'm becoming invisible in this relationship. Barely talking, barely existing, barely being listened to.

But it will change. Things will get better.

Anyway, why I'd remembered this article in the middle of the night when Daryl called is beyond me, but I figured a bit of praise for the fact he'd actually listened to me and bothered calling for once to let me know what was going on would go a long way. Maybe he'd realise it really was good to call home and keep me informed, instead of simply avoiding giving me information in case I got angry with him if he gave me bad news.

Of course the real irony – and this didn't escape me even as I turned my too hot pillow over to its cooler side and tried to get back to sleep again – was that he always says he doesn't tell me because I'll get annoyed with him. He always makes out like I have a bad temper. Yet whenever I run our arguments back in my mind it's always him who is angry. Maybe I'm going mad, but sometimes I wonder if I'm being manipulated a bit.

No, that's just silly, middle-of-the-night thoughts. Funny how you always get silly thoughts in the middle of the night – good job people sleep then!

Really did appreciate the call though. Maybe he's finally listening to me and realising that what I ask from him really isn't much; just a little courtesy, a little respect, a little love and consideration.

Weds 6

It was the engine that gave the game away. I was sitting on the bed, gazing into the mirror and putting the last touches to my eye shadow as I got ready for work. Then I heard it: that deep thrumming that could almost be felt in the ground, rising up through the soles of my feet and coming to rest in my solar plexus; the psssht of the hydraulic brakes; the tiny squeal that was almost too high to be heard by humans.

For a second I met my own shocked look in the mirror as I realised what it meant, rejected it, then decided it really was the only option – and my cheeks went all pink at the prospect. Chucking down my make-up brush, I raced to the bedroom window and looked down.

Yes! Daryl was here! He grinned at me from the cab, waved, then clambered down.

'Surprise!' he called.

I laughed, catching his excited mood immediately. He was really buzzed up, eyes bright, body almost trembling with nervous energy as he jumped down and strode to the front door with such purpose that my breath caught.

Lots of men in films and books are described as striding, but Daryl really does. At 6ft 3in, he has the kind of long legs that can do that, and broad shoulders too; he towers over me by more than a foot. He's incredibly powerfully built, and somehow his bald head seems to emphasise it, showing off the muscles of his jaw and neck. Phwoar!

I raced down the stairs in time to run into his arms, no hesitation; not when he was so happy. His massive arms wrapped round me and swung me round, then he gave me a huge, passionate kiss that made my stomach flip.

'Hey Gorgeous,' he boomed. So strong, so...extreme and over-the-top. But this is my Daryl, the man I love and it makes me feel alive when he's like this, as though some of that energy somehow transfers to me, and all thoughts of being peed off with my marriage disappear.

'Thought I'd surprise you. I finished my run sooner than I thought,' he said. His grin grew even wider at some memory, probably of some crazy driving or something he'd had to do to achieve this early finish. 'Yeah, it was a lot more successful than I thought it would be,' he nodded, attention snapping suddenly back to me. 'So who better to celebrate with than my babe?'

It's funny really, how he never calls me by my name. I am Gorgeous, Babe, even Stroppy Mare sometimes, but never, ever does he say my name. When we first got together I thought it was wonderful to have a pet name, as though somehow it bound us closer because it was a secret between the two of us. Sometimes now though, it just makes me feel even more that I am disappearing, the real me unseen and nameless.

But I refused to think such sad things today, not while Daryl was in a glorious mood, the sun was shining, and I was in his arms.

Full of joy, I buried my head in the funny little hollow in his chest where his muscles don't quite meet, the bit he hates because he thinks it makes him look puny, but which I love because it feels like it's made just for me, and squeezed him tight. Breathed in that wonderful Daryl smell, a unique mix of diesel, engine oil and Lynx Africa that always clung to him.

Yes, my man was really home, had come to surprise me and spend the whole day with me. My smile grew against his jumper. Then it faltered. Hesitantly, I looked up. 'Oh no, I can't spend the day with you,' I half groaned, half whispered. 'I've got to go to work.'

'That doesn't matter, take the day off,' he breezed. Actually breezed, like it was obvious. 'Come on, how often do we get a whole day together?'

I suppose I should have been insulted really that he just assumed I would drop everything for him without so much as a moment's notice, but...come on, who was I kidding. A day's work or a day with my fella? When he's in this mood and we won't be sitting awkwardly in front of the telly? It wasn't exactly a hard choice.

Before I'd had a chance to worry or change my mind, I was on the phone, faking a sore throat. My distraction must have only added to the bad acting, making me sound more convincing, because Daryl wasn't even waiting for me to finish the conversation before nibbling at my neck from behind and ripping open my blouse, hands cupping my breasts almost aggressively. Where the hell had this come from?

Well, I wasn't going to stop to question it – and honestly, when he's in the mood there's no stopping him anyway! With a squeaky 'Got to go, feel a bit...hot and wobbly!' to my boss, Keith, I put the phone down and surrendered myself to my man.

We don't have sex much any more, not since he developed the 'little problem' that I'm not allowed to mention. Apparently all men go through it at some stage, I just never thought he'd be one of them, and I know it sounds selfish but it makes me feels like it's my fault, like I'm no longer attractive enough for him… But to be swept off my feet like that was, wow. It was lovely.

You see, we can be romantic sometimes! For all my boredom and frustration, I do love Daryl and want to be with him. In fact, that's what causes the problems. If I didn't feel that way it'd be easy to just walk away and leave him.

Afterwards I felt so relaxed. Closer to him than I have in months, like something invisible had reconnected. Twisting in his arms, I turned to him, looking into those bright, cold-blue eyes as I idly ran my fingers through the dark curls of hair scattered over his chest. In that instant, for once feeling brave and in control and calm – and positive – I told Daryl that I wasn't happy and that things had to change. Said he had two choices.

'Either you can talk to a counsellor and get over this mental block about kids and well, your temper sometimes, or you could tackle it yourself. It's up to you,' I said gently, straightening a hair and watching it spring back into shape, unchanged, unchangeable. Running a finger over his collar bones and up his neck, trying to keep him soothed and calm like I might an injured dog that may growl and lash out unexpectedly at any second. 'Things have to change between the two of us. We're in trouble. And I want children, you know I do. It's time, I'm ready, and I don't want to put it off any longer. But you're not ready...'

Daryl didn't seem to know what to say. But he didn't fly off the handle and that is a good start. Didn't start saying how I was the one with the problem so I should look at fixing myself before having a go at him – that's the kind of thing he generally throws at me. Anything rather than discuss the actual problems we're having.

I understand why he's so emotionally closed off and hesitant to have children, what with his past. I'll never forget that time he told me about his mum, way back when we'd very first started dating nine long years ago.

He'd looked like a little boy then, those massive hands of his twisting the hem of his shirt backwards and forwards like he'd been trying to wring the life out of it.

I hadn't dared move, in case I'd broken the spell; I'd had a feeling something big was about to happen. Those bright blue eyes of his, so piercing that sometimes they feel like they can laser-beam straight into my soul, had come up so suddenly to meet mine. There'd been the strangest look on his face as he'd forced his fingers to still, his hands to stop wringing. Something almost dangerous; they'd been such a cold, steely blue that they'd reminded me of the dead eyes of sharks. I'd realised why as he'd spoken.

'Me and Mum aren't close,' he'd admitted softly. And the second he'd said those words his eyes had softened back to the more usual bright blue. I've never known anyone before whose eyes seem almost to change colour with his mood, but Daryl's do. Right then, I'd known he'd made a momentous decision about me, something I couldn't understand.

He'd decided to let me in, just the tiniest bit.

'I used to get bullied at school. These g-' he'd stopped short then continued. Had he been about to say girls, or had he just cleared his throat? 'These kids made my life a misery. Called me rubberlips. All the time, it never stopped.'

Daryl has full lips. All right, so his top lip is quite long, a bit like that old prime minister we had, who was it? Yeah, John Major. But that's the only thing he has in common with him; my Daryl is tall, strapping, handsome, with pale skin but not pasty. He even suits having his hair shaved off, since his dark wavy hair started receding badly two years ago. And he always has the most wonderful, comforting smell to him. Diesel and oil mixed with aftershave to create something so uniquely him that whenever I inhale it I feel like I'm home. After all these years of working around engines the aroma is impregnated into his skin; no matter how much he showers he can never get rid of it. It's another thing he hates about himself, but that I love.

Anyway, I've gone off the subject – but suffice to say, anyone picking on my fella's lips is just being rotten for rotten's sake.

Still, I hadn't said any of that to him, not right at that moment nine years ago; still too scared to break the spell. He'd picked up his coffee then, taken a slurp as if to lubricate the passage of the words that were stuck in his throat. Then his big hands had cupped it protectively – like it was protecting him like a shield, I mean, not the other way round. His fingers had obscured bits of the 'World's best trucker' logo that ran round it front and back, making it look a bit rude if you were trying to piece together what it said just from the fragments left showing.

My own coffee had been going cold, but I hadn't cared. Because I'd known that what he was about to tell me was about more than just being bullied by kids.

'They picked on me all the time. I'd tried holding my lips in to make them less big, less ugly,' he'd continued finally. 'Thought if I trained my muscles that somehow they'd start doing it automatically and hey presto, no stupid, big, fat rubber lips any more. Didn't work that way, of course. Nothing stopped me looking the way I did, nothing stopped the bullies.

'They'd scrawl my nickname on the board at school, chant it in the playground until it felt like the whole world was joining in, leave notes in my bag or desk threatening to rip my lips off if I told anyone what was happening. They'd steal my sports kit and throw it on top of the flat roof of one of the classrooms so that they could watch me trying to climb up and get it back; or just stuff rubbish into the bag or pour yoghurt over it so that then I'd get into trouble with the teacher for not having my kit – I couldn't tell them what had actually happened or my life would have been made an even bigger misery.

'I just reached a stage where I couldn't take any more. I ran home one day, told Mum about it because I knew I couldn't deal with it alone any more. Told her things were so bad that I wanted to die. "So what, dear?" she said. Just like that, "so what". Like it wasn't a big deal.'

Bloody Cynthia, I could just imagine her saying something like that. I can't stand the woman, she's so odd, so cold and unemotional. And she calls everyone 'Dear' yet manages to makes it sounds nothing like an endearment...it's quite a skill.

Daryl's words had seemed freerer suddenly at the moment, like the coffee had washed away whatever had been causing the blockage of emotion. He'd taken another sip to be sure, then carried on.

'When she said that, I'd realised then that I really was totally alone. There wasn't a single person in the world who gave a stuff about me. I'd run up to my room then, locked myself in. She didn't bother coming upstairs to check on me...not for three days.'

I hadn't been able to stop myself then. 'Three days?!' I'd gasped.

That couldn't be right. What mum would do that to their own kid, just let them hide for days on end because they were so traumatised, and not even be bothered to comfort them. His dad had died in a car crash before Daryl was born, so there had only been Daryl and his mum, no one else for him to turn to.

At that moment I'd been able to imagine him – still can – a poor little confused kid, longing for someone to hug him and tell him everything's going to be all right; longing for someone to get angry and take on the battle for him, saying 'I'll get straight down that school and sort this – I'll give them what for!'

Poor kid should have had his mum making him his favourite comfort food of sausage and mash to cheer him up, then cuddling up and watching his top programme on telly too. Even letting him stay up a bit later than usual as a treat, so he knows he's not in trouble.

Certainly what any sane parent would not do is leave their kid alone after something like that. And definitely not for three whole days. So I'd reckoned I'd clearly misheard him.

But no. His flaming mother had let him sob his little heart out for half a week, starve himself because he didn't come out for meals even. God knows what his bedroom must have smelled like, with him not going out even to the loo…

That's why I hate Daryl's mum, Cynthia. And yes, I do understand why he's not mad keen on having kids himself. Poor bloke's probably terrified he'll be about as good a parent as she was. But we can get past this thing, together – with a little help from a counsellor maybe.

That's what I told him as we lay in bed today. He said he'll think about seeing a therapist.

'I'll be there for you,' I whispered. I know the thought of talking to a stranger terrifies him and I'm very proud of him for taking this step. Hope we make it.

Thurs 7

Met up with Kim for lunch today. Although we work in the same office we don't get the chance to chat much, so it's always good to take our break together.

After our usual round of slagging off the boss and saying how much better a job we could do than him if only we were in charge, we got down to the real business – exchanging gossip and having a catch up. I couldn't wait to tell her about my glorious day of skiving with Daryl.

I knew it wouldn't go any further, we tell each other everything, could both blackmail each other from here to kingdom come with the amount of information we've got on each other. Besides, I know for a fact that that '24 hour stomach bug' she had the other week was actually her staying at home with her boyfriend (why she would want to let that weasely runt near her with a bargepole is not something I shall dwell on).

So I expected her to be happy for me. Instead, she looked like she'd just sipped sour milk and was trying not to let it show, her mouth twisting to one side slightly in a weird cross between grimace and smile, her cat-shaped eyes narrowing almost imperceptibly. It took the shine right off my mood, I can tell you.

'What?' I demanded, aiming for jokey, sounding closer to snappy.

'Well…just…' I could tell she was choosing her words carefully, her eyes glued to her chips as she dunked one into the yolk of her fried egg, breaking its delicate skin so that the contents spilled out across the plate. Finally, as she lifted the yellow-nubbed fry to her mouth she looked up at me and hurled the words out in a hurry. 'Don't you think sometimes you end up doing more what he wants than what you want?'

As a full stop, she shoved the chip quickly into her mouth, as if to stop herself from saying more that she might regret.

'No, I wanted to stay at home with my husband. I wanted to spend time with him, and frankly I wanted to have great sex. So, no, I reckon I did exactly what I wanted, and can't see a problem with it.'

I forced my voice to stay light, even though my heart was thumping a bit and I could feel the heat storming across my skin and making my cheeks flame.

I really, really hate confrontation, but there was no way I was going to take criticism from a woman whose own relationship is a total and utter mess and she can't even see it! Seriously, our nickname for her fella, Sam, is Psycho. Says it all really, doesn't it.

Bracing myself for a row, I pushed my chair back slightly with a high-pitched scrape, while at the same time easing my plate away from me. I couldn't face food, not now.

But instead of an argument, Kim did something even worse. She just looked at me, mouth smiling, but eyebrows knitted together and raised so high in the middle that they did a pretty good impression of Kilimanjaro. It was a pitying look she was giving me.

'I just worry about you,' she said apologetically. Her brow had so many ridges in it that it almost looked frilly. Then it smoothed as she shrugged and sank another chip into the egg. End of subject. To show we were still mates, I nicked a chip off her plate.

I didn't bother telling her about the rest of my day with Daryl though. About how I'd felt all warm and fuzzy inside ever since, like someone in a Mills and Boon. I refused to let her negativity seep in and slowly cool my warm glow and make my fuzzy all sharp again.

The problem is, people just don't understand me and Daryl. There's no point in me talking to anyone about us, because they just don't get it.

Fri 8

Ooooh, lunchtime gossip was that Kim has decided to finish with Psycho Sam. Hurray!

Sat 9

Okay, what I'm trying to think of right now is 'what the hell can I do for Valentine's Day?' Ah, the eternal question. Something nice and romantic, which shows I really do care, but not off-puttingly sloppy. At first I tried to think of things men would like but drew a blank. Then I tried to think of things I'd like and came up with quite a few ideas.

Then I got depressed because I realised that what I actually wanted was for Daryl to do something like this for me, not the other way round. I want so much for him to give me stupid, big gestures and thoughtful stuff. To show me he cares. Maybe I actually want to change him. Or maybe it's not that he's not like that…maybe it's that he's not like that *for me.* Because he doesn't love me enough.

So now I'm scared. I was supposed to be planning Valentine's Day and instead I'm depressed.

What's more, I'm fat. I don't just feel fat, I am fat. 10st. And under one week until VD (that actually looks really wrong written down!) so no chance of losing any pounds, really. Bet Daryl won't even be around either, bet he's working. He's always bloody working. God, I feel so alone.

One thing's for sure, sitting here moping won't make me feel any better. So…my romantic ideas are:

1 List the reasons why I love Daryl, and what makes him unique. Put each one on a bit of paper and pin up round the room. I read about this one in a magazine. Sweet but, to my mind, verging on obsessive. Maybe just list in a card instead?

2 Have an indoor picnic, with finger food and low lights and candles, in the lounge. Feed one another, then dance to his favourite Barry White CD, and our song: You're My First, My Last, My Everything.

3 Take him to a show (he'd probably hate that though, so more for me than him!)

I wish he'd do something like this for me. I know it's pathetic and needy, but I genuinely really do need something wonderful right now. Need a bit of magic. Feeling a bit low, actually.

Still, Daryl's going to start seeing a therapist and I'm really proud of him for that. But that's for him, not me. If I'm honest I'm terrified he'll turn around after a few sessions and say, 'Thanks for standing by me and being there for me but actually I've realised our problems stem from the fact I don't love you. That's why I can't commit properly to this marriage. That's why I work all hours and am never around. That's why I don't want kids…with you.'
I don't want to be alone.

Tues 12
Daryl really genuinely is making the effort with me. He called me at work today, at 11.30am, and asked if I could nip out – because he was outside waiting for me! So we went to a café round the corner for half an hour. Very naughty!
I was terrified I'd be caught and get a telling off from the boss, and it meant I was behind for the rest of the day, but I don't care! I'll put my headphones on tomorrow and ignore the world and get the report typed up double-quick. I always work better under pressure.
Anyway, back to D. Yes, he is making an effort. He even called me tonight at 10pm, before he started work, just to say hello. Sweet. Mind you, when I asked him earlier when his appointment with the counsellor was he said it was 'top of his list of priorities to sort' today. And he didn't mention it just now on the phone so I bet he hasn't done it. That will be the real test of how much effort he's making, whether he really does start seeing someone or if he was just agreeing to keep me happy…
Change of subject! Kim sent me a text yesterday morning saying she and Sam had had a big row and he'd hit he. She has a black eye! Very dramatic and very worrying. She

hasn't told me what happened properly yet, but presumably she finished with him like she said she was going to, and it all kicked off.

Well, at least a black eye should show her once and for all that he is to be steered well clear of, that there is no going back after something like that

I'm sorry, but ever since she got together with runty Sam her life has been one drama after another. She's a gorgeous, model-like 5ft 10in Asian woman who has the shiniest waist-length black hair like flipping Rapunzel. The problem is, she is a single mum to little Henry, a cheeky three-year-old who keeps her on her toes – and makes her convinced that as a single mum she will never be able to find a decent man who will take her on. So she puts up with Psycho Sam instead, who has mousey-coloured hair to go with his rat-like features, weak build and 5ft 9in stature. I'd like to say he's got a nice personality, but no, he's possessive and weird. It's no surprise to me that such a wimp feels the need to 'prove himself a real man' by slapping his girlfriend around and belittling her. Pathetic!

When I see her I'll have to sit her down and have a proper good chat with her. Get the whole story, and talk some sense into her. To think, she says she worries about me and Daryl! Oh the irony! Not that I'm going to say anything to her like that, of course, because the fact is I'm dead worried for her. She needs to get out of that relationship before that nutter hurts her.

At the moment though, the poor love is in hiding at home from what I can make out, because she has a black eye and is too ashamed to be seen in work. She'll have to come back in eventually though, she can't stay away until it fades altogether surely; that'll be days and days and she just can't afford to miss so much work.

I'm tempted to call her. I keep staring at the phone as though somehow the useless lump of plastic will help me know what the right thing is to do. I've even picked it up a couple of times, stared at it a bit more, then put it down with a sigh.

If I call her and Sam is there and answers it, will he guess I know what happened? Will I just make things worse for her? But what if she's all alone and feeling like no one cares? I really don't know what to do, but at the moment I'm opting for doing nothing. Interfering in people's private lives is never a good idea, is it? Kim will come to me when she wants someone to talk to.

Weds 13
Daryl and I went for a walk along the beach today because I finished work early. It was perfect. We were looking at all the shells and Daryl found a beautiful little white rock, rubbed smooth by the sea, with a black, flint hole worn through the middle of it that shone.

'It's beautiful,' I smiled.

'Not as beautiful as you. Nowhere near,' he shrugged. 'You're my Gorgeous.' Then he put his arm round me and we watched the sun setting over the waves. It was one of those rare, perfect times. I popped the rock in my pocket. I'll remember that moment forever.

That's when it hit me, what I should give him for Valentine's Day. I'll give him the rock. It's symbolic of that perfect moment we shared, of all the perfect moments we've shared, and the fact that he's my rock.

He's the person I want to spend my life with, and I can always rely on him to be there for me. Maybe not immediately, because of his job, but when it comes down to it he'd drop everything and be there for me, I'm certain. If my life were in danger, like happens in films sometimes, the first person I'd call would be Daryl. There's something so strong and capable about him, he's so able to think outside the box and just is unlike other people. I know he'd take on the world without hesitation if someone tried to hurt me. He's a very physical man; yes he lacks a bit of the emotional expression sometimes, but he's my rock, unchanging, reliable, beautiful in his hardness. I feel really pleased by the idea.

Thurs 14
I gave him a rock. 'Because you're my rock,' I explained to him. He looked down at the stone with the hole in it, the one we'd picked up together on the beach, and his face was totally blank. He didn't get it. It meant nothing to him. And I felt like a total prat.
I gave him a rock. What the hell was I thinking?

Fri 15
Keep thinking about Kim. I wonder how she's doing?
I haven't heard from Daryl today. Very paranoid he'll let me down. Don't know what is wrong with me, am very emotional. Cried on train to work this morning, cried in the loos at work…am crying all the time, at the drop of a hat, in fact. Also very changeable. For a second I wondered if it was crazy hormones, and got so excited because I thought I might be pregnant. Then I got nervous at the idea of it actually being real, and was kind of relieved when I realised I couldn't possibly be pregnant.
It got me thinking though. How would Daryl actually feel if I were expecting? I mean, if an 'accident' were to happen? Maybe I should just plan an accident…? But the thought

makes me feel panicky and tight in the chest, like I'm being constricted. It feels...wrong.

The thing is I do desperately want a child but Daryl needs to be around more otherwise I might as well be a single mother. Raising a child is hard work and if he's still away trucking all the time then I don't think I can cope. I want a family not just a child – baby, mum and dad, all together, not just with dad popping in occasionally when he feels like it, enjoying all the good bits.

Sometimes he does agree to trying but within hours he is denying it, or moving the goalposts. 'In two years' is his favourite thing. 'We'll try in two years,' he says. But he's been saying that for the last six years, and yet somehow the right time still hasn't arrived. I'm like little orphan bloody Annie, singing about how 'tomorrow is always a day away'.

Besides, there's a slightly cynical bit of me that suspects Daryl when he decides he wants me to have a kid. I feel like he suggests it to shut me up and maybe to control me a bit more. It's terrible of me to think like that, isn't it. Truly, if I think he's capable of such manipulation then why on earth am I with him? No, he couldn't do such an awful thing.

He can be so changeable though. Sometimes I feel like I'm riding a rollercoaster, our relationship is that same mix of euphoria and terror and out-of-control feeling and everything is just rushing towards me but it's too quick for me to react, to take it in or understand it, it's just an emotional blur and only when I get off at some point, with shaky legs and hammering heart, will I be able to stand back and look at it for what it is. And think 'wow, I survived that!' and laugh because it's brilliant and fun, and a bit scary. And want to do it again.

INVISIBLE

I mean, just look at the last month. I've been reading back some of the stuff I've written (so glad I started keeping this diary!) and I'm all over the place. Bored, wanting to finish things, paranoid that Daryl is manipulating me – then desperate for a baby, head over heels in love.

He's right, the problem is me not him.

But life with him can be...not scary, but definitely...unpredictable and heart-racing. He's always either one extreme or the other, there is no halfway with him. Of course that's also what attracts me to him, I suppose. He does have an air of danger about him, but he also has the biggest, loudest laugh and a grin that just transforms his sometimes stern-looking face. I mean, he actually throws his head back with laughter; how many people do that?

When I try to describe him to people he sounds like a caricature almost. He's too large for life. His laugh too big, his smile too wide, his temper too huge. How can I best explain it to someone who doesn't know him? Well, there is one way of illustrating it...

After heavy rain, we love to go for a walk. There's something exhilarating about the heavy, tinny, soil smell that hangs in the air, the charge of electricity that seems to stay there and freshen everything up. As we walk, Daryl will stop and pick up wriggling earthworms which have strayed onto the pavement.

'They'll get squashed by people,' he explains. He carefully handles them, like they are the most precious cargo in the world, and places them onto a nearby grass verge.

Our walks always take forever after a rainstorm, but I never mind because seeing this strapping, muscular man with massive hands delicately saving worms is one of the most heart-melting sights in the world to me. Imagine that.

Then imagine the day I heard a meow in the house. I'd thought I was going mad as I'd looked around, because there wasn't any sign of a cat. Then it had come again, sounding really muffled, and I'd slowly realised it seemed to be coming from the cupboard under the stairs.

The poor thing must have sneaked into the house when I'd left the front door open while I was backwards and forwards washing the car, I'd thought in horror, and got trapped somehow in the cupboard. So I'd opened it up expecting to find a hungry, thirsty and possibly very annoyed cat. But I couldn't see one anywhere.

When I'd heard the meow again I'd frozen because…there was one of those free rucksacks you get on magazines and stuff sometimes, you know, the really light, thin ones…and it had just moved.

For a second, maybe even longer to be honest, I'd just stood there, stock still, thinking: 'It's moving, and the meow is coming from there, which means there's a cat in there. But there can't be a cat in there, how could there be a cat in there? I mean, how the bloody hell would it manage to not only sneak into the house and get trapped in the cupboard, but also clamber for some unknown reason into a bag – and then pulled the drawstring tight behind it so that it couldn't get out. Oh, and tie a knot in that drawstring too.'

Like someone had cut the strings holding me in place, I'd moved suddenly. Leapt forward, shaky fingers undoing the knot, pulling the bag open, and lifting a terrified moggy free of its prison.

Then Daryl's voice had sounded behind me. 'That'll teach the little shit to come in here again,' he'd said. Then he'd laughed. Well, chuckled. Which in a way is more sinister, because a chuckle is so kind of little and light-hearted, isn't it; more sort of innocent.

And you know how sometimes people say they felt like their blood froze in their veins? Well, I reckon mine did too. I went shivery cold from head to toe, actually got goosebumps all over. I couldn't move, couldn't speak, because I was terrified. Terrified of my fella. The man I share a bed with, tell my secrets to, have vowed to stay with until the day I die.

Even remembering that day makes me feel cold. But then I remember the earthworms and realise that I was just being silly. I've got an overactive imagination; Mum's always said so. But see what I mean about Daryl? Two extremes, never a middle ground. Roaring with laughter, roaring with rage. Supportive, cutting. Cruel, kind.

There have been so many ups and downs between us lately that it'll do me good to get away and have a good think. I'm meant to be going to Salzburg a week today with Amy and Hannah, but although I've booked the ticket I'm not convinced it will happen. I thought it would be a laugh but now Hannah has dropped out with some muttered, crappy excuse so it'll just be me and Amy.

I get the feeling Han and Amy are peed off with me for some reason. Don't have the faintest idea why. I always used to get invited to stuff with them and now I don't. Every time I arrange to see Han she cancels on me at the last minute. Amy has been distinctly cool of late too. Think will email Han tomorrow and have it out. Let's face it, what do I have to lose? Reckon I've already lost their friendship.

Wonder if Daryl will come home tomorrow, or even bother calling me. He said he'd call today, but I was in a very weird mood last night and probably scared him off! Fancy getting so upset that he didn't like a silly stone. Reacting like it was the end of the world because he didn't understand my stupid, schmaltzy, over-the-top sentiments.

And now, because I got in a mood, I've probably hurt his feelings. The poor bloke can't know what on earth is going on. I mean, he bought me six red roses and a box of chocs, how sweet is that? And I still wasn't satisfied! Though the card was a bit of a disappointment, but it's Daryl's sense of humour, he loves a smutty joke and is a very physical man. Bit obsessed with sex actually (though all talk and little action these days)....

Yes, he could have been more romantic, but what the hell am I complaining about when he bought me presents that most women can only dream of? It doesn't get more romantic than flowers and chocs!

Oh, I'm being silly wondering if he's coming home tomorrow. He has to because we're seeing Zoe and Rick from the Florida holiday tomorrow. Might be fun. That holiday last year was such a laugh, it'll be good for me and him to have a night out together and relive a bit of it. Might help us reconnect, meeting up with the old crowd. You know what it's like on holiday, people always have good intentions of staying in touch, but looks like we really meant it, us Florida lot!

Sat 16
Wonderful. So far today I've been blown out by Daryl, who couldn't come home because he got a last minute job (he was actually really apologetic, so I'm not mad with him). Then by Amy, who told me she's not going to Salzburg for various pathetic reasons. She got the wrong weekend and has arranged to see her mum, she's skint, tra la la. Rubbish.

INVISIBLE

There's something else going on here, I'm not stupid. I just wish I knew what the hell it was.

Then I decided to have a word with Han (well, an email). I'd spoken to Kim about it and she agreed that it was the right plan of action. So I asked if I'd offended Hannah in some way because she seems weird and stuff, and things aren't right between us. To be honest, I felt like a kid in the playground again, a grown woman should not have to have a conversation like this! Still…

She replied she could ask me the same thing because I've been weird with her! Well maybe I have but only because she started it. Not that I could say that of course, because that would sound really childish in this already regressive situation.

After a bit of to-ing and fro-ing we seemed to thaw things out and ended with saying stuff like 'it's great to have you back because I've missed you' and all that silliness. Well, I say it's silliness but actually I do have to admit to having a bit of a warm, fuzzy feeling afterwards, am so relieved things are sorted. And yet… I still get the funny feeling things aren't right.

Anyway. When Amy let me down I sent Daryl a text telling him and asking if he fancied an impromptu dirty weekend in Salzburg. I mean, how are we meant to even consider trying for a baby when we barely see each other and when we do we hardly ever have sex. Not that I sent that bit to him, of course.

As soon as I sent the text, my phone rang. 'Hey Gorgeous, this sounds like a great idea!' said Daryl. He sounded so up for it – brilliant! He'd got me on speakerphone because he was driving, but even over the engine noise, I could tell he really meant it, and was in a fantastic mood.

'Wonderful! Well the seats are all booked and paid for so it seems a shame for them to go to waste,' I smiled. 'Finally I'm starting to look forward to this weekend! I'll have to revise my whole getaway wardrobe now that it isn't a girlie break...'

'Well don't get too excited,' he warned. 'I'll have to check the roster first, see if I can get the time off.' I could hear a shuffling noise as he opened and closed compartments, searching for the elusive piece of paper he had his jobs jotted down on. It's a flipping mystery that bit of paper, by the way – I can never catch so much of a glimpse of it, and it seems to change at the drop of a hat...well, unless I actually want it to change, then it seems even more set in stone than the Ten Commandments.

The rustling and thumping continued, and I started to get really excited. 'Hey, keep your eyes on the road,' I teased. He seemed in a good enough mood that I could risk teasing him a little.

As he grunted a reply and carried on searching, I started compiling a list in my head of things I needed to take. I'd have to include some sexy undies – maybe I should nip out and buy some new stuff, surprise Daryl. Something lacy and black and red and obvious? No, not Daryl's thing; he absolutely loves virginal white underwear. He doesn't like tarty stuff at all, even though he is always trying to peer down my top!

Then I heard that growly groan he does when he's disappointed. My stomach dropped like I'd missed a step going down the stairs. 'Sorry babe, I'm free on Friday, but on the Saturday I'm doing a job, Manchester to Tilbury Docks, 700 mile round trip of pulp for a paper mill. Want to come?' he said.

'Tilbury docks?' I asked, trying desperately to make the leap from romantic weekend abroad, luxuriating in a posh hotel, taking in the incredible architecture, and hopefully making love an awful lot, to a night in a smelly truck, visiting a papermill. Still, maybe it wasn't as bad as it sounded… 'You go there a lot don't you? What's it like?

'Yeah, it's massive. The size of 425 footy pitches.' Well, I'd asked for that, hadn't I? Cue lots of dull facts and figures. Fascinating, I'm sure, but I just nodded in the right places (then realised he couldn't see, so made 'ooh, right' and 'that sounds amazing noises every now and again) while making the shopping list in my head. Not for sexy undies any more, no it was a shopping list of things like wet wipes, dry shampoo, and a travel-sized hairbrush.

The thing is I feel so guilty now, so ungrateful. I'm not looking forward to sleeping over in his stupid lorry. I mean, it's a bit of a step down from what I'd had in mind and besides, we'll be trapped together with no entertainment and are bound to get on each other's nerves. But the fact is, by suggesting this Daryl is actually really making an effort, once again, and if I don't meet him halfway and drum up some enthusiasm then…what does it say about me and my commitment to us?

Why am I so convinced something is wrong with us anyway? He's come home early to surprise me, he's surprised me at work, and now he's trying to take me away somewhere. What more do I want?

I hope we work but I feel like, or rather am scared that, I'm clinging onto something in its death throes. It's a bit like we're on a life support machine at the moment – we look like we're alive and still breathing but actually we're dead. Still, I have to give it my best shot or I'll always regret it. Besides, we've been together for so long now. Nine whole years. It's too long for me to walk away; I've put so many years into this and they can't be wasted, I refuse to accept that. Romance is all well and good but it fades in every relationship, doesn't it, and in the end you have to be realistic. The reality is that I love Daryl and he loves me and I can't imagine life without him.

And yes, his job drives me mad and he drives me mad but we work, somehow, against the odds. We'll have a baby and be a happy family, and grow old together, and all that wonderful stuff. This is just a blip.

So actually, the day hasn't ended too badly really, because although Daryl couldn't come tonight, we did arrange our weekend away, plus…I met up with Zoe and Rick and had a bloody good time anyway! It was so nice to have a catch up with them, and we chatted and chatted for hours – the night flew by! What's more, we're making tentative plans to perhaps meet up next year in Florida too. Hurray!

Mon 18

Have to say, have had great day today, everything's gone like clockwork – better, in fact. I hit all my deadlines at work, even got a pat on the back from the boss, and then hit the shops! Everyone else seemed to have had the same idea, inevitably, but even though they were as desperate for a bargain as me, they all seemed in as good a mood as me too! No annoying stroppy, 'shopping-rage' people at all!

I bought loads of cosmetics (kidding myself they are for the weekend – like I'll be able to use them in a teensy lorry cab), some great smellies (telling myself same lie), and even some new undies!

Bit worried about Kim though. She had to borrow another £20 today. 'I'm really sorry,' she said, looking totally mortified when she cornered me by the photocopier. 'I just…I'm short on the rent. To be honest I almost didn't come to work today because I can't afford the bus fare, I had to raid that bottle full of pennies I keep in the kitchen. The driver was not happy when I poured a load of coppers out of my purse. He muttered something about shrapnel and I didn't think he was going to accept it...'

Her eyes (one shadowy with bruises) were starting to look dangerously sparkly, like tears were gathering, and her voice was thickening. I glanced round the office to see if anyone had noticed. That's the trouble with an open plan office, everyone can see everything, there's nowhere to have a private conversation. But by a miracle everyone seemed to actually be doing their jobs, staring at computer screens in concentration or calling clients and chatting to them as though they were bezzie mates, before putting the phone down and muttering 'what a cock.' All far too preoccupied to notice Kim's mini meltdown.

'Don't be daft,' I told her, 'I can lend you some money, it's no trouble.' Before she could say anything more, I scurried back to my desk to grab my purse and give it to her there and then. That's £120 she owes me now. Still, that's what friends are for, eh, being there for each other. I just hope Daryl doesn't find out, he'll go nuts if he discovers I've been lending out money.

After a couple of minutes I found a pretext to go over to her desk, hiding the money in a file and pretending to be checking inside it to refer to something official as I actually surreptitiously slipped the note to her.

'And I'm buying you lunch today too,' I hissed. She nodded gratefully, then brought the curtain of her glossy hair back over her face to obscure it a little while quickly turning back to her computer.

I could still hear her bashing the keys theatrically as I walked away. She's no actress, that one. I just hope no one else noticed, goodness knows people are gossiping enough about her since she came to work on Friday with a shiner and a pathetic excuse about opening a kitchen cupboard into her own face. The last thing she needs is people picking up on her money worries too.

Later we had a chance to chat over lasagne and chips. Today was my first chance to get the full story on what on earth had happened last week, and I wasn't going to let it pass – or the opportunity to feed her. She looks so skinny at the moment.

I softened her up first, just chatting about work and telling her about Daryl taking me on a road trip this weekend. I wanted her relaxed, knew she'd open up to me in her own time, and if I asked too many questions, pushed her too much, she'd just clam up.

We must have looked like every other person in there. A woman sat nearby who had taken accessorising to a whole new level by matching her fake tan to the exact shade of her coat. A cashier behind the till wiped her nose on a tissue then kindly handed someone a knife and fork using the same hand. A waitress twirled her hair round and round her finger while flirting with a handsome man sat at one of the tables, repeating the same phrase again and again: 'Aww, it doesn't matter, honest. But you should have come to me really! I'd have sorted it for you. Come to me next time. Come to me next time.' A couple at the next table getting increasingly annoyed as they tried to get her attention...

Yes, we must have looked just like everyone else, but I felt like I was on some kind of mission to get this information from Kim, like a spy. One false move and I'd never get the truth. So I chatted seemingly aimlessly, all the time hoping that soon she'd feel comfortable enough to start talking herself.

INVISIBLE

'Thanks for the money,' she said suddenly. She put her knife and fork together despite her plate being still half full, then sat back in her seat and rolled her head back, staring at the ceiling and I knew that finally the time had come. I shovelled a mouthful of by-now lukewarm lasagne in, letting the creamy sauce, pasta and mince plug my mouth up and stop me from saying anything to ruin the moment. As I'd hoped, she carried on talking, still looking up, as though she couldn't bring herself to meet my eye while she told her story.

'God, last week was a nightmare. I finished with Sam, just like I said I was going to. He seemed all right actually, but it was all just a loony act, of course. I didn't know that, obviously, but I went out with some mates because I wanted to get out of the flat anyway, get away from him. I bloody knew he'd kick off and I was dreading it, so took Henry to his aunt's and tried to put as much distance between me and Sam as possible.'

Her head came forward now, but she still didn't look at me. Instead she gazed down, apparently fascinated with some crumbs left by the previous customers at the table. 'There I am having a drink and a laugh, when I turn round and…there he is! He'd only gone and followed me.'

Somehow I managed to stop myself speaking or gasping in amazement or anything. I forced myself to just stay quiet and listen. But I couldn't eat any more either, just sat there, holding a fork-full of food that was rapidly going cold and would almost certainly never make it to my mouth.

Kim reached out, slim fingers moving the crumbs around as she continued.

'I went mental. I mean, talk about a stalker! And you know what he said? "God help any bloke who tries to talk to you tonight." The look in his eyes when he said it, too. He was crazy. But I didn't feel scared of him, just abso-bloody-lutely furious. Honest to God, I could have killed him there and then.

'So I stropped off out of the place and started to walk home, and Sam followed me there too. All the way home he trailed after me. We were screaming at each other. He just makes me angrier than any other person in the world. When I'm with him I'm just…ugly. You know? He makes me an ugly person, but there's nothing I can do to stop it. I'm just helpless around him…

'When we got in he was still screaming on at me – I'm a bitch, I'm a slut, he loves me, how can I do this to him, the usual stuff. Then we started pushing each other around. He caught me right on my eye, gave me this black eye,' Kim said, waving her hand in front of her face.

Her voice dropped even lower, and she leaned forward, still looking down, ashamed. 'But the really bad thing is what I did. I-I-I picked up a plate that was on the drainer and smashed it over his head! I was so angry I didn't even stop and think, just…just did it. I could have killed him right then and wouldn't have been bothered.

'And then, I felt so guilty that…,' she shrugged. Clearly she'd felt so guilty that they'd ended up having sex and getting back together. Inside I shuddered, scared for her, but I held every muscle tight so that it wouldn't show. I mean, hello, he's a total psycho! He's insane and dangerous, and is sending her over the edge too. Why can't my lovely mate see that she's worth so much more than this? Why she can't just leave him is beyond me, but then they do say love is blind. Blind, deaf, and mentally incapacitated in this case, by the sound of it…

'It's like I'm addicted to him,' she explained, talking more to the crumbs than me. 'I don't love him. I don't even like him much. But I can't seem to give him up. He's bad for me, I'm bad for him, but the pull towards each other just seems overwhelming. We crave each other, like crack addicts.

'Everyone keeps telling me what a prize shit he is. And they're right – I mean, I'm not thick, of course I know that. But it's as much my fault as his when we get physical; I give as good as I get, you know. He slaps me, I smash a plate on him,' she insisted.

Hardly the point. But I made myself just nod. Everyone is telling Kim the same thing about how she should leave Sam and she isn't listening. So clearly a different approach is needed. My theory is, if I join in and tell her exactly what I think, I'll wind up being consigned to the friend scrapheap, she'll stop confiding in me, and then where will she be? At some point though, she's going to realise she is in an abusive relationship, no matter how much she tries to justify it to herself by claiming she is as much at fault as him – and then she's going to need someone to turn to, someone who won't say 'I told you so.' Hopefully she'll know that person is me.

With a sigh she scooped the crumbs into a little pile with one hand, then swiped them into the other hand that was outstretched just below the table. Then she wiped her hands together, slap, slap, slap, cleaning away the crumbs and the subject with the movement. Our hour was up, time to go back to work.

I kept thinking about her for the rest of the afternoon. The rest of the day. I really hope she's all right. Bad enough to be in a bit of a sticky situation money-wise, but fella-wise too? It makes me realise how lucky I am to have Daryl. If I were in a relationship with someone as dodgy as Sam I'd scarper pretty damn quick.

Mon 25

Hmm, well, how best to describe my weekend with Daryl? Not sure if there is one word to sum it up. Maybe if I write it down and commit it to memory forever that will help.

He came over on Friday and I got all packed up and we got on the road. I haven't had a look round his rig for a very long time. When we first got together I'd go with him all over the country but, well, life gets in the way and enthusiasm drains away for trips in a noisy truck, especially after we bought our house together. Fact is, I wanted to be in my comfy home, sitting on my big cream leather sofa and watching telly rather than going glorified camping in my bloke's workplace. But Daryl has seriously pimped up the cab of his truck – it's really cool!

He's got his laptop in the centre console so he can listen to music on it as well as keep in touch with me and work. There's a mini fridge stuffed with food and drinks, the bed tucks away so neatly behind a curtain that runs behind the two seats – oh yeah, and how comfy are those seats?! They're incredible, in fact they almost rival our sofa, and because they are fully sprung they move with the cab, absorbing any bumps in the road so that I didn't feel a thing. A totally smooth ride.

We were going along merrily, countryside whizzing past us, when Daryl glanced over at me and smiled, his blue eyes crinkling at the corners. 'Hey, in one of the glove compartments there's a CD I think you'll want to hear,' he said.

Bemused, I reached up to the locker that ran all the way across the top of the windscreen. 'Not there!' shouted Daryl, his voice sharp and angry. I pulled my hand back as though from fire. 'They're always locked,' he explained. 'It's safer, otherwise they might burst open if I brake suddenly. With stuff tumbling out it might make me swerve and hit something, it could cause a crash. Last thing I want is to get hit in the face by half a dozen spare rolls for the tacho.'

Okay, okay. Lecture over, I popped open the glove compartment right in front of me. Inside were some CDs and the one on top had me grinning immediately. 'Barry White!' I laughed. 'No way! Let's put it on!'

Seconds later, the opening beat of our song, *You're My First, My Last, My Everything*, was pumping out of the impressive surround sound speakers. Daryl started shuffling round in his seat as if he had ants in his pants, head moving back and forth like a demented pigeon.

'Nice groove face,' I snorted, closing my eyes, biting my bottom lip and scrunching up my face in mimicry. We bobbed and weaved in time to the music, singing along at the tops of our voices. Daryl doing Barry's bits, and me joining in as a backing singer, 'Ooooh, ooo-oooh, ooo-ooooh, oooo-ooooooooh!'

What a laugh! Even Daryl's 'ironic' collection of nodding dogs of various sizes seemed to join in our seated dancing. As soon as it ended... 'Again!' I begged.

'Again,' nodded Daryl, pressing the button. I couldn't hear enough of our song, it was just exactly what we needed to get this trip off to the right start. We'd been on our very first date when I'd initially heard it.

We'd met at a house party – wow, I haven't been to one of those in a few years, but back when I was 22 everyone had them. Me and Hannah had been checking out the place, walking from room to room. Hannah had walked into the lounge and I'd been right behind her but spotted someone I hadn't seen for ages so took a step back, hanging onto the doorjamb as I leaned in and shouted 'hi' over the music.

I was only a second but by the time I turned, Hannah had already reached the other side of the room and was stepping through the patio doors. Right behind her were two blokes, leaning against the frame and totally checking her out, smirks on their faces as they nodded appreciatively. I'd grinned and rolled my eyes at them as I'd hurried by – never guessing that I'd end up married to one of them.

Of course, as soon as I'd caught up with Hannah I'd asked her who the men were. In the darkness of the room, under the flashing disco lights standing on the mantelpiece, she hadn't even noticed the way they were looking at her, their tongues virtually hanging out of their mouths! Turned out she vaguely knew one of them though, Andy, and he was best mates with Daryl.

I'd spent the rest of the night alternating between taking the mickey out of them for standing with their tongues hanging out over Hannah, and staring at this gorgeous, tall, mesmerising bloke in front of me who had the coolest, steely-bright blue eyes I'd ever seen. Back then he'd had a head full of dark brown wavy hair that made my fingers just itch to touch it, although now I think of it, even then he had a high forehead.

'I've got wavy hair; it's waving goodbye,' that was the joke he'd always said back then.

Neither of us could believe how we knew all the same people and went to the same places yet had never bumped into one another before. I'm the kind of person who tends to take a long time to get to know someone but with him for some reason the attraction was instant. A lightening bolt from the blue.

Did I ask for his number or did he ask for mine? To be honest I can't remember – I was a bit worse for wear by the end of the night. But by the time Hannah and I had left together in a taxi, I'd had a big grin plastered on my face and the oddest feeling that this man was going to change my life forever. It wasn't necessarily love at first sight, but it was definitely something big.

It'd taken a month to arrange a date though. Daryl had hurt his foot at five-a-side or something, so was resting it for ages, basically stuck at home alone – I'd been so impressed that he was only 25 and already owned his own flat. An older man with a mortgage, a bod to die for, and who was a laugh? He'd seemed too good to be true. I hadn't been able to believe my luck, so holding out for a month had been a pain but worth it.

Still, that first date couldn't have come fast enough as far as I'd been concerned. We'd talked on the phone though, bonding over telly programmes we watched – as far as I can remember we were both addicted to an amazing new American forensics show, CSI. Ha, that programme's ancient now, but at the time it seemed so ground-breaking. But then, everything that's exhilarating at first feels ordinary eventually. Maybe that's what has happened to me and Daryl too…

I'd had such a time deciding what to wear for that first date though because, typical Daryl, he'd been really vague about what we would be doing; maybe eating, maybe go to a pub, maybe even the cinema, he hadn't decided at that point. My entire wardrobe had been tried on, discarded onto the bed, then dug out from the bottom of the ever-growing pile, tried on again with different shoes, different jewellery, different attitude…discarded again. After all that, I think I ended up playing it safe and wearing jeans and a spangly top, plus a leather jacket, reckoning that would cover every sartorial eventuality a date could throw at me.

When I'd heard the beep of his car horn I'd almost jumped out of my skin. I can still vividly remember peering through the net curtains of the small side window in my old bedroom at my parent's house, and seeing him standing there. He'd got out of the car and was leaning on the open door, waiting for me, watching me as I walked towards him, a big smile on his face as he took me in. His look had set my heart racing. I'd been a gonner from then, really.

Then, as we'd set off, I'd ask him if we could have some music on. He'd pulled a face, looked like he'd been put on the spot. 'I've got a CD stuck in the player,' he'd grimaced. 'It's the only thing that'll play and, err, it's a bit embarrassing.'

'What is it?' I'd asked, immediately curious.

He'd sighed the sigh of someone who was resigned to his fate; he'd known there was no getting out of confessing now. 'It's Barry White…'

'The Lurve Walrus?' I'd burst out, smile widening to a grin.

'Yeah, yeah, I know. I bought it for a laugh the other day and it's stuck. I've tried thumping it but it doesn't make any difference, so what can I do?' he'd shrugged.

'Go on…play it,' I'd coaxed, teasing. And he had. *You're My First, My Last, My Everything* had started up, and we'd ended up singing along to it as it played over and over again until Daryl had pulled into a gastro pub where we ate.

I can't tell you what we talked about for the rest of the night, although clearly the date went well because here we are all these years on and still together. But I will always, always remember singing along to Barry White, and the sheer joy of that moment, the connection I felt with this man as we messed around.

And now, in the cab of his truck, I felt that same connection with him as we bombed along the motorway. Yes, this trip away had been a good idea.

INVISIBLE

As we drove Daryl told me about the rig and motorways and life on the road as a 'tramper' (I find the slang name for truck drivers hilarious, but there you go. Sounds like he puts it about a bit, and I do love the expression on people's faces when they ask what my husband does for a living and I reply 'Oh, he's a tramper.' Then I have to explain that it's the name for a lorry driver who lives in his truck all week, which is actually quite dull). He was telling me stuff I'd heard a million times before but for once I didn't just shut him out and daydream, I tried to listen. Well, if he's making an effort then I have to. Although sometimes it was hard work…

'When you've 44 tonne on the back of the truck you don't know what's going to happen. It's a killing machine; you brake too hard or go into a bend too quick and…game over,' he said. 'It takes a real man to drive one of these, to control it.'

He looked so serious. He really thinks driving a big truck is the manliest thing in the world. Wow, if a Porche or a Ferrari is a penis extension, what the hell is a truck? Still, I nodded, wide-eyed. He didn't look in the mood for a laugh, he looked like he was desperate to impress me and have me in awe of him the way I had been when we first started dating. It made me sad, to be honest, because I can't be that young woman again, so in love that just the thought of seeing Daryl would make me feel the biggest rush that I swear he should have been made illegal, like a drug.

After a few hours we pulled into a café and had a cuppa, then while Daryl tinkered with the engine I had a lie down on the bed. It was surprisingly comfy and I closed my eyes, tired from the early start and all that travelling – honestly, how Daryl manages to do so much driving without falling asleep is beyond me. I seem to get shattered just from the motion of a vehicle, be it a car, train or lorry, and the constant hum of the engine acts as instant lullaby. Well, it works on babies, doesn't it, that's why so many parents drive round for hours with their kids in a car seat, and I must be the same.

The truck door opening toppled me over the edge from dozing to wakefulness. Daryl had clambered into the cab and was just pulling on a pair of thin latex gloves, like surgeons wear.

'Something wrong?' I murmured, shading my eyes from the low, bright sun that was slanting through the windscreen and half blinding me.

'No, no, just going to clean off one of the spark plugs a bit, that's all, ' he said, holding the wrist end of the glove with one hand and opening and closing the other to pull it down until it was entirely encased. He let go and it made an audible snap against his skin.

Clean freak that he is, he always wears these gloves if he has to mess with the engine. The oil gets everywhere and he hates the way it ingrains itself into the skin around and under his fingernails, making him look like he hasn't washed in months. Says it makes him feel like he looks homeless because they are so blackened and dirty. It doesn't look great, I have to admit, and it's virtually impossible to get off – and as for clothes…! It's a real pain, has ruined many a decent shirt of his. That's why he's started wearing a kind of boiler suit when he is driving, that way he can whip it off in a flash if needs be to reveal a smart shirt and trousers beneath. Then all he has to do is pop on a tie and voila, he is ready in seconds to have a meeting with clients even at short notice. He still chucks shirts away every so often though; he'll go out with one then come home without one, saying it's been ruined. Wish he'd just bring them home so I could at least try to get the oil out, but never mind.

Normally I think he looks quite sexy in his overalls, in a rough kind of way. But those gloves… Yuck! Enough to put anyone off. 'You look like a gynaecologist when you're wearing them,' I said, wrinkling my nose. 'Like you're ready to give some poor unfortunate woman an internal.'

He wriggled his eyebrows up and down suggestively, posing with his hands in the air like some kind of magician's assistant. 'Oh yeah?' His eyebrows were working overtime. 'Hmmm, I'll give you an internal right now, if you want.'

'Eurgh!' I blurted. Then he wriggled onto the bed, pinning me down with his weight and almost knocking the breath out of me. He is 14 stone of solid muscle, so I didn't stand a chance as I giggled and bucked beneath him, pretending to try to kick him off.

'Now then, keep still, this won't hurt a bit,' he promised, kissing me, latex-clad fingers exploring my body….

Bloody hell, was the sex HOT. Bit weird that he kept the gloves on the whole time, but there was no time to rip them off, he was like a man possessed. We did everything, and I mean everything. It was sweaty, crazy stuff that was enough to make the watching nodding dogs on the dashboard blush; it hasn't felt like that in a while, umm, if ever, actually! It certainly wasn't making love, but we both just…exploded. Sometimes, just his kisses turn me on, and his hands were all over me, those massive, massive hands that are so strong but so gentle.

Afterwards we hit the road for another couple of hours then went to bed early. Snuggled down and popped on the night heater for a little while to make things extra cosy. And lay in total silence. We'd got nothing to say to each other at all. For a few hours I'd been fooled into thinking things were improving already, just because our sex life is looking up.

What an idiot I am to think it was going to be that easy to fix things.

I'm ashamed to say it, but I pretended I was asleep. Well it had to be better than us blatantly lying side by side in awkward, hideous silence. At least this way, it seemed like we weren't speaking for a reason, and that has to be an improvement. Right?

Saturday dawned bright and early, and we got on the road again. 'Can't hang around, can't be late. Come on, hurry up,' Daryl romantically told me as soon as I woke.

Maybe he'd guessed I hadn't been asleep, but the good mood he'd been in the day before had disappeared. Conversation was stilted and hard work, and I found myself wracking my brains for things to say. And as soon as I do that it always has the opposite effect, because it seems to make my mind freeze completely so that all I can think is, 'think of something!' which isn't very helpful really.

Perhaps the only reason why we work is because we never see each other. He's away so much with his trucking job that he's only home a few days a week at most. Perhaps, for all I complain about it, that's actually what keeps us going. Because as our weekend together progressed, I had this horrible realisation. I feel disloyal even thinking it let alone writing it down, but here goes…

Sometimes when we spend a lot of time together I realise I don't actually like Daryl.

There, I've said it. I am a horrible, horrible person.

I do love him, most definitely, but I don't like him that much. I wouldn't want to be his friend. We'd never just hang out together. Thing is, I feel on edge so much of the time when he's around. I'll be trying to guess what kind of mood he'll be in. And if he's in a bad mood I'll bend over backwards to change it; if he's in a good mood then even when we're having fun there is a bit of me holding back, analysing, making sure I don't do anything to ruin the atmosphere.

Oh, and he's always telling me the 'right way' of doing things, but what he really means is his way. Making a cup of tea, washing the car, filling up the car with petrol (you must always, always, always, give the pump a little wiggle before pulling it out of your car because there are a couple of drops of petrol that will fall from it. The logic is that as you've paid for them so you're entitled to them, and if you don't take them, think of how much petrol you're wasting over a lifetime. 'You've paid for it but never taken it? Then you're stupid,' he always says. I'm willing to bet that if I saved it all it would only be enough to turn the engine on and then for it to die, but the way Daryl talks it is probably enough to fly me to the moon and back, or possibly for me to become the next oil tycoon, a new JR Ewing). Apparently I wasn't even capable of stacking washing up properly until he came into my life and set me on the path of enlightenment.

Anyway, we went to Tilbury Docks. It wasn't the same as Salzburg, funnily enough. Another day in the cab, making conversation about landmarks. I even went through the newspaper, reading bits out of The Sun to Daryl so that we could talk about them – that was quite nice actually. He loves the news, is fascinated by it, from politics to nasty crimes. I'm not bothered really, but I suppose that's why he's cleverer than me. I don't know though, I just felt a bit…awkward and depressed. Even sleeping in the cab had lost a bit of its novelty value.

To be honest, it was a relief to get home yesterday at lunchtime. First thing I did was nip to the corner shop for some chocolate. Just hearing the cheery ting of the bell made me relax, grabbing a bar of something yummy made me feel even better. By the time Ric had grinned from behind the counter, 'Have a lovely evening, lady, thank you so much' the world was a better place.

Back at home, I had a bloody long soak in the bath and munched on my treat; it felt great to be alone again for a while. I could hear Daryl pacing up and down the hallway, talking on the phone. From the tension in his voice I guessed it was his mum. He really can't stand Cynthia… I once found a birthday card she'd sent him, screwed up and chucked in the bin.

MARCH

Saturday 2

I'm so angry. Daryl is always in control, always in the driving seat. I can't even phone him if he doesn't feel like it; he's always switching his sodding mobile off because he says the boss has a real thing about the possibility of him even talking on the phone while driving and does spot checks to see if they've been using them. Pah!

There are two things that make me not believe him. First, he's freelance, so even though he pretty much constantly works for one company because they are always subcontracting to him, he is in fact his own boss; and Daryl is not a man who likes being told what to do by anyone, especially if he is meant to be the one in charge. And secondly, it's amazing how he breaks the 'no calls' rule when he wants to talk to me, but suddenly when I talk to him it is a different story. And yes, it could be argued that he is sweet and wonderful for ever breaking the rules for me and that I should be grateful instead of narky, but I am really not currently in the mood for accepting that sort of thing. Grrrr!

We've just had an argument and the childish git put the phone down on me and has switched it off so I can't call him back. It's so typical of him – if in doubt run away, put your head in the sand and ignore the problem. Make the other person sweat so that then at least he feels he has control over the situation. It's pathetic, infuriating, patronising, and has all the hallmarks of a control-freak who has to be in control because they're too damn cowardly to trust anyone else. Manipulative bollocks!

The bastard actually said he fancied Kim the other day (actually what he said was…and it is so un-PC I can barely make myself write it… 'That chinky mate of yours is all right looking; I'd have her.' His nickname for her used to be Thai Bride until I pointed out that she was born in Chelmsford and that her mum is originally from China. I'd foolishly thought it might make him remember her by her name, but instead he simply started calling her That Chinky Mate). I was annoyed by his comment, of course, but held it in. I shouldn't have done that, should have let rip there and then but of course I didn't because it's not my way, for all he calls me a stroppy mare. So in a way it's my fault. I let it fester. But he shouldn't have said it in the first place! After all the talks we've had recently, the fragile state of our marriage, it's hardly surprising I'm feeling a little insecure. The last thing I need to hear is that he'd 'have her'. Flipping great! I can't believe the insensitivity of the man. He really has no idea at all.

So I tried to talk to him about it last night. 'Christ, I've just had a really stressful day; an accident happened right in front of me, virtually. I got stuck in a massive tailback because of it, and wound up delivering late. I'm so tired. We'll talk about it tomorrow, promise,' he sighed.

That got my goat a bit but I tried to understand. But when he called today he didn't mention it, instead simply asked me what I was doing. 'Cooking salmon,' I told him tersely. Then he just went on about his bloody rota, which sounds more like a work of fiction the more he talks about it (am convinced he has more say in it than he makes out).

All I wanted him to say was: 'Sorry about last night, let's talk about it now.' It should have been the first thing he said to me. It wasn't. So I waited and waited, listening to him more and more impatiently and becoming increasingly furious and frustrated.

Finally he realised something was wrong and made some half-arsed attempt to find out what. 'So what's up with you? This about the other night?' he grunted.

'I don't think I can be bothered to talk about it, seen as you attach so little importance to it,' I huffed.

'Fuck off,' he said - and put the phone down. Wanker.

Bet he thinks it's all my fault. Well, stuff him. I'm off out tonight and I'm going to look bloody glamorous and have lots of fun. I'm meeting Sophie, Amy, Hannah and Una tonight at a bar on Charing Cross Road. I'm really looking forward to it because I never travel into London for a night out, really. I refuse to sit moping around in floods of tears because of Daryl, although it's tempting.

2am - Before I went though I did spend quite some time obsessively dialling Daryl's phone. And despite having an absolutely wonderful time with my friends (Hannah cried out at the last minute, but she wasn't missed much!) every time I ducked to the loo I rang him too...and on the way home I hit redial until I actually got a sore finger... It's ringing out and he's not answering. Cunning, because now he can see the amount of calls he's missed and will know I've been repeat dialling him.

He knows damn well the one thing guaranteed to drive me insane is for him to drop off the face of the earth. I get so that I can't rest until I've spoken to him, even if I've nothing to say. It's his little control device and the sad thing is, it works every time.

Tomorrow I must: tidy house, change bed sheets and towels, do washing up, exercise, sort present for Sarah (birthday in a week's time, but got to allow time to post it to her house in Lincoln), bikini line, deep condition hair, shave legs, because

Daryl is coming home tomorrow night. But for now I'm going to bed and forgetting about men!

Sunday 3
Well, I did the housework but that was about it. Deep conditioned hair then waxed bikini line - possibly the most painful experience of my life and it turns out I've done it for no reason at all. Just as I was about to shave my legs, Daryl called. He's being sent direct to Sweden, won't be home until 12th. Gutted.
But we had a good talk about him refusing to talk to me after rows, and he actually apologised, which is pretty much unheard of. And he was almost crying because I said: 'When you tell me stuff like this, that we won't be seeing each other for ages, you sound so business-like. I feel like you don't care.'
He explained that it's because he's so nervous and is really het up, so just comes out with it. 'I know I'll just, if I try to tell you how sorry I really am for what I do, I'll just...and if I say how much I love you...I'll get all nervous, trip over my words,' he said. He certainly started to stutter and stumble when he said that bit.
My heart melted then, I don't mind admitting; a warmth spreading through me, out from my chest. He's seems so big and strong and blokey, and really it's all a huge act to hide an insecure boy. It's easy to forget that sometimes and only see the façade he puts up. Then something will happen to make me think of that bullied child he used to be and I don't think there are words to describe how I feel. Protective of him, angry for him, guilty that I could forget for even a second the tough life he's had and why he's the way he is.

INVISIBLE

I told him I just need him to keep telling me what's happening and how he feels, or else I'll get worried. I didn't mention that stuff about him fancying Kim, what's the point? I understand now that it was just about him putting his 'big man' act on.

Monday 4
Very sweet today. Daryl gave me a call before he went to work. 'Just to say hi and I'm thinking of you and miss you and love you,' he said. That really made my day!

Wednesday 5
Why is it that you never get everything right in life? If work's fine, then chances are the relationship is struggling; if the relationship's fine, then there's a problem with the family. As up and down as Daryl and I are, it feels like we're slowly making headway – I mean, at least we're finally talking about our problems a bit instead of just ignoring them and hoping they will go away. He has promised to try to get round to booking a counselling session this week, too. So that's good, and work is good. But this situation with Hannah is really bugging me.

Even thinking about it makes me feel like a kid again, it's all so childish, and I can't help feeling that as grown women we should both be handling things a bit better. But I'm not invited to nights out with her and Amy any more, and when I ask her for a drink she can't make it because she's skint or busy or something, but she always seems to make it to nights out with other people.

I asked her to that night out on Saturday and she cried out right at the very last minute because she'd no money. Fair enough. But I found out today that she went out with a group of other mates instead.

The problem isn't, of course, that she's gone out with other people, it's that she lied. If it were just once then fair enough, I'd think maybe she did it to spare my feelings or because she felt awkward, but she always has an excuse. Something has happened between us, and although I've tried hard to think what it can be, I've no idea. I've asked her continually what the problem is but she doesn't want to tell me.

We've been friends since primary school. Surely she knows me well enough to know she can tell me anything, and that if there is a problem I'll want to try my best to sort it out. She's my oldest friend.

Clearly I'm just going to have to be the bigger person in all this. I can't and won't keep offering the olive branch forever though, but I am willing to give it one more go. This morning I sent her a text message asking if she was in tonight so I could talk to her, as I really want to clear the air. If she's still weird after this, then tough, because it's been going on for months and I'm bored. No more effort will be made on my part to find out what is wrong or build bridges. I'm not a doormat, and if she can't be bothered to tell her friend (me!!) what is up then it wasn't much of a friendship in the first place. Whatever I have done wrong in her eyes, it can't be that bad – it's not like I've murdered someone or something, so I'd have hoped I deserved a bit of honesty, a bit of leeway and support. Like I'm giving her.

6pm –Still no reply from Hannah. Stuff her.

On a far more important note, I've lost 4lb for no reason whatsoever. I was 10st exactly on Monday, but not any more! It's given me the incentive I need to start exercising. I'm doing a Body Blitz dvd followed by yoga before I go to bed tonight.

INVISIBLE

10.35pm – Heard from Hannah at about 7pm. She sent me a text saying she'd been working all day and was going to watch footie tonight. Said she'd come round tomorrow though. We'll see. Wish I weren't so suspicious-natured.

Anyway, I have done my workout and my legs feel all satisfyingly wibbly now. I feel great, and much less stressed.

Saturday 8

Typical. I go all the way through winter without so much as a sniffle, and just as spring starts I get a stonker. I came home Thursday night thinking 'hmm, feel a bit dodgy all of a sudden.' By yesterday morning I had a full on cold. My nose, bunged up and hot, feels like it's swollen until it has taken over half my face. Eyes water continually, limbs ache, my voice is really croaky - and not even in a sexy, husky way; more of an old crone way. I'm like the 'before' in a Tunes ad.

And I've got nothing to eat in the house, so am basically eating a mismatch of leftovers, because of course Daryl is away and I am too ill to face going outside let alone doing battle in a supermarket. Seriously, I may as well be single. What's the point of being married if he's not around when I need him?

Mind you, it's probably just as well. Once he's fetched me half of Boots pharmacy, bought some Lucozade, and fixed me some food, he'd only start bugging me. Far better I be left alone while I lie on the sofa, wrapped up in a sweaty, Olbas oil-soaked duvet, free to watch whatever rubbish I want as I come round from one nap and float into another, surrounded by a drift of used tissues.

4pm - Eek, just made the mistake of looking in the mirror. I have a very white face and a very red nose, like a washed out clown, all framed with greasy hair. In fact, my nose is so sore that even thinking about blowing it makes me wince.

I'm feeling pretty sorry for myself as I sit here wiping at my watery eyes so I can see what on earth I'm writing – I am constantly on the verge of sneezing.

5.30pm - Bless her, Kim text to see if I needed anything but I didn't feel right asking her to run errands for me. Not when she has so much to worry about in her personal life. She's a good friend though. Ah, talking of good friends... Hannah. Can't believe she blew me out on Thursday night. To be honest I was going to cancel on her because I felt so rotten but she got in first, using the catch-all phrase 'something has come up'. Pathetic.

I've no energy to be annoyed though. I'm using it all up on keeping my mouth hanging open and breathing in and out. I want my nose back!!

Sunday 9

I'm snoring. I know this because I actually woke myself with a particularly loud one. Gross. I'm sooooooo tired. Can't sleep for more than an hour or so in one hit because my nose is so bunged up I can't breathe. I wake with a dry mouth from sleeping with it wide open, while my nose runs like a tap, and my chest feels heavy from the mucus gathering on it. Eurgh, having a cold is rotten.

I really need a cuddle and my stupid husband is miles away, working hard and earning a crust so he can keep me in tissues – and believe me, I'm getting through them at a rate of knots. Well, actually, I've used up all the tissues I've bought and have moved on to loo roll. Let's hope I either get better soon or Daryl comes home because I don't even want to think about what will happen if I run out of that...

The problem with lying on the sofa, mad with lack of sleep, is that my mind has free reign to dwell on things without distraction (I don't count constant reruns on telly of CSI and Time Team as a distraction). As I lie here, waiting and hoping for Daryl's return, I realised that my whole life is spent waiting, waiting, waiting. It's on hold. I put off doing anything because I always think it'll be nicer to do it with Daryl than do it alone – and then we never get round to it. I don't even get to cook for him and look after him; we live on takeaways when he's around because although I do want to look after him, I don't want to waste our precious time together messing around in the kitchen.

Oh the guilt. I'm a bad wife.

I really, really miss Daryl. I just want him here, making everything okay. Just hearing his voice would be good but he doesn't like to call when abroad because of the cost.

Bored, bored, bored. Ooh, phone's ringing!

It was Mum checking up on me. She said: 'I wish I didn't live so far away so I could pop over to look after you. But then again I know all you want is Daryl back; you'll feel better once he's around again, and so will I.'

She's a big fan of his, especially since I told her about his childhood. I think she wants to be his replacement mum.

I've just ricked something in my neck while sneezing. Going to try to sleep now…

Monday 10

Amy and Hannah came over after work today to check on the sickie. When I got Amy's text I managed to galvanise myself to pick up the tissues strewn all over the floor, which were almost ankle-deep round the sofa and bed, so I must be feeling a bit better. Even yesterday I couldn't have contemplated that level of movement.

I was looking forward to the visit, bored of my own company, with nothing to think of but mucus. But the minute I saw their faces I knew something was up. I felt like

I was standing in front of a firing squad, waiting for them to speak. They managed a minute or so of nervous small-talk about how they'd brought some magazines over to keep me occupied, and as Amy handed them to me I noticed her give Hannah the tiniest nudge with her elbow.

'Erm, look I know you've been thinking something's wrong for a while,' Hannah said. When she gets nervous she really talks with her hands. They were suddenly very busy. 'Well, the thing is…you're right!'

Definitely nervous – she said this last bit inappropriately brightly, like a magician's assistant saying 'ta-da', her voice going right up. She seemed to realise and cleared her throat before carrying on. 'Thing is we didn't go to Salzburg, and we are being funny with you, for a reason. Because we hate Daryl.'

I blinked. I took a deep breath in, heart thumping as I tried to comprehend, and then huffed the air out. And smiled. 'This is a joke, right?' I looked from one to the other and back again, still smiling. They weren't laughing. No surprise there, it wasn't a funny joke.

Hannah glanced at Amy for reassurance, then looked me right in the eye and carried on, her hands in full flow. 'A few months back, back in January, we popped round to see if you fancied going shopping with us. He made us feel really uncomfortable.'

'Really uncomfortable?' I repeated slowly. My heart was banging against my chest now, like I'd run a marathon, and I felt so shaky from the cold or the adrenaline, I'm not sure, that I sank down onto the sofa.

All kinds of things were running through my mind, wondering what the hell he'd said or done. Perhaps he'd got bored of me and decided to try it on with them. I mean, he'd said the other day, and I quote, 'That Kim is a bit of all right. I would.' Perhaps it wasn't just her that 'he would', perhaps it was all my friends. Suddenly I felt a bit sick.

'Tell me exactly what happened.' I hadn't meant to whisper but that was all the sound I seemed able to muster.

'We came over and asked for you. Daryl invited us in, told us that you shouldn't be too long because you'd just nipped to the supermarket. He said we should wait for you, offered us a cup of coffee...' said Hannah. 'Then, as we sat on the sofa, we got talking and suddenly he...he gave me this look.'

A look.

'This, this, this terrible look. There was just a terrible atmosphere. He gave this knowing sort of look, like he was thinking something terrible, like he was capable of doing something terrible,' she plunged on, running her hands through her pixie crop. She used the word terrible a lot – clearly her vocabulary is...terrible.

Amy agreed. 'Honestly, I know it sounds over the top, but you weren't there. The atmosphere...' she shuddered. I was tempted to ask if it was terrible, but I couldn't seem to speak or move, I was locked in place as I listened to her continue. 'I just wanted to get the hell out of there as quickly as possible. He said we could wait for you but no way was I going to. I was scared.'

That's when the anger exploded. 'Scared?! You were scared of...a look? An indescribable yet "terrible" look?' I shouted, ignoring the razor blades that seemed to score at my swollen tonsils. 'He made you feel uncomfortable. Good grief, have you any idea how petty and ridiculous you sound. What did you think he was going to do, leap on you and ravage you? Hold you hostage? Slit your throat?'

'You weren't there,' said Hannah.

'No, but I'm here now, hoping you can offer me something more than this. Christ, you've got in a moody with me

because I wasn't in when you deigned to come and see me; that's what's put your nose out of joint. If you were genuinely so scared you could have told me this crap weeks ago but instead you've waited and waited – and you know why? Because it's a nothing, a nonsense. You just always have to be in control of our friendship, be Little Miss Popularity bestowing your friendship on me. Well I don't want your friendship. Stuff you!'
I gave it to her with both barrels. She stepped back from me, amazed that I've finally stood up to her because we have never, ever had a row before as I always just go along with what she wants, for an easier life. Ever since school she has been the one in charge, and she hasn't been keen on Daryl from the start simply because he took me away from her and she didn't like the fact that someone else had more influence over me than her. She's not used to being challenged, was always so popular at school; sporty, clever, the first to get picked on teams, while I hung on to her coat tails a bit and was popular purely by association with her. This was the first time I had ever challenged her, and she didn't know what to do. It was empowering to see her step back like that, stunned.
I could understand her reaction though because I was pretty stunned myself. But I just carried on, for once feeling strong and unafraid of confrontation – I think it was my protective streak that gave me the strength; she was being so unfair on Daryl and hadn't even given him a chance to defend himself.
'You just feel bad because you know damn well how unreasonable you've been lately, and now, desperate for any excuse, you've decided to blame Daryl,' I ranted. 'You come

here and announce you hate my husband because - ooh, scary - he looked at you.'

I'm quite proud of myself because I spat the last bit out while doing a kind of jazz hands movement, totally taking the pee. I was so furious it gave me the guts to be sarky. Even now, I'm so angry I'm almost shaking. All right, so Daryl isn't the easiest of people. Even I freely admit that he's often a tosser when in company, seems to have this need to push people's buttons and act like a knob, but you just have to learn to ignore him. He's not scary!!!!

By the end of it, Hannah had got all sniffy, as though somehow I was being unreasonable. Silly cow. At least Amy had the courtesy to look mortified by the whole thing. 'We didn't mean to hurt you…' she began, but I cut her off. They both should have thought of that before they came to my house talking rubbish.

Tuesday 11

Still annoyed about yesterday. I'm not going to tell Daryl about it though because he'd, fair enough, go absolutely mental. He'd be so hurt. Poor bloke has little enough self-esteem as it is after all those years of being bullied at school and undermined by his mum, without people laying into him now. Tell you what though, if Hannah and Amy were terrified of one of his looks I reckon they'd wet themselves if he went to see them to give them a piece of his mind. The thought almost makes me tempted to tell him, but no, it's not fair on him. Shame though.

Anyway, the good news is, the tonsils have come right down to normal size and I am starting to feel human again. I don't like to boast but I washed my hair this morning. I had to, otherwise it might have walked off and washed itself, it was in such a state.

Afterwards I sat and read the mags Amy and Hannah had brought round (at least the visit was good for something). There was an article in it about 'How to spot if he's having an affair'. Elusive behaviour, hard to pin down, irritable, frequently unreachable on the phone… Should I be worried that Daryl ticks every one? Well theoretically, yes. The thing is though…he's always been the same. So unless he has been having an affair for the last nine years, the entire time we've been together, then I'm not too worried. Boy would he have to have an understanding mistress!

We even joke about it sometimes when, for example, he'll mention having been to the cinema to see something and he'll think we've been together. 'No, that was with your other woman,' I'll laugh, and he cracks up too.

Or sometimes he forgets he's told me things and will either not have told me at all or told me 20 times and he'll snigger and say: 'Ah no, I must have told the other woman, not you.' I've even asked him before if he is seeing someone else – not in an accusing way though because that would just cause a row; in a jovial, funny way. He just gives me an exasperated but sympathetic look and says: 'How the hell could I have an affair? Even if I wanted to I don't have time for one. I can barely find the time to be with you and I love you to bits.' Sometimes he is such a sweetheart and knows just what to say to make me feel better. Can't wait to see him tomorrow.

Thursday 13
Daryl is home. These ten days away have seemed so long, too long. When he climbed into bed beside me last night it felt odd for a second. The bed seems so different with him, the duvet too small to cover us both, the mattress tension firmer because it is stretched further with the weight of two

bodies instead of one, and he gives off so much heat that I am roasting and have to poke a foot out from under the duvet to try to sneakily cool down.

But then he throws his arm around me and pulls me in to him, and somehow our bodies just fit together like two pieces of a jigsaw. We know each so well that we automatically twist to one another without any thought. My leg over his, his leg over mine, a knotty tangle that no one could undo. Then my nose nuzzles into his neck and I breathe in the oil, diesel, Lynx, Daryl smell and I smile to myself like an idiot as happiness rushes through me, and suddenly everything seems so right. Daryl is home and all is good with the world.

Saturday 15

I am so lucky to have a man like Daryl. Seriously. I very nearly cocked us up permanently today, and feel queasy every time I think about it. Bloody Hannah and Amy, it's all their fault.

I kept thinking about that stupid magazine article. Unable to shake the paranoia gnawing at me, I sneaked downstairs this morning and - eurgh, I'm ashamed to write it down and have a permanent record – I sneaked a look through Daryl's phone.

How awful is that?! I kept thinking about how he ticked virtually every single one of the criteria in the feature, and had worked myself up into a real tizz. Convinced myself that that was why Hannah had felt afraid of Daryl, too, because he had given her one of his smouldering, lustful looks. They can be pretty impressive, and they certainly take my breath away.

So I scrolled through all of his messages. And I found absolutely nothing. The relief! And the guilt... I burst into tears and went straight up to the bedroom, prodding Daryl awake. He knew from the look on my face that something was wrong, I think, because he looked worried as he propped himself up on a pillow.

When he gets in a bad mood his face reminds me of one of those speeded up film sequences where the clear sky is suddenly blotted out by clouds racing across and turning blacker. His face changes that quickly. There's that saying isn't there, 'a face like thunder'. That's literally what he has.

I sat on the edge of the bed, telling him everything and watching him carefully, keyed up and waiting for that time lapse camera moment, for his expression to change from worried to angry…but it never came.

After I'd tearfully confessed all, my poor, bemused husband was so fantastic. He didn't say a word, just sat up and gently pulled me against him, letting me cry against his chest. I could barely look at him, so he held me close and kissed the top of my head, breathing into my hair in that funny way of his until it was all hot.

'It's okay, it's all okay, hush,' he soothed again and again.

How can I doubt someone so understanding; because I'd go nuts if he did the same to me, accusing me of things, of secrets and lies. But that's decided me once and for all. I am fighting for this marriage. We've been great before, and we'll be great again. I will not give up on us just because I feel a bit bored and not quite right about things.

Sunday 16

Argh! Remembered today that I have completely missed Sarah's birthday. So I rushed out and bought her a jumper from the supermarket in the end. Well, supermarket stuff is great these days so I'm sure she'll like it. But wrapping has never exactly been my strong point…

INVISIBLE

'I've got to send Sarah's present to her, but I'm worried the package will fall apart,' I moaned to Daryl, showing him the flimsy parcel I'd created. It looked like a three-year-old had wrapped it.

'I've got some duct tape you can use, that will hold most things in place.' He smirked, as though at some private joke. Yes, well, the parcel did look pretty funny; I had made a poor job of it. Ha bloody ha.

He went out to his truck and came back seconds later brandishing the tough silver tape, still sniggering away to himself. He quickly unfurled it, covering almost the whole package with it. Daryl's strong fingers worked rapidly, tearing the tape with a strength and well-practiced technique that surprised me, until only the tiniest amount of brown paper peeked out here and there.

'Job done,' he said, patting it, satisfied.

'My hero,' I grinned. And I meant it.

APRIL

Thursday 3

If only everyone could be as happy as me right now. Sounds pretty smug, doesn't it, but I don't care. Everything is so great between Daryl and me. Why? Because not only is he still making an effort despite me acting so badly, but also I have finally learned the secret of happiness too. I simply let things go.

I'm so much more relaxed, and am not letting myself get annoyed by stuff, or dwell on questioning things; I'm just going with the flow. And when Daryl does bug me, I just take a deep breath and count to ten and tell myself it doesn't matter. I'm thinking big picture now, i.e. saving my marriage, not sweating the details by getting annoyed when he doesn't always do exactly what I want.

I am using my new-found happiness to try to encourage Kim to split from Psycho Sam. 'There is a wonderful man somewhere out there, just waiting to make you happy. But until you split from Sam you will never meet them, because you're not ready. Break free from his control, take control of your life again, and things will change for the better,' I coach. She actually seems to be listening.

Amy has really apologised as well for what she said about Daryl. She still insists they were scared but admits there was no actual reason for it at all and they over-reacted, and the more they talked about it together the more they cranked it up to be something bigger in their imaginations than it actually was.

I haven't heard from Hannah though...

Saturday 12

'How is Saggy Tits? Not seen her around lately,' Daryl asked suddenly over breakfast this morning.

So he's noticed Amy and I have had a bit of a falling out. Instead of letting him wind me up though, I just told him that wasn't a nice way to speak about my friends, said it in a very neutral way – lightly, even, so he had nothing to trigger off and we wouldn't row. Since I've determined to be more of a grown up and stop reacting to him, things have been much better between us.

He wouldn't let it go though.

'She's a bit of a whore though, isn't she,' he said, mimicking my matter-of-fact tone.

'Daryl!' Okay, I bit, but he was definitely asking for it.

'What?' he grinned. 'She is. She puts it about a bit. A right cunt.'

I screwed my eyes closed and shook my head. I hate that word! And he knows it, was just using it for a reaction. So instead I just forced my eyes open and smiled. 'Well she's a big girl, and not hurting anyone else, so who cares how many people she does or doesn't sleep with. You don't have to worry about her sex life, just mine.'

Keen to get him off the subject of Amy, because then I might have to explain what we'd fallen out over, and emboldened by the success of my 'go with the flow' plan, I stepped towards him and gave him what my dear departed gran would have described as a 'come hither' look.

'She can never have what I've got, no matter how many people she sleeps with,' I said as huskily as I could muster. 'She can never have you. Why don't you show me what she's missing?'

Well, my lust-fuelled idea worked in one respect. It took Daryl's mind off Amy. Sadly it didn't get his mind on to me though. He gulped down his coffee and set his mug down, suddenly full of purpose.

'Right, I need to clear the cab of my lorry out,' he said. And instead of coming hither, he went outside.

Monday 14

Kim has dumped Psycho Sam!!!! And this time she actually seems to mean it!

She came into work today smiling but nervous, and I knew immediately something had happened. I went into the kitchen to make a cuppa, and put two mugs out, knowing she'd join me any moment.

'I've done it,' she whispered the second she appeared, eyes all bright and sparkly like they haven't been in months and months (unless you count times where they've twinkled with tears).

'You've...?' I said, letting the sentence hang there, not daring to finish it the way I suspected it would end, just in case.

'I've finished with Sam.'

'Oh my God!' I shouted. We both ducked instinctively, grimaced at how loud I'd been, then giggled. As we held onto each other, unable to stop, I tried to mouth sorry, but it just made us laugh even more. I think we were both hysterical with joy that Psycho Sam had been given the elbow at long last.

Finally, I pulled myself together with one last cheery sigh. 'So what happened? What's different this time?'

She shrugged. 'Nothing. Despite our whole relationship being one big drama, there was no huge, earth-shattering explosion of emotion. It was everything, you know? The constant atmosphere, the walking on eggshells, the rowing, and the person he was turning me into; I didn't recognise myself any more, was nothing like I'd been when we'd first met. Putting up with all kinds of crap, having my self-esteem chipped away, getting into physical fights. He'd even started complaining about the way I dressed – and I was listening and changing.

'I told myself they were little things, and that the problem was with me, but that wasn't true…and it all piled up until I couldn't take it any more. And instead of getting angry and shouting, I was just very calm and told him I couldn't do this, it wasn't what I wanted or needed. That I was happy for him to stay with me for a month, to sort out a place to live, but that he would be sleeping on the sofa until he left.'

'Wow,' I breathed. 'And how did he take it? Did he go mental?' Beside me the kettle boiled, the button clicking off as steam poured upwards, but I ignored it.

'You know what? He seemed to accept it. Seemed defeated. Mind you, he probably thinks I'll change my mind, that this is just like all the other times we've split.'

'But it isn't?'

Reaching past me, she picked up the kettle and poured water into the waiting mugs. 'No chance. This time I really mean it.'

And you know what? For some reason, it does feel different this time; she does seem stronger, calmer, more in control. Actually, she seems more like the Kim I met three years ago when I started at the company.

Finally everything seems to be coming together and everyone is getting a step closer to their happy endings. I've just got to keep up my 'stay calm, don't argue, go with the flow' mantra.

Wednesday 23

Poor Daryl sent me a text message tonight saying how much he missed me. He sounded tired. Does that sound funny? Yes, but he did. There was nothing in particular he said in it to hint at that, but you just know someone inside out after so many years don't you. I know him so well I can even tell how he's feeling just from a text message.

Still, he'll be home this weekend, and I can't wait. We'll spend a bit of quality time together, maybe go for a meal or something or the cinema.

MAY

Saturday 9
Blimey, it's been over a fortnight since I've written my diary. I suppose that now things have settled down between Daryl and me, there's less need for it – it's a great way of pouring out my feelings and sorting through stuff, but I need to do that less now. But today I have big news, because I'm going on holiday! Woo hoo!
Daryl has, by a small miracle, managed to book the same time off as me. It's normally a total nightmare co-ordinating holidays, but this was stunningly simple. And so we're off on a last minute break. Hu-blinking-rah!
Aside from that, nothing much has changed really. Kim is doing well after her split with Sam. He's found a place to move into, and leaves next week. He wants to stay in touch and Kim is staying neutral about the idea at the moment because she doesn't want him to kick off, but actually she's no intention of having anything to do with him ever again.
What else? Hannah still hasn't been in touch and I'm sure as hell not contacting her. She needs to apologise to me. And although on the surface Amy and I seem okay, I'm wary of her, and she seems the same of me. I'll never fully trust her again, I don't think, because she really hurt me, and for no reason at all.

Saturday 30
Wow. What a day. What a glorious, fabulous day. Daryl and I are finally on our holidays!!
He arrived last night after working all day, then driving over to me, arriving home at 10pm. As soon as I opened the

door he ran past me saying: 'I'm gonna be sick, I'm gonna be sick.'

Luckily he made it to the loo. That's the first time in all these years together that I've ever known him vomit.

Anyway, I suggested he go to bed for a couple of hours before we had to go to the airport. We had a lovely chat in bed because he felt much better and he just stroked my hair and face for ages as we talked. It was so relaxing, and finally we very gently made love.

Think we've really turned a corner because not only are we getting on well, but then something really amazing happened.

We had to get up at midnight, and I was rushing round double-checking that we'd packed our passports, tickets, suntan lotion, insect repellent, enough undies to last us... Daryl was sitting on the sofa watching me, head moving back and forth like he was watching a tennis match because I was running backwards and forwards with everything.

Suddenly his hand shot out and grabbed me, stopping me in my tracks – with hands his size, he could stop a juggernaut he's so strong. I just looked at him, surprised, eyebrows up near my hairline.

'I think we should go for it,' he said, nodding in determination. He must have seen the confused look on my face, because then he clarified. 'I think we should try for a baby, start a family.'

Yes! I felt like punching the air, or running around with my top over my head like blokes do when they've just scored a goal. Maybe throw in a somersault or two for good luck. Instead, I just let myself be pulled onto his lap and gazed into those blue eyes of his, as bright as icicles, and let my

smile spread as the reality of what he'd said sank in. Finally, I'm going to be a mum! Well, soon anyway, if things go well. I can't believe he finally he wants us to go for it. The only problem is (and I do feel bad even thinking about whinging when I'm so happy) I really would like Daryl to be at home more before we have a child. He spends so many days away, and has to work such crazily long hours because those gits who run the haulage business are making him break the law all the time on his hours. How they manage to rig the taco is beyond me, but Daryl works loads more hours than is legal.
We chatted about it while we were at the airport, waiting to board our flight. Well, I nagged about it.
'Maybe you should just refuse,' I said. 'They can't force you to break the law.'
He gave me a look that showed how naive he thought I was being, but took my hand and twined his fingers with mine. For the first time I noticed he'd got a nasty graze on his knuckles and they looked swollen, but now wasn't the time to ask how he'd managed that, so instead I gently stroked the back of his hand with my free hand.
'I'm scared I'll lose my contract,' he sighed. 'They've not outright said that, of course, but it's definitely been hinted at. What choice have I got? I have to do what they say, because if they get rid of me I don't even get severance pay because I'm freelance. There's nothing to stop them turning round tomorrow and telling me they don't need me any more.'
I looked down at our hands, which formed a cage the way our fingers were woven together. He's a lot more trapped than my digits, and it makes me so angry on his behalf. It's not fair!
Anyway, I'm determined to leave all that behind for a week. Who cares about work! We're on holiday and we're trying for a baby. I don't think I could get happier! Daryl seems

really cheery and content too, though I think it's partly relief that he no longer needs to dodge the 'when are you going to make an appointment with a counsellor' question any more, since clearly he no longer needs to see anyone to work through his problems now he has got past his phobia of having a family.

So, we're now in Olu Deniz, Turkey. After a late lunch we wandered down to the beach. This is our second trip here, and it felt lovely to be back, like saying hello to an old friend – I was overjoyed when Daryl said he'd managed to book our break here. We went to the left side of the beach rather than the lagoon, as last time we were here we never really got round to exploring that bit.

Exploring is too active a word though. Actually I lay there looking at literally turquoise sea, pure white surf crashing onto the pebbles; the sight and the sound was hypnotising. Sunbathed, read, splashed around with Daryl, who couldn't stop laughing.

JUNE

Monday 1
Went out for a meal last night and then back to hotel for 'a quick nightcap'. Turned into a bit of a session, and we drank and chatted to other couples until 3am. Good fun. Felt a bit wobbly this morning!
We've done loads though. First we went by boat to the mud baths at Dalyan. Stripped down to our swimwear and sat in a big pool of warm mud to cover ourselves from head to toe in the thick, sticky substance.
'Poo! It stinks like rotten eggs,' I gasped, wrinkling my nose as Daryl scooped up a massive handful and slapped it onto his arm, smearing it across his skin with grim determination. I thought it might sting his bad hand but it didn't seem to bother him.
'That's the sulphur in it.' He pointed to a placard that explained why the mud was so good for you, and all about the sulphur. I'd completely failed to notice it, of course, but my gaze was dragged away from it by Daryl puffing out his chest towards me. 'Come on, babe, lay it on me. Then I'll do you, it'll be easier,' he insisted.
It was the weirdest beauty treatment in the world. There we were, surrounded by equally mud-caked tourists, all of us stinking to high heaven and loving it. I could imagine people all through the ages doing just as we were, even Romans relaxing in the muck.
I put the finishing touch to Daryl's face, carefully applying it with my fingertips until only his eyes were untouched. When he smiled, his teeth shone through, brilliant white. I smiled back, feeling the already drying mud tighten then crack slightly at the movement.

'How do I look?' I mumbled, like a bad ventriloquist, trying not to move my mouth too much.

He leaned back to take in my full, reeking glory. 'You've never look better – or smelled it,' he joked. Ha, ha.

We both baked gently in the sun until the mud hardened, then rinsed off in a shower before dipping in a hot thermal bath. Wonderful! My skin felt so very soft afterwards.

Then we went by boat again to the beach where the loggerhead turtles lay their eggs. The surf there is massive but the sea is also very shallow for a very long way out. We both went out into the surf, and the crashing waves kept almost pulling my bikini off! We were jumping over the big waves like kids and laughing. Great fun. Then we dried off in the sun before sailing back. It was just glorious sitting at the head of the boat, lying on the flat bulkhead, sunbathing.

Tues 2

It's 10am and already uncomfortably hot. I've arranged to meet Daryl downstairs in 15 mins because he wanted to finish off his breakfast, while I panicked about burning so decided to come to the room and slap on the factor 30! We've a hectic day ahead of us...

Weds 3

Well yesterday got off to a good start. Daryl had really splashed out and hired a sort of yacht called a gullet. Where he got the money from God knows but, hey, I'm just glad he's spending it on treats for me! We sunbathed on the deck, beneath the masts and every now and again the captain would pull into a secluded harbour and we'd climb down the rope ladder and swim in the sea from the boat. Fab.

INVISIBLE

I was a bit wary at first about swimming straight from the boat because obviously I couldn't put my feet down on the floor, but the warm, bright blue sea is so salty there that I was incredibly buoyant, so it wasn't a problem. It was amazing swimming round and round the boat. Then it was back to a bit more sunbathing!

Daryl was getting a bit amorous on deck, but I wasn't having a bar of it. Honestly, he's terrible! Can't keep his hands off me sometimes, and he does love a bit of al fresco action.

'Come on, Gorgeous, the captain won't notice,' he insisted, hands sliding up my thigh. I slapped him away, but laughed. He pouted – those big lips of his are built for that expression. Then he had an idea, grabbed the towel and flung it over my bottom half. 'I could touch you under this...' he began. Before I had a chance to say no, his fingers slipped under my bikini bottoms.

I rolled away, scandalised. 'No chance,' I hissed, giving him a stern look. Not too stern, but enough to show I meant business. I think he gets off on the thrill of possibly being discovered – but let's face it, when you're on a tiny boat and there's only three of you, chances are you're going to be caught in the act!!

Anyway, I got absolutely hammered last night. We got back from the boat trip and went to our hotel room and tried to have sex but...Daryl's problem made a re-appearance.

We didn't talk about it, of course, we never do, and I pretended not to notice when things failed to rise to the occasion. But it makes me feels so rejected, and Daryl always seems so deflated afterwards. Ooh, unfortunate turn of phrase there... But it definitely put a dampener on the mood, which had been really buoyant up until then.

This problem of his has been happening on and off for the last two years or so, and seems to have got worse since I really started hammering home how much I want a baby. I'd hoped that him agreeing to that would mean the problem wouldn't happen again, but seems I was wrong.

Am I not enough woman for him? Don't I turn him on? Maybe I'm just really bad in bed. Oh heck, how embarrassing. I bet it's me. It can't be him, he's always so rampant and up for it. One look at me is enough to turn him limp though.

Afterward we'd got dressed; we'd decided to go for a nice meal in nearby Hisaronou and we shared a bottle of wine…then another bottle…then we went to a bar and had another bottle, plus a couple of cocktails. I was steaming and we had a row.

'If you want to fuck that bloke, why don't you just go over to him?' Daryl snapped at me suddenly. I'd immediately tensed up, even in my drunken state, knowing that he was picking a row with me for no reason because he was in a bad mood about our abortive sex. A row would make him feel a bit better, more in control. So I tried to stay calm.

'I'm not looking at anyone,' I said, looking him in the eye. Admittedly, it was quite hard to do because the room was swimming a bit as I'd had so much to drink. It may have been an unsteady look, but it was still sincere though.

'Do you think I'm stupid? You've been looking at him ever since we got in here. At least have the respect to not rub my face in it.'

The storm clouds had well and truly gathered, his face like thunder. I made myself take a deep breath, didn't want to panic and make things even worse. I tried to soften my voice, like an FBI agent in a film trying to negotiate with a mad bomber or something.

'Daryl, I'm not looking at anyone but you. I don't want anyone but you. I don't even know what bloke you're talking about.'

'Don't treat me like I'm an idiot,' he shouted, the barstool clattering to the floor as he stood up. He leaned right down over me, his face almost touching mine and I flinched back. 'Don't ever treat me like I'm a fucking idiot.'

Then he stropped off and left me alone. At first I was a bit relieved, but as adrenaline made me sober up slightly, I started to get teary, then really angry.

Furious, I stomped after him but there was no sign. I walked round and round that pub for ages looking for him, even asked a fella to check the gents for me, but he'd gone. Eventually I got a cab back, but he wasn't at the hotel room either. God knows what time he did arrive – I was dead to the world by then; passed out, if I'm honest.

So we've spent most of today barely talking. He still seems to think the whole thing is my fault and that I should apologise. Keeps muttering about me eyeing up some ginger bloke. I don't even remember seeing a red-head, let alone giving him the eye, but Daryl won't listen and every time I try to tell him it jut sparks another row. He says I'm treating him like he's stupid, that I'm showing him no respect, that I'm just a tart. It's so crushing after the wonderful start to the holiday, and I don't know what to do.

Maybe, this is payback for me going through his phone. But at least when I did that I realised immediately how terrible I was being, how wrongly I was acting, and confessed all to him in a bid to make things right.

So no, I'm not apologising to him until he apologises to me. He's the one in the wrong, I haven't done anything. Besides, I've got a stonking headache that's putting me in a very bad mood, so there is no way I'm giving in on this.

Thurs 4

Okay, so I apologised to Daryl this morning. It's day two of the hangover (seriously, I can't handle my drink now I'm in my 30s. I remember when I used to drink loads then wake up bright and breezy the next day. Now it takes me two days to get over a big night. Two days!!) and I didn't have the strength to keep up hostilities.

So this morning I tried to give him a hug in bed. He shook me off. I knew what I had to do. 'I'm so sorry,' I said in a small voice. 'I was drunk, I honestly don't remember what I did, but I never, ever intended to upset you. Please...forgive me?'

Did it put a smile on Daryl's face? No. He was still in a right old grump. But at least things thawed between us slightly and I knew it was only a matter of time before I was in his good books again.

Still, when he grunted at me that he wanted a Turkish bath, I just couldn't face it. The thought of getting all sweaty and claustrophobic in a tiny cubicle then having someone pummel me...no thanks, not with my stomach still so delicate, and my head still woozy and thumping.

Instead I said I'd just lie round the pool...and I heard something terrible. The gossip poolside is that a woman was attacked last night and raped. Awful.

The other holidaymakers reckon that the police and the hotel staff are all keeping it quiet because they don't want tourism affected – but I think that's disgusting, if it's true.

I don't know how much I believe, the details are a bit sketchy, but, well, it's shaken me up. This girl was attacked on her way back to her hotel after leaving a nightclub – one not far from where Daryl and I were.

INVISIBLE

When I told Daryl, I freaked out a bit. 'I was stumbling round last night, really drunk and…it could have been me!' I said. 'You left me on my own…it could have been me.'

All thoughts of our stupid row were forgotten instantly. He gave me a big hug and said: 'No one's touching you, they'd have to get through me first.'

Bless him, I always feel so safe with him. He must have been worried too though, because he actually apologised for leaving me alone.

'I'm an idiot, I shouldn't have done that,' he admitted. 'I won't leave you again for the rest of the holiday – promise.

'No matter how stroppy you get,' he added, the cheeky devil.

Fri 5

Our last day. I've been lying on the beach all day thinking about the little boy or girl I'm going to have one day soon. Who will our child take after most? My eyes or Daryl's? My lips or Daryl's? My temperament or Daryl's?

JULY

Sunday 12
2am – I need to write this all down to make it real. Or maybe I shouldn't write it down, maybe it shouldn't be real. I don't want it to be real.
3.15am – I've been pacing. Kim is staying with me. Bless her, she dropped everything when I called her. Everyone did. But she offered to stay, knew I didn't want to be alone. In a minute I'm going to write down what happened. I think. I feel like I'm going mad, or am the butt of a very sick joke or something. I want to curl up and pretend that what's happened hasn't happened at all…
Let me start small. I've been arrested. I'm staring at those three words now, hoping to drill them into my brain so I'll accept and somehow reboot myself so that I work again, because at the moment I feel like a faulty computer. My programme is frozen and no matter how hard someone punches the keys, I can't respond with anything other than a whirling 'wheel of death'.
So, I've been arrested. The next bit to write is why, and I don't think I can face those words. Not yet. Not yet. Too soon. I'll have to work my way up to it.
Daryl was home last night – well, the night before last, now, I suppose; I don't know where I am any more. Anyway, it was Friday he came home. He was in one of his moods, but I'm used to that. I just hid in the kitchen for a while, stretched out cooking for as long as possible, hoping that

eventually he'd crack a smile. Or at least not have a go at me.

Made him a cup of tea, made sure I got it exactly the right colour for him. Put the telly on, let him watch whatever he wanted, while I loitered, giving the countertops a good wipe down, getting the sink sparkling.

It wasn't too bad a night in the end, he did cheer up a bit. I just let him slag off every telly programme and that seemed to vent most of his mood. Let him have sex – I mean, it's no hardship really to do it. I enjoy it most of the time. But it was one of those horrible nights when he wasn't making love to me, wasn't even having sex, I just ended up lying there while he pounded me. It took everything I'd got not to cry. He didn't look at me, just pounded away.

It doesn't happen often, but when he's like that I always feel like I could be anyone, like I'm just a hole he's shagging. There's no connection. He had that dead-eyed look, when his eyes remind me of a shark's. Bright, cold blue, and devoid of emotion. Where does he go when he looks like that?

But I made myself make all the right noises, do all the right moves, so that he'd think it was good, and eventually he finished. He withdrew for that. I remember thinking: 'How am I ever going to get pregnant if he doesn't do the deed inside me?' and feeling hurt about it. Knowing that at some point I'd have to ask him, and trying to work out the best time to tackle it, the best way of phrasing it so that it didn't seem like I was having a go at him. We'll probably never have that conversation now though.

Afterwards, we curled up and fell asleep quickly. It was the bang that woke me. The sound of the door hitting the wall as it exploded open, only of course I'd no idea that was what the sound was at the time. All I knew was that some bloody loud noise had made me jump from sleep to wake in a microsecond, my heart thumping away as suddenly it looked like aliens had taken over the bedroom, all these lights bobbing up and down, shining onto the bed, people shouting, shouting, shouting. So many people shouting at once, the noise overwhelming.

I couldn't make head or tail of what was happening, my brain still too heavy with sleep to work. I just lay there, scrabbling around for the duvet and pulling it up under my chin like it would somehow protect me. Were we being burgled? Had Daryl somehow annoyed the wrong person? I had no idea, didn't really have time to think.

It shows how quick it happened, because Daryl didn't even have time to jump up and get angry, although he was on his feet before I realised what was going on.

Just then my addled brain worked out what the hell everyone was shouting. 'Police! Stay down, stay down! Stay where you are!' And Daryl was up now, shouting back, his words drowned out by the din. Out of the darkness someone in black grabbed him.

The lights were wobbling all over the places, torches held by these blokes. Wobbling from me to Daryl, Daryl to me. I'm amazed there was enough room in our bedroom for so many people – I mean, it's quite a tight fit between the wardrobe and the bed.

And that's what I kept thinking as someone read Daryl his rights and arrested him. I just kept thinking: 'How do they all fit in here, all these policemen? How many of them are there, because there are a lot of torches...'

Think I must have been in shock.

By the time an officer had flicked the big light on, Daryl was already in cuffs, completely starkers, and I'd totally missed why he'd been arrested.

That's when I noticed they were all holding what looked like little machine guns. If I'd been scared before, now I was terrified.

As he was led out, a woman came over and sat on the side of the bed, like she was a friend. That just confused me even more. She said I was coming to the station too, but instead of asking questions I just pulled the duvet a bit higher and nodded.

'Where does your husband keep his clothes?' she asked. I pointed to the chest of drawers and she opened it up and took a jumper and some jeans out for him, then opened up a couple of other drawers and chucked some of my clothes onto the bed for me. 'I'll leave you alone to get dressed,' she added.

When the door closed, I was alone. I stared at the wall for a minute or so, stunned, literally stunned, then shook my head and got up, trying to move quickly then as I realised someone could burst into the room any second. It's hard work putting on clothes when you're shaking and there's a bunch of strange blokes standing on the other side of the door, and it's 3am and you've just been shocked out of sleep. I couldn't even stand on one leg to pull my socks on, had to sit down as I was trembling so much.

After all that shouting the quiet seemed so eerie and my ears rang so loudly – which only goes to show that silence really can be deafening, but only if you've got tinnitus.

The officers were ever so nice though, as they read me my rights and arrested me. Honestly I couldn't take in what they said, their words fading in and out of my consciousness like someone was turning the volume on a radio up and down, up and down, very quickly.

Charges...aiding and abetting...multiple persons or person...

So I just assumed I'd misheard the whole thing, that what they had said couldn't be true.

'Are you going to handcuff me?' I asked, dazed. I even offered my wrists. Well, I didn't want to annoy them, wanted them to know I was a nice person and had absolutely no flipping idea what they were on about. I mean, how could I have anything to do with breaking the law? How could I have anything to do with the terrible thing they believed I'd done; something so awful that my whole mind and body rebelled every time the words flashed through my brain.

The officer just glanced at my proffered wrists then gave me a look. Sort of pitying and exasperated all at once, in his cool little SWAT team type dark navy clothes – you know, those little boiler suit type things, with 'firearms officer' written on the back.

'No, you don't exactly look like a flight risk,' he sighed,

I'm writing all of this down now and it doesn't seem real. It's like a scene from a film...or a sitcom. I mean, my husband and I had just been arrested, and I didn't dare check why because I'd been told already and didn't want them to think I was stupid.

Next thing I know I'm in the back of a police car being driven to the station (no sign of Daryl, they'd put him in a separate car). I was shaking and juddering like an ancient diesel engine. I tried to stop, tried to get my body under control even if I couldn't marshal my thoughts yet, but no matter how hard I tensed up and willed myself to stay still, the trembling continued.

I only came to myself when I realised we'd gone round the same roundabout twice. By the third time it was obvious that we were a bit lost. Before I quite knew what I was doing I found myself piping up from the back: 'Umm, are you okay? Only there's an A-Z back at the house; we could go back and get it if you like?'

The officers exchanged sidelong glances. I'm a decent person, you see. I don't deserve to be questioned for a heinous crime because actually I'm so nice and polite that I even offer to help out police officers who've arrested me. I don't think they knew what to say, not sure they'd ever dealt with anyone like me before. Probably more used to people swearing and spitting at them, but I respect the police force, think they do a hard job under tough conditions. Well, I wouldn't want to do that job…

In the end the one in the passenger seat replied. 'It's okay, we'll radio the station for directions. We've, umm, not been to this station before, aren't from round here.'

That was clear, by now we were on our fifth go round the roundabout and I was starting to feel a bit ill. Luckily, the female driver took a punt on one of the roads next time round and turned out she was right, according to the directions they got over the radio seconds later.

You'd think I'd have been angry, or trying to figure out what all this was about. But honestly? I wasn't. I think I'd kind of shut down. All I knew was I was really, really scared and nervous, but just thought everything would work out in the end because, well, I'm innocent. I speed occasionally, I once drove without realising my tax had run out…and then carried on driving for a week or so knowing it had run out because I didn't have two pennies to rub together…but aside from that, I've always been law abiding. I don't even drop litter, disgusting habit.

I hoped Daryl wasn't getting too angry, hoped he was okay. He'd be spitting feathers, and quoting all kinds of rights at the officers. He'd sort this mess out quick smart, I knew, I just hoped he didn't start threatening to sue them and getting up their nose. I wanted this over as quickly as possible and if he annoyed them they might drag their heels just to spite him. You get further being nice, I always find.

Once we'd found the huge police station, we parked up at the back and I was led inside through a grey, depressing concrete passageway. I looked round but couldn't see Daryl anywhere and just tried to avoid anyone else's eye. God knows what those people were being questioned for, and the last thing I wanted was to have some hard nut think I was staring at them.

Instead I just kept my eyes on the floor, and once again tried to stop the shaking, especially as now I had to sign things. I don't even know what it was I was signing – it was all explained to me, and I was asked if I understood, and I definitely nodded but, come on, who understands in those circumstances. I reckon only the guilty would be able to keep a clear enough head to start asking about terms and conditions.

'Hand over your jewellery, shoes and belt, please,' ordered the duty sergeant.

What? I just stood there, opening and closing my mouth like a goldfish or a cartoon character, before finally finding my voice. 'Wh...?' It came out a hoarse whisper and I cleared my throat, licked my dry lips, before trying again. 'Why?'

'To stop you using anything to harm yourself,' he explained. He looked quite sorry for me as he said it. That meant a lot, that little show of humanity, and it gave me the courage to slip my shoes off then undo my belt and slide it through the guides.

Only problem was, in the confusion I'd just slipped on what the policewoman had picked out for me and thrown on the bed, and she'd chosen my old jeans. They're really big. Without a belt, I had to use one hand constantly to stop them falling down. They wouldn't have gone all the way, of course, but I didn't really want crims and coppers to see even the tops of my knickers. Mortifying.

Like someone in a film, I found myself having my mugshot taken. 'Face left, face front, face right,' I was told, and I was so stupid-scared in case I annoyed the man by turning the wrong way in my muddle. Of all the things to be scared by.

'Fingerprints next,' said the officer. He wasn't unkind, simply business-like. I suppose this was just another day in the office for him. Funny, how one person's disaster, their life crashing down around their ears, can just be someone else's dull, typical day. So over I shuffled, careful not to trip over the bottom of my jeans, which pooled on the floor round my socked feet despite me tugging them up.

'Put your right hand onto the glass and press down gently,' I was told. Doing as I was told, I saw a light from underneath scan across, like on a photocopier. No ink. I didn't realise they didn't ink fingers any more to get prints. I was oddly disappointed by that.

Once I'd also rolled every individual finger and my thumb across the glass as well, and even done the side of my palm (why?!) I then held my trousers up with my right hand and repeated the whole process with my left.

Finally, a DNA sample was taken. A little swab brushed against my cheek, like a Popsicle, while I stood with my mouth open, fighting the childish urge to go 'ahhh' like I would if a doctor were checking out my tonsils. Now there will be a little piece of me held on the nation's database for all time.

Then I was put in a cell. Actually locked up. The metal door clanged shut, I heard the key turn in the lock, then I was alone.

The shaking, which had eased a bit, got worse again as I looked around that tiny little room. It wasn't dirty, in fact it was surprisingly clean, and painted that special, industrial creamy yellow that institutions choose when they're trying to be cheerful. Whose bright idea it was to pain a cell that colour I couldn't tell you.

My legs were feeling weak and wibbly, were starting to give out, so even though I didn't want to sit on the thin mattress that was placed over the concrete ledge that clearly served as a bed, I finally let go of my jeans and perched on the very edge of it. Drew my socked feet up and balanced my heels on the edge too, wrapping my arms round my knees as I tried to take in the reality of the fact I was here in a police cell, having been arrested.

'Daryl will sort it,' I told myself. How was he doing, I wondered. Was he locked in a cell too, feeling sorry for himself?

I couldn't imagine it somehow, could more imagine him ranting at people. Or, actually now I'd thought of it the most likely scenario was that he'd smooth-talked the policemen, made friends with them, and was having a chat with them in reception right now, charming them. He could turn on the magic when he wanted. He'd probably forgotten about me and would remember in an hour or so, and fling open the door eventually, having a laugh about 'my babe in a police cell!'

I shifted uncomfortably as I thought. About two inches thick, the mattress wasn't exactly comfy and my bum was starting to go numb but I couldn't move. Didn't want to. I wanted as little physical contact as possible with anything in that room – I'd have hovered above the floor if I could.

How long had I been in there? I'd no idea; they'd taken my watch and rings when they'd taken my shoes and belt. At one point I did stand and, clutching the waistband of my jeans, paced the cell to get the circulation moving again in my legs, stiff from sitting in one position for so long.

The fear started to be eroded by boredom, which made room for a bit of anger at this stupid situation. Why was I even here? It made no sense. They should be speaking to me, trying to clear this mess up.

For a moment I contemplated knocking on the door and asking to be dealt with – not in a nasty way, just in a firm manner. Pah, who was I kidding, there was no way I'd do something like that, it's just not my style.

Pressing as all this was, the police seemed in no hurry to clear things up and tell me what the hell was going on, and there were certain physical problems starting to rear their ugly head. Like, I started to need the loo.

There was a little, low wall in the cell and I had a horrible feeling…yes, when I peered round it, there was a shiny, stainless steel toilet. I couldn't use that! God knows who'd used it. Credit where credit's due, it looked like it had been scrubbed to within an inch of its life – it positively sparkled – but even so, I baulked at the thought. Apart from the hygiene reason, what if an officer walked in as I was mid business? Didn't bear thinking about.

Such are the daft things that went through my head during this. Because as weird as things were, my life was still essentially the same at that moment. I'd no idea what was coming next. People talk about having their world torn apart and yes, that's the closest description I can find for what happened.

I've been arrested. And now I've worked myself up until I'm ready to tell why. Ready to write the words down and face them. No point hiding from them any more.

Daryl is a rapist. A serial rapist who has attacked at least five women, and murdered one.

Even though I'm staring at the words, this feels no more real. What's wrong with me? Why can't I take it in? I'm still in my bubble of shock, I think. I feel removed from it all, like I'm hiding in the corner of the room watching it all pan out and none of it really affects me. How do you deal with something like this? How do you accept that the man you love is vicious, twisted, evil and you didn't even notice? How could I not have noticed?

What do you do when you realise your whole life has been a lie? I don't know. Somebody tell me, please.

Monday 13

It's 6am. My mind is whirling too much to sleep, though I did manage an hour or so. My eyes feel full of grit, my head full of cotton wool. And my heart? I don't know. I don't know.

But, as I keep replaying everything over and over in my head anyway, maybe it'll help to write it down. Hell, it might even help me make sense of things, if that's possible. There has to be some way of me getting a grip. So, here's the rest of what happened on Saturday…

When I was finally taken into the interview room I had no idea what to expect. There was a skinny man in there already, his incredibly thick, black hair stood up here and there like straw, even though I could tell he'd tried desperately to smooth it down, and he had the kind of stubble shadow on his pale face that is ever-present on very dark-haired men, even immediately after shaving.

'Hi, I'm Peter Simpson, the duty solicitor who has been designated to represent you at this time. Are you happy with that or do you have your own solicitor you wish to contact?' Business-like, but friendly.

INVISIBLE

Despite his suit seeming too big for him, adding to the whole impression that he was young and new to this game, I somehow felt I could trust him. I nodded timidly.

Then he told me why Daryl had been arrested. I shook my head, refusing to take it in. Patiently, he repeated the words, as though he was talking to a child. I just stared at my hands and continued to shake my head.

'Do you realise why you're here?' he ploughed on. More head shaking. He continued: 'You have been arrested as an accessory. The police think you may have helped him. But as far as I can tell there is no evidence to support that. I have to ask…did you?'

My head shot up then and I looked into his eyes. 'No!' I replied. It was whispered but still had force behind it. 'I would never hurt anyone. And neither would Daryl.'

I stuck to that, even when a man I hadn't seen so far walked in. I could tell from the way he held himself that he was in charge. He had that air, that confidence, bit like Daryl until you broke through the swagger to the scared child inside. Was this officer like that, I wondered?

He introduced himself as Detective Inspector Baxter and the woman beside him was Detective Sergeant Chapman. Just like I've seen on telly, they explained about how the interview would be taped, gave the date and time, and my name, then the fun began.

When I say fun, I'm being ironic.

For the next goodness knows how many hours I was basically asked the same questions over and over again: *Where were you on this date? Where was your husband on that date? What happened on the other date?*

'I'm really bad with things like this,' I tried to explain. 'If you asked me what I did yesterday I'd be hard pressed to remember.'

Still they asked. So many dates, going all the way back from nine months right up until a few weeks ago.

'Where were you on Tuesday the second of June this year?' the DS asked.

Automatically, I opened my mouth to say I couldn't remember, but then I did. 'Turkey! We were in Olu Deniz on a week's holiday,' I said triumphantly.

At least I could help with that one, so didn't feel completely useless. Ha! Daryl couldn't have hurt anyone when he wasn't even in the country.

But judging from the way DI Baxter pursed his lips he still wasn't happy, because then he just asked me tons of questions about the exact timing of every little thing we'd done while there. The more I tried to remember the more fuddled I seemed to get.

'We went on a boat that day…or was that the day I just stayed round the pool…? No, no, we went on a boat to a beach called, ummm…' I waved my hands, as if the whirring motion they made would help my brain turn a bit faster. Then I slumped.

'I don't remember the name of it, but it's where the turtles lay their eggs,' I said apologetically. 'But if you really need to know all these things, I do have a diary. All the info will be in there.'

That seemed to cheer the DS up, she seemed to sit a little straighter in her chair. The DI pursed his lips again though, drawing them together so that they reminded me of a dog's bum. Still, I wanted to help, I really did, because this had to be one big mistake and the sooner we got it cleared up the faster Daryl and I could go back to our old lives. And Daryl could probably sue the police for wrongful arrest…

INVISIBLE

After hours and hours of this, I was exhausted and still didn't feel like I'd helped either the police or Daryl, although I had remembered a couple more of the dates they'd asked me about, just because it had been Daryl's birthday and the like. I answered as honestly and fully as I could, but it's not as easy as it looks on telly and I was still so scared – especially of saying the wrong thing.

Then they start asking me about my love life! Does Daryl have any weird fetishes? Is he ever violent with me? Does he like it rough? Do I like it rough! Do we role play? It was mortifying. I wanted to be helpful but come on, some things are just off limits with strangers – what business was it of theirs what we did in private?

'Everything is perfectly normal, thank you,' I said primly.

Which it is! Like I'm going to start telling them about his occasional problem getting it up, or anything else we do. Some of the questions though…they made me squirm with embarrassment. DS Chapman tried to make out like we were having some kind of girlie chat together instead of sitting in a windowless interview room that smelt vaguely of farts (either that or someone had been boiling sprouts in there. I think not.)

'Come on, we've all been there; sometimes you go along with stuff your fella wants just for an easier life, even though it doesn't really do it for you. Just agree and get it over with, eh? Like, maybe some kinky stuff,' she said, leaning forward in a conspiratorial way and nodding gently, presumably at her foolishness in the sack.

'I-I don't…no,' I replied, confused.

Why was she saying this stuff to me? I'm sorry, but what happens between me and my husband is private; it's got nothing to do with anyone but us. I'm not one of those people who just tells all and sundry what I've been up to in bed. I don't even go into details with Kim, for goodness sake, and she's my closest friend!

'I don't know what you want me to say. Everything is fine and normal between us,' I said. DI Baxter did his dog bum impression again.

Finally the duty solicitor stepped in. 'It seems clear to me that my client knows nothing more than she has already told you.' And after a couple more minutes of waffling between the three of them a decision seemed to be made. Next thing I knew I was back at the reception desk signing yet another form to get my shoes and so on back.

'Here's a key to your place,' said the duty sergeant. I took it and stared at him, confused. 'New locks had to be fitted after they knocked your door in with the Big Red Key during the raid,' he added.

That just confused me even more. Big Red Key? But apparently that's the police nickname for the battering ram they use.

'Umm, what about my husband?' I asked timidly. 'Where is he? Is he coming home now too?'

'He's at a different station, still being questioned,' came the swift reply. I just nodded and wandered outside feeling like I'd been hit over the head.

Standing outside, the daylight seemed strange after leaving the house in the dark, then spending all that time in artificial light. I'd lost track of time. I looked around the car park, hoping for answers. Or at least a lift home. Stared at the big concrete building. It stared back, offering me nothing in reply to my questioning glance. So finally I turned and walked away, hands in my jeans pockets, towards the bus station.

INVISIBLE

I felt tired, grubby, confused, terrified for Daryl...and distinctly annoyed at having been swept from my home only to be dumped in the middle of town, miles away. How was I supposed to get home? There were so many other, bigger things to worry about, but as everything else was out of my control I concentrated on the one thing I could solve. If only I'd thought to pick up my purse before leaving the house, but it hadn't seemed a priority at the time.

I'd never really thought about what happens to people after they've been arrested. I mean, I suppose the police are far too busy to be used as a taxi service but it does seem a bit much to take you out of your home by force, and not offer you a lift back.

Finally I remembered about reverse charges calls, and found a working phonebox and rang Kim. Unable to face explaining everything to her, I simply said: 'I need you to come get me. It's an emergency, a proper emergency. Sorry to sound so dramatic but...'

'I'll be right there,' she replied quickly. Maybe it was my voice that made her realise, although I sounded very calm, I think.

Perhaps I sounded too calm. I feel too calm. I feel like I am very brittle and will shatter if I start to cry or allow emotions to take over.

We journeyed home in total silence. I did try to get my head together enough to explain, but...I just couldn't find the words. It was mental. Finally, as we pulled up, I cleared my throat.

'Erm, I'm not sure what the place will look like,' I apologised. 'The police raided us this morning, so they might have left a mess.' Did they leave mess? Or did they tidy up after themselves? I'd no idea what to expect. Maybe they'd have helped themselves to all our goods and chattels in their crazy quest to find evidence.

She nodded thoughtfully, then folded her hands in her lap. 'Love, what's going on?' she asked.

Time to spill the beans. She seemed to take it all in her stride. Maybe she didn't and I just didn't notice. I don't know. I don't know anything any more. At some point we clambered from the car and into the house, the new lock slightly stiff. Aside from that, you'd never have guessed anything had happened here. A couple of splinters of wood were scattered across the brightly-striped welcome mat, and the front door's white paint will need to be redone because there are some gashes on both sides of it... The police don't seem to have taken anything from the house either, apart from some work clothes of Daryl's and some shoes...and they've emptied the washing basket for some odd reason. Aside from that though, the place was pristine. It was surreal, as though the raid had been one of those very vivid dreams you have where you wake up thinking it's real, feeling it's real, but knowing it wasn't.

I slumped down onto the cream leather sofa from a great height, the cushions giving a puffy, huffy sigh as the air was forced from them. Kim offered to cook me some food, but I refused. Then she offered to get me a drink. I didn't refuse that.

I cupped the large vodka and tiny tonic in my hands, watching the liquid quiver and realising I hadn't stopped shaking all day. Certainly my world had been shaken apart, so maybe my body would be next. I took a big gulp.

'Hey, I can't taste the vodka,' I said, confused. 'Did you put any in?'

'I put in enough to poleaxe an elephant. You're in shock,' she said simply, squeezing my shoulder.

I nodded. It made sense, I suppose, though I'd never realised before that shock even affected tastebuds. Whatever, I took another big gulp. But what was the point when I couldn't taste it, couldn't feel it warming me and relaxing me. I knocked it back anyway and didn't so much as grimace – I've seen people in films do that and laughed at how unrealistic it is because you can't help but shudder if you take a massive, burning glug of a spirit, but now I realise how completely accurate it is. Shock has robbed me of everything, even my ability to taste. Nothing will ever be normal again.

As I put the empty tumbler on the glass coffee table, I frowned. I'd spent ages finding that and a matching dining table, which was just like one Daryl had seen in a magazine and announced he wanted. He'd barely even noticed when I'd tracked them down and proudly shown him, had just smiled in a vague way and muttered 'very nice'. What was I doing thinking about something like that at a time like this? It annoyed the hell out of me, as though I was somehow linking his ingratitude with his ability to be a killer.

'Where's Daryl now?' Kim asked. Filling the silence between us. Quiet as the grave, they say. It feels like someone has died.

'Still being questioned. I've got to find a solicitor from somewhere I suppose. I...I don't know what to do or how to do it or...anything.'

'I'll help. Everyone will help. I've got to go and fetch Henry from my mum's right now though. Are you going to be okay alone? I don't want to leave you. Shall I call your mum and dad?'

I let her, while I stared at the pale blue swirls on the cream rug as though I wanted to wear the pattern away through sheer force of will. Then I felt a hand on my wrist, shocking me from my reverie and making me look up.

'Will you be okay?' asked Kim again. 'I've called your parents; you mum is setting off right now, but it'll still be a couple of hours before she arrives.'

Mum would have to drive from Cambridge; it was a journey she hated and I was suddenly surprised that she was doing it. Wow, things must be bad - things must be as bad as I think they are – for her to brave that.

Kim was staring at me, waiting for an answer. I made myself nod, act normal.

'Okay, well, I've got to go,' Kim continued gently. Then she hesitated, mouth twitching before finally speaking again. 'Do…do you think there's anything to these allegations?'

I don't know. I don't. And I hate that I don't. I should be rushing round like a headless chicken, defending his name to all and sundry. Why aren't I? Because there is the tiniest sliver of doubt and I feel awful for it, but maybe this is why I've felt for a while that something isn't right, and I can't believe myself, can't believe my betrayal of the man I love, and how could I love someone who was capable of something like that, and what does it say about me if he did, and what does it say about me if he didn't and I'm sat here with a sliver of doubt slicing at my heart and soul, and I don't want to think about this, am not capable of dealing with this, I want to lie down and go to sleep, I want to watch Coronation Street and worry about what to cook for dinner, I want everything to be normal again, I want it to be yesterday, I want to be me, bored and wishing something exciting would happen, I want…

But of course I can't admit that to anyone. So instead I said: 'Of course there's nothing to this! It's all a horrible mistake. And I'm going to do everything I can to clear his name –

then we'll sue the arse off the police for this. They can't be allowed to get away with it.'

She looked at me for what can only have been a few heartbeats but seemed to last forever. What was in that gaze? So calm, so steady. It felt like she was making her mind up about something. The moment passed, she nodded, hugged me tight, then promised to come back as soon as she could, as soon as she'd sorted Henry.

Afraid to be left alone, I found myself calling anyone and everyone I could think of, even Amy and Hannah. Even as I repeated the words 'arrested…rape…murder' again and again, I still felt detached from everything and sort of calm whilst strangely agitated. I don't know how to describe it, how to explain that two completely warring feelings can control a person all at once. The closest thing I can describe it as is the way plunging your hand into an icy lake would feel like it was both freezing and burning you, two opposite things happening at once.

Amy was amazing. I was surprised by that. 'Oh my God! I'm in the middle of Tesco with a trolley full of shopping,' she babbled. 'Look, I'll just…there, I've just dumped it in the aisle; I can get a bus to you and be with you in what…30 minutes. Okay? I'll be with you in half an hour. Will you be okay until then? Just sit tight until then.'

Hannah's phone went straight to answerphone but I left a message, my voice suddenly breaking where before it had been so strong. Weird. Maybe it was the incongruity of leaving such a voicemail for someone. 'Something's happened to me and Daryl. I really need all my friends right now. Please call me as soon as you get this…please.'

In the end, within the hour I had Amy, Una and her husband Andy, and Kim round at mine. Almost a party. Or a wake. Together we talked about Daryl, about the charges, about how crazy it was. Yet somehow people seemed to lack the passionate conviction I needed from them.

By the time mum arrived I felt annoyed by everyone and just wanted to be left alone. I lay down in the bedroom, curled up like a baby, and tried to sleep but couldn't even close my eyes. How could I relax in that room when last time I'd been in there people had forced their way in and…

Feeling like a lost soul, I wandered back into the living room, hovering uncomfortably, as if this wasn't my own home.

'What does Daryl's mother make of this, love?' asked Mum.

Christ! I'd forgotten about her; she didn't even know!

Well, that phonecall was a barrel of laughs. She was funny from the start, but then I always find Cynthia a cold fish, but instead of biting I ploughed straight on with the news…

'Now you don't need to worry, I'm certain it's going to be sorted out quickly,' I fibbed. 'But the fact is Daryl's been arrested.'

I paused, expecting a reaction. A gasp of shock at the very least. Instead there was silence.

'Hello?' I checked.

'Yes, I'm still here, dear,' came the reply. 'Why has my son been arrest?'

Cold bitch. She must have to defrost her knickers every night when she gets undressed.

'The police have made an awful mistake,' I replied, just about keeping my temper in check. 'They think he's attacked someone, a woman, but we're sorting it out. I just thought you ought to know.'

'Attacked a woman? In what way exactly?' Still her voice sounded steady as a rock. It was as if she was asking me what depot Daryl was driving to or something.

'Well…I didn't want to say the details…but as you ask…ummm, rape.'

'I see. Well they must have evidence of some sort. No smoke without fire.'

I shook myself, stunned. 'Excuse me?'

'They must have a reason why they think he did it, dear,' Cynthia replied. 'I have to go now, I'm afraid. Goodbye.'

'Umm, bye.'

Unbelievable. Poor Daryl, having a mother like that. No wonder he's a funny devil sometimes.

My mum on the other hand was great, actually. She even called the police station to try and find out what was going on, and she's so shy that she normally hates calling people she doesn't know. In fact, I think at some point every one of us called the station to discover when Daryl would be released. The only thing we were told was that they'd been granted permission to extend the time they could question him.

That can't be good news, can it…?

So now I face another day of uncertainty. I'm exhausted, I haven't slept in what feels like forever, I can't think. Please God, let the madness stop.

12.30pm – Still no news. Feel like I'm going mad. I'm trying to remember something, anything that can prove Daryl didn't do these crimes. Nothing so far. But I've taken my diary to the station where I was questioned and handed it over; maybe something in there will help. I tried to see Daryl, but they wouldn't even tell me which station he's being held at, said he was 'still helping with enquiries'.

I didn't realise, but they've taken the rig too, so they can run tests, search it for evidence, or whatever it is they need to do. Fingers crossed they will find proof that he is innocent – a receipt, maybe, to show he was nowhere near when the crimes occurred.

6pm – It's the worst news. I can't, I can't deal with this, I can't process this, I can't react. Daryl has been charged. Amy and everyone came round again after work, and she called the police station about 40 minutes ago and we got the news. Despite me calling incessantly, somehow I've missed the whole thing.

'It's up to him to call his wife and let her know he's been charged,' was what the duty sergeant told Amy to relay to me. Great. Well, I'd imagine Daryl had other things on his mind and maybe didn't want to worry me!

So my husband has been charged, and apparently he's already been to magistrate's court late this afternoon and remanded to appear at Crown Court in a week's time.

God, fancy having to face that alone, he must have been terrified as the crimes were read out: five counts of rape, one attempted rape, five assault by penetration, assault occasioning actual and grievous bodily harm, and one murder.

Amy had to write the list down, it was too big to remember, while I rocked back and forth on the sofa like some loony tunes person, moaning gently. When she handed it to me the paper was shaking so much I had to hold her hand in both of mine to keep it steady as I took in the words – but she pulled away from me as if I had acid for skin.

'I knew it,' she whispered. Her eyes were big, like a spooked horse's, and she took tiny steps away from me as she shook her head and sent her long, crazy curls dancing.

She was scared of me, was so terrified she couldn't drag her eyes from mine for one second in case I did something insane.

My stomach dropped. 'Knew what?' I'd already guessed the answer though.

INVISIBLE

'That day Hannah and I came round, I knew he was evil. We saw something in his eyes. Gut instinct warned us. But I told myself I was being stupid, over-reacting, because how could you be married to him if he were like that...?'

Her voice was low but every word clear as a bell. She knew what she was saying. Still her eyes bored into mine, and I saw fear harden into anger. 'This is the proof though. He's raped. He's murdered!'

This last word was almost screeched. It broke the spell holding everyone in place, suddenly people were all talking at once, rushing between me and her.

Kim's voice rang out clearest over everyone else's. 'This isn't proof, Amy. He's been accused but we don't know what's happened. Whatever Daryl's guilty of, you can't seriously think she knew.' She jerked her head in my direction.

I didn't move a muscle, my throat so constricted I couldn't swallow let alone speak. Let it all play out in front of me, knowing, knowing what was going to be said.

'How could she not know? She's his wife! He must have acted weird; there must have been some clues! If I could see it, why couldn't she?' Amy didn't wait for an answer. She grabbed her stuff up in both arms and ran from the room, from the house. The front door slammed, then silence.

There it was. She believed Daryl was guilty, and if he was then so was I. My horror rose, along with some bile. I swallowed down the bitter taste, trying to think.

Andy was next to break. He cleared his throat, Mr Reasonable after Amy's hysterics. 'The erm, the police wouldn't charge Daryl unless they had some pretty hard evidence, surely? And he's been denied bail...'

Una reached out gently and touched his arm. 'People are found innocent in court sometimes you know. Innocent until proven guilty and all that,' she said to him, then looked at me. 'But look, you probably need a bit of time alone to process this bombshell. We'd best go too, don't want to leave the grandparents looking after Jacob for too long, he'll be getting antsy soon. You know what five-year-olds are like!' She laughed, then realised her mistake and left it hanging in the air.

I swallowed quickly, my mouth suddenly full of saliva. 'Yes, yes, you'd best go home,' I replied thickly. Hugged her goodbye. As they drove away I ran to the loo, stomach heaving, and threw up.

I'll never see them again, I bet. If friends believe he's guilty then what will the rest of the world think? What will a jury think?

What will everyone think of me?

I'm scared.

No, we'll get through this, we'll be fine because there'll be a trial and no one will find him guilty because he isn't guilty.

Tuesday 14

Normal life is completely suspended until this…mistake is over. Yesterday, on top of everything else, I had to call my boss and explain that I was taking a couple of days off for personal reasons. He wasn't pleased about it until I said I'd suffered a bereavement – that's what it feels like so the lie came quickly and easily to me. Normally I'm so bad at fibbing, I get tongue-tied and my brain doesn't seem to work fast enough; only afterwards do I think: 'ooh, I should have said so and so, that would have been great. Why didn't I think of it at the time?'

So my boss swallowed the lie…until the newspapers came out today.

Daryl's name and picture everywhere (where the hell did they get the photo?!) there was even information about him:

his job, the fact he's married, even the street we live on. I'm just appalled they've done that. What if some weirdo actually thinks he's done all these things and comes round to the house to get revenge? I feel scared in my own home now. Thanks a bunch, my life wasn't crappy enough already.

They've given Daryl a moniker too. The newspapers. I should have seen it coming really, I mean, they always name people. Sometimes cool, sometimes eerie, sometimes a bit silly, but the name the papers give is the one that becomes synonymous with the crimes. Think about it. The Moors Murderers. The Night Stalker. The M25 rapist. The Suffolk Strangler. It seems like giving the label is almost as important as finding out the perpetrator's real name. More important in fact, as it takes them a step away from humanity, from us normal people, in the same way that a superhero's catchy name does.

If Batman had just gone around permanently as plain old Bruce Wayne no one would have taken him seriously. 'Bruce, stop wearing that silly utility belt and whizzing round in that fast car, you'll get yourself killed,' pals would have nagged. Because he'd have been normal, see. But give him a cool name, Batman, and he's capable of anything, because he clearly isn't like the rest of us. He's capable of much, much greater things.

Well, I reckon that's why the need is so great to label killers, rapist, and 'baddies'. To show that they aren't one of us, either, and that's why they are capable of doing such terrible, twisted deeds.

So, Daryl isn't Daryl any more. He's The Port Pervert. Does it make it any easier for me to deal with? I'm not sure. Part of me feels relieved. He's not the man I loved any more, he the Port Pervert. How could I have known what he was up to when no one else guessed either?

Look at the way Clark Kent fooled Lois Lane for all those years, and he saved people right in front of her face. It's so easy to be taken in by a secret identity when you're right in the middle of it – but of course the people on the outside can see it so clearly. How many times have people rolled their eyes at the TV screen while Lois once again failed to notice that Clark and Superman are never in the room together, and that they look exactly the same? I feel sorry for her. Because I've been fooled too. And now the world is shouting at me, not the telly, screaming: 'How could you not have noticed? How stupid are you?!'

If he really is guilty, the answer is 'monumentally'.

I don't know the Port Pervert, I know my husband, I know Daryl. If he hurt these women then I never really knew him at all. All those shared memories built up over nine years together are nothing. Lies, lies, lies. Can I believe that nine years of my life was spent with a stranger? I can't, it's madness. These accusations just don't sound right to me. Amy's right about one thing: if he had done these awful crimes I'd have seen something, known. You can't be that close to someone and not know what they're capable of.

So no, I don't believe my husband is the Port Pervert.

Bless him, he must be so scared. I can't imagine how I'd have felt if the police hadn't released me. Thinking of being locked up in that horrible cell makes me shiver all over again. That's why he didn't call me, I'm sure, not because he didn't want to let me know what was happening, not because he didn't long to hear my voice, but because he was trying to protect me from worry. I'm desperate to speak to him; as soon as I hear his voice I'll feel better, more confident that things really will turn out okay in the end.

Right now I feel lost.

INVISIBLE

There's no time to feel sorry for myself though. There's so much to think about, but the first thing I have to sort is a lawyer for Daryl. One of those top flight ones, like you see on telly...but I'm not exactly sure how you go about getting one.

I started with Yellow Pages. Called all the ones in there; it took forever.

It's not exactly the kind of thing I'm used to doing, explaining that my fella's in the clink. I was so nervous I'd jotted down a few notes so I wouldn't forget anything, and launched into the explanation as soon as the first person answered the phone.

'Umm, hello! I've – my husband – well, he's been arrested – we were arrested – you might have seen it on telly - they barged in at 3am – the police, I mean – and now they've charged him with,' quick glance at notes, 'five counts of rape, attempted rape, assault by penetration, assault occasioning actual and grievous bodily harm, and one murder – they can't, well, they can, but they can't – well, you know – so I need someone for him – for court - can you help?'

'You want a criminal lawyer,' sighed a woman. 'We only do family law; it does say so in the advert.'

Did it? Yeah, actually, when I checked it did indeed. 'But this is kind of family law, isn't it?' I said. 'Our little family, mine and Daryl's, is being ripped apart by the police's mistake.'

Mum and Dad (he's taken some time off work and arrived this morning) gave me an encouraging thumbs up, as out of their depth as me in all this.

'You want a criminal lawyer,' the woman repeated down the phone, sounding bored. 'Goodbye.' The dialling tone sounded as she hung up. Well, sorry my humdrum little problem of my life falling apart was so sodding dull for her.

Still, it taught me a lesson. From then on I read the ads better before ringing. After a couple of goes I even stopped gabbling and was able to encapsulate the problem in seconds, not minutes. 'I need a criminal lawyer; my husband has been arrested for rape and murder,' seemed to cover it.

By the end I was exhausted and my voice a little croaky from over-use. Mum offered to take over, but I refused. This is my problem.

She made me a cup of tea afterwards, the hot liquid soon soothing my throat as I curled up on my big, squishy armchair. She sat down at the end of the sofa closest to me, at a right angle to me, with her knees almost touching mine.

'Umm, your father and I would like a word,' she said. On cue Dad walked into the room then, looking sheepish but determined as he sat beside her. They both leaned forward intently. I felt like a little girl about to be gently told off for letting go of their hand and wandering off while shopping.

'Don't be annoyed…but are you sure you want to stand by Daryl?' asked Mum. I opened my mouth to argue but she raised her voice just slightly and continued as kindly as she could at the increased volume. 'I mean, what if he's guilty, love? Have you thought about that? You've seen the way your friends have reacted…'

'Mum, it's fine. This will be sorted out soon. He'll be home in a couple of days, probably,' I insisted.

'We're worried for you, love,' said Dad. He sounded like a gruff bear in a kids' cartoon; he doesn't do touchy feely emotional stuff much. In fact, he doesn't really talk much, thinking about it. My dad has been a silent man, quietly getting on with his life of work, gardening, and reading the newspaper. Sometimes he disappears into his shed for hours and tinkers with bits of wood or something; and as I gazed at him now I realised…I don't really know him much.

In fact, as Mum and Dad talked on, I found myself staring at them and trying to think about them as people instead of My Parents. I don't know them. I don't know their innermost secrets and desires. I don't know what makes them tick. For instance, there must be more to Mum than an ability to listen to me whine about life while making sympathetic noises, a gift for baking seriously nice cakes, and a penchant for kitsch stuff (and not in an ironic way). But if there is, I don't actually know what…

They're both so quiet, so accepting of life. Maybe that's where I get it from, my inability to question things, or to speak up for myself. We're more a stoic, put-up-and-shut-up kind of family.

Anyway, eventually they stopped talking and I carried on staring at them until the silence became really quite awkward, and finally I cleared my throat and said: 'I'll definitely think about what you've said. Honest.' Of course I can't though, because I wasn't listening.

Oh, and before I called those solicitors I gave my boss another bell. Told the truth.

'Oh! Oh gosh, that's terrible,' Kevin said, pretending to be surprised. 'Take all the time off you need, call me next week.' He couldn't get off the phone from me fast enough, had clearly seen the news.

Still, it's one less thing for me to worry about.

Wednesday 15

Great day, not. I woke with my face buried in Daryl's pillow convinced I was snuggled up beside him, to the sound of something thumping against the front door. Eggs and shit were what I discovered had been chucked when I opened it; they smeared the paint, creating a stinking, gelatinous mess.

Someone had also spray painted 'scum' in massive letters on the side of the house. It took me and my parents ages to scrub the graffiti off (the shitty mix on the front door came away easily though, so that was something) and as we worked Clare from next door appeared on her doorstep, arms folded.

'Disgusting,' she tutted.

'I know,' I smiled apologetically. 'It's unbelievable, isn't it.'

'Not that,' she sneered. 'You. You're disgusting and so's that husband of yours. You should both be locked up for life. Scum!'

Her husband, John, appeared beside her, alerted by her increasingly shrill voice, and grabbed her shoulders, dragging her inside.

'Don't give her the satisfaction, babe,' he said to her.

'Oy, was this you?' demanded Dad, pointing to the remains of the mess. The only answer he got was the sound of their front door slamming shut. Ears burning, I carried on scrubbing…

Later, still furious, I sat on the sofa clutching my usual early morning coffee (see, even in this mess, some things never change, some routines are still adhered to) and fantasised about chucking the mug across the room. Hearing the jangling explosion as it hit the wall, seeing it shatter into splinters and shards. God, that would be so satisfying.

Then I thought about having to clear it up. Knowing my luck I'd cut myself. And the coffee would definitely stain the cream carpet, so then I'd have to spend ages scrubbing it with carpet shampoo and I'd be annoyed at myself for ever throwing it. Rage rarely achieves anything, I find, apart from make a mess you later regret.

Still, I couldn't shake the anger. Then inspiration struck. I decided to call up one of the newspapers that had printed my address and tear a strip off them. I hunted down a number, and as soon as I said who I was I got put through to the writer whose name was on the piece. I felt rather smug about that; clearly they'd realised their error and are going to take my complaint seriously.

'My life's been ruined by this. People have attacked my home,' I pointed out, describing what had happened that morning. 'Daryl's innocent, but if you keep printing your lies people will start believing it. You can't keep printing my address, it's disgraceful.'

'Well we have to give the street name in case someone else of the same name lives in the town; we wouldn't want people mixing them up with a criminal, would we?' the reporter replied.

'But Daryl isn't a criminal! He's innocent!' I flung back. I said a bunch of other stuff too, and the reporter actually seemed really nice and listened to everything I had to say.

'We'll definitely run a piece putting across your point of view,' she promised.

'With an apology?' I pressed.

'I'll certainly be mentioning it to the editor.' Excellent!

Minutes later I heard the soft snap of the letterbox. When I saw what had arrived, I was stunned – it was a letter from Daryl. My hands shook as soon as I saw his writing. Couldn't help hoping that maybe this was it, the thing that would explain everything away and prove this is a terrible mistake.

I was so dead keen to get into the letter that I tore the envelope diagonally, ripped it apart. This is what it said:

'Hi Gorgeous, You are the only angel in this seething cesspit. Do not ever get tainted by my shit, you are well above me. I admire you so much. I wish I could be like you. In so many ways I am

better for having known you. No matter what, I did and do love you and I have never deserved you. I so wish I could have. If you should ever need anything it's yours, All my love, Daryl xxxx.'

At the end of it was the prison's date stamp. So, at least I know where he is now.

This is the first contact I've had with him since the police burst into our home. So of course I've read it over and over, analysing every word for their obvious meaning first, then the hidden ones behind them. Sometimes I think it's a goodbye note, others an apology, or maybe he's just sad…?.

I don't really think there is much of a hidden message though, Daryl was never that good with words, and this is surprisingly eloquent. He must have spent a long time putting it together. Then again what do I know; maybe I don't know the bloke at all.

No, mustn't think like that. Bad wife. Bad wife!

The thing that gets me is…there's no denial. Not even a hint of denial. Instead he just goes on about me. Bless him, because he really is innocent it doesn't even occur to him that he'd have to deny anything to his own wife. What a cow I am, what a horrible person for allowing myself even that transitory moment of doubt.

The more I read it the note, the more hopeless and helpless he sounded. I cried, imagining him in a cold, grey prison cell from Dickensian times, hunched over as he wrote this note.

Poor, poor Daryl. I hate myself for entertaining even for a second a tiny bit of doubt about him. If he's so evil, how did I manage to escape his clutches? Why did he choose to settle down with me and have a normal life for nine years? It's daft; a weirdo pervert would never act like that. Imagine how cold and calculating you'd have to be to pull off something like that; impossible!

INVISIBLE

Well at least I'll be able to see him soon. In a post script he let me know he'll be appearing in Crown Court on Monday 20th to request bail. Please, please, please let him get it….

I can't sleep in that bloody bedroom either. The memory of the raid is too strong, too traumatic. As soon as I close my eyes images of it flash, like blotches of colour against closed eyelids after you've accidentally glanced at the sun.

Instead I drag the duvet and pillows into the lounge, curl up on the sofa, watch telly until exhaustion takes me for an hour or so, surrounded by the smell of Daryl. Links Africa, diesel and him.

3am – Dad's unplugged the landline. From 11pm the phone started ringing constantly. When I answered it, it was horrible. People shouting disgusting abuse at me – men and women – screaming that I'm a murderer, scum, sick, twisted, that I got off on Daryl's crimes, and I deserve to burn in hell. I'm speechless. Do people really think that? The worst calls though were the silent ones. I could tell someone was there, listening to me listening to them. Somehow that scared me more than the spewing abuse.

'Don't answer it, love,' urged Mum, trying to hold me back after the phone rang for the umpteenth time.

'I have to,' I whispered, voice hoarse from tension. I couldn't leave the phone just ringing. It wasn't simply that the noise did my head in, it was more that I needed to hear what they had to say. Needed to torture myself, like a kid picking a scab.

The funny thing is, I didn't even cry. I just sat silently, numb, taking whatever the callers had to throw at me. That's probably what disconcerted my parents the most.

Finally, Dad didn't give a word of warning, simply stood up, walked over to the phone socket and unclipped the lead. 'Get some sleep,' he said calmly, then walked from the room.

Thursday 16

What a bloody idiot! I stared at the newspaper headline that Dad had shoved under my nose, and blinked a couple of times as if I could somehow make it disappear. Tearing a strip off the newspaper has made things a hundred thousand billion times worse. What was I thinking? Sat there all smug, feeling like I'd finally taken control of the situation when actually…

'I'll stand by my man,' vows Port Pervert's wife. That was the headline on the front page. The front bloody page! Then there was a load of stuff about how I'm 'claiming' he is innocent. The way they've written it, I sound delusional, hysterical, my arguments making no sense at all… The quotes are accurate enough it's the stuff in between that's the problem; it's so clever the way they've twisted it all and given it their own spin. They didn't say anything about me being victimised with malicious calls. And they printed my street name again.

I've made things worse. I've made them so much worse. I didn't think it was possible. Why won't anyone listen to me? I feel ignored, forgotten, unimportant. How can I be unimportant when it's MY LIFE that's turning to shit? My husband's in jail for a crime he didn't commit, my friends want nothing to do with me, my parents think I'm insane for sticking by Daryl, and to top it off I look like I've been positively boasting to the national newspapers.

Mum suggested I call that solicitor, Peter Simpson, and see if he could help me because he'd been so great when I was arrested.

INVISIBLE

'Last time I tried to take control and do something I made them worse, remember?' I said, brandishing the newspaper like a weapon.

Dad cleared his throat. 'I don't think you can make them any worse.' Fair point.

So I called Peter. I've an appointment to see him tomorrow. Fingers crossed.

The heat in the house was starting to feel oppressive, and I automatically walked over to a window to open it, then realised I didn't dare in case someone shouted something obscene or chucked something. As for setting foot in the garden to cool off…it's out of bounds now that my neighbours hate me. I feel too self-conscious; can see their curtains twitching the minute I step outside. I'm trapped figuratively and literally in my life.

With so much going on, it's hard to imagine that there's any room left in my head to think about Daryl. Sounds selfish, but in a way I wish that were true. The reality is that, of course, he's on my mind constantly. It's like there is a little background monologue running all the time, which can be heard in my brain no matter what else I'm thinking or doing: How's he doing? How's he feeling? How's he coping? What if he gets picked on in prison? Sometimes he's bolshie, sometimes he's such an introverted little boy, which way will he go in there; which will help him survive best? Why hasn't he called me…?

Then there all the times I catch myself forgetting for a split second and automatically thinking 'must tell Daryl that', or 'must ask Daryl to sort this', or even 'God, I need a hug'. Or my mobile will ring and I'll for the briefest instant feel that excitement as I assume it's Daryl. Then I remember. That's when my stomach drops like I'm on a rollercoaster and I sometimes gasp out loud as I realise all over again where he is and what is happening.

Why hasn't he tried to call me even? I can only think it's because he is too scared himself and needs time to sort his head out because he'll think he has to be strong for me. He needs time to create that front. I've tried calling the prison to see if I can be put through to him, but have been told repeatedly that it isn't possible. It's silly that in the midst of all else that is going on, I'm hurt by the lack of contact.

Still, only a few more days until I see him, even if it is only in a court room. Hopefully he'll get bail and be coming home with me. Can't wait. Literally cannot wait.

Friday 17
This morning I opened up my curtains to discover journalists had sprung up like mushrooms overnight and are now permanently on the pavement outside the house. Nothing surprises me any more though. I think there's only so much stress and 'stunning' a person can take before they just go 'wow, another bag of crap thrown at me. Okay, cool,' and simply carry on regardless.

I already can't think, can't eat, can't sleep, my body aches constantly from my muscles being always held tense, the skin round my eyes and cheeks hurts because it is chapped from so many tears (I didn't know that was physically possible, but lucky me, I've discovered it is) and even my eyeballs throb.

I traipsed away from the window with a sigh, thinking about how the neighbours will hate me even more now, and went to the bathroom and cleaned my teeth. As I spat into the sink, I caught sight of myself in the mirror and literally didn't recognise myself. I don't look like me any more, and not just because I've already lost half a stone from stress; it's more the haunted, hunted look in the eyes that's changed me.

This time last week I was me. A bored wife hoping something exciting would happen to her. Be careful what you wish for, it might just come true.

For the first time this week though, I washed my hair, brushed it neatly, and carefully chose something smart to wear. The pencil skirt hangs a little loose now, the waist resting on my hips instead thanks to the weight-loss, but it looked fine. I even put on some make up. Not that I give a toss what I look like, but somehow seeing a solicitor feels like something I should make an effort for.

Then I kissed my parents goodbye (they were too afraid to come outside with me) and opened the front door... So many camera flashes went off it was like the strobe effect in a bad nightclub. Half blinded, I put my arm up across my face to keep out the light and scurried to the car as best I could in the stupid skirt; in my hurry my ankle going over painfully in the ridiculous heels I'd decided to wear.

The whole time, the journalists yelled at me, all shouting different questions at once like an aural version of the strobing, but as I fell into the car and slammed the door shut one question made it through the wall of sound: 'How do you feel?'

I sat staring at the steering wheel, key in hand, telling myself to put it in the ignition and turn it, but the query had brought me up short. More media bods thronged round the car, more pictures were taken as I sat there like a crash test dummy. How did I feel?! What a bloody stupid question.

But when I thought about it (and I kept thinking of it, for some reason) I realised it was really quite clever. It's simple, but gets to the heart of the matter. How *do* I feel? God knows. When I figure out the answer, I won't be bothering to tell that journalist though. I've a funny feeling that if I did my words would be used against me because, actually, no one gives a shit about me in all this mess.

Finally I arrived at Peter's office, having successfully remembered how to start a car. He looked genuinely pleased to see me – and genuinely concerned about what was going on.

Still, as we talked, I couldn't help thinking about how much money every syllable we uttered to each other was costing me. No matter how kind he seemed, I couldn't relax, felt as if I was an actress playing a part, because I'm just not the kind of person who says: 'I'm going to consult my solicitor.'

I sat with my legs crossed neatly at the ankles, which felt really unnatural, but it seemed like the kind of place where ladies (not women, ladies. You have to act like a lady in this place) sit like that, and I kept my back ramrod straight too, even though it ached like hell and I'd really quite have liked to have gone into a teenage-style slump instead. My handbag stayed firmly on my lap, gripped like some talisman that would keep me safe from dodgy lawyers and other evils.

'Can you stop the newspaper printing things?' I begged, fiddling with the handbag clasp to stop my hands from shaking.

Peter shook his head sadly, as though this was all a game, not my life, and I was stupidly refusing to understand the rules. No, that's unkind. He did look like he wanted to help, kept running his hands through his dark hair in a concerned manner as I spoke; amazing how such short hair can be so unruly. But I feel like being mean because it seems no one can help me.

'This isn't my area of expertise but after your call yesterday I phoned some colleagues for advice. Basically, if I act against the press it won't make any positive difference,' he said. 'And if you antagonise them, it will just make them worse. They will turn on you, lose any sympathy they are currently showing for you, and potentially could totally destroy your reputation.'

The handbag got hoicked a bit higher, protecting me from his words like a shield. I had an idea. 'Okay, well maybe I should talk to only one of the papers then.' I could see him starting to shake his head but I ploughed on desperately anyway. 'Or maybe a TV interview. Bit like Princess Di…' I know, I know. I've no idea where that last bit came from.

'You talk to one paper,' he replied slowly, every word dropping into place like it weighed ten tonnes, 'and the ones you haven't talked to will turn on you instead. And they'll be even more vicious, desperate to discredit the story their rival has published. It'll be a matter of honour to prove that you are an evil, lying, manipulative bitch who was complicit with what her husband did, and should face the jury herself.'

By then the handbag was at chest level; any more bad news and I wouldn't be able to see over it.

Peter changed the subject. 'Have you found someone to represent Daryl in court yet? He'll need someone pretty good; I could recommend a few people if you like.'

'Could you do it?' I asked. He hesitated.

'I could,' he replied, stretching out the words, 'but as I'm now acting on your behalf to a certain extent, I believe it would be better for you to keep things separate.' I gave a shruggy nod and he continued. 'Now that he's on remand it's important to find someone as good as possible as quickly as possible so they can start building a case immediately. It'll take almost a year to come to court, probably, which sounds a long time but really isn't.'

'A year?' I gasped. I'd convinced myself it would be a matter of weeks, maybe a couple of months at worst case scenario. This can't go on for that long, it' so unfair, how will we manage?!

Depressed but armed with a couple of barristers rated by Peter, I could barely drag myself back to the car and the waiting media, who somehow had managed to track me down to Peter's office. The fun wasn't over yet, either. When I got home I discovered my parents had spotted that the crowd of journos and cameramen outside had thinned significantly after I'd left, so had grabbed the chance to leave the house. They'd nipped to the corner shop. To buy a newspaper.

Why do they keep doing this? Why??

A number of the tabloid rags have run stories about Daryl's life, upbringing, job, when and where we married… Picture-wise they've surpassed themselves by finding a wedding shot; one of the official ones, not a snap taken by a family friend. I got straight on the phone to Peter.

'Surely they can't just print any pictures of me and Daryl they happen to come across?' I demanded despairingly.

'The copyright of a wedding picture remains with the official photographer. He owns it and therefore he can do whatever he wants with it,' came the patient reply. 'In this case, if he chooses to sell it to a tabloid for a small fortune, he is at liberty to do so.'

Fan-freaking-tastic. How come everyone else can do exactly as they please but me? Why do I seem to be the only one all at sea in this situation?

Then I picked up the paper again and like a rubbernecker unable to take their eyes off a car crash, I found myself scanning the article. And for the first time I thought properly about those poor women who have been attacked. What a bitch. I honestly can't believe I've been so self-absorbed that I've barely given them a second thought apart from an abstract, micro-second-long 'poor cows'.

Imagine it, walking home on a winter's evening after a night out. It's still quite early and you've maybe had a couple of drinks that are enough to keep the chill away but certainly not enough to make you drunk and silly. It's only a two minute walk from the bus stop to your front door, and you know the area so well that you feel confident, at ease here; it's not like a strange place, full of weird shadows and noises that might make you jump every minute, it's your stamping ground. Then…wham! From out of nowhere someone grabs you, hits you, threatens you. You don't know what's happening, all you know is you're terrified, heart pounding. You maybe try to scream, but all that comes out through the fingers clamped over your mouth is a muffled, barely audible cry. And then…and then…

Even my over-active imagination runs out at this point. I can't begin to put myself in their place. I've no idea what their ordeal must have been like. I don't want to know, if I'm honest. Yet still I made myself read that article.

Timeline of Terror was the heading on the box that caught my eye initially. All those dates I'd been questioned about at the police station that had meant nothing to me. As I stared at them now though, without pressure on me, I suddenly remembered something.

December 18. That's Daryl's birthday, and also the date of one of the attacks. In my fluster I'd told police he'd have been with me, that I'd have cooked a meal as usual and we'd have eaten it together. Which is sort of true.

He'd actually turned up late for his meal, I remembered now. He'd already seemed in a bad mood, then I'd made some comment that had meant to be cheery to ease the tension, but that had actually seemed to make him grumpier.

'This could be our last celebration as a couple; this time next year it'd be nice if we had a baby. Just imagine!' I'd smiled hesitantly. I'd pushed the boat out, making his favourite pork roast, buying a birthday cake and candles, got dressed up in a nice dress for him. I'd even cut different-sized heart shapes out of red tissue paper I'd bought, and scattered them over the bed.

'What were you thinking of, cooking a meal? Why did you assume what time I'd arrive?' he'd frowned furiously. 'Jesus, you want to control everything about me.'

I'd stood there, confused, hurt, upset. Unable to understand what I'd done wrong. He'd said he'd be home by 7pm, and he'd been late…but instead of me making any kind of critical reference to it I'd let it slide and then he'd had a go at me. When he gets like that, shouting at me like that, I feel like I'm going mad because I believe him, believe I'm in the wrong, and only afterwards do I think, 'hold on, that seems maybe a bit unreasonable.'

He'd stomped out, turned his mobile phone off. I'd called and called but only been able to get through to his answerphone. I'd left a stroppy message (I'm always braver after the fact and when he isn't actually around) but by the next day I still hadn't heard from him so had wound up sending him a text saying: 'Are you ready to talk yet?' A few hours later, he'd finally deigned to switch on his mobile and receive my calls. In my relief at getting through to him I'd swallowed down my anger, a puppy grateful that the master had come home after being ignored all day.

Why hadn't I remembered this when the police were questioning me? I don't know. Possibly it was the terror of being arrested in the middle of the night. Perhaps it was because I got in a flap as they fired date after date at me until my head span. It could even be that I'd blocked it out, smoothed over it as I always tend to do when Daryl's been in one of his moods; life's easier that way. Whatever, I'd remembered it now, which left me with another problem.

Should I tell the police what I've remembered?

Oh God, I have to, don't I. Because he's innocent, right, so what difference can it make? Just because he hasn't a solid alibi for one of the attacks doesn't mean he's guilty. It doesn't.

I realised I'd scrunched the paper up in my fist as the memory had come to me. I threw it to the floor as if it burned me. 'No more reading tabloid nonsense, it's just going to upset me,' I told myself.

I walked from the room into the kitchen, leaving the screwed up ball where it had fallen, and flicked on the kettle. Stared at it. Stared at the kettle. Stared at the teabags in the jar. Sighed, walked back into the lounge and reached down, smoothing the crinkles from the story.

Honestly? I had to know more; I'm still that rubbernecker at the car crash scene. So once again I started to read the Timeline of Terror. My stomach lurched with nerves, I put the paper down again. Picked it up.

'Stop being a baby,' I muttered out loud angrily, forcing myself to read on.

'In June police identified the existence of an extremely dangerous serial rapist who is believed to have attacked at least six women - killing one victim and the very next day conducting a depraved assault on another.

'His hunting ground is believed to have stretched from Manchester to as far afield as Turkey, but his favoured location for his sickening rape spree appears to have been around Tilbury Docks, Essex, where he found four of his six victims – and became dubbed the Port Pervert.

'Often he'd gain the woman's trust by wearing smart clothes that gave the appearance of a security guard or office worker, before launching a blistering attack, frequently punching his victims in the face to incapacitate them.

'Essex and Manchester police joined forces with Interpol to launch a massive manhunt named Operation Globe. Within just one month of its launch, they'd made an arrest.'

My stomach lurched, my breathing quickening as if I was running rather than rooted to the spot. Manchester, Tilbury, Turkey…all places Daryl knew well. He couldn't be capable of these crimes though; if he did, how come I managed to escape his evil clutches? No, he's a mardy arse sometimes but he's such a gentle, loving bloke – when he comes home after a long break, he gets into bed with me, spoons up behind me, gives a huge sigh of contentment and says: 'Ah, thank God I'm home. I know I'm home when I've got your freezing cold feet against mine. I bloody love those blocks-of-ice feet.' That is not how a rapist and murderer acts.

I ignored the burning bile at the back of my throat, and ploughed on. Stared at the list of dates, willing more memories to come. 18 December, 14 January, 3 February, 2 March, 29 May, 2 June.

Nothing would come, why wouldn't anything come?! Then another date jumped out at me: Friday 29 May. According to the newspaper, the Port Pervert murdered a woman that night.

God help me, but I almost danced with glee at that news.

Daryl can't be the killer. On Friday 29 May he was on a plane, flying to Turkey with me. Being trapped 30,000ft in the air with over a hundred witnesses has to be the most airtight alibi ever. I know I mentioned it during my interview, so why on earth haven't they corroborated it yet and released Daryl? Lazy, useless buggers!

I hadn't realised I'd been holding my breath until I let it out in a great big huff of relief. Now I knew for certain – not just certain enough to defend him to friends, family, the world, but to *know* to the depths of my soul. Now I can focus all my energy on supporting my husband and getting him freed. And getting justice for those poor women too; they deserve seeing the real criminal jailed rather than some poor hapless bloke the police have chosen for no apparent reason.

Smiling for the first time since my husband was banged up for a crime he didn't commit, I shouted to my parents. 'He's innocent,' I said, almost laughing as they ran into the room looking comically panicked. 'Everything's going to be fine. I'm going to get Daryl out.' Then I explained everything. They smiled too, gave me a massive hug. Didn't realise I saw the worried look they exchanged.

'Mu-um, Da-ad,' I said in warning.

'Umm, it's just...' began Mum.

'There have been more calls, love. While you were out we plugged the phone back in. Some of the stuff was, well, I'm just glad you didn't hear it,' explained Dad.

Stupid me. Just because I'd realised the truth doesn't mean others will. That moment won't come until the trial, a whole year away from now.

'Well, don't worry about it now,' Mum told me with fake brightness, then shot Dad a look and told him in a stage whisper: 'I knew we shouldn't have said anything.' She walked from the room then came straight back holding a box. 'Anyway, this package came for you. Is it something exciting? It always cheers me up, getting a delivery through the post; almost like getting a present, somehow.'

She smiled and shrugged at her silliness as she handed it over.

I stared at it, confused. 'I haven't ordered anything.' She was right though, I did feel a thrill of curiosity and excitement as I tore into the box, and plunged through the plastic bag inside to reach the contents.

I reeled back in horror, a terrible stench making me want to gag.

It was a dead rat. Attached to it was a note: 'This is what happens to vermin. You're next.'

Saturday 18
The police came round last night and took the package away after Dad called them. Thank goodness he was here; I couldn't have done it… I'd been busy having a bit of a breakdown while it was all going on, to be honest.

Fear, lack of sleep, the strain of what's happening all built up to a point where I couldn't take any more. I've never felt like that. I'd literally no strength in my legs or my body (or my soul, it felt like) and I sank to the floor right where I'd been standing and curled up, sobbing. Couldn't have moved if my life had depended on it. I just wanted the world to stop for a while so I could have a break and get the chance to catch up, cope.

Mum pulled at my arm ineffectively, saying 'oh, love, don't, don't', then gave up and sat beside me, her arm wrapped around me while Dad talked down the phone about 'deaths threats', 'protection', 'it's simply not good enough', oh and of course 'she's in fear of her life'.

Someone out there wants me dead. Even if they'd never go through with the threat and actually kill me, they still want it. Not in a transitory way, that split second moment in a row where you shout petulantly: 'I hate you! I wish you were dead!' Instead they'd taken the time to write it down and tell me. I can't imagine thinking that about anyone; not really, truly.

Turns out they aren't the only ones either. The postman knocked on the door this morning with a thick handful of letters and suspicious-looking packages. Mum, Dad, and I went through them warily, with wrinkled noses, touching things gingerly, fingertips only. Most were poorly spelled messages of vitriol and spite. We quickly became able to spot them without having to read anything. A quick peek, a guttural noise of terror and then they were flung to one side into the growing pile; it would have become mechanical had it not been for the fear.

People hate me. People want me dead. People want to kill me.

I can't take this any more. This is not my life. I'm bloody well going to get my life back though.

So I picked up the pile of hatred, stuffed it into a carrier bag, and stepped out. Noise erupted, flashes exploded. Bloody journalists. I put my head down and marched straight to the car with a stony face and drove to the police station. There I gave a fresh statement to DI Baxter about what I'd remembered.

'Oh, and I'm fairly certain that if you look in my diary – I dropped it in the day after my arrest, did you get it?'

He nodded.

'Well, if you look in my diary I'm fairly certain it will back up what I've just told you.'

He doesn't give much away, DI Baxter, but I swear he gave a shadow of a smile as I spoke; perhaps he's been having second thoughts about Daryl's guilt too.

Then I explained about the threats and handed over the bag. 'I'm really scared. Is there anything you can do? Everyone knows where I live because the telly and newspapers keep mentioning the road I live in, well, Daryl lives in, so...'

The detective did his by now familiar dog bum impression, pursing his lips. Ah, that brought back happy memories of the last time he and I had spoken, but I brushed off the revulsion, instead hoping this time I'd get help.

'I'm aware of your father's call last night and the subsequent package an officer picked up from your house,' he nodded. 'We're taking these threats very seriously, and will be investigating. In the meantime, because of the nature of the threats we're assigning protection officers to you.'

'You are?' I was stunned, relieved...but also kind of more scared. It sounds ridiculous, doesn't it, but I couldn't help thinking: 'Blimey, if the police are taking this seriously then there really is something to worry about. They don't think this is just a sick joke; it's real.' Of course I'd known it was real, but now it was really real, sort of thing...

'We'll deploy plain clothes officers to be outside your home at all times,' he said. 'There will be two officers working 12-hour shifts, and we'll try to keep to the same people as much as possible so that you get to know them by sight – it will help to put you at ease instead of worrying about who the strange people outside your house are.'

Wow. I could have hugged him, aside from the rather massive matter of him wrongfully arresting Daryl and me.

Back home and feeling safer already, Dad told me he'd organised for an alarm to be fitted. 'He's due any minute; I told him it was an emergency,' he said.

As if on cue, there was a knock on the door. Dad opened it and a chipper-looking bloke with a scrubbed face and glowing cheeks managed a cheery smile despite his confused expression.

'Hi, I'm Paul, here to fit your alarm,' he said, bustling in. 'What's that lot all about then?'

'The crowds of people?' I asked. Stupidly. 'They're, umm, they're here for me. That's why we need the alarm.'

'Ooookay,' he frowned, nodding. He was only short, couldn't have been much over 5ft 5in, but looked so capable that just his presence made me feel calmer and safer. I was in good hands, I was sure.

'So, Mr...' he glanced at the form on his clipboard, '...Miles, is this alarm for you? Can you sign just here for me, please?'

'Er, no, it's for my daughter,' Dad explained.

'Righty-o. Can I just make a note of your name?' he asked me. I didn't think of giving a fake name until afterwards. With hindsight, telling him my real name was a stupid mistake, because as soon as I did it was like a switch flicking inside him. Instant recognition – and repulsion.

He screwed his face up as if he'd bitten into an apple and found a wriggling maggot. 'Hold up, you're that bloke's wife? That-that rapist fella? Port Pervert. Jesus!'

He reminded me of a Jack Russell terrier the way he kept edging back then dancing forward, then edging back again, nervously warring between the urge to stand his ground and desire to get away from me in case I infect him with 'murder flu' or something that would instantly turn him into a perv too. The cheeky chappie who'd arrive on my doorstep minutes before was unrecognisable.

'I don't want your money. Sorry, but no, no way, no, it's disgusting what he's done. I'm not helping a scumbag like him. Find someone else to fit your alarm.'

'Now just a second, sonny Jim,' said Dad, waggling his finger. 'Our money's as good as anyone else's...'

'Pffffft,' was the huffed reply, as the alarm man opened the front door. Cue lights and shouting... And then slammed the door shut.

Dad turned this way and that, unsure what to do with himself or his annoyance. 'The cheek, the bloody cheek,' he muttered. Mum stood in the doorway between the lounge and the hall, white-faced, her hand over her mouth in shock. I think that's when it really hit home for all of us. This is the way life's going to be from now on. It's not just a handful of nutters who hate my very existence, it's everyone.//
It's a hard thing to get your head round.//
I'm a nice person. I am!//
And if I'm getting a reaction like this on the outside, what the hell is happening to Daryl in prison? Suspected sex offenders get a really hard time inside, don't they? They're targeted by other inmates, picked on, beaten up. I've never been one for religion, but suddenly I find myself praying.//
Please let him be okay, please God let him get through this.//
Curling up on the sofa in my now favourite foetal position, I thought about my lovely husband and how he simply doesn't deserve to be in this position. How the hell did we find ourselves in the middle of this tornado of insanity? What will I find when I see him on Monday? I just want to hold him, tell him everything will be okay.//
I sniffed at the tear that had tickled its way diagonally across my face and now hung on the end of my nose. It dropped onto the cushion beneath my head, quickly joined by another and another until they started a little damp patch.//
Desperate to escape the constant misery I forced myself to think about something nice. What though? Ah, Daryl's proposal – that always brought a smile to my face. We'd only been together a couple of months at the time but already I'd moved into his little house, and although others might have called it a whirlwind romance it hadn't seem fast to us. It had seemed just exactly right.

INVISIBLE

Never having lived with a man before, I'd found every little domesticated thing thrilling somehow and felt incredibly grown up buying new towels for us or the odd ornament. Even cooking and cleaning had seemed fun because they were a bit of a novelty.

One night I'd been ironing with a soppy smile of contentment on my face when I'd realised Daryl was staring at me. 'What? Do I have something on my face?' I'd laughed, quickly rubbing at my nose and cheeks.

'What would you say if I asked you to marry me?' he'd replied, matter-of-fact.

I'd broken into a grin, then quickly looked down and continued ironing, determined to be as casual as he. 'Well, I'd say yes, I'd imagine.'

'Hmmm. Excellent. Shall we get a ring tomorrow?'

'No, no, no; not until you've proposed. That wasn't a proper proposal.'

'It was! I asked, you said yes.'

'You asked what I'd say if you asked,' I'd argued with a smile, setting the iron down, going over to him, and reaching up to wrap my arms around his neck. Then stared into his ice blue eyes. 'But you didn't actually ask.'

He'd pretended to consider this, then nodded fake-grudgingly. 'Maybe I can do better,' he'd conceded.

The next few days had been spent in a frenzy of anticipation. It had been like waiting for Christmas to arrive but not being sure of the date. Daryl had been impossible to read though, giving nothing away, and slowly I'd started to calm down and feel a bit disappointed.

'Let's go for a walk,' he'd announced one day. I'd looked out at the lashing rain and raised my eyebrows. 'Come on, it'll be bracing,' he'd added.

'That's one word for it,' I'd agreed sarcastically. 'I'm cosy here, thanks.'

'Come on!' He'd gone and got my coat, held it out for me.
'Daryl, I don't want to go out. Not in this weather.'
He'd made a little growling noise of frustration and hung his head. 'But you've got to come outside,' he'd whispered to the floor.
'Why? Oh -' Of course, it was obvious once I'd put my brain into gear. This was it, the big proposal! So despite the pelting rain, I'd buttoned up my coat and gone outside. Holding his hand, we'd raced along the pavement, me squealing occasionally, and then turned quickly to go through gates that led to the local school's playing field, which was empty with it being a Saturday.
There'd been a helicopter there, waiting for us!
'I know you've always wanted to go in a helicopter, so this is for you. I want to make all your dreams come true,' Daryl had said, suddenly sinking onto one knee despite the mud. 'Let me spend my life trying to make that happen; will you marry me?'
My hair had been plastered to my head and I was shivering with cold, but it was the most incredible moment of my entire life as I'd nodded happily. He'd even sorted the ring, a little diamond solitaire.
The helicopter ride had only been short because of the awful weather, but I'd barely noticed in my euphoric state – and besides, I hadn't been looking at the scenery anyway because I hadn't been able to drag my eyes away from my sparkling ring or Daryl's proud smile.
We'd married just four months later. That had been the first day I'd seen him with a bald head. 'I wanted to surprise you; got sick of having receding hair, decided to just get rid,' he'd whispered to me at the altar, grinning at the look of

amazement on my face. Everyone had been talking about his new look!

Of course, our first dance had been to that all-time cheesey classic 'My First, My Last, My Everything.' All our friends and family had been in fits of giggles as Barry White's voice boomed out, but of course not all of them knew the significance of the song for us and the happy first date memories it brought.

Over the years, Daryl has kept his promise and tried to make my dreams come true. They aren't big, expensive, exotic things, so I suppose it hasn't been hard for him, but that's not the point is it? The point is, he knows me inside out, knows what I want, and gives it to me. Took me to Turkey twice, a place I'd always wanted to go; nips out and buys a curry whenever I fancy one; and he gives a mean foot rub with those big, strong hands of his. And best of all he's agreed to try for a baby, something I want with all my heart.

After nine years of marriage, I was bored, I admit. Took him for granted. Goodness knows it's easily done. My God, has all this business made me re-evaluate though. We'll come out the other side stronger and happier than ever. Nothing's ever going to tear us apart.

Monday 20

Okay, now I'm really angry. Daryl didn't get bail! The judge didn't even seem to consider it for a second, just dismissed it out of hand. Bastard! As for the person representing Daryl, who was just the bloke who'd acted as his duty solicitor, well, we have to replace him asap. Now I know exactly why Peter has recommended I find someone good.

I've been researching on the internet for days though and making calls and honestly I feel lost in this world I suddenly find myself in. I wish Daryl were here, he'd take charge immediately and sort it all out.

Friday 24
I think I've sorted out a barrister for Daryl. She sounds perfect, and has handled a couple of high-profile cases already.
That's how I found her actually. I was reading some newspaper cuts about other people who have been charged with similar things to Daryl, and her name cropped up a couple of times. Though I'm not sure I really approve of her, as some of these blokes sounded guilty as sin. Still, if she can get them off, she can definitely get an innocent man like Daryl off.
I also got another letter from Daryl, well, more of a note really telling me to call a certain number and book a visit to come see him on Monday. My heart skipped when I saw that. Finally I'll be able to talk to him, hug him, comfort him. It feels like forever since I've had one of his cuddles.

Sunday 26
In preparation for tomorrow, I've been online to find out what to expect. I don't know anyone who has ever been in prison as a visitor or otherwise; it's really not the sort of circles I move in, so there's no one I can ask.
Anyway, I've found out that while Daryl's on remand I can send as many letters as I want (something I hadn't realised, so haven't done – argh! Feel terrible. But then again, maybe Daryl didn't tell me because sometimes hearing from someone makes you miss them all the more and he's worried it'll make him even more miserable. I am both looking forward to and dreading this visit, I have to confess.)

INVISIBLE

According to the website, the minimum visiting allowance for someone like Daryl, who is waiting to go on trial, is ninety minutes every week; and if I'm lucky we might even get a bit longer. It's more than I'd dare hope, so I'm feeling a little better about things.

To be honest though, the confusion and helplessness I've been feeling since this happened is starting to give way to anger, and all the visiting time in the world doesn't change the fact that we shouldn't be in this position in the first place. Maybe I should write to my MP or something about this, get them on side. I've never done anything like that before but surely I can't be the only one to see that there's a miscarriage of justice going on.

Anyway, I'm not going to rant about it when I see Daryl; seeing me upset and angry is the last thing he needs. I've got to make myself positive and upbeat for him, so I'm just trying to concentrate on the fact that at least we'll get to spend a half-decent amount of time together from now on. I've checked with the prison and it'll be 45 minutes a day, three times a week, that I can see him, and apparently, if he's well behaved (which he will be, of course) he might even be given something called privilege visits as a reward, so that's great news.

I called Daryl's mum, too. 'Hi, I'm visiting him tomorrow and wondered if you were going too – I've just discovered three people can see him at a time so we could go together if you like,' I explained, trying to keep my tone friendly despite my dislike of her.

'You're visiting him?' Cynthia scoffed. 'My dear, what would you do a stupid thing like that for? No, I've decided I want nothing to do with him. He's disgusting.'

'Okay! Thanks, bye!' I said sarcastically, slamming the phone down.

What I wanted to do was rant at her. Bitch. How can she wash her hands of her own flesh and blood? But maybe, just maybe, the evil old cow will realise her mistake and come round. The last thing I want to do for Daryl right now is burn any bridges for him, so I fought the constant urge to redial her and say something rude, and concentrated on something inane instead – what to wear tomorrow.

It's hard to know what to choose. I want to wear something fairly nice for Daryl, you know, I want to look good for him. But then again, it's a prison, so I also very much want to go in my scruffiest clothes, no make-up and my hair scraped into a ponytail so that I don't stand out...

Monday 27

I parked the car at the prison and deliberately didn't give myself time to think. My stomach had already been in knots all morning, and I'd felt sick for the whole journey, so the last thing I needed was a chance to get even more worked up. So I jumped quickly from the car and started hurrying to the entrance of the visitors' centre, a funny little building that was slightly separate from the rest of the prison.

Then had to nip back to leave my mobile behind; they aren't allowed inside the prison.

That's when I caught sight of myself in the wing mirror and despaired. I'd so wanted to look nice for Daryl, but I look washed out and drab; my skin pasty and a bit spotty even under the make-up I'd forced myself to slap on; my hair flat and lifeless. Oh well, there was no point worrying about it, hopefully he'd just be as glad to see me as I was to see him, no matter what state I looked.

Luckily I'd remembered to bring my driving licence with me to hand to the guards once I finally made it inside, so they could confirm I'm really who I claim to be. Name, address, date of birth, all were taken and double checked.

'We just need to take a quick photo of you,' a guard told me. It reminded me of my arrest, as I sat there being snapped and having my fingerprints scanned. I've gone my whole life without having my fingerprints taken and now it's happened twice in just over a fortnight. Madness.

The staff, though, were very kind. Despite my nerves and obvious confusion about what to expect, they stayed patient with me, steering me towards the lockers, where I had to leave my handbag and car keys because you can't take them into the visiting room. I hadn't realised that.

'Well, that makes sense,' I found myself laughing nervously, 'I could have a file inside there or something.'

The guard's mouth barely twitched. I bet if he had a penny for every time he'd heard some overwrought visitor tell that rubbish joke in a desperate bid to alleviate the tension, well, he might not be a millionaire but he'd probably be able to afford a nice holiday somewhere.

He spotted me glancing anxiously at the clock, though, and this time gave a genuine smile to soothe me. 'My little tip for first timers is to always arrive about half an hour before your visit is booked,' he said. 'That way being checked in doesn't eat into any of your time together.'

'That's-that's really helpful, thank you,' I bumbled, honestly touched. He nodded, business-like again, and pointed over to the exit.

'Now go out there and into the main prison building. There you'll be searched, and after that, you'll be able to see your husband.'

The search was only a pat down like you'd get in an airport, and obviously they went through my handbag with a fine-tooth comb. It wasn't too traumatic really but...okay, sounds obvious but I felt like a common criminal. Thanks to my over-developed sense of guilt, I blushed constantly too, as if I'd done something wrong.

'Lovely dogs,' I found myself babbling inanely to the woman running her hand up the inside of my leg. Why can't I just keep quiet when I'm nervous? She didn't reply, didn't even acknowledge my comment, but it didn't shut me up.

'They're very well behaved, aren't they?' I added, watching as one that looked like a springer spaniel or something wandered away from its handler and sat beside another woman who'd just entered the room. It just sat there quietly, wagging its tail gently and looking rather pleased with itself. I half wished it had come over to me instead as patting it might have calmed my nerves, but then I noticed a couple of officers go swiftly over to the dog and suddenly lead the woman away, holding onto her elbows.

'It's a load of rubbish,' she exploded. 'I don't know why the dog thinks it can smell drugs on me. Maybe I sat next to a junkie on the bus over here. Yeah, that's right, come to think of it, the fella I sat by did look dodgy...' No one seemed to be listening to her protests though, and her words faded away as the door closed behind her.

The rest of the room hadn't skipped a beat. Me? I was totally confused. 'What just...? Was she...? Did they find drugs on her?!'

The guard had finished patting me down. 'Aye, maybe,' she said in a broad Glaswegian accent. 'The dogs are trained to go sit by anyone they smell drugs on. They don't bark, just sit quiet, like. When we see that, we know to check the visitor out proper-like.'

'Right. Right. Right, okay,' I stuttered. What the hell world am I now moving in? Rape, murder, drug smuggling...

Finally, we were all allowed to go into the visiting room. The room was full of tiny tables and orange plastic chairs, so it reminded me of a school hall during exam time, and I scanned it anxiously. Men all wearing identical outfits of blue shirts and jeans looked up from their seats, many seeming equally eager and anxious. I watched as their faces changed to smiles when they saw their loved one…and then I saw Daryl.

Oh my God, to describe that moment… I felt like I was flying through the air and plummeting off a building all at once. It was so wonderful to see him, but horrid because of the surroundings. Sounds corny, but I ran across the room and threw myself at him, calling his name like a teenager in a bad romance, and trying to breath in his smell.

He hugged me back but quickly extricated himself from my grasp as a guard loomed and barked: 'No long or passionate kisses or embraces allowed. Do it again and the visit will be terminated.'

Bloody hell. We hadn't seen each other in a fortnight, had been through absolute hell, but we could barely touch. I could look though; nothing could stop me doing that. I found myself gazing at him, trying to imprint every little look, line and crinkle onto my brain, trying to memorise every tiny thing he said. Trying to store him in my head until next time we met.

'You look…well, thank God, you look okay,' I smiled hesitantly through my frown. But his blue eyes looked so sad and wary, and there were dark circles beneath them. He looked like he'd lost weight too. 'How are you though? How are you coping?'

Everything I asked or said seemed trite and ridiculous. How was he? How's he meant to be?! He's banged up for a crime he didn't commit, so funnily enough he isn't exactly hunky dory. Worse, he's listed as a sex offender in the prison, although luckily that does mean he's marked out as vulnerable so he's been put on special obs.

The conversation was stilted somehow, as though we were two people who barely knew each other and suddenly found themselves stuck in a lift together or something.

'Have you any cash with you?' he asked suddenly. I nodded, a bit nonplussed by the question.

'Great. Go to reception afterwards and deposit as much as you can into my IPC.' He caught my frown and explained: 'Inmate's Personal Cash; it's an account I can access to buy phone credit, groceries, toiletries, sweets, that kind of thing. The maximum amount allowed is £500.'

Good job, because I don't have more than £500 to give. I don't have £500 in fact. Not that I told Daryl this. Actually, I'm a bit worried about money. I'm not sure I can run the house just on my wage, and I need to check our joint account because I'm fairly certain there's not much in it because we cleaned it out to pay for our holiday.

Still, me whining about money problems is the last thing Daryl needs right now, so I stayed quiet; and besides, he's got to be able to buy phone credit otherwise we'll never speak. These two weeks without contact have driven me nuts. Mind you, together at last in that visitor's room I felt so awkward.

'You seem to know all the lingo,' I hazarded. 'That's good. You're settling in. Finding friends. Discovering how it all works...'

Heck, there was nothing else to say. I had to think of something.

'I need the loo,' I said suddenly, nerves apparently putting my bladder into overdrive as much as my mouth. 'Do you know where the ladies' is?'

'Oh, well if you go then you'll be accompanied by a female officer, who will search you before and after you go,' explained Daryl.

'Right, fine, I'll...just hold it until after the visit, eh?'

'Look, sorry,' he sighed, rubbing the top of his bald head like he always does when he's stressed. 'I'm making your nervous, aren't I? This is just really difficult. I've had to build some barriers to keep myself sane and protected and in here and...well, it's hard to suddenly drop them and talk as if we're safe at home.'

Of course. I totally understood. 'Hey, you should not be apologising. You've done nothing wrong. And I think you're coping brilliantly; I'm proud of you.' Tears started blurring my vision as his eyes locked on to me and seemed to laser beam right into my soul. 'I'm proud of you,' I repeated, sniffing.

He reached towards my hand, hesitated, glanced over at the guard for confirmation that it was okay, then continued until my hand was cradled inside his huge paw. Suddenly, I felt safe again. Like somehow, someway, everything's going to be okay. Wish I could bottle that feeling.

'I love you, Gorgeous. Never forget that,' he whispered.

'Never,' I promised. After a minute of gazing at each other, I sniffed again, straightened myself up and wiped the tears from my cheeks, determined to be strong for him. That meant knowing exactly what we are facing.

'So, did the police say why they'd picked on you for these crimes? It makes no sense to me. We have to get a bloody good lawyer, quick. The solicitor who helped me when I was arrested has recommended a couple of names –'

'I've got a barrister,' Daryl interrupted. 'I got talking to another inmate and he recommended someone. That's all sorted. Give them a call when you leave here, introduce yourself; I'm sure they'll be keen to speak to you and they've already started putting the defence together.'

Bit of a shock that, but I nodded eagerly. 'Great. I just can't believe the police even charged you. They didn't seem to listen to a word I said – was it the same with you?'

'Oh, I didn't tell them anything. "No comment" was as much as they got from me.'

'But…isn't that a bit daft? It looks bad, doesn't it?'

'I wasn't going to say anything they could twist and use against me; it's up to them to prove their case, I'm not going to help them.'

His face went from sombre to suddenly smiling at me indulgently, eyes crinkling. 'Gorgeous, don't worry about it. Seriously, I don't want you worrying about any of this, or even thinking about it too much. It's all going to be handled, don't worry. All you have to do is come and visit me whenever possible, keep the house ticking over, and support me in court. And just be as gorgeous as ever. Look at you, so sweet and innocent, in a place like this – it's obvious you don't belong here.'

He squeezed my hand gently, the oddest, faraway look on his face. 'The judge and jury will take one look at my baby and know someone like you could never be with a monster,' he whispered, voice thick with emotion.

Even in all of this he is thinking of me first. I'm blown away by how strong he is being. If it's possible for one good thing to come out of this nightmare it's that I'm falling in love with my husband all over again.

Wednesday 29

He took care of all the bills. I don't even know which utility group we're with let alone the account number and I'm buggered if I know where Daryl kept all that stuff.

After a root around I managed to find the information I needed, and get payments changed to be taken from my account rather than his as he's no longer earning. Flipping hope he gets out soon because I can't keep paying everything on my own, will have to dip into our savings to keep my head above water – and there's precious little of those thanks to our break in Turkey.

When I came to change the water bill the woman on the end of the line said: 'Oooh, how unfortunate, your poor husband's got the same name as that rapist, the Port Pervert. He'll have to change it!'

She laughed. I didn't.

Fri 31

So, the day that changed my life was Friday 10 July. It's now three weeks on from that and the weight is dropping off me because I'm having trouble eating. I've been signed off work sick (stress) and have lost 9lb in a fortnight. To be honest, I'd have thought it'd be more considering Mum made me weigh myself after five days and it turned out I'd lost half a stone.

It might seem strange that I'm obsessing about this when my entire world has fallen apart, but believe me, if I start thinking about that other stuff I'm going to fall apart too.

I feel…broken. People always say 'numb' in these situations don't they? And I suppose I can understand why because it is the oddest emotional experience I've ever had: I feel like I'm in the eye of a storm and everything is raging round me. But I'm not numb. That seems to imply a lack of sensation and feeling, but if I am numb it's not in the normal way, it's more like…okay, it's like the time I burned myself on the iron. For a good second or so my body didn't seem to register the pain, almost as if it was so hot that my nerve-endings were overwhelmed. Then finally the body and brain caught on to what was happening, and boy did my arm hurt as I finally whipped it away! Now it's the same sort of feeling somehow; I've too many emotions tearing at me and I've overloaded and can't react. What I wouldn't give to simply feel numb.

The craziest thing is the constant deluge of death threats. I don't understand why people want to hurt me; I'm a decent human being who's done nothing wrong. But they don't seem to think of me as a person…

Why can't people leave me alone? Well, because the press won't let them forget about me and Daryl, I suppose. Journalists are everywhere, all the time – not that they can currently write much about me because they'll be in contempt of court right now if they put too much about the case. Peter assures me that this is the calm before the storm and that things will be worse after the trial, but I'm not worried about that; after the trial, when Daryl's home again, I'll want to tell our story anyway, so that the world can know the hell this innocent man's been through.

I've learnt a new technique to help with sleeping, incidentally. I turn one pillow sideways so it lies alongside me, and I put my arm over it, as if it's Daryl's chest. Tragic, isn't it, pretending I've got my arms around my husband. At least I'm now managing about three hours' sleep a night, on and off. Still not enough. I still feel wide-eyed and on the edge. But at least I don't feel like I'm literally going mental any more. Well, not so much, anyway.

AUGUST

Monday 3
The moment of truth couldn't be put off any longer; today I had to go back to work. I'm exhausted from being a figure of so much hate. No one could look me in the eye, and yet everyone was staring at me the minute they thought my back was turned. No one spoke to me, yet I was the only topic of conversation. As for my boss, he danced around me like a barefoot tourist hopping across hot sand at the beach.
I may have to quit. I can't afford to quit. I really, really want to quit.
Kim wasn't even there. I didn't ask where she was because that would have involved talking to someone and the prospect was way too awkward. I want to contact Kim, she if she's okay, but the fact she hasn't been in touch with me speaks volumes. I'm hurt by the way mates have dumped me but in a weird way I'm not that surprised – but I did expect more from Kim. And knowing there was just one friendly face in the office would have made the day tolerable.
As it was it felt like torture. Every single second seemed to last forever, I'd glance at the clock constantly and be stunned that just a minute had passed by, and I couldn't even kill time by making a cuppa because the kitchen became a no-go area. I'd walk into it and conversation would be killed instantly, everyone disappearing like mist so that I was left alone, feeling even more awkward than before.
At lunchtime, unable to eat because my stomach was churning too much, I wound up walking the streets around the office. Even that didn't feel like escape though; I felt

exposed and scared that someone would recognise me from the news, so scuttled along, head down and my shoulders tense around my ears. At least I had the protection officers with me, trailing along behind, to make me feel safer.

I don't think I did a jot of work either. I couldn't concentrate, paranoia sapped all my energy. I don't know about resigning, at this rate I might be sacked.

Thank God for Mum and Dad though. It was good to get home to friendly faces, and Mum had done a lovely roast chicken. I could get used to that treatment, and managed to eat a good few mouthfuls.

But as I tucked in Dad cleared his throat, which is always a precursor to him saying something he isn't looking forward to.

'We're going to have to go back home tomorrow, love,' he said.

'It's Dad's job,' added Mum. 'We don't want to leave you, but your father has to get back to work, like you have.'

I swallowed, the chicken almost sticking in my suddenly dry throat, and forced a smile. 'It's fine, honestly. I don't expect you to stay here forever. We've all got to try to get on with life until, well, Daryl's released and we can really get back to normal.'

Normal. What's that? It seems so long ago that I honestly don't seem able to remember.

Tues 4
Kim called late last night! She'd heard through the gossip grapevine that I'd been into work and about the wall of silence that had met me. It was so good to hear a friendly voice, I've been feeling very isolated and abandoned since, well, everything.

She asked about me and Daryl, of course, and what could I say? That it's all horrific but we're trying to stay strong for each other? Nothing I say can cover it, so that's pretty much all I said. Instead I wanted to hear all about her.

'I'm all right,' she replied. But I could tell from her voice she wasn't. Eager to hear about anything to take my mind off my own troubles, I pushed her for more info. Finally she caved.

'It's Sam,' she sighed. 'He's been back on the scene, making a nuisance of himself. I shouldn't be burdening you with all this though, you've enough on your plate. That's why I haven't been in touch sooner though; I've been trying to deal with all this.'

'Well what do you mean, he's back on the scene? In what way?' Then I gasped in horror as a thought occurred to me. 'You're not back together are you?'

'No! God, no! But I thought he'd gone forever; he took it so well when we split and he moved out that I should have known I hadn't heard the last of him though... You know what, honestly, you don't need to hear about this.'

'Tell me!' I demanded. It's amazing, the restorative powers of hearing about someone else's problems. That sounds awful, and I don't mean it as if I'm enjoying it, just that I suddenly felt more awake, more connected with the world again than I had in a long time. I felt needed and human again, I suppose. Maybe this was a problem I could actually help solve, instead of feeling like a useless piece of flotsam.

'Okay...he broke in the other night.' She was trying to sound matter of fact, but her voice cracked just a little. 'I woke up and just knew someone was in the room. I flicked on my bedside lamp and he was standing there, staring at me.'

'What did he want?' I whispered.

'H-he wanted me. He was raving on about how he wanted me back, couldn't live without me. Then he...'

My heart pounded as I waited for her to explain. Had he hurt her? Forced himself on her? She seemed to read my mind.

'He pulled out a knife. I thought he was going to kill me and Henry, and I was just frozen to the bed, too scared to defend myself. He stepped towards me...then slit his wrists. Said again and again that he couldn't live without me.'

'So what happened then?' I wondered.

'He burst into tears. He wasn't a threat any more as he stood there like a little boy, all sobbing and snotty, and falling to his knees to beg me to take him back. I called an ambulance and the police, and they took him away. He hadn't even cut himself properly, they were just scratches, it was all for drama and show...

'That was just after Daryl was arrested, and I've been sorting out an injunction to keep him away forever; in fact, your solicitor, Peter Simpson, has been helping me a lot and giving me advice. I contacted him because you seemed so impressed with him and the way he put you at ease.'

'Well, I'm glad I've helped somehow, even without knowing it,' I smiled, relieved. I'm so, so glad she's finally seen what we all could have told her a long time ago; that Sam is a proper, full on, looney tunes nutter. Why couldn't she have seen it earlier?

'Are you sleeping okay after all that?' I asked.

She gave a wry laugh. 'Not so great. You?'

'Bloody awful,' I smiled back. 'Listen, if you're awake in the small hours, feeling a bit crazy and lonely, just call me. I'll be awake. I'm always awake.'

She said she might just take me up on that. I hope she does. There is no lonelier time than the hours between 3am and 4am. Everyone in the world seems to be asleep and peaceful but you. That's how I always feel, anyway, and it's when the worst thoughts stalk me: will Daryl ever get out, is he really innocent, will someone somehow get into the house and hurt me...?

Anyway, today I endured another day of being ignored and hated at work. Shame Kim chose this week to take off as holiday, but never mind; simply knowing I still had one friend in the world made things a little easier to deal with.

On the way home I remembered I needed some milk. To be honest I need quite a few things but I couldn't face the supermarket and I'm not exactly eating a lot right now anyway so... I nipped to the corner shop for the first time since, well, the arrest. Mum and Dad have been getting bits in for me. Anyway, just like the good old days, I walked into the shop and the bell over the door tinged. Ric looked up, usual smile on his face...which rapidly slid away when he saw me.

Still, I grabbed the milk and went to the counter smiling hesitantly, proffering a couple of quid.

'It's gone up,' he said.

'Oh, right,' I said, flustered. 'The, er, the price says £1.50 still.'

'It's gone up.' This time he folded his arms, set his head back a little so he seemed to be looking down his nose at me.

'How much?' I asked, digging around in my purse.

'More than you can afford, lady.'

My insides seemed to solidify into something cold and hard, but my mouth babbled on. 'I've a tenner in here somewhere, that be enough?'

I meant it too, I'd actually have paid £10 just to get this awful episode over, and get the hell out of there with the milk.

Ric shook his head.

The thought of leaving without the milk seemed too mortifying to contemplate, so I tried again. 'Come on Ric, please, I've been coming here for years, you know me…'
'I don't want your kind in here, lady.' He said it slowly, deliberately, as if I were a child.
The shop bell gave a cheery ting again that was totally at odds with the atmosphere. I couldn't look away from Ric though, nor he me. His eyes didn't leave mine even as he spoke to whoever was behind me: 'Don't worry, this person was just leaving.'
I held his gaze for another beat, then hung my head and scurried to the door, feeling sick to my stomach.
I am hated. I am vilified. I am utterly rejected. That person who wrote the graffiti got it right: I am scum.
I ran home, tears streaming down my face so fast I could barely see. Hands shaking, I shoved the key in the door, desperate to get inside, then slammed it shut and leaned heavily against it, hysterical now. Crying so hard I could barely breathe, the sobs that racked my whole body sounded like an asthmatic donkey as I sank to the floor and curled up on the Welcome mat. It was 15 minutes before I could move, and then it was only to reach up and put the chain and bolt across.
It may be stiflingly hot and stuffy inside, it may be inescapable because it is surrounded by journalists, it may be in danger of being blown up or something, but this house is the only place I feel safe now.

Monday 17
Even the worst time of your life becomes mundane eventually. I visit Daryl twice a week, plus receive two letters from him and get a call every single night without

fail. In some ways we have more contact than when he was working and life was normal.

Conversation between us is often awkward though. There's not much to say. His life never changes, his daily routine remains a constant – the most exciting thing to happen to him is that he decided to try a different brand of body spray, so now he doesn't even smell like he used to. And I can't tell him about my life: money worries, death threats, aching loneliness. We avoid talking about the future, terrified we'll jinx it, and he refuses to discuss the trial, which is frustrating but he thinks he's stopping me from worrying about it by pretending it isn't happening. I don't feel in a position to argue and therefore add to his own worries; I want to stay upbeat and cheer him along his way somehow. Often we end up talking about telly programmes.

I've got used to seeing the plain clothes police officers outside my house all the time, and bring them a cuppa every morning when I make my own brew. I know all their names now, and although I wouldn't even remotely say we're friends we are friendly. I know Terry (PC Cole) is getting married in two months' time; Luke (PC Christie) is waiting anxiously for a call about his baby daughter arriving because his girlfriend is due to go into labour any day now; and Senga (PC Wallace) is just buying a house. The only one who doesn't say anything beyond the professional is PC Derek Yeoh, but he's nice enough really.

The journalists seem to have got bored, as one day I opened my curtains and they weren't there any more.

Work's a worry though. No one is talking to me still; no surprise there. I just keep my head down and try to get on with it. Keeping busy is the best way through the day. But I'm not doing a brilliant job, to be honest, because I do have problems concentrating and at inopportune times I'll realise I've drifted off and started worrying about Daryl or money or if someone will go through with their threat of planting a bomb under my car and blowing me to smithereens.

As a result, Keith has given me an official warning. It was done in a very touchy feely, caring and sharing way where he pretended to be worried about me, but I could tell that he'd be relieved to be rid of me. I expect I'm quite bad for office morale…

I wish I could feel, even just for a moment, normal again. I wish I could stop the churning worry in my stomach, and the fears rattling round and round my head. The only thing keeping me going is that eventually this will end, Daryl will be home and life will be normal again. Everyone who has given us a hard time will realise their awful mistake.

The one and only person who has stood by me is Kim. She's been fantastic. Often I'll text her at 3am, asking if she's awake, and she almost always is. Then she'll ring me and we'll chat for ages about how crap life is, or exchange advice on how to keep going.

Ultimately though, the best advice is the simplest.

'We've just got to get through it,' Kim always says. 'In the story of our lives, this is just a couple of pages, even though it feels huge right now.'

'After every rain storm there is sunshine,' I add. And we both repeat it, then say goodbye as the sky turns pre-dawn grey.

Saturday 22

More good news (can you sense the sarcasm?). There's a benefit available to help people with the cost of visiting their loved ones in prison. I'm not eligible for help though.

Daryl being in prison is costing me a fortune – of all the problems involved with having an imprisoned spouse that

INVISIBLE

wasn't one that ever occurred to me. But things are tight enough paying all the usual bills on just my wage...then there's the fact that I send him £500 every month. I write a cheque for that amount making sure to remember to write his prisoner number beneath his name.

SEPTEMBER

Saturday 12
You know what? I'm sick of feeling miserable and sorry for myself. I'm going to get through this and so is Daryl. I'm going to channel all the energy I've been using to be a miserable git into keeping everything going for Daryl. When he comes home everything will be exactly the same, and we can pick up where we left off – only things will be much better.

Sunday 20
I'm so annoyed with all my so-called friends. How could they just abandon me like this? I feel like phoning every single one of the buggers and giving them a piece of my mind.
Take Hannah; she's meant to be my best friend. We've known each other since we were knee high, been through all sorts. I've supported her through all the problems with her asthma; and when she dumped Karl but then changed her mind and he didn't want anything to do with her any more; and even when she had that affair with the married man (which I didn't actually approve of at all, but I kept quiet because it's none of my business, really, is it) and he wound up choosing to stay with his wife.
All sorts of things I've counselled her through, going way back to when she'd get detention at school for not doing her homework, then sound off for hours about how unfair it was. I'd nod, and agree with her, though technically it *was* fair because it was her fault.

INVISIBLE

Now, for the first time ever I need her. And where is she? Nowhere to be seen, that's where!

But they're all as bad as each other. I've helped all of them out in one way or another over the years, and never asked for anything back. I'd been lucky, I'd had a nice, smooth-running, straightforward life until now, although I reckon I'm now paying for it by having more drama than most people can pack into one lifetime... So the least I should expect right now is that my mates rally round me, right? Wrong. It's been ages since I've heard from any of them.

I got lonely the other night, sitting watching telly all alone having spent an entire day at work being ignored by everyone but Kim (even Kevin seems to avoid telling me what to do if he can help it, and he's my boss for goodness sake) and I found myself sending a little text out to them all. Just saying *'Hi, how you doing? Been ages, hope all's ok. Be great to hear from you xx'*

I thought that might open the door a bit, if they were worried that they'd left it so long to contact me that I now no longer wanted anything to do with them. I wanted to let them know that if they made a move to get in touch, we could get past this silly blip where they'd got all scared and judgemental (not that I'd ever have been able to forget it, mind, but I'd have been the bigger person and forgiven them).

The message went out to each of my so-called close friends: Una, Amy, Hannah, Sarah. I didn't receive a single reply. They all ignored me.

I found myself checking my phone every hour over the following days; making excuses for them that perhaps there had been a problem with the network and the message had only just been delivered, or they were busy, or they were struggling to find the right words to apologise to me for ignoring me for weeks on end...

But no, I haven't had anything back from them. They want nothing to do with me. Gits.

How dare they sit in judgement of Daryl and me? What do they know of the facts? They haven't even bothered asking me whether or not I think he's guilty. Well, the smug smiles will be wiped from their stupid faces after the trial when the truth comes out. I will never, ever forgive them for what they've done – because I wouldn't have dreamed of treating any of them this way.

OCTOBER

Thursday 15

Kim went to see Peter today to get more advice on how to deal with Psycho Sam. The flipping weirdo keeps stalking poor Kim. The wire to her phone and satellite TV were both cut the other day when she got home, and though she has no proof, it doesn't take a genius to work out who is responsible. She's only just replaced her car's windscreen too, after it was 'mysteriously' smashed one night.

I worry about her. And she worries about me. In a weird way I think it helps us both, distracting us from our own troubles. We still often call each other at obscene hours of the night, when the rest of the world is asleep. Without her, I think I'd probably have gone mad. I'm glad I've been able to help her in a practical way too, by putting her in touch with Peter. He seems a really genuinely lovely man, always willing to put himself out for people. Every time I meet him I find myself warming to him more and more.

NOVEMBER

Wednesday 20
People in the office are making plans for Christmas and getting excited. They all pointedly leave me out of the conversation. Kim tries to make it up by asking me in a loud voice what my plans are, or making a song and dance out of us going for lunch together, but I'm afraid that all her efforts just mean she is ostracised too. Not to the extent I am, as Kim is one of those lovely, smiley people everyone instantly loves and warms to, but even so there is a lack of warmth sometimes in the way they are with her, and a definite confusion in the glances thrown her way. They don't get why someone as nice as her would have anything to do with someone as vile as me, presumably.
Mum and Dad are trying their best to get enthusiastic about Christmas too, bless them. They've invited me over to theirs and Mum's planning on making all my favourite foods by the sound of it. They keep saying that I've got to enjoy myself, 'it's what Daryl would want' (as though he is dead).
They're right though, it is what he wants. Even he has made encouraging noises about how I should be going out and having fun. He has absolutely no idea how crap my life is, thinks I'm just carrying on as normal. I can't tell him the truth.

Monday 25
4am – Just got off the phone from Kim. What a nightmare! She was woken at just gone midnight by the sound of

someone outside. She called the police immediately, and luckily they arrived quickly because they know of her history of being stalked. Of course, they found good old Sam outside, trying to break in again.

As he was arrested she reckons he was moaning: 'I love her! We're meant to be together!'

Luckily Henry slept through the whole thing, only waking once Psycho Sam had been taken away. Apparently the little boy had been overjoyed to meet officers and try on their hats. But how much longer can Kim hide the frightening truth from her son?

'Why can't Sam just leave me alone?' she sighed down the phone to me just now.

'Are you scared of what he might do next? Scared for you and Henry?'

'I was that first time he broke in, but not any more,' she admitted. 'I didn't know what to expect that first time, seeing him standing there with a knife in his hands. But he looked so pathetic when he stood there crying, with a couple of scratches on his arms, that all the fear disappeared. So even this time, I wasn't afraid really, just…I don't know, all I feel is pity for him; but not the kind that will make me want him back or anything. He's broken and needs to be fixed by experts. There's nothing I can do for him. There's certainly nothing to love about him.'

Although I can see what she means, I can't help admiring her because I just don't think I'd react in the same way at all. I wouldn't feel pity, I'd be scared stiff. Then again…

'It's amazing what people can cope with once life chucks horrible things at them,' I pointed out. 'I never thought I'd get used to death threats and police officers outside my door almost permanently, but somehow I barely give them a thought these days.'

'You just have to get on with life,' agreed Kim. Then she repeated our little saying, 'After every rain storm there is sunshine.'

Yes, but when you're in the middle of the monsoon and it's starting to cause a flood, it can be hard sometimes to imagine the sun every coming out again.

DECEMBER

Thursday 13

The smashing of glass, instantly followed by shouting, sounds of running, pandemonium, had me wide-eyed and out of bed in one movement. I was standing up, looking round the room, heart pounding, before I was even awake properly. Head flashing this way and that trying to find the source of the chaos, taking everything in in snapshots.

Bedroom empty, still dark - this wasn't another raid. Hammering on the front door. Someone shouting my name. Then a high-pitched screeching rent the air, and my heart hitched higher into my throat as I realised: it was the smoke alarm.

Oh God, oh God, someone had set fire to my home.

I still hadn't switched a light on, instead raced and stumbled blindly along the landing that I knew off by heart. Skittered down the stairs, nearly missing steps in my hurry. Almost at the bottom a smell hit me, so thick and acrid it was virtually a solid wall: petrol fumes and smoke. I coughed and wheezed as I breathed it in, my eyes starting to sting.

Shivering fingers felt for the hall light switch, and I blinked rapidly as my watering eyes adjusted, expecting to be blinded for a second or so. I wasn't though, instead I gazed dumbly at black smoke rising taller than me and swaying lazily, and flames eager to join in the dance were licking at the bottom of the front door.

Panic froze me until another shout, more hammering, made me jump. 'The back door,' someone yelled. 'Get to the back door! Get out!'

Right, of course! My brain was still unscrambling but my legs were already moving. Down the dimly-lit hallway, past the lounge-come-dining-room door, plunging on into the kitchen, almost ricocheting off the breakfast bar in my hurry, legs somehow tangling with the bar stools and bringing me crashing to the floor.

Pain flared in my right hip as I hit the ground, coughing still. More shouts from outside, hammering on the door replaced suddenly with a loud thump that made the wood shudder. I lay on the floor like an upturned beetle, kicking and kicking, finally extricating myself.

Another massive thump on the back door.

I jumped up, feeling blindly for the key. Got it! Turned it with a click and flung the door open, just as PC Yeoh was about to take another kick at it and break it down. We almost fell into each other, and he grabbed me, dragging me from the house and into the garden.

His colleague, Senga, appeared round the corner, panting even harder than we were, her face smudged with black.

'Got the little scrote,' she gasped.

'Who…? My house, it's on fire,' I screamed.

Senga put her hands on her hips, took a big breath, then smiled reassuringly. 'The fire's out,' pant, 'I put it out,' pant, 'extinguisher in car.' Another couple of big breaths, then: 'Looks like he chucked a homemade petrol bomb at your front door. Stupid sod didn't seem to realise we're watching the place. I arrested him before he'd got more than a few feet away, and Derek came round the back to make sure you were okay.'

I felt weak. Thank God they'd been here. Thank God. I could have been killed!

Senga stepped towards me, waving her hands in a placating manner. 'It's was just a dumb teenager doing it for fun; it wasn't a serious threat,' she said. She was trying to soothe me but that just made it worse. A kid with no grudge against me at all, apart from what he'd read about or heard in the media, had decided to try and burn my house down with me in it. If that's not a serious threat then I dread to think what someone who was serious would do to me.

Shakily, I made my way round to the front of the house, not caring that I was in my pyjamas, or that my feet were rapidly freezing on the icy path.

The front door was scorched all over, and beneath the foam of the extinguisher I could make out black marks radiating out from the centre where the petrol bomb had been lobbed with unerring accuracy and shattered. The bottom of the door had borne the brunt of the burning, of course, as the petrol had dripped down and taken the flames with it.

I held my breath, peering at it through the tears that were falling now adrenaline had abandoned me. Prodded at the wood – ouch! Still hot!

From behind me I heard a sigh. 'You'd best get on to your insurance people,' said PC Yeoh.

I shook my head. 'No, it's fine. The door looks solid enough. I'll just buy some paint and gloss over the damage.' After all, that's what I do with my whole life these days, gloss over the damage...

Friday 14

I've received a couple of early Christmas presents as a result of last night. The police have fitted tiny CCTV cameras at the front and back of the house, and the fire brigade have fitted a lockable letterbox cover to my singed and blackened front door, along with extra smoke alarms, in case someone else decided to kill me in the hope I'll burn in hell forever.

I'd almost got used to living in a permanent state of terror that had become as mundane as sifting through the post for death threats. Now it's come into sharp focus again.

People want to kill me. They don't see me as a person, don't think I deserve sympathy because my life's been torn apart for reasons I don't understand.

So much for peace and goodwill to all mankind, eh?

Tuesday 18

Today's Daryl's birthday. I wanted to make it special, especially as I'm not allowed to visit today, so sent him a big padded card with love hearts all over it...and got into trouble with the prison because apparently that sort of thing is banned. They had to rip into it to check nothing had been smuggled inside the padding - that news made me cry quite a lot, in the privacy of the toilets at work.

I've got quite good at crying in secret. Lock myself into the cubicle, sit down on the toilet lid, then lean forward so that the tears drip straight down my eyelashes and onto the floor, rather than down my face. It means my make-up doesn't get ruined, and helps stop my skin from going blotchy, so that once I pull myself together I can return to my desk faster, and no one can tell what I've been doing by looking at me. The only problem is my nose is often still red and swollen, but hopefully people just think I have allergies.

I'm probably going to spend quite a lot of time in the toilets tomorrow; it's the works Christmas party. I'd decided to defiantly go, just to show everyone that I don't care what they think, and that I have nothing to be ashamed of, but now the reality is getting closer and I'm not sure I've the courage to go through with it. I wish Daryl were here and we could march into the room arm in arm,

Thursday 20

Ah, the good old Christmas party. What fun that was.

Mind you, any party staged on a Wednesday is doomed to failure, in my opinion.

Because it's a lunch that carries on into the evening I find it weird at the best of times, walking into the office on party day. It's incongruous to see people sitting at their desks or doing a spot of photocopying whilst in their best going out gear.

That wasn't what really got me this time though. It was more the scandalised looks on people's faces when they saw me in my red silk dress and realised I'd be joining them at the do. It was like a scene from a movie the way quiet descended as every eye turned to me. Inside I was a quivering jelly, but I wasn't going to let them know it. I smiled sweetly at them then pushed my chin up and walked proudly to my desk, plonked down onto my chair, and flicked my computer on.

Only when I felt the glares slide away and heard the noise levels rise as everyone hissed 'how could she?', 'what's she thinking', etc, to one another did I start to blink rapidly to clear the tears that threatened.

Minutes later Kim arrived and made a beeline for me. Perched on my desk and bent forward so her glossy black hair fell into a natural curtain between us and the rest of the world.

'You look lovely,' she smiled but her eyes were worried. 'Are you sure you want to come though? It's not going to be fun for you…'

'Not about fun. I'm proving a point,' I said stubbornly, fiddling with some paperclips as distraction. 'Anyway, any Psycho Sam news?'

'He's been quiet for the last couple of weeks, ever since he was arrested a second time for trying to break in,' Kim confessed, her face a mixture of horror and relief. 'Peter's been so fantastic sorting injunctions and keeping on at the police. He even arranged for some CCTV to be fitted…'

'Oh, snap, I've got some too!' I grinned. Inappropriate, but we couldn't help giggling. What the hell have our lives come to?!

The morning wore on and people shot me evil looks more and more openly. I started to wonder exactly what point I was trying to prove – and to whom. Sheer bloody-mindedness was the only thing that kept me from running from the building to the safety of my home.

At 12.30pm the stampede for the loos started as the women went to fix their make-up and touch up their hair. The fog of perfume and hairspray hit my nose like a punch, then slid down my throat, making me cough and splutter. Lauren the office manager turned to me boldly.

'Sounds like you should go home,' she said bitchily.

'And miss the chance to spread festive goodwill with all my favourite people? Never,' I mock pouted, even as my heart tried to batter through my ribcage. God, I hate confrontations. Still, I felt proud of myself though because not so long ago I would have made that remark in my head but not had the courage to say it out loud.

The atmosphere was even worse when we arrived at the restaurant and people scurried to sit down so they wouldn't wind up stuck next to me. I finished up sandwiched between Kim (hurray!) and Kevin (boo! Poor bloke; as boss, no one wants to sit beside him either). Kim did her best to chat to me, but I found myself sinking into depressed silence.

Thing is, it's all well and good being stubborn, but I was making myself as miserable as I was making everyone else.

Finally the meal was over, the tables cleared away, and it was time for the music to start. It was easier to hide in the dim light of the dance floor. I felt more anonymous and at ease, watching as everyone else had fun.

I even made myself have a dance, all on my own, to Wham's Last Christmas. Why shouldn't I have fun? I have as much right as the next person; I've done nothing to be ashamed of.

And with that thought ringing in my ears, I hurried home, frankly relieved. I reckon that was the longest day of my entire life, and given I've spent time in a police cell that's saying something.

When Daryl called he asked me all about the party, wanting to hear everything as if to live vicariously. I made the whole thing up, right down to me and Keith doing a rousing rendition of Slade's Merry Christmas Everyone on the karaoke and me almost bursting a blood vessel screaming 'it's Chriiiistmaaaaaas!' Daryl made me do an action replay of that bit.

I am a total fraud. I can remember when I couldn't tell a lie without stuttering, stammering and blushing my way through it. Now they trip off the tongue. Still, they are in a good cause. He doesn't know anything about the fire either; I don't want to worry him.

Friday 21

Thank God it's Friday. Another week over.

The only thing keeping me going is the thought of Daryl coming home, and that's bloody months away.

Saturday 22

Today was my final chance to see Daryl before Christmas. Nothing says festive like a prison visit... Instead of a snog under the mistletoe, I had a security pat down from a total stranger. Instead of the sound of carols, there were only barked orders.

Inside the visiting room the only concession to the time of year that had been made in the horrible sombre grey room was a paper chain across one wall, and the oldest, ugliest Christmas lantern that hung rattily in the middle of the room, one side sagging, and a couple of its dangling fronds missing.

Daryl didn't seem to notice though; he only had eyes for me. His arms wrapped all the way around me and he held me so tight, flush against him for as long as we could get away with. God that felt good. It's been so long since we were together.

The guards seemed a bit easier going, maybe because it's Christmas, and let the embrace last for a couple of seconds before we were told: 'Come on, break it up, you know the rules.'

We released each other reluctantly, but I didn't want to break physical contact. My hand slid down the front of Daryl's regulation blue cotton shirt, feeling his hard muscles underneath, and then grabbed his hand, our fingers automatically twisting together. Hand in hand, we slowly sank into our seats, gazing at each other.

'Merry Christmas, and Happy Birthday,' I smiled. 'Did you get my Christmas card? I made sure this one wasn't padded or musical or anything that's against the rules.'

Daryl chuckled, shaking his head. 'Typical you, not reading the rules properly. My gorgeous air head.'

Umm, bit patronising. I found myself bristling at the comment, when normally I'd have just giggled along with it. I wanted to argue back and say 'actually, this air head is managing to keep the household going all on her own; I'd like to see you try.' But I bit it back because of course I am being a right old grumpy cow. It's not Daryl's fault that we're in this situation, I shouldn't take my anger out on him.

'So…is there a special Christmas meal or anything in here?' I asked, struggling to find something to change the subject to.

Daryl ran his free hand over his bald head. 'Dunno,' he shrugged. 'But me and you'll have a massive celebration next year.'

'It's not fair, we should be having a massive celebration now. You shouldn't be here,' I pouted like a three-year-old having a tantrum. I knew it wasn't helpful of me but I couldn't help myself.

Silence. There really wasn't anything to say. I cast around the room as I searched my head for a suitable subject. The Christmas lantern's few remaining sparkly plastic fronds rippled in the draught from the heating system.

I was reminded of all those silent nights Daryl and I had spent in front of the telly. How not long before all this happened I'd been thinking of leaving him, thinking I wasn't even sure if I liked him. I huffed and pulled a face, impatient with myself for even thinking something like that here and now, when Daryl needs all the support and love he can get. I'm a terrible person.

'God, if it's that boring you can just go,' snapped Daryl, letting go of my hand. He must have been watching my expression the whole time without me realising it.

'No, no, sorry, the sigh was frustration because of being here, not boredom,' I placated. 'I'm sorry if it seemed like something else. I just can't wait for you to be out of here…'

Ah, that gave me inspiration for our conversation. 'So, how's your defence coming on? Are you happy with your barrister?'

'I don't want to talk about that now,' snapped Daryl impatiently. 'Can I enjoy just one day without being nagged by you about the sodding trial.'

I sat back, chastised. Stupid, stupid idiot that I am, fancy going on at him when he must be feeling so down. An image of him spending Christmas Day in a tiny cell instead of in our cosy home with me flared in my head.

'I just wanted to see how things are going. You never tell me anything about it and I worry for you; I want to be involved,' I said in a small voice.

'You don't need to fret about it, I've told you that. All you have to do is turn up to court every day looking pretty - the judge and jury will look at you and know I must be a good man if I'm with someone as good as you. Now just leave it.'

He sat back, the orange plastic chair making a little groan of protest as his heavy, muscular frame slumped against its back.

Another extended moment of silence, then: 'You got the decorations up then?' Daryl asked. 'The ones I like? It helps me, when I'm sitting in my cell, to imagine you at home surrounded by our things.'

'Oh…yeah, of course,' I lied. The last thing I've wanted to do is put up cheery, twinkly decorations.

And so the conversation went on, in fits and starts of awkwardness and closeness. Finally the hour was up and with a quick embrace we said our goodbyes, my face aching with the effort of being cheery and upbeat. It'll be new year before I see him again…

By the time I got home, I was angry again. That's the main emotion that keeps me pushing on, to be honest. Fury at this injustice.

INVISIBLE

That and the drive to keep things going for Daryl. So I dug out the baubles, tinsel and lights and put them all up. Felt like I owed it to my husband to act as normal, so that he could imagine the place. I even used the white decorations he likes, rather than the colourful ones I prefer – he likes everything to match.

Tuesday 25
At first I admit I was really miserable today. Instead of feeling even vaguely excited about getting out of bed and opening my presents I found myself cynically thinking 'What do you get the girl who has nothing?'
Then I remembered Daryl in his cell, whose only comfort is imagining what a good time I'm having. He wanted me to put the decorations up and I did, and he'd want me to enjoy Christmas Day with my family too. So although it was a bit of a struggle, I made myself enthusiastically rip off the wrapping paper of the various presents Mum and Dad had insisted on buying me. Every time I found myself sinking into misery I'd remind myself about Daryl and slap a smile on my face for his sake. Anything else felt like a betrayal of him somehow.
And next year we'll be together, and we can celebrate double.

Monday 31
Well it's New Year's Eve and I'm on my own – I came home the day after Boxing Day. Much as they made every effort to keep me happy and cheery (and I'm grateful, I really am) I found myself longing to be home, surrounded by my and Daryl's things, and our memories. It makes me feel closer to him, somehow. I've even been wearing some of his jumpers.
I won't be bothering to stay up for midnight. Instead I've shuffled off the sofa at 10pm, having forced myself to watch

all the cheery telly programmes because I refuse to allow myself to wallow and feel miserable. I have to stay upbeat and positive; it's the only thing that will keep me going until Daryl's release. If I allow myself to get all bitter and twisted then Daryl won't recognise me when he finally comes home. Sometimes it feels like such draining hard work though. Still, it'll be worth it in the end…

Anyway, it's good that it's New Year's Eve. I can't wait to be rid of this terrible year. Next one will be better, I just know it. It has to be.

If someone could see me now I'm sure they'd laugh though. I've pulled the duvet over my head to muffle the sounds of celebration going on around me, and am scribbling furiously in my diary by the light of a torch that's normally only used when a fuse blows at night. I feel like a child, and it's actually quite comforting.

Inevitably, I keep thinking back to previous New Year's Eves, especially last year. If I'd known then what was coming, I think I'd have packed my bags and done a runner from the country. Instead we'd been in blissful ignorance. We'd actually arranged to go out with Una and Andy for a few drinks at the local pub, but at the last minute we'd cried out – one look at the freezing cold weather had been enough to make us change our minds. Besides, I always get a bit over-emotional if I go out on NYE, for some reason.

'We should do something though,' Daryl had insisted. 'I don't want to sit around watching telly, this is a special night. I know…' He'd disappeared into the kitchen and come out brandishing a book of cocktail recipes we'd been bought by a mate years before but never used. 'How about we try some of these out? We've a load of booze left over from Christmas.'

He'd stood there doing a little dance, mimicking the staff in cocktail bars as they slung bottles around their bodies, in the air, and caught them behind their backs, before shaking the mixer either side of them. Blue eyes laughing as he bit on his lower lip in fake concentration.

'Impressive, but best not try that with any real bottles or we'll have a truly smashing time,' I'd joked.

'Come on, what do you think? Yeah?' He hadn't stopped dancing yet...

'Yeah, why not,' I'd grinned.

Two hours later the kitchen had looked like a mini-tornado had swept through it, dragging bottles of alcohol and mixers out of cupboards, along with the odd glace cherry; we'd even dug out a couple of cocktail umbrellas we'd found – goodness knows where they'd come from. In the lounge, music had thumped out, drowning out our merry giggles as we'd danced around. It was freezing outside, but we were snuggly-warm inside and having a whale of a time.

'Rave!' I'd shouted, turning the music up another notch when Chase and Status's Lost and Not Found came on. Flapping our arms round almost uncontrollably, we'd wobbled, laughed, jumped up and down and finally flopped on the sofa breathlessly.

'That's my babe,' Daryl had grinned. 'That's what I love about you, that we can do daft stuff like this. Makes me realise how much I love you. Happy New Year.'

Fireworks had gone off as we'd kissed. It had felt magical. The disconnect I'd felt growing between us during the previous few months had disappeared momentarily and I'd felt truly happy. It's one of my favourite memories. Hard to believe it was only a year ago, it feels like a lifetime.

Midnight – well, just after actually. Happy New Year! I'm surrounded by the sound of fireworks going off. This is going to be a good year, I can just feel it, although still tough. I feel really positive, lighter even, to be rid of last year. It can sod off; only good times ahead, especially once the trial is out of the way.

JANUARY

Tuesday 29

Daryl says this is the lull before the storm; that soon the gearing up for the trial will begin properly and everything will be a last minute rush. I have to take his word for it as I'm still not allowed to talk about the trial with him. Instead we talk about TV programmes or about Kim's stalker problems; Daryl can never remember her name (still got that inability with my friends) but he does seem genuinely fascinated with Psycho Sam and the way he's terrorising Kim. He's outraged on her behalf.

His lawyers tell me nothing about the upcoming trial either – a few times I've called them and tried to find out how things are going, but they tell me they can't discuss the case with me because of client confidentiality.

'Even though I'm Daryl's wife?' I check every time.

'I'm afraid so,' I'm always told.

All I know is that they've no plans to call me as a witness. I don't understand why. The prosecution wanted me to appear on their behalf at one point for some odd reason, but Daryl's solicitors did sort that one. Apparently I can't be forced to give evidence against my husband – though what they think I would say anyway is beyond me.

So there you go, no one wants to tell me anything. I somehow thought I'd be a lot more involved than this. I feel like I'm jumping up and down, shouting for attention, but no one can see me or hear me.

MARCH

Sunday 3

The trial starts tomorrow. I saw Daryl on Friday and he seems remarkably calm. I so admire the way he's handled this whole thing. He's been incredibly strong, and never once broken down (or if he has, he's never let me see it. What amazing strength of will it must take to hide your feelings like that in order to protect the one you love; I just hope I've been able to fool him the same way, but I doubt it; he can read me like a book).

Everything's been such a last minute rush. Daryl's defence team had asked me to approach people to act as character witnesses for him, but I've not had much luck. In fact, I've had none. It's unbelievable the way people have abandoned us. So much for innocent until proven guilty, as far as our former friends are concerned I think they'd happily see Daryl at the guillotine, and they'd knit merrily away as it chopped his head off. Even his own mum has declined to come to the trial. I don't understand her; after all these years of knowing her though I've given up even trying to.

On Friday I finally had a proper meeting with Daryl's lawyers. After delivering the news that no one was willing to speak up for him, I was given a long speech about how it was now even more important that I attend court every day – like I needed telling.

'You have to be highly visible throughout the whole proceedings so that people can be in no doubt you are on your husband's side,' lectured his QC, Mr Jenkins (his first name is Richard, but he's one of those people who simply doesn't suit a first name; somehow without any conscious effort he commands a formal address only). 'The court is as much a show as anything else and it's important the jury see that people, especially women, are standing by the accused. It's a show of solidarity.'

I nodded eagerly. 'Just try and stop me being there for him!'

He gave a small, slightly forced smile, just enough to show his needle-sharp incisors that reminded me of Dracula. His receding hairline made quite an impressive widow's peak too, so perhaps he actually is a vampire in disguise.

I do wish my brain didn't default to random sarcasm mode whenever under pressure. Banishing thoughts of Vlad the Impaler, I tried to concentrate on what he was saying. This was it, at last my chance to have a proper conversation about Daryl's defence and find out what the plan was.

'Can I help in any other way?' I asked, summoning up the courage to speak and risk seeing those menacing fangs again. 'I'm more than happy to give evidence for Daryl. Surely I can do more than just sit there looking supportive?'

Mr Jenkins looked me up and down, and again gave that tight little smile. 'I know it must be frustrating being on the sidelines, as it were, but that is truly the best place for you. Nothing you can say on the stand can help your husband.'

'I can tell people he definitely has an alibi for one of the crimes; he was with me. That's the key piece of evidence you have to get him off, surely.' He didn't respond, just met my gaze. 'I just don't understand why I'm not being called when that's such a vital occurrence.'

Mr Jenkins tilted his head slightly, but still didn't look away. 'I'm afraid I cannot discuss our strategy for your husband's defence, Mrs –'

'Well, that's another thing I don't understand,' I cut across him.

'It's client confidentiality,' he said, with me chiming along beside him in mimicry. Bloody client bloody confidentiality, I'm sick of hearing about it.

'Even though he's my husband, and my future hangs in the balance as much as his?' I demanded.

'I'm sorry. It isn't personal, these are the rules that we are tied to in all cases. Unless your husband gives us direct instructions to share information with you, our hands are tied.'

'And he hasn't,' I said sadly.

Honestly, I know Daryl thinks he is protecting me from worry this way, but it's having the opposite effect. I feel sick with nerves about tomorrow.

Kim offered to come with me to the court for a bit of moral support, but Peter advised her against it. He says it might cause trouble for her, and I can understand that, as much as I am tempted to gloss over it so I can selfishly have someone with me. I don't want to be alone, I'm not sure I can face it. But I have to, I know that. And I also know that I can't ask anyone else to put themselves in the firing line for my sake; that's why I've told Mum and Dad to stay away too. They're having a hard enough time without having their photos plastered everywhere and everyone knowing they're supporting the supposed Port Pervert and his wife.

Soon though, in a matter of weeks, Daryl will be home, and we can get on with the rest of our lives. The house will be safe again with both of us earning (honestly, the trial couldn't have come soon enough. I've got myself into serious debt keeping everything going single-handed. But I've managed to keep going this long, I can cling on a bit longer. And hey, Daryl might even get some compensation for being wrongfully imprisoned or something).

INVISIBLE

We can start trying for a child again too, as soon as Daryl settles back into normal life.

When I try to imagine it I shake my head because it seems the stuff of dreams: Daryl home, and me pregnant. But it will be happening soon. I can't wait. I truly cannot wait.

I keep finding myself staring at the photos on the mantelpiece, especially the one of Daryl leaning forward at a precarious forty-five degree angle, arms open wide as if he's trying to fly, mouth even wider in a grin, and eyes popping with exhilaration. What a laugh we were having when I took that!

We'd been on a short, four-day break in the Yorkshire Dales one February, and had had a terrible row that morning – what about I can't even remember. To make matters worse, the weather had grown stormier and stormier, to match our moods. Then suddenly Daryl had broken off mid-sentence, looked out at the howling wind, and just grabbed my hand and pulled me towards the door of the cottage we were staying in.

'Come on, let's get out of here,' he'd urged, face suddenly alight with urgency.

'What…?' I'd resisted, trying to tug away but his huge hands had had too good a grip on my arms. I might as well have been fighting to keep the tide at bay as fight Daryl; resistance was futile, even if I was still annoyed with him.

'Come on, quick! Listen to that wind! Let's jump in the car and drive up to the top of the moors and see how crazy the weather gets,' he'd grinned, his expression transformed from thunder to sunshine.

'Oh, Daryl, I don't know…' I'd still hung back, not willing to forgive and forget as quickly as him. But his enthusiasm had been infectious; a couple of seconds of looking at his sparkling eyes and I'd given in.

We'd pulled on coats, hats, scarves, gloves, and driven the couple of minutes to the top of the moors. As soon as we'd jumped out of the car we'd been battered and buffeted by the high winds. What a buzz!

Shrieking in delight we'd raced around like a couple of kids, first seeing how fast we could go with the gale behind us, then how much slower it was trying to run into it; we could barely move!

'Hey, hey, I've got an idea,' Daryl had gasped suddenly, unzipping his jacket. I'd frowned, confused, wondering what the heck he was doing. He'd grasped the edges of his now open waist-length jacket and held them open like wings as he faced into the wind; it had blown up like a balloon.

'Woah!' he'd yelled, staggering backwards with the force of the gust.

'Lean into it. Quick, lean into the wind,' I'd urged, twigging on and grabbing my camera. He'd yelled in glee, then with feet firmly planted on the ground he'd pushed his top half forward until he looked like Michael Jackson in the Smooth Criminal video. Click! I'd captured the moment.

We'd carried on doing that for another twenty minutes or so, both screaming, yelling, and giggling like we were drunk on life. It was fantastic.

Maybe we should book a break as soon as Daryl gets home. It'd be nice to get away. Then again he might just want to enjoy relaxing at home for a while. I'll run the idea past him though, see how he feels.

Oh, I've remembered what we were arguing about. I'd suggested we go to the pub that night to have a meal, but he'd reckoned I only wanted to go so I could flirt with some bloke behind the bar. Of all the stupid things! Once he's home I'll never pick such a silly row with him again. Promise.

Monday 4

The reporters were screaming at me from the second I got out of the car outside court. A wall of sound where my name wasn't really my name, was no longer the two syllables my parents had bestowed on me, instead it ran into one long exhalation of a word, all melting together, unrecognisable, punching my ears until it felt like they might bleed. They'd turned my name into a weapon.

Faces were shoved into mine; I couldn't see a way through. I felt all panicky, started to have trouble breathing. I'm only short and all I could see were chests, shoulders and heads all in front of me, above me, I couldn't see past them as I fought to get to the courtroom door.

I was being pushed and pulled, and all the time, even worse than anything else, were the flashes of the cameras. It was like being in a nightmare where you can only see tiny slivers of the action, and it isn't enough for your brain to be able to process. It was only because of the burly policemen standing beside me, holding my arm so firmly it almost hurt as they forced their way through the baying pack of people, that I managed to get to safety.

It sounds impressive doesn't it, that I had these police officers looking after me. It wasn't said outright, but it was made abundantly clear that it wasn't out of sympathy for me or what I had been through; it was purely to stop any public order problems that my presence might cause. There you go I'm the problem, apparently, not the people shoving me around and sticking cameras and microphones into my face so hard that sometimes they hit me, bruise me, almost make me fall.

But what do I expect? I'm not a victim in this mess.

I was just thinking that rather bitterly when I saw her. Only for the briefest of moments. But it was enough to catch the brittle strength holding her together, to recognise the façade so like mine that she'd carefully constructed to fool people into thinking she was strong. She was one of the victims – I knew it instantly.

My God, my God, she looked like me. The petite frame, the shoulder-length hair, the eyes, the set of the mouth... She could have been a long lost sister.

With a flash of blonde hair, she was gone. It had only taken the time of a blink of the eye but it was enough to steal my strength.

My knees did go then. Strong hands under my armpits lifted me up and I was half-walked, half-carried through the entrance of the court with my legs dancing uselessly beneath me, and put on a seat in the atrium. My head sank between my knees and as I forced myself to breathe slowly in and out, in and out until the wooziness passed, the noise of the crowd was dampened down to a quiet roar as the doors closed.

Finally the sensation that I was going to faint passed, but I still didn't lift my head. Instead I stared intently at some stitching on my shoes, trying to fight the panic and the bad thoughts.

How come that woman looked like me? Coincidence? Or was Daryl really somehow connected to this? Had...

No, I snapped my head up, forced myself upright, trying to physically move away from my questions.

I know he is innocent. I know it because it's inconceivable that he's guilty. I know because he was with me the night one poor victim died. So that's the end of that.

For all I know, the person I saw was simply a passer-by, not even connected to the case at all. Or perhaps adrenaline from being pushed around by the crowd made me imagine things that weren't real, and if I were to see her again I'd realise she's nothing like me at all. Yes, now I think about it, her hair was more mousey than blonde and she was a chunkier build and her features were all wrong.

Anyway, I was taken from the main atrium to a separate waiting room. It was odd sitting there nervously, knowing that somewhere in the building, in another waiting room, were strangers ready to give evidence that could see my innocent husband locked away for 20 years or more.

When in court, I looked around but couldn't see any sign of that woman. There was Daryl's barrister, looking formal in his black gown and white wig as he busied himself shuffling papers and looking things up on his laptop, while around him buzzed other members of his team eager to do his bidding; and beside him was his opposite, the prosecution, doing exactly the same.

More craning round and I spotted a group of people sitting separate from the public gallery where I was. Who were they? I only worked it out when they brought out notepads and pens; of course, even here there was no escape from the press.

Still I couldn't stop looking for that woman. I only stopped rubbernecking the minute Daryl was brought up to the dock. He took his seat behind his brief, and his eyes searched round the room. I leaned forward, wanting to wave but feeling stupid. Luckily, the movement caught his attention, and he smiled gratefully at me, the custody officer beside him seemingly oblivious.

A court usher sonorously pronounced: 'All rise'. It felt so odd and scarily formal having to stand, reducing me to a little girl waiting to be scolded. The judge walked in from a side door, took his seat beneath a coat of arms and with a nod he let us all be seated.

The prosecution then outlined how they'd make their case. It sounded...horrific. Whoever did these things is evil. I looked over at Daryl and we stared fiercely at each other as those awful words washed over us. We were one person then, both fighting the urge to stand up and shout that it was all lies, both knowing the only realistic alternative was to shut the horror out. Somehow in that gaze we escaped to miles away, were free and holding each other. 'Soon,' I tried to tell him with my gaze, 'soon this will be over and we'll be together again. It will all be fine in the end.'

Even when the defence summarised their case, we barely looked away. Right then nothing mattered but us – because when this is over, that's what will be left. Stronger, better than ever, thanks to this mess.

The prosecution then called their first witness, introduced as Miss A. This was the supposed Port Pervert's first victim. I expected her to walk in, and was confused when it was explained she'd be giving evidence via video link.

As the TV screen opposite the jury was fired up and she appeared I felt totally disconnected from what was happening. This wasn't real; it was a programme I was watching, like a soap opera or crime drama or something. The woman on the screen had a strawberry blonde bob that accentuated her chubby cheeks, and the kind of button nose that automatically made her look even more baby-faced. If she'd have smiled she'd have looked so pretty.

But her eyes...her eyes were so sad that she looked like she'd never smile again.

'Can you describe the events of the night of 18 December please?' asked the QC. When he said the location of the attack I was stunned – it had happened in our town! I don't even remember hearing anything about it. Oh, actually, I do recollect seeing some of those 'Did you see this crime' appeal posters up around New Year but I didn't bother reading them because I never see anything interesting happen...

'It was a works night out, our Christmas do,' said Miss A, voice ringing out strong and steady, as though she'd practised this moment in her head. To be honest, it just added to my sense of detachment, as though she were an actress.

'Everyone was just starting to get really drunken, and so I thought if I left then no one would really notice. I'd had fun, it's just I wanted to get home because my boyfriend and me had just moved in together and I loved being in our new home. So I made my excuses at about 10.30pm and text my boyfriend that I was on my way. He offered to come pick me up, but I told him not to bother because it was only a five minute walk to our flat. So he said he'd start walking from ours and meet me halfway.

'I'd only been walking about a minute when I noticed a man coming towards me. I didn't take much notice of him because, well, the street was brightly-lit and this bloke was wearing what looked like a suit so I assumed he was either a security guard or businessman who'd been out straight after work himself and was now on his way home. Stupid, if he'd been wearing a hoodie and jeans I'd have been more suspicious, but someone in a suit...they just look more trustworthy somehow. We were just passing each other when...'

She took a deep breath to steady herself. All eyes were glued to the screen. I glanced at Daryl just as he looked at me, and I gave him the tiniest hint of a smile, so he knew I was with him, willing him to stay strong. I knew that what we were about to hear would be upsetting.

'We were just passing each other,' Miss A repeated, 'when suddenly he punched me. I didn't see it coming, just felt the pain and I think I fell to my knees. I was so dazed it was confusing what was happening, but I felt myself being half dragged, half carried. The light disappeared, it was dark – I didn't know then but I'd been taken down a small alleyway and put on the ground behind some big wheelie bins. I tried to kick out, was with it enough to know I needed to fight, but my feet didn't connect with anything and I couldn't see properly. But I did manage to scratch him; that earned me another punch and I was knocked out.

'I-I don't remember anything after that until I heard my boyfriend's voice calling me. Everything hurt, the lower part of my body... I shouted out and my boyfriend found me, called an ambulance and the police...'

The poor woman had been raped, punched, and strangled. She was lucky to be alive. The whole attack can only have taken minutes because her boyfriend had found her just 15 minutes after she'd set off from the bar she'd been in. It's incredible to think that she was so close to the man she loved, so close to colleagues and friends, and just seconds from a busy main road, while some beast had almost killed her. Even that felt like a plot from a programme though, rather than real life.

'It was the smell of him,' she continued as if someone had asked her, mouth curling in disgust. 'That's what stayed with me more than anything. A mix of fuel fumes and strong cheap aftershave... Then one day I walked past a bloke in Superdrug testing out some Links Africa; you know spraying it into the cap and sniffing it to see if he liked it. It took me right back…the terror…I was back there for an instant, thought he was coming for me… I knew then that that was what my attacker had been wearing. I curled up in the foetal position and yelped like a wounded puppy, too scared to even scream properly. That's what he's done to me. I'll never be the same person again, she was stolen by that man and I wish I knew how to get her back… But I never will.'

Tears dripped from her chin, but she didn't let it show in her expression or her voice at all. Her baby face belied her strength. The Crown Prosecutor thanked her for her testimony, adding to the jury: 'Please note that you will hear from all the victims that they noted the same smell from their attacker: that of fuel, or diesel, and Links Africa. The relevance of this will become clear later.'

What did he mean by that? From Daryl's expression he was as confused as me.

'Please, tell us a little more about the impact the rape has had on your life,' the barrister added gently.

'Well, I can't stand to be alone. I'm afraid of the dark and have to sleep with a light on. I've split up with my boyfriend because the thought of being…' For the first time her voice faded away, but then it punched back as strong as ever. '…Of being sexual with him was too much. One day we were messing about, actually having a laugh for once, and he tickled me; I freaked out because I felt like I was being held down, confined, even though I wasn't. That was the final straw. And I've moved back in with my parents; like I said, I can't stand to be alone and they help me deal with my nightmares.'

Then it was the defence's turn to question her. I almost cheered. Yes, she's been through a terrible ordeal, but nothing she's said has made me think that it was my husband who did it.

'Did you get a good look at your attacker?' asked Daryl's lawyer – good to see him finally earning his money.

'No, I said, I didn't take much notice of him. He was wearing a suit or some sort of smart outfit, and I wasn't really looking at him. I think he was bald or balding…'

'Balding? Well, that describes half the men in this room,' said our QC, moving his arm expansively to illustrate. I looked round and nodded, and was pleased to see the jurors doing the same. 'But surely when you were up close you managed to see his features properly.'

She looked flustered. 'No, no, he'd hit me, I'd almost passed out, and everything happened so quickly.'

'So you couldn't, for example, pick your attacker out if he were in this room?' asked the barrister. 'Can you see him in this room? Can you say with absolute certainty that he is here?'

'I…the police said…'

'Could you recognise your attacker?'

'No. No, I can't.' She looked defiantly from the screen.

'Thank you, that will be all.'

One nil to us, I believe.

It was only when the judge closed the session and I had to watch Daryl being led away by his guards that I realised that hours had passed. He twisted his head, craning over his shoulder to keep looking at me. Tears poured down my cheeks as he mouthed a simple message: 'I love you.' All I could do was nod back as despair washed over me and he disappeared from sight.

Stiff and exhausted, I stretched my legs one by one, knees cracking as they changed position for the first time all day. Rolled my neck, pushed my shoulders back. Stood with a groan. A moment's pause to pull my brittle façade around me, then I stepped out of court and back into the crowd again...

Back at home, wiped out, I put the telly on to try and find something to block out my thoughts, to stop me going over and over what had been said today. The news flashed on. There I was, in glorious Technicolor, being pushed through the crowd, head down, face white, mouth grim. It felt like a lifetime ago.

In the sea of people I spotted several brandishing placards that I hadn't noticed at the time: Die Port Pervert, Rot in Hell, Justice for Julie. It was the last one that made my throat catch. Selfish, selfish cow that I am, I tend to concentrate so heavily on the miscarriage of justice going on, and how mine and Daryl's lives have been ruined, and...well, I don't think about those poor women much, especially Julie, the one who was murdered. Maybe I don't want to, my mind dancing away from that because thinking about them makes them real and a part of my life and I don't want that. Even hearing that victim today give her evidence made me feel very little. This is nothing to do with Daryl or me.

Although it does make me furious for me, Daryl and the victims that the police have made such a monumental cock up of this investigation, because the monster who raped and killed is still out there somewhere.

Tuesday 5

The white noise of the crowd screaming hadn't lessened because a day had passed; if anything it seemed fuller of fury than yesterday. It's terrifying. I forced myself to take deep breaths to keep the panic at bay, and tried to let myself go with the surges of the mob as they pushed this way and that, rather than fight my way through, but it made no difference. I was grabbed, pinched, shoved as I stumbled across the pavement towards the court entrance, blinded by camera flashes, my police officer bodyguards almost as helpless as I.

I only realised once I was in the building that someone had spat on me, the gobbet of saliva showing clearly against my black jacket lapel. I had to hurry to the loo to get rid of it before entering the courtroom, and dabbing at it made me feel sick. How could someone do that? I've done nothing wrong. Standing by your husband does not warrant that kind of response. You don't see me spitting on police - and they've actually done something terrible to me!

Once in the courtroom I sat in the same spot as yesterday – and had another look round for that woman who I thought looked like me and now I can't decide. But there was no sign, so that's that. Then the judge came in again, and it felt like I was reliving yesterday. Most of the women will apparently be giving evidence via television link like yesterday, too. Funny to think of them in a room just down the corridor, all alone, answering questions via a link when they're almost within shouting distance.

Anyway, another day, another poor woman describing being raped. This one happened in a district of Manchester....why this bloke is called the Port Pervert is beyond me, so far he's been nowhere near a flipping port. Typical over-excited media making up silly names – the M25 rapist did attacks elsewhere too.

This incident happened on 14 January; I certainly don't remember anything particularly exciting about that date in all honesty, and although I feel for the women, I just want this bloody trial to be over and done so Daryl can come home and we can finally get our lives on track again.

But once again the television screen came on, and Miss B appeared. She seemed more nervous than the previous witness, and as she talked she kept looking down into her lap as though it held some kind of escape.

All the time below Miss B's on-screen face the stenographer sat at her desk, fingers moved constantly, taking everything down. At first as Miss B talked I didn't look at her, instead I found myself fascinated by those flying fingers that were recording the horror for posterity. Try as I might, I couldn't block out the testimony though.

Again, her attacker was wearing a suit. He'd come over to her and asked for directions as she'd walked home, past a nearby park, at 8pm-ish having just finished her shift in the supermarket she worked in.

'It was freezing cold and I just wanted to get home, that's all that was on my mind really,' she said, her long blonde hair a curtain she hid behind as she gazed down. 'I turned to point in the direction he needed to go, and suddenly his…his arm was around my neck…squeezing. He'd had his hands in his pockets before, but now I realised he was wearing those thin latex gloves, like doctors wear - I can't be examined by doctors any more because their gloves are exactly like the ones he wore.

'H-he was very calm as he wh-whispered in my ear to do exactly as he said and walk with him. He was sort of behind me, had me in a choke hold, I could feel my windpipe being crushed, could only take tiny little breaths. I was so scared, so scared.'

As she grimaced I noticed her skin twisting oddly and realised she had a nasty scar across her right cheek that make up failed to hide.

'We-we went into the park, and he pushed me to the ground behind some bushes. I begged him to take my mobile, my purse, anything he wanted. He just sh-shook his head and told me to look at him. I didn't want to, thought if I got a good look at his face he might kill me. But he said it again so

I looked up, straight into his cold blue eyes, as he told me: "If I wanted your stuff I'd have taken them by now. This is about me taking something else from whores like you." Then he…then he…'

Her shoulder shook with the tears that choked off her speech. The judge cleared his throat. 'Would you like to take a break?' he asked.

She shook her head, wiping at her nose with the backs of her hands until she remembered the tissues she already clutched. Still talking to her lap, she managed to continue, voice quavering with the effort.

'He told me to…' Her hand made a gesture, trying to get us all to guess what her attacker's orders had been because she couldn't face saying the words. But the prosecution lawyer gently encouraged her to speak. '…He told me to give him oral sex, said if I did he might let me off.' The last word was a choked squeak of despair as she disintegrated into sobs.

A break was ordered and it was twenty minutes before we reconvened. I did feel for the poor woman, she was clearly traumatised. Despite more tears she managed to hold it together enough to finish her testimony – because, of course, her attacker hadn't kept his word and 'let her off' once she'd done as he'd ordered. Instead he'd pinned her down and raped her, telling her he had a knife in his pocket and would kill her if she screamed.

'He said it in such a reasonable voice, calm, like, cold,' she sobbed. 'I didn't have any doubt that he meant what he said. So I l-let him rape me. I just wanted to live. I kept thinking about my kids, wondering if I'd ever see them again, while he was… But when he was done and took his condom off, instead of feeling better he seemed angry. He c-called me a whore and a…a cunt, and suddenly he started kicking me as I lay on the ground.

'I tried to curl up in a ball to protect myself, put my arms round my head, and begged him to stop but he kept kicking me and kicking me. I felt something in my face crack, and my lungs hurt, I couldn't breathe properly – I found out after that he'd fractured my skull and jaw, broken my cheekbone, and several of my ribs were snapped, my spleen had ruptured, and my bladder was damaged; I have to use a colostomy bag now.

'He got on top of me again, I think he wanted to rape me again, but h-he couldn't seem to. I could see it in his eyes then, that he was going to kill me. He was pulling something out of his briefcase or laptop carrier or whatever it was… I didn't want to die there, like that; I didn't want my kids to grow up without a mum. I-I kicked, screaming and screaming and just ran. I didn't know what direction I ran, where I was going, how I did it, but I ran and ran and all the time expected to feel his hands on me again. Only I didn't.' She shook her head amazed.

'I found myself on the street again, and literally ran into a couple. I only realised the state I must look when I saw their horrified faces. They called the emergency services, held me until help arrived. I was convinced my attacker was going to appear again, and even in hospital I was terrified. Doctors couldn't believe I was still standing, let alone able to run from that man, not with the injuries I'd sustained. No one knows how I got away. I don't. Someone up there was looking out for me that night.'

I admit it; I wiped a tear from my own eye then. What she'd been through…I hadn't been able to stop myself from imagining it as she'd spoken, wondering if I'd have had the strength to fight back and run for it.

But then the prosecution asked her a question, and her answer made me hate her. 'Do you see your attacker here today?'

'Yes. He's in the dock,' she said.

Wednesday 6

I'm still reeling from that woman's lie yesterday. I know, I know, it's not really a lie as such; she's said it because she's confused, and after what she's been through who can blame her. She's just imagining that Daryl is her attacker because he happens to be right there in front of her, and because people are telling her that he is. Can't she see that by saying that though she's actually allowing the real criminal to get away? Poor Daryl had looked absolutely poleaxed when Miss B said she recognised him as her rapist; it was the last thing he'd expected to happen.

Obviously Daryl's lawyer made mincemeat of her this morning during cross-examination, pointing out that when you're in a high-adrenaline situation such as she was that it's hard to recall exact details. I thought it was particularly clever when he asked her what colour her rescuer's coat was and she said blue but actually it was green. He even implied that she'd made up the bit where she'd seen her rapist properly, because why would he let her see his face yet wear gloves and a condom to protect against leaving fingerprints and DNA evidence?

So ultimately I don't think the jury were swayed by her pointing out Daryl – she's clearly unreliable, and now I've calmed down I do feel sorry for her.

Once she left the stand, victim number three was called: the imaginatively-named Mrs C. Finally an attack that happened in a port; although is Tilbury Docks technically a port? I don't know…and I can't believe that even during all this drama random thoughts like that still pop into my head. I'm tired though. I don't want to listen to any more horrifying testimony; I've heard more disturbing things in the last few days than most people hear in a lifetime.

This isn't me, I don't know how I got here; one day I woke up in someone else's life, and I'm sick of the drama, sick of being pushed around and spat on and jeered at and glared at and screeched at and people setting fire to me or sending me threats and poo – I'm really sick of the poo - and I feel like I've held it together, just about, by the skin of my teeth for so long, but I'm not sure I can go on another second longer. I want my life back!

Sadly, falling apart isn't a viable option though. I've just got to keep going for a little bit longer. Just a little bit longer. Then everything will be okay again. But today, in court, I just wanted to sit with my eyes screwed shut and my fingers in my ears, singing 'la la la, not listening!' Actually, I didn't even want to go to court, but knew that would look terrible, so I dragged myself there and tried to look like I was listening while actually desperately trying to block everything out. I couldn't even bring myself to look at Daryl in case my despair leeched through to him. I have to stay strong for him.

Can you think of anything more depressing than hearing a woman talk about her 30-minute rape ordeal at the docks at 12.30am on 3 February though? This bloke didn't even just rape, he bound her with duct tape first so that she was helpless to stop him as he…well, he…you know what, I don't need to write that down, it's seared in my memory already.

He was clever enough to make sure he wore the latex gloves and condom again though, bastard. Dressed in his smart suit, he must have looked trustworthy, but he sounds like an utter monster, and seems to have totally got off on the power trip, telling her: 'Listen, whore, I'm not going to lie, this is going to be very bad. But if you behave, you'll be fine. If you're a stupid cunt and don't behave…well, you know what the consequences will be, don't you?'

I don't want to know any of this stuff. I want to wipe my brain clean.

I'm going to bed. I'll think about that night, 3 February, when Daryl called me in the small hours and was in such a lovely, jolly mood, and really wanted to talk to me, bless him. I'm going to pretend that I'm back there, at that moment, and we're both happy and carefree. And I'm going to eat half a ton of chocolate, have a large whiskey, then, please God, go to sleep.

Thursday 7

The thought of going back to that courtroom again makes me feel physically ill. Since finally getting home tonight, I've spent most of my time kneeling on the floor, virtually hugging the toilet bowl. That's where I'm writing, right now, in a bid to sort out my utterly messed up head.

The day started (and ended) with the usual vitriol pointed at me; screaming, pushing, photograph-taking fun. Then the television was once more put on and Mrs D, yet another blonde (this time the kind of dirty blonde that occurs when natural blondes get a bit older and the brightness of their hair fades away) gave her evidence about her 2 March attack in Tilbury.

As she described her rape in eye-watering detail that made me wince, I glanced over to Daryl. Having been so utterly rubbish yesterday, I wanted to let him know I was there for him one hundred per cent, and I was worried that he'd be as upset as me at hearing what this woman had been through, at what he was accused of doing.

What I saw made my stomach curdle.

He was smirking. Leaning forward intently and drinking in the lurid descriptions. Something lit up his face: enjoyment.

Daryl must have spotted me frozen to the spot and gawping at him in horror, and realised what was going on because he suddenly rearranged his features into a look of sympathy. Sighed and shook his head sadly and even pretended to wipe a tear away.

Maybe he did wipe away a tear. Maybe I imagined this scene? I've a horrible feeling I didn't…

Right at that moment though, I was convinced by what I'd seen – and it sickened me, my stomach doing a rollercoaster drop. I remember that day, March 2 last year. Daryl and I had a row and he told me to eff off and slammed the phone down on me. I was repeat dialling him for hours but it just rang out. What exactly had he been doing for all that time?

See, I hate myself for even asking questions like that, even in the privacy of my own head, but the expression in my husband's face had made me doubt him for one horrible second. Until I talked myself down, reminding myself of the irrefutable evidence of his innocence: his cast iron aeroplane alibi on the night of the murder.

All these thoughts flashed through me in the blink of an eye. Still I couldn't take my eyes off Daryl. Then I wondered: had the jury noticed his slip up? I stared keenly at the twelve members of the public whose job it would be to decide Daryl's fate, but if they'd spotted anything they gave nothing away. All were rapt by the evidence still being given.

'When it was over, as he stood over me and pulled his suit trousers up, all I could do was lie there. The pain…' The woman's voice caught, but she gathered herself enough to continue. 'Then he looked straight at me. His eyes, they were a very cold blue; I'll always remember that, I'm haunted by them. That, and the smell of him. Sorry.'

Tears flowed down her face, and she wiped constantly at her nose, desperately trying to hold it together.

'He...he said: "I hope you realise that was your fault, you fucking whore. Never forget you're just a cunt, nothing more," and: "I'm going now, but if you scream, if you move, if you try and get help, I'll know. I'll come back, and then things will go very badly for you. Very badly indeed." Then he picked up his briefcase and walked away. I, umm, I didn't dare move.

'I don't know how long I lay curled up on the pavement, but I-I-I think it was about, umm, ten...ten minutes or so. I only found the strength to move because I suddenly thought he might come back anyway. Don't know how I did it, it's a bit of a blur, but I forced myself to sit up. There was...God, there was so much blood...between my legs...and... My hands were still taped together in front of me... I remember putting my hands to my face and it feeling really sticky. When I looked at my hands in the half- light they looked black with the sticky stuff – I didn't...didn't realise it was blood too, couldn't figure it out.'

She looked lost, head down and shaking slightly as she looked this way and that as if back on that dark, deserted side street. Mouth working constantly, while voice dropped to almost a whisper. 'I couldn't stand up. My legs were sprawled out in front of me and I couldn't seem to make them work. Doctors said afterwards it was severe shock and trauma that had temporarily shut my body down...'

'Objection! Hearsay. The witness is not a medical expert.' The words came out like bullets, making us all blink in shock. I'd almost forgotten we were in court as I'd imagined what that poor woman had been through.

'Sustained,' agreed the judge. 'We will be hearing from medical experts on this matter later though,' he added in the direction of the jury.

Given the go-ahead to continue, Mrs D took a deep, shuddering breath. But I wasn't watching her; I was looking at Daryl again, trying to gauge his expression. All I saw was genuine sadness and concern.

'I, umm, I scooted forward on my bum and got my handbag and shoved my stuff back into it; it had burst open when it fell to the ground, and everything had gone everywhere, see. I don't, I don't even know why I did that. Automatic,' said Mrs D, words tumbling out now as she neared the end of her story.

'Then I pulled myself forward, dragging my legs behind me, reached the main street and carried on going, sort of pulling myself along on my elbows, which was easier than using my hands because they were still taped up.' She held her wrists together and bent her arms to demonstrate. 'Knew I had to keep going otherwise I'd die, or he might come back or something and then I saw headlights and…and I remember screaming and screaming and screaming because I thought it was him…but it was a cabbie…I was saved…'

I'd say she was lucky to escape with her life, but how can you call someone lucky when they've suffered such horror?

Her words had been so powerful and affecting that when Daryl's defence team started questioning Mrs D, I felt sorry for her. Instead of wanting to cheer at every hole they pulled in her evidence, I felt uncomfortable. Instead of feeling annoyed when the Crown's barrister asked the defence to tone down their questioning because they were being too aggressive, and were backed by the judge, I felt secretly pleased.

This is so messed up and wrong. I've tried so hard not to let these women in; I don't want to feel for them because although I know they are victims of terrible crimes it is easier to think of them almost as the enemy. They must be beaten, because the alternative is that Daryl goes to prison for something he simply didn't do. Yet here I am, softening towards them and almost rooting for them, and imagining things about my husband.

If only a judgement on one's side favour didn't brand the other side liars and worse.

So I have to harden myself to these women and their ordeals. I can't show I care about them or the jury could misread it and think I doubt Daryl. I feel like a total bitch though. That's why I'm hanging over the loo, feeling nauseous: because I know Daryl is innocent, and yet this stupid court case has made me question everything even when I know it is an absolute; has made me imagine nonsense; and because I'm having to hate rape victims.

The only consolation about today is that Daryl has no idea about the turmoil my head was in. Instead I must have appeared as solid as ever when we once again mouthed 'I love you' to one another as he was led away at the end of the court session. I spotted one of the jurors looking at us and smiling gently; that's got to be a good sign.

Friday 8

There was a different atmosphere in court today. I could feel it as soon as everyone settled into their places (even I've managed to find a 'usual spot', always sitting in the same place. It's nice, means Daryl always knows where to look for me). There was a sense of anticipation almost because today a victim was going to give her testimony in the stand rather than via a video link. We all knew this was going to seem way more real – sometimes it's easy to kid yourself the person isn't real, that it's simply a programme you're watching when it's on the screen.

When the woman was called, I saw the back of her head as she walked over to the witness box directly opposite the jury and entered it…then gasped as she turned. It was her – the woman who looked like me.

There could be no doubting it now that she was right in front of me. We were a similar age and height, our hair the same colour and texture, though hers was slightly shorter and choppier; our lips, eyes, basic shape of face… We weren't identical, but it was enough similarity to freak me out, and I heard whispers of surprise rustle through the courtroom as others noticed.

There was one very important difference between us though: she was heavily pregnant. I hadn't noticed it when I'd spotted her briefly the other day because the crowd had hidden all but her face, but actually her stomach was huge and she looked ready to drop any day.

She was allowed to sit as she gave evidence and settled with one hand over her bump, the other just below, rubbing it comfortingly.

This is the woman who was raped in Turkey…

'Please, Miss E, can you describe what happened to you whilst on your holiday in Olu Deniz on Tuesday 2 June last year?' asked the prosecution.

Olu Deniz. I'd know the attack had happened in Turkey, but hadn't realised it was in the same resort we'd stayed in. Then I remembered – the day after Daryl and I had had a huge row I'd heard about a young woman being raped. Of course, I should have put two and two together.

I swallowed hard, trying not to show on my face the worry I was feeling inside. The fact that we were in the same place at the same time as this crime was going to look bad, very bad. Miss E spoke in a calm manner; the only sign of anxiety was her hand constantly circling her tummy. 'I'd gone on holiday with a group of girl friends. I'd just split up with my boyfriend and so getting away had seemed like the perfect way to relax and get over things. We spent several days at the resort and felt very comfortable there; it's a wonderful place, with the turquoise sea, gorgeous beach, friendly locals, and it's very family orientated too so none of us girls felt intimidated about going out at night. It wasn't a meat market, like some resorts can feel, you know?

'That Tuesday the four of us had spent the day relaxing by the hotel swimming pool, and that night there was some entertainment being laid on at the hotel too. Two of my friends wanted to stay and see it, but my other friend and I fancied a change of scenery so decided to go to the town.

'We walked down to some of the seafront bars; it's only a small place so we got there in about five minutes, and had a couple of cocktails and watched the sun set over the sea, then caught a dolmus – they're like minibuses, that's how everyone gets around – into Hisaronu, which is still fairly quiet but a bit livelier than Olu Deniz itself. We fancied having a bit of a dance, you see.

'Some lads came over to chat to us. My mate really liked one of them but I wasn't interested, so I decided to go back to the hotel alone. Like I said, we felt really safe in the resorts, there were dolmus coming every couple of minutes, so it didn't feel like a reckless thing to do. I was more worried about leaving my friend alone in the club than me walking to the bus stop, and arranged to call her in half an hour to check she was okay – we even sorted out a word she could use to secretly tell me if there was a problem: we chose "inconceivable".'

Miss E paused then, appearing to gather her strength. The courtroom seemed to hold its breath as we waited for the horror we knew was coming, and I realised I was on the edge of my seat, leaning forward. The hard wooden ledge was cutting off the circulation to my legs but I barely noticed. Everything she'd said had been so familiar to me that I'd imagined every step she'd taken…

'I started walking to the dolmus stop. The main street is very well lit and there were lots of people around so I felt confident, although I did of course look around every now and again to check there was no one dodgy around. The stop I was walking to was on the edge of town, but still well-lit thanks to all the street lamps and lights from restaurants, bars and shops.

'I was almost there when I suddenly became aware of someone behind me and as I turned my head to look over my shoulder, wham, I was punched in the face. I was totally dazed by it, but I tried to scream, but there was a hand over my mouth and an arm around me dragging me backwards. I remember being struck by how efficiently he moved, it was like he was well practised…'

'Objection. Conjecture.'

'Sustained.'

She took a steadying breath, apparently determined not to get flustered or phased – or at least not to let it show. 'Where I was taken to was dark, and the noise from the street seemed very muffled somehow even though it had taken scant seconds to get there. I couldn't see the man's face because he was behind me, but sensed he was quite tall and muscular, powerfully built, and at one point I sort of saw the top of his head and realised he was bald.

'I could smell him too, he was wearing the same body spray as my ex-boyfriend had worn, Lynx Africa, but there was something else as well, something that seemed almost ingrained into his skin. I knew that every detail I could remember about him would be important afterwards, so I concentrated on staying calm and trying to identify it. It was diesel.
'I tried to scream again, but he got me in some sort of choke hold and told me to keep quiet...'
The Crown Prosecutor stood up for a moment. 'Can you remember the exact words he used?'
'Yes, definitely. He whispered right into my ear: 'Dirty whores like you need to be taught a lesson. I'll teach you a lesson you'll never forget.' As he spoke, he squeezed my throat until I could barely breathe and my vision went black around the edges and finally I lost consciousness.'
There was no sense of uncertainty or fear about her at all as she spoke. Despite her inner steel though, she looked vulnerable as her hand circled round and round her pregnant belly.
'When I came round I was in an ambulance. Apparently some locals had heard my mobile phone ringing and followed the sound until they'd found me down a back alley; my friend was calling me, worried when I hadn't contacted her as arranged. When they saw me, unconscious, they'd called for help and I was rushed to hospital where it was immediately obvious that I'd been raped.'
'Can you tell us about how the brutal assault has changed your life?' asked the QC.
For a moment the hand stopped its circular motion, then started again as she spoke. 'My life was turned upside down that night,' she said, still sounding strong and sure. 'At first I

blamed myself, thinking that I must have done something terrible to somehow deserve what had happened to me, wondering why I was picked out over countless others. Then I discovered I was pregnant by my rapist.'

I gasped, stunned. Judging from the hiss that rippled through the courtroom I wasn't the only one.

'At first I wanted to get rid of it…the thought of having something growing inside me that was anything to do with that man…I even though about killing myself…' Her voice juddered with emotion for the first time. She took a moment then continued.

'I was raised a Catholic though, and in my time of need I turned again to my religion. With my parents' support, I made the decision to keep my baby – I have an innocent life growing inside me, one that shouldn't be punished for the horrific way it was conceived. It wasn't easy at first, but as time has passed I've realised I can love this child. She is mine and will never have anything to do with the monster who fathered her.

'That's one of the reasons why I wanted to give evidence in person today, rather than have my testimony read out or give it in a different room. I want to face my attacker and for him to see the consequences of his actions. And to know he will never have anything to do with his child.'

'Objection!' said Daryl's lawyer, jumping to his feet. 'The witness is talking as though her attacker is in the room when in fact she didn't see him and is unable to identify him.'

'Sustained,' agreed the judge.

The defence soon got their chance to tear into Miss E though. I settled back into my seat, back aching from having spent so long leaning forward, and tried to push down any pity I felt for her. It was time for us to score some points…

'When you went on holiday you were getting over the break-up of your relationship, is that correct?'

'Yes.'

'With some other single female friends?'

'That's correct.'

'All single ladies together, having a few drinks and a holiday romance or two; that would be fair to say, would it not?'

'I can't speak for the others, but I wasn't interested in having a holiday romance.'

'Oh come, all girls together, what happens in Turkey stays in Turkey…'

It reminded me of when I'd been questioned by the police about my sex life, and DS Chapman had tried desperately to get me to admit to stuff that plain wasn't true. All misleading insinuations and pathetic attempts to create a fake connection to get me to 'open up'. Seeing it happen to someone else now was infuriating; despite myself, I could feel anger rising.

Miss E wasn't falling into their trap any more than I had though. She answered every question calmly. I don't know how she did it; she stayed far stronger than I had.

They threw it all at her, implying she was a party girl who'd got drunk and had sex with anything that moved on holiday, despite there being no evidence of this. They sank to an all-time low though when they basically said that she was lying about her pregnancy. She was using the rape to cover the fact that she was actually pregnant by her ex-boyfriend, the barrister said, and that she'd been forced into such desperate measures because, as a Catholic, her parents would otherwise have disowned her for becoming pregnant out of wedlock.

How dare they? Hasn't she been through enough already? Could I have kept a child conceived in such a way? I don't think so. No one knows for certain how they'll react until they're actually in a situation of course, but I think I'd look at that baby and feel disgust. I'd see its father, relive that horrific attack every time, and be scared it had inherited his bad blood. I felt she should be applauded not vilified.

This was my team attacking her now though. They were the people I was supposed to be rooting for. Instead I felt horrified. I wanted to jump up and defend her.

At least Daryl looked as thunderstruck as me by what was happening. After her cross-examination had ended and she was told she could leave the witness box, he couldn't take his eyes off her as she walked from court. Still, at the end of the session he gathered himself as his guards led him away, looked over at me and, as had become our little ritual, we mouthed 'I love you' to one another.

Outside, the news that the Port Pervert had fathered a child seemed to have driven the crowd into an even greater frenzy. The noise was almost ear-bleeding as faces and cameras were shoved at me. Beside me one of the protection officers stumbled, almost going down as he tried and failed to absorb the ebb and flow of the storming mob.

I was terrified, my heart hammering painfully against my chest, lungs burning as if I was running a marathon rather than walking slower than a death march as I pushed on, on, on, through the wall of baying people, head constantly flashing this way and that as I tried to see a way forward.

Even in the car I wasn't safe, people hammering on the windows and roof, hailing down blow after blow and stopping me from driving away. I had to fight the urge to floor it, scattering bodies this way and that in my desperation to break free, and instead edge forward slowly, oh so slowly like a ship making its way through an ice flow.

Thank God the house was free of media – they all seem to have taken themselves off to the court. I parked the car and ran like a woman possessed to the front door, keys jangling in my shaking hands. Once through it, I slammed the door shut, ran to the sofa and curled up on it like a child, hugging one of Daryl's jumpers and trying to breathe in his smell, although it's disappeared now. Trying to imagine the time (hopefully just days away now) when he will be home and I can hug at last the real thing.

Sunday 10
It's 11.30pm and I've just got home. I spent the weekend at my parents' house, and it was so lovely to get away for it all for a while. I spent a lot of time in the garden just looking at the flowers coming up and taking in that wonderful 'spring has sprung' feel. It all feels a world away from court. I don't get to go out into my garden any more, too paranoid of the neighbours glaring at me or shouting something (or even throwing something over the fence, then denying it) so it's fantastic to get some fresh air.
While I was there Kim called to see how I was doing. We had a good old catch up chinwag, and she asked all about how I was coping with the trial. I've noticed she does that a lot, carefully choosing her words – I don't think she actually believes Daryl is innocent but has vowed to stand by me and support me all the way, and I really appreciate that. I get the feeling that if she asked how the court case itself were going she wouldn't be able to keep her own judgement from her voice, so instead she always asks how I am feeling about things. She doesn't give a toss about Daryl, but she doesn't have to; I know she cares about me as my absolute greatest friend (probably my only friend these days, but that's a technicality) and for that I love her to bits.

INVISIBLE

So, I told her how I was feeling. How am I feeling? A weird mixture of trepidation, fear, and excitement. I just want this to be over, and finally I can see the finish line. Afterwards we talked about her, but when I asked her what she'd been up to lately I noticed she kept letting the conversation slide away. I tried three or four times but to no avail.

'Oh, we don't need to talk about me', 'It's the same old same old', and the classic 'yeah, I'm good…so anyway, how are you feeling about tomorrow' subject change were just some of the things she said to avoid talking about herself. Is she keeping something secret from me?

Anyway, it's time for me to go to bed. I need to be fresh for tomorrow. I'm really looking forward to it: tomorrow's the day when the bombshell is dropped and proof that Daryl is innocent will be produced. I'm hoping that once that happens the case will be dismissed. Just think, it's possible that this time tomorrow I could be going to bed with my husband!

Monday 11

It's only the second week of court and already I feel like a battle-scarred veteran. Standing in the hallway trying to find the courage to leave the house; facing the screaming crowd; fear, security pat down, find my seat; the nervous, jangling calm of the court just before the session begins. I somehow face it all and survive. As stressful and horrifying as everything is, I could face it this morning with renewed strength and even excitement, thinking to myself: 'This could be the last time you'll ever have to do it.'

As I looked around the room as people in the public gallery took their seats, I was shocked to spot her: Miss E, my pregnant doppelganger. I found myself staring at her, fascinated and horrified all at once. She's actually going to sit through the rest of the court case? She's the only one of the women who's chosen to do that though.

She must have nerves of steel, because if I believed my rapist was in the room I wouldn't have the courage to be in there with him unless I absolutely had to – unless of course she doesn't truly believe it is Daryl, now that she's seen him in the flesh. Not that she got a look at her attacker, but if…well, at that moment my mind ran away with a crazy scenario where she suddenly decided to speak out in Daryl's defence, saying it wasn't him who hurt her.

But that wasn't the only reason I kept looking at my 'twin'. I couldn't help thinking that hopefully this time next year I'd be like her; heavily pregnant with my own child.

As my gaze slid away, I felt her turning to study me. It must be as odd for her really. I wonder what ran through her mind as she realised I was Daryl's wife.

First to take the stand today was the murder victim's husband, Tony Scrivens. Julie Scrivens was found beaten, raped and dumped on some wasteland, cast aside like she didn't matter.

The court was shown some photos of her and Tony; they looked really happy together, always seemed to be laughing. He painted a picture of an ordinary woman with ordinary dreams; someone like me. Both of us had been going along with our lives, minding our own business when suddenly through no fault of our own something horrific had happened. Poor Julie though had paid with her life.

Tony talked of how Julie had been going on a rare night out to the pub with some friends, leaving straight after work. Cried as he confessed that she hadn't wanted to go, but he'd pushed her because he wanted her to have some fun as her mum had died a few months before and it had affected her profoundly. Poor fella obviously blamed himself. The last time he'd seen her had been that morning, at 7.30am, when he'd kissed her goodbye and left for work as a bus driver.

'If I'd known it was the last time I'd ever see her...' he sobbed. '...I didn't know...' I wasn't the only person in the room who was wiping tears from their face as he spoke. 'T-to think, she didn't even make it to her n-n-night out,' he spluttered, before disintegrating into tears.

Confusion washed over me. She didn't make it to her drinks out? But she was attacked at night wasn't she? That's what I'd understood from the scant newspaper reports I'd read.

DI Baxter was next in the witness box, and swore his oath. He started by explaining that police had first become aware of a serial rapist on a violent spree because of the Tilbury attacks, which had included two rapes and one attempted rape that had escalated to murder.

'It was only when Interpol contacted local police in connection with the crime in Turkey that the accused came to our attention. He'd become a person of interest to them because his description matched the attacker in Olu Deniz, they knew he'd been in the area at the time, and they'd tracked him down to his hometown. They were contacting the local police, asking them to go to his home and bring him in for questioning,' DI Baxter said.

I tilted my head, interested. So that's how Daryl wound up in this mess; this was all new to me.

'The officer who happened to take the call had by coincidence just moved constabularies. Previously he'd had some involvement with the Tilbury inquiry, and noticed some similarities between the attacks.'

I frowned, confused. What similarities? The Turkey victim hadn't been bound with duct tape, a condom clearly hadn't been used, no weird latex gloves had been worn... To me this sounded like desperation; they were trying to see clues where there were none.

DI Baxter continued. 'The officer made some calls to the Essex police force, and also did some digging on his new patch. Thanks to his hard work, he realised that there had also been a similar incident in his new locality. A taskforce was created and Operation Global was launched, which I headed, as we realised that the accused was the common link to all the crimes – he lived a few miles from the first attack, and in his capacity as a lorry driver he was familiar with Tilbury Docks and surrounding area having often picked up or dropped off goods there. In addition, he had holidayed in the resort of Olu Deniz at the same time as a rape was conducted.'

'Coincidence,' I breathed, not loud enough for anyone to hear. I just wanted to reach the bit where they realised Daryl was 30,000 feet in the air at the time of the murder, surrounded by around 200 witnesses. But the inspector just droned on.

'We started to look at his work as a lorry driver, identifying that the accused often did a run from a paper mill in Manchester to Tilbury Docks and back again. This was how we made the connection between him and the second rape in what we now know to be a six-crime series.'

Then he described how Daryl had been arrested – and the most bizarre pantomime I've ever seen was then played out. He and the Crown Prosecutor produced identical-looking pieces of paper that turned out to be transcripts of my husband's police interview, and then they read them aloud, like a script. DI Baxter played himself, while the QC played Daryl. It was so odd I almost felt like laughing, but instead chose simply sitting there with my mouth open in amazement.

'The accused said "no comment" to all questions apart from the following,' explained the inspector, setting the scene. He cleared his throat, an actor preparing for his role... 'Were you in Tilbury on the night of Sunday 3 February?'

'I'm not saying anything that might incriminate me,' the barrister for the prosecution playing Daryl read from the script.

'What if we said to you we could prove you were?'

'You've got nothing. I know you've got nothing.'

'We have all kinds of evidence, Daryl. Come on, you'll feel better if you tell us everything.'

'No comment. Except...surely someone doing something like this would wear gloves or protection or something. Can't be evidence if they did that. Bit thick, aren't you, plod?'

Both 'actors' then put their scripts down, having finished reading the interview aloud. Apparently that had been the only time Daryl had deviated from his 'no comment'. I can only assume he got annoyed by the constant questioning and decided to goad the officers a little – well, I can understand that having been through it myself, but I'm worried other people might think it looks like a boastful criminal. Honestly, sometimes my husband can be such an idiot, if only he'd kept his mouth shut! And to think that initially I'd thought not giving a proper interview had been a bad idea...

Twisting my wedding ring round and round nervously, I silently urged Baxter to get to the good bit of his testimony. Sounds terrible, but I needed him to start talking about details of the murder, which we hadn't heard about yet. Instead he started droning on about Tilbury Docks; how it's located on the River Thames at Tilbury, Essex, and is the principal port for London; it's the main port for importing paper, and is the third largest container port in the UK. Who bloody cares?!

Tension bubbled into hysteria and I fought back the urge to giggle as I flashed back to the road trip Daryl and I had taken together to Tilbury that time; how Daryl had bored me with dull facts like this. I felt like shouting to the stand: 'You two should get together after the case, you have a lot in common.'

Finally, though... 'The body of a female woman was found in bushes near the grounds of Tilbury Fort at 7am on Saturday 30 May by a dog walker,' said the inspector. 'Through dental records she was identified as Julie Scrivens, 26, who worked behind the counter of a local convenience store. Tests indicated that her time of death was approximately 7pm the previous night, Friday 29 May, and this was further established by witness statements and CCTV footage.'

Goosebumps shivered over my skin. I suddenly felt feverish, hot and cold all at once. She was killed at 7pm, on her way to meet friends at the pub after work. Daryl didn't arrive at our home until 10pm. Oh my God, he doesn't have an alibi.

All hopes of having my husband home that night melted away faster than an ice lolly in the desert.

Even as I shivered in despair, Baxter continued his monologue. He described how the victim ('Julie, call her Julie,' I wanted to shout) had been found stuffed under a bush.

'Her lower half was naked, her upper half clothed, but the top pushed up to expose her chest and cover her face. She had been restrained with duct tape at the wrists, and been severely beaten until her facial features were no longer recognisable.'

Revulsion made me look away from him, as though that would somehow block out his words. As I did so, my eyes landed briefly on Daryl. For a second he smirked. Just the tiniest flicker, but enough for me to know I hadn't imagined it this time, as I'd thought I had the other day.

My insides turned to ice as efficiently as if someone had poured liquid nitrogen into them. I once saw someone instantly freeze a beautiful red rose that way and been amazed by how perfectly the bloom had been preserved – until they'd shattered it to show how brittle it had become. And I swear, if someone had touched me or looked at me right at that moment, I'd have exploded into a million pieces too until nothing was left of me but splinters.

Loathing twisted through me so suddenly I couldn't breathe. I felt like I didn't know this man at all; that I'd spent nine years of my life with a person I don't recognise. It makes me think of the medieval myths of changelings; trolls secretly left in place of a stolen human baby. Someone stole my husband and replaced him with a monster. And I didn't even notice.

Daryl didn't seem to realise I'd seen his mask momentarily slip. Our lawyer started cross-examining the DI, at him like a Rottweiler, making him look a fool who hadn't done his job properly. I tried to feel pleased but I couldn't shake my sense of disorientation. What had I just seen? Had my husband really been amused by that horrifying description of Julie's discarded body? I shook my head to physically shake off the fear that gripped me, and tried to listen to what was being said.

'Did you even consider anyone else as the culprit in this case?' the barrister asked

'No, he was the person we concentrated on.'

'A little blinkered, is it not? Considering the attacks were scattered not just across the country but the globe? Is it inconceivable that someone else might have committed the crime?'

The inspector pursed his lips, annoyed, pulling his dog-bum face. 'As I said, we concentrated on the accused.'

'Some might say you took the easy option. To cut off all other possible avenues seems very hasty. Within 75 miles of Tilbury Docks alone there are 18 million people, and you're saying not one of them was worth considering? You decided to concentrate on just one man? Some may say that's a brave decision…others foolish…'

Foolish, foolish, foolish, that's what it was, I told myself over and over. Repeated it silently like a mantra. But why had the police been so sure it was Daryl? Why hadn't they even looked at anyone else? He had no alibi for any of the attacks…

By the end of that day's court session my head hurt from the confusion swirling round it. As Daryl was led away, I stared straight ahead, stunned and scared. From the corner of my eye though I saw him try to make me look up so he could tell me he loved me. I couldn't bring myself to look at him.

The second he disappeared from sight though I knew I'd made a terrible mistake – I needed to see him, right away, if I was to get rid of the fear and doubt at the back of my mind that was like an itch I couldn't scratch.

I raced over to Daryl's defence team. 'I want to see him,' I demanded. 'I have to see him.' I needed to confront him.

'No one can visit him until he's given evidence,' I was told with an exasperated huff.

'I need to see him!' I said, voice rising hysterically.

'Well…legally it is possible…but it's a logistical nightmare.'

I repeated the sentence a fourth time, urgency robbing me of originality. Finally they gave in. 'You'll have to make your way to the prison, and it'll only be for a few minutes.'

That was fine. A couple of quick calls and everything was arranged. I drove like a loony to the prison, racing against the beat of my heart. Then I sat down with Daryl. Just seeing him instantly made me feel calmer, my resolution to confront him sliding away. I had to ask though.

'I need you to tell me the truth, babe,' I urged. 'It's just me and you, no one else is listening. Did…did you hurt those women.'

The shock and betrayal in his eyes brought tears to my own. 'I can't believe you'd think that,' he said finally, his anger clear but controlled. 'Don't you know me at all? Do we have a marriage left, if that's what you believe I'm capable of? When do I get the time to go off all over the place hurting women when I'm working all hours to keep a roof over our heads?'

'I'm sorry, so sorry.' I reached out to grab his hand but he shook me off. Sat back, massive hands folded in his lap, trying to get as far away from me as he physically could. Panicked and guilty, I apologised again and again for the hurt I was inflicting on him. 'I know it sounds stupid but I had to ask, I thought I saw…'

What did I think I'd seen? It seemed ridiculous now I was away from the courtroom and actually sitting centimetres away from my husband, the man I loved and who I knew inside out.

Finally he relented, grudgingly said he forgave. 'The atmosphere in court is enough to get to anyone. I just thought we were stronger than that,' he said, clearly disappointed in me.

As he was taken from the room though, he turned from the guard and those beautiful ice blue eyes of his bored into mine. 'I love you,' he said. My face lit up with relief.
'I love you, too,' I said desperately.
Back at the car though, I hunched over the steering wheel and cried, great racking sobs that threatened to shake my whole body apart. What am I going to believe? I was always taught to believe the good in people not the bad. The doubts are driving me insane, my head hurts with trying to figure out if he's guilty. If he is, surely he'd have admitted it though – at least to me, after all this time, so I could know exactly what I'm dealing with?
This is just a bad dream; he's never laid a finger on me.

Friday 15
A bad night's sleep had followed Monday's bad day at court…and was followed up with…well, I don't know how to describe it. There's been an avalanche of evidence and I'm buried under the snow, hoping someone will dig me out, but I can't see anything but white, can't hear anything, oxygen is running out. It's cold, so cold, and I'm so tired that I want the end to come. I'd welcome it.
The blizzard that started the avalanche was the forensics expert. When the police had taken Daryl's lorry away and searched it, they'd found what was described as a 'rape kit' in the locked overhead glove compartment – that compartment I hadn't been allowed to touch when I'd been in the cab with him during our weekend trip away.
Still, I told myself that describing silver Gaffa tape, latex gloves, and condoms as a rape kit was a bit over the top…even if it was odd that they were stuffed inside a briefcase. After all, I know he used those gloves to stop

getting oil and dirt under his nails when tinkering with the engine, and duct tape comes in handy for quick repairs sometimes too. The condoms were harder to explain though. The forensics officer started talking. It was really complicated but I tried my best to follow. Basically, they proved that the duct tape was exactly the same brand as the rapist had used to truss up his victims – something to do with the same chemical signature or something. I wasn't convinced; lots of people must use that same brand, and I didn't see them in the dock.

Then she started showing pictures of the end of the tape, where Daryl had torn it off. Alongside that she brought up a snap of the bloodstained end of duct tape the killer had used on Julie. Both torn ends slotted together like jigsaw puzzle pieces, a perfect match for one another. Julie's attacker had used Daryl's silver duct tape.

That was when the avalanche smashed over me. I should have had hysterics. I should have had a total meltdown. There it was, simple but inarguable proof than my Daryl was a killer; I knew I to be true now, there was no room for my denials and excuses any more.

A leaden sense of inevitability had settled over me then.

At the end of the session I couldn't help myself. I'd looked at Daryl as he was led away. He smiled as his eyes met mine, eyes like a shark's now that the truth was out.

'I love you,' he mouthed, still grinning.

My stomach lurched, saliva filling my mouth. I jumped from my seat, shoving people out of the way, running, running, running to the ladies, cubicle door punched open and rebounding onto me as I heaved. I barely got there in time, some yellow vomit splashing onto my navy suede shoes.

Over the following days more and more pieces of evidence slammed into me, each one making me cower down further and further. I couldn't stop going to court though, had to know the truth. It was almost a relief to finally have everything slot into place. To have the doubt finally brought to an end.

They'd found the all-in-one, boiler-suit-type overalls he liked to drive in. The outside was clean as a whistle, but on the inside…

'We found blood stains and hair from a number of the victims. We have concluded that the accused would approach his victims in smart trousers, shirt and tie in order to look business-like and gain their trust,' the forensics officer said.

He'd then attack them, using his strength to overpower them and sometimes pretending to have a knife. In order to not leave any evidence behind of fingerprints or DNA, he wore the gloves; and used condoms during most of the attacks, taking the used ones with him in the briefcase so they wouldn't be left behind. Then, the clever devil would quickly slip his overalls on, over the top of his by-now bloodstained smart clothes, and walk away without a care in the world, knowing no one would link this overalled lorry driver with the businessman rapist.

The smug bastard wasn't as cunning as he'd thought though. Despite his best attempts, he'd left DNA evidence at a number of the attacks. The first woman, in our home town, had been littered with evidence – he hadn't even bothered wearing a condom then; and of course the skin under the victim's fingernails from her scratching him had also been a match to Daryl.

They reckon that during the second rape, in Manchester, he'd been so cocksure he wouldn't be caught due to lack of forensic evidence thanks to his DIY rape kit, that he'd made the woman look at him. He'd been on a total power trip, his over-inflated ego and arrogance dooming him in that case.

He'd have probably got away with the third rape though, the first attack near Tilbury Docks...but he forgot to switch his mobile phone off. Using its signal, the police had been able to prove he was in the vicinity of every single crime he was accused of, including that one.

All those times we'd argued and I'd repeat dialed him and couldn't get through, was that what he'd been busy doing? Was this all my fault somehow?

A single pubic hair was left on victim number four. Unlucky for him, lucky for everyone else. And one end of the ripped piece of duct tape used during this attack matched an end of the adhesive that had been used to restrain poor murder victim Julie - the other end of that piece had, of course, been a direct match to the tape in Daryl's briefcase in the truck.

As for the Turkey rape, the silly sod had clearly been so angry with me that he'd just lost control and grabbed the first woman he'd seen. If he thought at all, he'd probably simply assumed that it wouldn't be traced back to him because we were abroad. It's not much logic, but I'm fairly certain I can say logic probably hasn't played much of a part in Daryl's life for a while. Mine either.

Then there was the murder. As well as the ends of duct tape matching up, Daryl had apparently punched Julie in the face again and again with such ferocity that he had smashed some of her teeth, ripping open his latex glove and cutting his own skin in the process. He'd left behind a smear of his own blood, mingling with hers on her lips.

It was what the Americans would call a slam dunk case. He did it. No doubts. No uncertainty. Nothing open to interpretation. I'm married to a killer, a rapist, the lowest of the low. To add insult to injury, it turns out he hadn't been working extra hours, or selling days off, or even driving on the continent. What he was doing with all that spare time away from me is anyone's guess. Conducting more attacks?

They even got a linguistics expert to prove that the speech patterns the Port Pervert had used meant that it was definitely all the same man. Daryl. Well, he was always keen on using words like 'whore' and 'cunt' to describe my friends...

I sound all right, don't I? Like I'm handling the news of his guilt. I'm not. Some of the stuff I've sat through is so graphic, so disgusting, that I've vomited until even my stomach lining has come up. That someone I know is capable of doing those things...no, I can't comprehend. That someone I love could...

It's unthinkable. What I mean by that is I literally can't think of it. I try. My brain refuses to work, goes utterly blank.

I'm as numb as an ice statue. I'm in the heart of the avalanche, frozen solid, can't feel, can't think, can't, can't, can't...

Saturday 16

Thank God for my parents. They arrived on Tuesday and once again are stuck with the job of holding me together as I fall apart. Before the trial I'd confidently insisted that I'd be fine alone and that I preferred to face the trial without their fussing (in the nicest possible way).

Of course that was when I thought my husband was innocent and would be home with me soon...I'd even started planning what meals I'd cook for him, was going to do all his favourites, even breakfasts were going to be lavish affairs. Now all my plans lie shattered.

At least I'm not back to the gibbering wreck I was when I was arrested, my mind going crazy. Instead, I seem to have shut down. I know I'm not being normal…the problem is I don't seem to be able to access normal any more. I think I've forgotten how to feel.

I looked like absolute shite though. Pasty, dark circles under my eyes, unable to sleep or eat. Ah well, I'll rest when I'm dead. I feel dead, so maybe it's not far off.

My parents are worried about me. They talk to me in low, gentle voices, as if I'm ill or so fragile that a loud noise might make me crumble. They don't understand why I have to keep going to court. Dad is particularly adamant that I stay away, but I can't. I know I should, but I can't.

This thing has swallowed my life whole and destroyed everything I thought I knew, and what, I'm supposed to just shrug and walk away? No, I have to see it through to the very bitter end.

Bitter. Yep, that's me.

I think it's my mum too. 'You need to get away from that place, those memories,' she said about the house. Almost spat the words. My mum has never hated anyone, but the venom she finds for Daryl now is …scary and inspirational all at once.

To distract herself, she rolled up her sleeves (literally. She actually rolled her long sleeved top up to over her elbows and gave me a meaningful look, so I felt obliged to do the same) ready to tidy the frankly disgusting house. I've sort of let things slide this past week.

Dad sighed, and opened the back door to let in some fresh air, then stepped outside to give us room. Judging from the look on Mum's face, he was worried he might accidentally get swept up with the rubbish and put in a bin bag.

Outside, from the neighbour's side, came the persistent, mesmerising drone of a lawn mower. Clearly they'd got used to the constant press presence and started getting their life back to a semblance of normality. As normal as life can be when you live next door to the building that once held the Port Pervert.

First Mum tidied up the kitchen, then the living room. I'd kind of forgotten how different the place looks when it's clean and everything isn't filed on the floor. Well, at least I knew where everything was.

I admit though that while I was enjoying wallowing in self-pity and chaos (as only seemed fitting, as it was a direct reflection of the state of my mind) it did make me feel better to see everything back to the way they used to be. It was weirdly comforting, as though the whole thing had been a bad dream.

It had a very different effect on Mum…

The more things went back to normal, the more annoyed she seemed to get. Her shoulders were going, twisting round and round like a Les Dawson character, like they were trying to burrow through her top and make their escape – the only part of her body to betray that she did want to escape.

After a valiant effort to control it, her face went too. She looked like she'd sucked a lemon.

By the time we reached the bedroom she'd really worked up a good head of steam, muttering under her breath, slagging Daryl off, asking how he could do such a thing to me.

To me? I should have been grateful, I suppose. Finally someone was on my side. Instead though, I just felt…not a lot really. Vaguely annoyed that she was talking about poor me when what Daryl had done to me was nothing in comparison to what he'd wreaked on those women.

Guilt gnawed at me, chewed on my very bones. How can I possibly feel sorry for myself? He's blasted apart my life, everything I thought I knew has turned out to be a lie, everything solid was quicksand, every memory of the past nine years is tainted. I can't trust anyone or anything – certainly can't trust myself because clearly I have terrible judgement and zero ability to spot liars and worse. Yet...

Yet for all that, when I think of those women and their families, I can't allow myself or anyone else to feel sorry for me. If this is a 'my life is crap' competition, they win hands down. And that's how it should be.

The only problem is that right now, if I can't feel angry or bereft or any of the myriad other feelings that threaten to tear at me, then I don't know how to feel. So I feel nothing. Good old icy numbness.

'Look at that bed!' Mum exploded suddenly, pointing, shocking me from my thoughts.

It seemed a bit of an over-dramatic reaction to the simple double divan that Daryl had bought dirt cheap from a mate two years ago, when we moved into the house, and we'd never got round to replacing.

Clearly she could tell that I was confused, so she expanded on the subject.

'It's cheap!' she raged. Actually quivered a bit. 'It's cheap and disgusting, just like that man.'

Yes, Daryl may now have two identities, his own and his Port Pervert pseudonym, but to Mum he has a third. He is like Lord Voldemort in Harry Potter, He Who Must Not Be Named. She never, ever says his name.

I put my head on one side and considered the bed. 'I never liked it much,' I admitted. 'I always wanted one with storage underneath, you know? It was just meant to tide us over until we saved up for a decent one.'

She was clearly dissatisfied with my response, so to show solidarity with her, I added: 'The mattress is a bit uncomfortable...'

My mum is a really mild mannered person. She never gets riled up about anything, or if she does, she doesn't let it show. She hasn't got a temper. So it was a bit weird seeing her so infuriated and offended by the bed. It wasn't a great bed, but it hadn't actually done anything wrong. Mum glared at it like she wanted it dead.

So she killed it.

Suddenly Mum leapt forward and kicked the bed. She even gave a little grunt of satisfaction.

I raised an eyebrow, a bit stunned. I'd never seen Mum get physical before. Ah well, I thought, if it makes her feel better, and there's no harm done...

'How could he treat you like this?' she shouted. 'That bed is like, like, like a symbol of how he treated you. It's cheap, nasty, common, worthless.'

Each word was punctuated with a kick, and with an audible tear the material gave way. The first times she'd landed her blows on the spindly wooden frame that held the bed together, but the last time she'd got lucky and hit material that was stretched between the cheap frame to give it the appearance of substance.

I've seen documentaries where packs of lions or wolves or whatever, once they see weakness, go into a kind of frenzy and attack. That was Mum once the bed tore. She didn't say a word after that, just went mad, lashing out.

'Umm, that's my bed,' I pointed out, but rather weakly, because I was kind of fascinated. She wasn't my every-day, mild mannered mum who wouldn't say boo to a goose, who refused to tackle the horrid neighbour she had who made her life a misery by making little comments about how leaves from her hanging baskets blew into his garden, and such other petty misdeeds. She'd been transformed into some kind of glorious avenging angel, her face twisted from the norm into something between sheer rage and heavenly joy.

It was strangely inspiring to see, and I was envious to be honest. She'd focused all her anger on that bed and was kicking the shit out of it – and loving every second. It was a release for her, acting like the valve in her pressure cooker. I wanted that. I wanted to feel the anger coursing through me and make someone or something pay.

But I just didn't have it in me. Instead I stood there, watching my mum quickly create matchsticks out of my bed. When there was nothing left of the flimsy little pine joists, she started on the material, ripping it to shreds.

Finally, panting heavily, she looked with some satisfaction at the little pile of debris.

Frankly, I'm not sure which surprised me more, her actions or the fact that my bed could be so easily destroyed, and had been made of nothing much more than matchsticks and cloth.

Mum smiled at me, looking relieved. Clearly she was all spent of anger.

'Sorry, love,' she panted, breathless after her exertions. 'It was just really pissing me off.'

Wow, another first; Mum swearing.

'That's okay,' I shrugged. 'Although I do have to spend money on a new bed now, as well as everything else.'

Mum had been standing with her hands on her hips, leaning forward slightly because she was so done in, but at those words she straightened and waved her hands airily. 'Oh, that doesn't matter; you can pick them up cheap enough.'

I wonder if she appreciated the irony of that comment.

Sunday 17

I spent all of today in bed (technically, I was just on the mattress, of course, as I no longer have a bed, just a pile of wood that's been shoved into bin bags and popped into the wheelie bins outside). Mum and Dad brought me a steady supply of tea and sympathy. The only time I moved was to go to the loo. The fact they didn't lecture me to pull myself together and at least get dressed shows their level of concern. They did, however, try to get me to 'see sense' about continuing to go to court.

'People will think you're supporting that man,' Mum insisted. In that one sentence alone her voice had gone from reasonable to worked up. Dad put a soothing hand on her forearm to stop her from saying more.

'Honestly, what he's put those poor families through. And then to make them give evidence, re-live it all...' she hiccupped, tears making her squeak. Then she ran from the room, crying, Dad going after her.

As I retreated once again under my duvet and pulled it over my head to soften the sound of Mum blowing her nose, I thought about what she'd said. Why is Daryl pleading innocent? I don't get it. What can someone who is so obviously guilty get out of pretending he didn't do it?

The image of his taunting shark's grin as he'd mouthed 'I love you' to me that one last time flashed into my mind. Of course. It was that obvious, that simple, and that demonic. He wants to taunt those women too, and their families. He wants to relive his glory one last time, exerting power over them once more.

Twisted, evil sicko. That's my husband.

Suddenly I flung the duvet back and with a grunt I hauled myself upright and marched to the phone. Dialed before I could change my mind. It rang a couple of times before a voice that always makes me tense up answered: Daryl's mum.

'How did you know and I didn't?' No preliminaries, no introduction, we didn't need it.

'Oh, hello,' sighed Cynthia. 'How did I know what, dear?'

Patronising cow. 'How did you know your son was guilty? I didn't. I had no idea; I thought he was innocent.' Each word shot out like machine gun fire. 'I take it you did know, from the way you've wanted nothing to do with him since his arrest.'

'He's…' she stretched the word out, thinking. 'He's never been right. That's the only way I can describe him. When I heard what he was accused of, it confirmed everything I've ever suspected of him, I'm afraid.'

'And you never thought to warn me?'

'Dear, that's not my place. For all I knew, you were fully aware of his defects and chose to be with him anyway. Perhaps you even liked them.'

'Fine, great, thank you for the information,' I stormed, about to launch into a full-on tirade.

'Please,' she interjected calmly, 'don't call me again. This is painful enough. Good luck for the future, dear. Goodbye.'

Now I'm back under the duvet trying to figure out how this living nightmare started. Was Daryl damaged irreversibly by his cold mum? Or did his mum withdraw from Daryl when she realised she'd given birth to someone so utterly broken?

And would it make any difference if I had the answers?

There's another obvious question too. How could I have been so stupid? I skim read the newspapers and assumed that Daryl had a cast iron alibi for the murder. I was in so much denial that if someone had held a piece of chalk up to my face I'd have sworn it was black not white if it had meant Daryl was innocent. Now I can finally see what was so searingly, staggeringly obvious to the rest of the whole world: Daryl's guilty as sin. I was so blind.

Monday 18
This morning I lay on my mattress for some time staring at the ceiling, occasionally stealing glances at the alarm clock. Was it time to get up yet? No, I could wait another couple of minutes. Then another couple of minutes. And another. Until finally I was reduced to telling myself that I'd get up once I'd counted to twenty…five.
Eventually I pulled myself together and got up, dressed, and ready for court. Dad stopped speaking to Mum as I appeared in my suit and he set down his cuppa; clearly they'd been discussing me. He cleared his throat.
'You're definitely going then.' Less a question, more a statement. His short, clever fingers ran round the handle of his mug, a nervous habit he can't seem to break.
I nodded, smoothed the front of my skirt down, then picked up the car keys. I know they think I'm nuts and I couldn't face a conversation about this.
'At least let me do you a decent breakfast to face the day,' sighed Mum, jumping up. Ah, they must have decided arguing with me was useless.
'Umm, no thanks. Just a coffee for me,' I said, wrinkling my nose. The thought of food making my stomach churn uncomfortably.
'You've got to eat, sweetheart…'
'Just a coffee. Thanks, Mum.'
I only took one big, scalding gulp, just to show willing, then hurried from the house, with Mum calling after me, 'We'll order you a new bed while you're out, love.'

'Don't bother, honestly,' I shouted back, slamming the door shut. Somewhere to sleep is the last thing on my mind currently.

The defence started their case today. Really, what hope do they have? At long last I can now understand their reticence about revealing their strategy to me.

Daryl was going to give evidence but I've heard a rumour that his defence team encouraged him not to. Good, because it's more than I could stand, the thought of seeing him try to lie his way out of this, spinning that mesmeric web of his until I can fight no longer and somehow, against logic and all evidence to the contrary, I fall under his spell of confusion, misdirection and half-truths. I'd go mad. Even madder than I already am.

With no character witnesses willing to speak out on his behalf either, his barrister was forced to immediately bring out the big guns. In this case, a consultant psychologist who was willing to somehow justify what he'd done and tell everyone that basically he needed a hug rather than punishment. What rubbish.

Because it turns out that this is all my fault.

'It is your opinion that the accused isn't responsible for his actions. That, unable to handle his emotions when he was put under pressure, he acted out in the only way he knew how; is that correct?' put his QC.

The psychologist tucked her raven black hair behind one ear and nodded seriously. 'Yes, and for that reason, simply put, he lacks the capacity to comprehend what he has done.'

A dismayed murmur ran through the court, everyone realising that this was a play to get Daryl's sentence reduced. Remembering the sick smile that I'd seen momentarily on his face while hearing evidence, it took everything I'd got not to shout: 'oh yeah, if he doesn't comprehend what he's done, how come he looks like he's enjoying himself so much?'

'Order please,' insisted the judge. 'Quiet in court.'

The barrister took a moment then turned to the expert witness again. 'Can you talk us through how this occurred?'

'Certainly. Through a series of conversation with the accused I built up a picture of his character and emotional make up, and also used his wife's diary as a reference.'

My heart jumped painfully. She was actually going to use my own words to back up her tin pot theories. I'd handed it over days after the arrest in order to prove Daryl's innocence, now it felt like it was being used against me.

'You will hear that he was under a lot of pressure to start a family, something he didn't want to do, and this I believe was the stressor that triggered the spree,' she added.

Hold on, hold on, what's so terrible about wanting to start a family?

'Throughout the diary there are references to the accused's sexual dysfunction. This will have affected the relationship deeply. He will have felt that he was letting his wife down, the rage building inside him. That, in addition to his feeling of losing control of his life because he doesn't want children, will have created a powder keg of emotion that would not take much to explode.'

'Can you talk us through the first attack, please?'

'Yes, this was clearly unplanned as it happened just miles away from his home. This indicates that he was out of control, acting on instinct. Then there is the level of violence involved and the lack of sophistication in his approach; this lack of finesse shows it was, as I have said, an explosion of emotion.'

Lack of sophistication? What did she mean; that he wasn't using chat up lines or something?

'The third rape is a particularly good illustration of the relationship between the accused and his spouse,' she continued. 'By now he has perfected his technique, which has become much more controlled – he is regaining the control in the rapes that he feels he has lost in life. The language he uses during the attacks really shows this; he is cool, calm, emotionally detached almost as he tells the women what he thinks of them.'

Then she read from a paper Daryl's words. *'Listen, whore, I'm not going to lie, this is going to be very bad. But if you behave, you'll be fine. If you're a stupid cunt and don't behave...well, you know what the consequences will be, don't you?'*

'After the third attack, he feels so happy and confident in his actions that he even calls his wife and talks cheerfully to her,' the psychologist explained. 'She describes him as being *"happy to hear my voice"* despite it being 2am. She says *"he was in a really good mood; the kind of mood that's contagious. Honestly, when he's like that being near him is like being near the sun".'*

I winced at the words. Remembering that feeling, that person, that innocence I had... Ignorance really was bliss, but now I couldn't believe I'd ever been that stupid.

Still the psychologist's voice boomed out confidently across the court room. She must have taken lessons in public speaking or something, because she certainly knew how to project. There was no chance of blocking her out...

'Rape number four occurred after the accused and his wife argued. Again, this will have triggered his feelings of uncontrollable rage. The following day, thanks to his purge, he called his wife and apologised to her for his behaviour during arguments. This proves that only his release allows him to handle his relationship.'

Right, so the only thing keeping us together was rape and violence? I'm so awful to be married to that I forced him to do those things? And I love her euphemistic terms for rape, by the way: 'purge' and 'release'. Purlease.

Daryl's lawyer prompted his witness again. 'I'd now like to ask you about poor Julie Scrivens's murder. According to the diary, there doesn't seem to have been any arguments in the accused's household. This doesn't seem to fit into the pattern you've described. Can you explain that?'

'The murder is different,' she nodded pensively, shiny black bob swinging. 'I believe that by this stage the accused was completely out of control. He was able to stop the attacks for some time, given that previously they'd been occurring around once a month or more, then suddenly there is an extended break of two months because his marriage is less tumultuous.'

There it was again, the dig at me. I didn't know whether to feel ashamed at myself, or furious at her. It's not really my fault is it? Is it? Oh God, what if it is...

'But it's no longer enough for him. He needs the thrill of the crimes,' the psychologist nodded more enthusiastically, really warming to her theme now. 'In addition, he is still suffering from erectile dysfunction issues within his marriage, and the only time he seems properly able to have full penetrative sex is during his crimes, when re-enacting them with his wife, or in the immediate aftermath of them when he is probably re-playing them in his mind.

'My theory about the trigger for the escalation from rape to murder is that he was unable to achieve erection during the attack – a post mortem showed Mrs Scrivens was not raped.

'One of his previous victims does mention that at one point during her attack he was unable to perform a second time, and this prompted a rage in him which resulted in her receiving a severe beating from him.

'I believe this happened again, but that this time he was so furious that he completely lost control – in the very situation he has created in order to feel control. His unleashed fury was catastrophic for his victim.'

You can say that again.

But she had more on the subject. 'The diary mentions that when he arrived home that night, immediately after the attack, he vomited. The following day he agrees to the very thing he dreads the most – having a child. These actions are clear illustrations of his panic...and most importantly his remorse.'

'No!' came a shout to the right of me. Julie's husband was shaking his head, furious. 'He's a monster, he doesn't care what he's done.'

The judge was not impressed. 'You will be quiet, please, or you will be taken from the court,' he warned.

You can't blame him for his outburst though – I certainly couldn't. Some of the graphic things we've heard have been horrific, but somehow listening to this woman trying to excuse Daryl's actions is even worse.

This witness had a last twist of her knife left for me though, involving the final rape, in Turkey.

'No one can have failed to notice how much his final victim resembles his spouse,' she said. I quickly stared down at my lap as all eyes turned to me momentarily, then swivelled back to the stand.

'He and his wife try to have sex but he can't manage it. Let me read this section: *"This problem of his has been happening on and off for the last two years or so, and seems to have got worse since I really started hammering home how much I want a baby. I'd hoped that him agreeing to that would mean the problem wouldn't happen again, but seems I was wrong. Am I not enough woman for him? Don't I turn him on?"*

'They have a huge row, and he immediately has to go in search of a victim because now it is the only way he knows for handling his rage. He finds a woman who looks just like the source of his anger…' Again, people looked at me, accusing rather than appraising this time. '…and while he is attacking her, ultimately he is attacking his wife, but lacks the emotional maturity to confront her.'

The defence lawyer turned to the jury. 'Lacks the emotional maturity,' he repeated slowly.

'Yes, and because of that, I believe he lacked the ability to control himself or his rages, and now lacks the capacity to comprehend what he has done, hence his 'not guilty' plea.'

No one said anything, but there was an uneasy stirring through the public gallery. But now it was the turn of the prosecution to cross examine the psychologist. I hoped to God he could undo any damage the defence had done to the chances of Daryl going down for life.

He made sure everyone had settled and was giving him their complete attention before he spoke in a gentle yet commanding voice. 'Surely you would agree that someone's partner desiring to have a child is not normally an excuse to go around raping and killing people?' he asked.

The witness frowned. 'Certainly not. But the right pressure exerted on the right personality type can definitely create extreme reactions.'

'The right personality type… And what personality type does the accused have.'

'He clearly has psychopathic traits, and some sociopathic too, I'd say by the way he is able to charm people. Characters such as this tend to have an inability to comprehend emotions, or the emotional impact of their own actions on others. The accused would have simply 'acted out' as a way of regaining control over a life he felt he was losing control over.'

'He's a psychopath?' checked the prosecuting barrister, throwing a knowing look at the jury. Well, being described like that isn't going to help Daryl – good.

'In her diary, his wife describes a trip to Tilbury and Manchester that the accused takes her on,' he added. Then he read out an excerpt where I described the great sex Daryl and I had in the cab, when he wore his latex gloves. I didn't think I could have been made to feel any worse, but having that private, intimate moment shared with a room of strangers managed it.

The psychologist nodded her understanding. 'He definitely would have enjoyed what in his mind was a re-enactment. Revisiting two sites where he raped women, then donning the type of gloves he used during those attacks would have excited him emotionally and physically a great deal.'

'At one point in another part of the diary the wife also mentions him wrapping a present with duct tape and smiling...'

'Yes, it would amuse him a great deal to know he was showing off his skill with the bindings, and she was clueless.'

'A show off, someone who relishes re-enacting his despicable crimes...this doesn't sound to me like a man who doesn't comprehend what he's done. It sounds like someone who is all too aware of his actions, and has thoroughly enjoyed himself,' the barrister said, his formerly gentle voice suddenly biting.

The room was silent, the psychologist didn't say a word, looking flatly at her adversary. He let his words sink in then continued. 'You say that the first attack was an unplanned explosion of anger. What about the following attacks? Why didn't they happen near his home? They show definite evidence of planning, do they not?'

'There was an element of planning, definitely. Although the victims were chosen opportunistically...'

'Tell us about the planning,' the QC interrupted.

'He would have chosen places that were away from his home deliberately, because he wouldn't want to be linked with the crimes; it lessened his chances of being caught and he knew it. At the same time, he wanted locations that he knew well and therefore felt comfortable in. That's why he chose places at either end of his regular trucking runs,' the expert admitted reluctantly.

Right, so basically, he was in control enough to know he didn't want to shit on his own doorstep! Ha, argue with that, bitch!

'Then there was the rape kit he put together, the disguise to put women at ease, the cunning way he then covered his tracks by covering his outfit with his overalls,' prompted the lawyer. 'These are the actions of someone who recognises what they are going to do, plans it, enjoys it, and does not wish to be caught. Correct?'

'Yes, but it's more complicated...'

'Yes or no answer, please.'

She narrowed her eyes. 'Yes.'

'Incidentally,' the lawyer added, having a Columbo moment, 'why bind the victims when the assailant is so powerfully built? He clearly is strong enough to overpower someone if he chose to. Could it be that it's about the ritual of binding more than the physical restraint?'

'There is evidence to suggest that, yes. The act of binding someone then being able to step back and see how helpless the victim is would heighten his pleasure,' she admitted reluctantly.

Her reward was a brilliant, triumphant smile from the prosecution as he thanked her and told her she was free to leave the witness box.

It's an odd feeling, wanting to cheer someone who is putting the nail in your husband's coffin. As well-trained as Pavlov's dog, I couldn't help feeling guilty, and glanced automatically over at Daryl.

He didn't look shocked or worried. He looked amused. Catching my eye, he smiled cheekily, like that first smile he'd given me all those years before, the first time I'd clapped eyes on him. Then he mouthed something. I frowned, unable to work it out.

A quick check around to see if anyone else was looking, and he silently repeated the words, pointing at me. 'Your fault.' Then he settled back in his seat, satisfied, a little grin playing across his face and his eyes twinkling.

Well, it's nice to know someone is happy with the psychologist's conclusions.

Tuesday 19

I was tempted to stay at home today yet I find myself, against all logic, unable to stay away from court. Macabre curiosity, maybe? A sado-masochistic tendency to have pain inflicted upon myself? No, more like I don't know what I'd do otherwise, so, on automatic pilot, I get ready while Mum and Dad look on in despair; drag myself through the crowds (rather hoping they'll succeed in their bid to tear me to pieces) and then sit in my usual seat and watch the court circus.

Both sides made their closing arguments, each taking about an hour and a half to summarize the case from their point of view. It basically went something like this - the prosecution:

he's guilty and evil; the defence: he's guilty but can't be held responsible, so technically he's not guilty.

Daryl just looked bored. Sitting slightly slumped in his seat, staring into space, all pretence of acting like the concerned, innocent man seemed to have disappeared. The mask was well and truly off.

The jury then disappeared, filing out slowly and solemnly. All that was left to do for the rest of us was wait...

Not for long though. Within two hours we were called back in. Victims and their families held hands, the atmosphere tense but hopeful. For a moment I felt an affinity with them; we all wanted the same outcome. But then, watching them, I felt...it's so wrong to admit, but I felt a stab of envy.

They are all in it together, and I'm all alone. They're helping one another, leaning on their support network. No one wants to come near me, as if I might contaminate them. As if Daryl's badness has rubbed off on me, and may infect them too. I get it; in their eyes I'm on his side. But I've never felt so alone.

In fairness, my parents ask every single day whether I want them to come with me, but I always so no. I can't possibly expose them to this, and besides...I am alone in this. No one can understand what I'm going through...

Quiet settled instantly as the judge walked in. All eyes were on the jury as they gave their verdict.

Guilty of all charges. Of course.

Cries of relief rang out, people hugging and cheering, it was chaos. The judge shouted for order. Daryl barely reacted though, apart from a roll of his eyes.

The crowd outside were euphoric as I left court. They barely noticed me as I slipped away.

All that's left to sort now is how long he will serve. Apparently court will reconvene on Friday for that.

I'm almost there now, almost at the end. I've just got to keep going for a little longer, and then I can collapse in an untidy heap. It can't come too soon; I'm running on empty, nothing but fumes keeping me going.

Wednesday 20

Why don't I feel anything? Angry, betrayed, devastated, something for all Daryl's done to me. Relieved even, now that the truth has come out and he has been found guilty? Instead, I am a ghost haunting my own body.

Thursday 21

Maybe the problem is that I can't get my head round what's happened. I went to court, I saw it all with my own eyes, heard things that, well… But there is a part of me that still doesn't believe.

I mean, I believe. I just don't believe…

Because Daryl is guilty. He did it. I've stood by a killer, a rapist, a pervert. I've loved him, missed him, longed for him, when all the time... My life has been destroyed, because I fell for the wrong man. It is, for want of a better word, unbelievable.

Friday 22

For one final time I pulled on my court outfit of smart suit and appropriately-named court shoes. Mum and Dad asked if I wanted them to come with me, but I shook my head, unable to summon the energy to speak.

Instead they will stay at home and scrub off the graffiti daubed across the front door. Why bother? It'll only be back again tomorrow, just like it always is. An eternal reminder that I am scum and should die.

At court, lead weights seemed attached not just to my limbs as they dragged through the crowd, but even to my eyelids. I seemed to be fighting a losing battle to keep going.

Halfway through my now-traditional early morning fight through a screaming mob, I suddenly stopped, swaying slightly as I looked around. I was in a bubble, even the sound deadened as I stood taking it all in. So much anger mixed with so much glee, they seemed to be enjoying themselves.

Seconds ticked by and still I simply stood. Finally my protection officers prodded me gently forward and I managed to remember how my legs move.

The same sense of detachment clung to me as I took my seat one final time in the public gallery. Slowly I became aware of a hissed conversation seeping through the membrane that seemed to be surrounding me.

'…should be ashamed. Why does she keep coming here?' stage whispered a woman.

'You'd think now he'd be found guilty she'd stay away,' came the reply.

Still I stared straight ahead, didn't flinch as the words washed over me.

'Sat there like she's so high and mighty when… She must have known, how could she not have known?'

'He must have come home with blood on his clothes, so why didn't she question him?'

'Because she knew! He must have been acting funny as well, but she didn't bat an eyelid, I bet.'

'Thank God they didn't manage to have kids.'

'Can you imagine the kind of feral beast they'd produce? When I think of that poor woman who's pregnant by him… Oh, there she is now…'

INVISIBLE

The bubble held me together. It stopped me from showing that each word was like a kick smashing my ribs and stopping me from breathing. Finally I was feeling something, but it all raged on the inside, while the outside looked as still as a statue. With the bubble's help I focused everything I had on not sinking to the floor and howling.

I wanted to cry, scream, rage. I remembered Mum kicking the bed apart, and wished I had something I could tear to pieces too. But there was nothing.

I wanted to shout: 'Me too! He destroyed me too! Look at me, feel my pain, see the evil that he did, how I'm holding on by the skin of my teeth because of what he's done.'

And then what? Then they'd shout too? 'No, look at my pain! How can you say you've been hurt when all you did was realise you'd been lied to! He held me down, he tortured me, he forced himself on me and I thought I'd die. How dare you compare your pain with mine?'

Then all the victims would unite in one baying mob of hurt. All of us wanting to prove whose pain was worse. But there's no answer. There's no competition. Everyone's hurt is different in its terribleness.

No, that's not true; my hurt can never, ever compare with theirs. I feel ashamed for feeling sorry for myself for even a second, I have no right. When I think of what they've been through... I swayed in my seat for a moment, but steeled myself.

'All rise,' said the usher, his voice cutting through and helping me keep the tears at bay. There will be plenty of time for crying in the days to come. Years of empty self-pity stretch ahead of me. For now though, I have to remember how to stand, how to sit, how to breathe, how to listen as the judge talks to Daryl.

'You are clearly a dangerous and clever man who used everything at your disposal to plan violent attacks on women, then launched a savage and perverted campaign against total strangers. You showed them no mercy. It is as clear to me as it possibly could be that there is a serious risk of harm to members of the public from you.

'If I could I would sentence you so that you are never released. Instead I can only apply the maximum the law allows. You are hereby sentenced to six life sentences, to serve a minimum of 18 years.'

Cries of triumph exploded around me, along with anger too. 'Rot in hell, scum!' screamed one woman.

Daryl picked his nails, only looking up when the custody officer patted him on the shoulder to lead him away. He'd just reached the doorway when he stopped suddenly, as if something had occurred to him. Then he turned, looked over at the public gallery and all those women and their relatives, the oddest look on his face. Was he feeling remorse? His eyes slid over them, over to me.

'Love you,' he shouted, as guards furiously tugged at his shoulders to move him on.

Why had he done that? Was he trying to cause trouble for me one last time? Or did he mean it? It disgusted me.

My legs wobbled as I too stood up. Sweat made my palms slick and I rubbed them on my skirt, then wiped my face with my sleeves as the room seemed to tip in front of me. Everyone seemed to be looking at me, no, sneering at me, and my heart pounded against my ribcage, pain starting to stretch around my chest like stitch but a million times worse. I couldn't catch my breath. I gasped in shallow mouthfuls of air, but the room was darkening, sliding away from me.

'Going for the sympathy vote? Actress!' someone shrieked at me. It was the last thing I heard as I crashed to the ground and darkness swallowed me whole.

INVISIBLE

When I blinked open my eyes everything swam in front of me as if I were in a snow globe, and then slowly settled. I was in a small room, two men I recognised as court ushers standing over me. How had I got there? I must have passed out and been carried from court.

Embarrassment washed over me as I remembered what had happened. Things were bad enough without people thinking I was pretending to faint for sympathy; or worse, believing I actually did faint, but because I was upset about my husband's sentence. Oh God, what if they thought that was the reason?

Gathering my things as quickly as possible I made my apologies and scurried from the room. They let me use an exit at the back of the building so I wouldn't have to face the crowd.

When I got home I peeled off the suit and court shoes and put everything into a plastic bag (everything. Even the underwear). Then carried it outside and dumped it in the wheelie bin. I could never wear any of that again without being reminded of where it's been.

If only I could peel my skin off too, slough away everything that's been touched by Daryl.

'At least it's over now,' Dad said, nodding his head sagely. 'You can start moving on, put everything behind you and start fresh.'

'Divorce that man, sell this house. Fresh start, like your dad says,' Mum chimed in.

Easy as that.

Only I don't think it will be.

There was something I could do though, to help rid Daryl from my life. I went to the kitchen, grabbed the roll of bin bags from the cupboard under the sink, then marched into the bedroom.

Flinging open the wardrobe door, I grabbed a handful of clothes and, still on their hangers, shoved them into the bags. Not just his clothes, mine too – outfits I'd worn on special occasions, clothes he'd touched, tops he'd liked, anything, everything. It didn't take long to fill up one bag, then another, the metal hooks of the hangers poking through the black plastic here and there, hedgehog-like.

Soon only a few lonely items swung in the emptiness of the wardrobe. But lying at the bottom, neatly set out, were Daryl's shoes. I swept them into a bag too, then moved on to the chest of drawers. Underwear, t-shirts, socks, toiletries, comb (why does a bald man own a comb?) all were dumped inside.

I wasn't like Mum had been that day she'd destroyed my bed; I wasn't like a woman possessed. Instead I moved calmly, methodically, mechanically. There was no emotion, it was simply a job that had to be done. All traces of Daryl had to be removed, so that's what I was doing.

I moved on to the bathroom. Razor, aftershave, toothbrush, shower gel. I'd been saving everything for him, had wanted him to come home to find things exactly as he'd left them. Bloody fool that I was. Now it all went into the refuse sacks. But as I shoved his shaving foam away I suddenly stopped and stared in revulsion at my hand...

...At my wedding band.

I didn't allow myself to feel anything as I tugged it off. It stuck at the joint, refusing to go over it. A panicky, claustrophobic feeling gripped me and I pulled harder. It wouldn't budge. I turned on the tap and rubbed soap all over the third finger of my left hand, then tried again desperately. This time it slid away easily. As I flipped it into the bag the calm enveloped me once more.

Dragging a laden sack behind me, I surveyed the living room next. Pictures of Daryl, pictures of us, adorned shelves. I'd become so used to them I'd stopped noticing them but now I snatched them up. Mum and Dad didn't say a word, simply stepped aside to make room for me.

I didn't so much as pause to look at the photos or remember the days they'd been taken. I've no desire to relive supposed happy memories; they sicken me now that I know what the good mood may have been fuelled by. Everything went into the bags without a second glance, each item giving me an all-too brief glimmer of relief. I was unburdening myself of my marriage.

That vase Daryl always liked and I hated, that went too. His books were next. By the time I moved on to CDs (the first one to go was The Best of Barry bloody White album, with *My First, My Last, My Everything* on it) and DVDs my legs and back were starting to ache but I kept on moving, sweeping away the crap with rhythmic movements. Step, sweep, step, sweep, step, sweep…

I didn't sit down until gone 2am, and felt almost peaceful.

Saturday 23

I'm avoiding the telly. And the newspapers. And the internet. And the phone. Oh, and people. Because everywhere I turn there seem to be images of Daryl (and often me, too). Various in-depths breakdowns of our relationship make up a large part of much of the coverage thanks to him shouting that he loved me as he was taken away. It seems people think I'm as bad as him; some even hint that I'm worse because they believe I could have stopped him somehow, either by reporting him to the police or by talking to him. They all seem to believe I must have known what was going on.

There's much dissection of his childhood too, along with the crimes; some places even have interviews with a couple of the women who have waived their automatic legal right to anonymity as rape victims and decided to speak out. Well, that's fair enough, they must deal with things however they choose, and if it can help just one other rape victim who is reading the article then it's worth it. Perhaps they find it cathartic too, re-telling their tales. But I can't face it. I've been steeped in Daryl's horror for too long, I've heard every vile detail of what he's done and I never want to think about it again.

Except of course I can't stop thinking about it.

After the case Detective Inspector Ian Baxter gave a quick statement to reporters outside the court. I hadn't realised his name was Ian, makes him seem more human – aside from the unfortunate arse-face photo that ran alongside the articles I've seen online.

'These women were subjected to some of the most appalling attacks I have seen in my policing career. We strongly suspect that these are not his only crimes and would urge any further victims to please come forward.'

That's the bit that got to me. As if what he's done isn't bad enough, they think my husband is guilty of further crimes. I'm…I'm just…what do I feel?

Sickened. Stunned. Disgusted. Angry. Confused. Betrayed. Horrified. Panicked. Embarrassed. Stupid.

Those are things I should feel, and don't. I especially wish I could feel hatred for Daryl; there must be something wrong with me because I don't. But there's nothing inside me, no emotions. I think I've died but my body just hasn't noticed yet, and is continuing on zombie-like. Automatic pilot.

INVISIBLE

My parents have asked this walking, talking cadaver to stay with them. They think a break will do me good. I've nothing to offer for or against this idea, so I've packed a bag.

Before we set off though, Dad took all the bags of rubbish to the dump; he was worried that otherwise people would go through them and try to sell stuff to the media or to weirdoes who wanted Port Pervert memorabilia. Welcome to my life.

Wednesday 27

I've been staring out of the window for days now. There's a squirrel that comes into my parents' garden and I watch him. He spends all his time rushing round trying to find the ultimate place to bury his acorns, and never seems to quite find it. Sometimes a robin watches him too.

I think I might be having a nervous breakdown.

Probably the fact I think I am means I'm probably not.

It might be nice to escape into madness. Or amnesia. Could I smash myself over the head with something really hard and lose my memory deliberately?

My finger feels naked without my wedding ring.

APRIL

Tuesday 2
I came home last night.
The press was waiting for me. They went into a frenzy when they saw me. Exhausted, I tried to shut out the blaze of noise by putting the telly on as soon as I got in. An extra-bright flash went off suddenly; someone must have been trying to take a photo through the glass of the window. Don't think it will work, but I pulled the curtains shut all the same.
I miss the squirrel.

Sunday 7
Without the distraction of the court case I've nothing to do but think. I don't want to think.
I try my best to shut it all out, and try to revisit in my mind all those hours spent peacefully staring at the squirrel at Mum and Dad's, that creature whose biggest worry was remembering where it hid its acorns, but it's useless. I'm trying desperately to shore up my protective bubble, because it's safe in there and I can't feel anything and nothing quite reaches me. But huge cracks are developing in it. Things are sneaking through it, memories and emotions that I don't want snake around me and I keep trying to push them away but they cling to me.
I want to go back to feeling nothing,
I'm not going to think. I won't think. I can't allow myself to think.
That silver, heavy duty duct tape he always had handy for quick engine fixes. I keep seeing it, his nimble fingers tearing

it up and sticking together packages for me, a secret smile playing on his lips.

Now I know the secret. I want to scream and run away. I want to curl up and cry. I want to ask him 'why?'

I want to ask him why.

I'm not going to think. I won't think. I can't allow myself to think.

He called me straight after one of the rapes. Why? Did he want to share his euphoria with someone? He was in such a good mood that night. I was so happy that he was happy, and honestly thought the call was a good sign of the state of our marriage. I believed he was making an effort and that we'd be okay.

The last thing I ever would have thought was that he was so cheery because he'd brutalized someone.

Don't think about it, don't think about him, that way lies madness.

He took me to the places where he'd raped those women, and got turned on by it. He wore those gloves and did things I thought were hot and horny at the time but that now make me want to rip my skin off in disgust.

Stop it. Stop it. Stop it.

He said he loved me. Shouted it out in the courtroom for all to hear.

I need to stop the madness. I need to take my brain out and pop it on a shelf, out of reach, until it stops working overtime with sick memories.

Those huge hands used to hold me so gently. He murdered a woman with them, beat her to an unrecognisable pulp, then came home and made love to me, tenderly, lovingly, stroking my body with the same fingers that smashed life from someone else. He said he wanted a baby with me. We held each other, gazed into one another's eyes. I didn't see a monster, could never have guessed…

Please don't think. Please no more memories.
He raped a woman because she looked like me.
He raped a woman because she looked like me.
He raped a woman because she looked like me.
No matter how many times I say it, it doesn't seem real. How does someone get over something like this? How do I 'move on' as my parents suggested. I don't know. I wish someone could tell me.

Monday 8
When I think of that man my flesh creeps, and I find myself scratching, trying to tear away the skin he has touched.

Wednesday 10
The journalists are now camped outside my home constantly. I can't go to the shop for a pint of milk without a photo and accompanying story running the next day in the tabloids, dissecting what I've bought and the possible hidden meaning behind it.
I don't bother buying the papers, of course, but it's hard to avoid them when their headlines are stuck outside shops on little posters, or there is a huge pile of them outside the local garage when I fill up my car with petrol.
Ah yes, my car. I've started referring to it as the cauliflower car now because it has so many dents and scrapes from people deliberately hitting it or keying it. They smash the windscreen too, or paint rude words on it. I can't afford to get it professionally re-sprayed all the time so I just do it with an aerosol can I buy from Halfords. It looks bloody awful.
I deserve everything I get though. And more. Because I loved a murderer.

Thursday 11

How could I not have noticed? How didn't I realise that my husband was…perverted, twisted, demonic? Instead I just sat there wittering on about how bored I was with my life. I loved him for God's sake! As much as it sickens me, I still love him. I just want to switch the feeling off but I can't, it doesn't seem possible, even though at the same time he utterly repels me.

I'm appalled. I look back and realise that the good times coincide with immediately after he's raped someone. It must have put him in a good mood, doing those unspeakable things to those poor women.

Every time I think of it I want to vomit, my whole torso spasms, but there's nothing to bring up because I can't eat. How can I? Yet for all that, there's a tiny voice inside me saying 'he couldn't have done those things.' Of course I know he did, the evidence is irrefutable. I'm just in denial I suppose, because what does it say about me now that I know I have spent years loving a monster?

Worse, I feel so bloody guilty. Not just because maybe if I'd realised what he was I could have saved a woman. No, the guilt's mainly because I keep thinking about myself: what this means for me; how my life has been torn apart and everything is a lie; how devastated I am. And how I'm going to be stigmatised forever because of my connection with that man, when I haven't even done anything wrong. I'm being punished for being a bloody idiot. I'm scared.

How can I possibly think of myself when Daryl's victims have been through so much. Stupid, selfish bitch, that's me. Maybe that's why I deserve what's happening.

My parents keep saying to me: 'you're strong, you'll get through this.' How? I don't bloody feel strong. I feel like I'm falling apart. I've fallen apart. I've not just been shattered into a million pieces, those pieces have then been ground down into dust and scattered to the four winds. I don't know if I'll ever be whole again.

Kim, who still calls me every night, tells me continuously: 'At least you didn't have children with him.' As though it's some consolation. But you know what? As awful as it sounds, as sick and evil as he is, I wish we had had kids. With a child, I'd have something to focus on, a reason to keep going. Someone to pour all my love into. Instead I'm all adrift. I'm lost. I'm drowning. I'm definitely feeling sorry for myself, selfish cow.

I keep thinking about my doppelganger, who is now expecting Daryl's child - hell, maybe she's even had it now. Is it wrong that mixed with the pity and admiration I felt for her, there was just the tiniest hint of jealousy.

I know, it's disgusting of me. I'm disgusted with myself. And what makes it worse is that I'm lying, even to myself. Because it wasn't the tiniest twinge of envy. It was a big, heart-squeezing, breath-taking surge. Totally unexpected, totally unwanted, but there all the same.

And I can never admit that, not to anyone. They'd never understand, they'd judge me, they'd think that I sympathised with Daryl at some level. I don't. I'm disgusted by him, by what he did. But...a baby. A beautiful baby. I didn't realise how much I wanted one until the chance was snatched away from me.

The reality is I'll probably never have a child now. I'm 32. I will probably never trust another man. Even if I do, it will take a long, long time. By then years will have passed. Precious years in fertility stakes. The older I get, the less chance there is I'll conceive.

INVISIBLE

Chances are I will never, ever have a baby. I'll never know what it's like to feel a life growing inside me, to get that much talked of rush of maternal love when I hold my child in my arms for the first time. I'll never have that heady mix of love and fear watching my child grow up and go into the world, through nursery, school, dating, all that life has to offer. A whole chunk of what it is to be a woman will forever be alien to me.

And all the time, that fucking rapist bastard has a child. So yes, I'm jealous.

Thursday 18

He's sent me a visiting order. Daryl. (I've noticed that I've stopped using his name. But it tastes bad in my mouth when I say it, clagging it up like a dry cracker so that I can't speak or swallow; I even had to force myself to write it down just now.)

Perhaps I should go and see him. Ask him why?

I've killed an entire day standing in the hallway staring at the order then putting it down, walking away, coming back and starting all over again.

Sometimes I mix it up by putting it in the bin, then picking it out again.

Monday 22

Kevin called today. I've been sacked. Too much time off work, apparently.

'We've been as understanding as we can be, but your absences have reached an untenable level, and this situation has been on-going for almost twelve months now,' he said. He sounded like he was reading from a script Human Resources had given him.

As I so often do, I went to anxiously twirl my wedding ring, my right hand fluttering away uselessly as I once again discovered it is no longer there.

Kevin continued. 'In addition, when you have been present your work has not been up to the standard required by this company, and as stated in your contract of employment. As such, I am afraid I have no choice but to inform you that your employment is being terminated with immediate effect.'

'Okay, thank you,' I croaked, my voice husky from lack of use, then put the phone down. No point arguing with him, he has a fair point.

I couldn't afford the house with just my wage. Now I have no wage. I should be getting worried and worked up about this. I should, but the good old numbness stops me. Oh dear.

I shuffled through to the hallway and stopped by the little table where I keep the post (well, the post that isn't obscene or threatening) and stared at the visiting order. Picked it up, twirled it in my fingers, then put it down again and shuffled away.

Kim called as soon as she'd put Henry to bed, having heard the news of my sacking on the work grapevine. As usual lately, when I tried to change the subject on to her and what she's been up to, she let the conversation slide away.

Am I losing her friendship as well? My world is shrinking, soon the only people I will speak to are my parents, bless them.

Sunday 28

Mum's come to stay for a few days. She and Dad are worried about me (still). They say I should be angry, that I should be expressing my emotions. But apart from scared, I don't know how I feel.

I did hide the visiting order though. Mum would go crazy if she saw it. I dread to think what she might kick apart this time, and I really can't afford to replace all my furniture.

Sarcasm aside, bless her for coming to stay with me, in the heart of the whirlwind of madness. I've tried to protect her as much as possible from what's going on, of course, but it's impossible. She and Dad are suffering the looks, the whispers, the abusive phone calls (and worse, the silent ones) almost as much as me. How anyone can hold a pair of 63-year-olds responsible for what's happened is beyond me. Most things are beyond me though.

Mum didn't even need to ring the doorbell when she arrived, she was heralded by cameras clicking as she walked up the garden path, their flashes epilepsy-inducing, and the cry of journalists shouting questions. They all yell at once and I can't make out half of what they're saying to me.

They've so many questions, how do they think of them all? Don't they ever get tired of asking and never getting an answer? Or have they never grown up, and like children they can ask for all eternity it feels: 'Why? But…why? Why?' It's amazing the stuff they ask.

They all call me by my first name, too, as though trying to prove that really they're my mate and if I open my heart to them they'll look after me. I can trust them, they're saying.

That's another thing. I get their cards stuffed through the letterbox, along with endless letters saying that they'd 'love to hear my side of the story'. That I'm being judged by people already and so it's only fair that I get to 'set the record straight' by speaking exclusively to them. Oh, and that while 'obviously it isn't about the money' they would be 'more than happy to pay a six figure fee'. So when it gets right down to it they think I'm some heartless bitch who will profit from what has happened.

The really obvious question though, the one I'm asked time and time again, is: 'Did you really have no idea?' Of course I had no bloody idea! Surely no one can truly believe I would know about what Daryl was up to and keep quiet.

Or…maybe they think I got some horrible thrill from it, or was somehow party to it? Maybe they think Daryl would come home afterwards and give me a blow by blow account over a cuppa, and I'd laugh and clap my hands in delight in all the right places as he got to the really gory details. And afterwards we'd sit and watch Coronation Street.

If people really believe that, they must be sick themselves.

But…then again, I have to remind myself about women like Rosemary West and Myra Hindley. They really did enjoy their bloke's crimes. In fact, they actively took part, loved every second of it, were a driving force behind it. Is my name going to be mentioned in the same breath as them now?

The thought makes me feel sick – I mean makes my stomach physically contract and I have to run to the loo or stand over a bin, retching, gagging.

I hate being sick, it scares me, but the second I feel scared, I feel guilty. I can't allow myself to feel anything any more, because nothing I feel can ever compare to what Daryl's victims feel.

I'm glad Mum's here. It gives me less time to think about that sort of thing. Of course, the second she arrived, she took charge. You know what? I didn't mind at all, in fact, it felt great. It took everything she had not to open the curtains, but I've got used to the half-light now, and it means the paparazzi can't sneakily take photos of me in my own home.

INVISIBLE

They do that, you know, sneak up to the window, press the camera right up against the pane then snap away. The photo quality isn't great, as I discovered when the first grainy shot of me was printed immediately after the verdict, when I got home and put the telly on to try and drown out the noise they were all making outside. No, it's not great, but it satisfied the appetite of the nation to see the 'monster's wife relaxing at the home they'd shared'.

Relaxing! I've already checked with Peter – they can't make any specific allegations against me, they can't outright say that I knew anything because then I could sue them for libel and defamation of character and all that. But with oh so subtle use of words they can imply so much. 'Relaxing' because I don't have a care in the world, 'relaxing' despite my fella being a killer and multiple rapist.

So Mum kept the curtains closed and instead cleaned up the mess in the twilight. I seem to have forgotten how to do the washing up, vacuuming, dusting…bathing, dressing, brushing my hair…

Then she offered to go shopping because apparently everything I own is past its use by date. 'You need to eat, keep your strength up,' she told me. I think she tells me that a lot, but her words, along with everything else in the real world, seem to have turned into a strange fug that is muffled from me, and everything I see is dulled through a mist. I don't exist any more. I am a ghost.

As she wittered on about eggs and bread and milk and vegetables, I simply grunted occasionally, but when she was about to open the front door reality hit along with panic.

'Wait!' I shouted, grabbing her arm and holding her back. 'Be careful out there, Mum.'

She looked at me, eyes widened in surprise that I was finally reacting to something.

'I mean it,' I begged. 'If people know you're anything to do with me they'll try to hurt you or have a go at you. Be careful.'

She nodded slowly. Placed her fingers over my hand and rubbed them gently until I stopped squeezing her arm. It soothed the hysterical fear that was building inside me and I cleared my throat, trying to regain control.

'Just…don't go to the local supermarket, people might recognise you, link you to me,' I instructed. 'Drive to that other one that's across town. Or the big one by the bypass. I tend to change which ones I go to, so that no one can ever guess where I'll be and plan an attack. Sometimes I even drive to different towns…'

I trailed off then, suddenly struck by the concern, fear, and fierce love all reflected in Mum's face. It must be so hard for her. I've got to try harder to pull myself together, if only for her sake.

I'll try. I promise I'll try. I just don't know how I'll manage it though.

MAY

Wednesday 1
Night time is the worst, I think. During the day I can distract myself. I can do things, talk to people (well, Mum, Dad, and Kim – that's it, everyone else has disappeared).
At night though, there's nothing for me to do but lie waiting and hoping for sleep to finally take me into oblivion for a while and offer me a few hours of respite. It rarely comes though. Instead I lie in the darkness, staring straight up, in a bed that seems abnormally huge. Cold and empty. I know I spent the majority of my time alone when Daryl and I were together, and then almost a year while he was on remand and I kidded myself that he'd be home because he was a good, innocent person…but somehow, knowing I am now truly alone and hopeless makes the bed seem bigger and emptier and lonelier.
I curl up and try to imagine arms around me, a warm body spooned behind me, but my imagination's not that good. Then I realise I'm thinking of him, my husband, and feel sick because now all I can think of is the Port Pervert.
How could I not have known? Why did he do this to us?
Those are the thoughts that keep me cold at night, shivering even when it's warm.

Thursday 2
Mum marched me down to the doctor's today and despite my protests she sat in on my appointment as if I was a little girl again.
'She doesn't eat, doesn't sleep, barely speaks, can't be bothered with anything and either stares out of the window

in an almost catatonic state for hours or jiggles non-stop, rocking like a lunatic,' Mum told the GP.

Wow, I hadn't realised I was quite that bad. But instead of arguing I just sat there, knee going up and down like the clappers.

'It sounds as if you're depressed,' the doctor replied directly to me. Her voice was sympathetic but her body language spoke volumes: if she'd sat any further back in her chair she'd be coming out the other side. Yes, she knew who I was and wasn't happy but was doing her best to be professional. 'I'm going to write a prescription for you that will help you deal with things.'

Finally I found my voice. 'No, I don't want that,' I blurted, shaking my head stubbornly. 'I'm not depressed, or, at least I am depressed probably but I know why; there's a reason why I feel this way and tablets aren't going to get rid of it. If I'm going to stand any chance of getting over this then I need to deal with it properly. Work through it.'

It was the most I'd said at one go since the trial started. Goodness knows where the determination came from, but I kept on talking, my brain seeming to work properly for a few moments, at least.

'Tablets will fog my brain up and make me feel better for now but it's just putting off the moment when I do have to face reality. I'd rather do that now, even though it's...' I searched for a word to sum everything up, but failed miserably, '...hard.'

'It doesn't really work like that,' the GP replied, voice gentler, unfolding her arms. 'The tablets would simply help you, but if you're certain you don't want them...'

'I am.' It felt good to be certain of something. Good that I was in control of some tiny aspect of my life. There was one problem I'd like help with though… 'I do have trouble sleeping, and it's making me feel like I'm losing my mind.'

'Lack of sleep can definitely make it harder to deal with everyday life,' she nodded. Leaning forward, she picked up her pen and started scribbling something down. 'I'm going to write you a prescription for some sleeping tablets. You don't have to use them every night, just as and when you struggle with sleep.' That's every night then. 'I also think you should consider having counselling to help you deal with your issues. You, err, have had to deal with a lot… Now I can put you down on a waiting list to see someone on the NHS, but it could take a year for an appointment to come through, or you can pay to see someone privately. Here's a list of practitioners I'd recommend.'

She pushed it and the prescription over to me and I reached for them but Mum got there first and popped them both into her handbag.

Later, at home, we went through it together. Counselling…I don't know. I don't think I can talk about this stuff. How can I talk when I don't know what's going on in my own head?

I keep thinking about what the Inspector said. That there may have been more rapes than they know about, more victims who are too scared to come forward. It haunts me. So now I keep going over every row Daryl and I ever had and wondering if it was a trigger for another attack; thinking of happy memories and being terrified that they were because he'd just hurt someone.

There isn't a single tender moment or happy memory I have from the last nine years that I can think of now and take any solace in. There's no refuge from Daryl's evil. Everything is tainted by horror.

Did he do something terrible the day he proposed to me? On birthdays and anniversaries? Even walks on the beach when he seemed happy, was he planning something? How can the man who shared his life with me be capable of such things? He moves worms out of harm's way when it rains, and yet... I once went away on a mate's hen weekend and when I opened up my overnight bag at the hotel I discovered that Daryl had gone through it and hidden love notes in every single item. I'd laughed, stunned, as they'd fluttered from tops I pulled out, jeans, my make-up bag, one in each high heeled shoe I'd brought...

'I'll miss you, Gorgeous', 'You are my one and only', 'My first, my last, my everything', each message was different. He'd even written 'I love' you' on the cellophane wrappers of every individual tampon I'd had to bring with me.

At the time I'd thought it incredible and rather wonderful that he'd gone to all that trouble. Now it freaks me out. Why did he do it? What triggered such a show of emotion? Had he hurt someone? Nothing can be taken on face value, not when you're thinking of a man who agrees to have a baby after murdering someone.

No, there isn't a single thing I can take from the last nine years of my life. My whole adult life had been based on lie after lie layered together until it gave the impression of something solid and reliable, when all the time it was waiting for the bloody great wrecking ball of truth to smash it apart.

How I wish I could go back in time and never have met him. If I just hadn't gone to that stupid party with Hannah, just think, I'd never have known Daryl. He was only at that party by chance, so if we hadn't got together there maybe we'd never have clapped eyes on one another. Think how different my life would have been. Maybe I'd have met someone else that very night, fallen for them instead and now I'd be married to someone honest and lovely.

INVISIBLE

I'd be curled up in bed next to him, and we'd be complaining about our couple of rug rats crawling in with us, but actually secretly pleased as they snuggled up with us, because that's what life is really all about when you get down to it: family. We'd laugh as we all squeezed together in our little double bed, complaining that someone was hogging the duvet when actually there simply wasn't enough to cover us all, then finally the kids would fall asleep again, their hot breath against my neck, their legs thrown over me and their dad in a tangle that seemed inextricable.

I've a stupid smile on my face as I imagine that, tears dribbling down my cheeks. That's the life I should have had. I wish I could turn back time.

Some people believe there are parallel universes out there, don't they. They think that every permutation of every decision we could have made is being lived out somewhere at the same time as we're living this life. I don't really understand it, but it's an oddly comforting thought that somewhere out there there is a me that got it all right and is happy. That somewhere that scene I imagined is reality, and I have children and I'm loved and I'm truly happy and have solidity, contentment, everything I ever wanted.

I've got to stop writing for a minute, the tears are making it hard to see the page.

Right, I'm back, that's better. Well, it is and it isn't because while I was crying I had another horrible thought.

That story about his mum leaving him for three days after he told her he was bullied. It can't be right. How could he have gone for three days without water? He made it up, of course.

God I'm stupid! He made everything up to make me feel sorry for him, to dupe me into falling in love with him and actually feeling protective of him – him, the evil monster that everyone actually needed protecting from!

Or did he make it up? Maybe it was real and that was what damaged him beyond repair? Could that be the beginning of him becoming twisted and sick?

He'd looked so serious and sad as he'd told me, surely it couldn't be yet another fabrication. The way his eyes had filled with tears, and he'd twisted his hands anxiously as he'd spoken. The odd expression on his face as he'd told me the story, as if he was making his mind up about something and letting me in…

Jesus, he'd been thinking about killing me, wringing my neck, that's why he was wringing his shirt hem; it was instead of my neck! What had it been about me that made him stop, not go through with what his heart told him to? Should I feel flattered? Or sickened? Maybe he saw in me some flaw that was equal to his, maybe he thought I was like him.

What if I'm evil and don't even realise it?

Thursday 9

Despite popping a sleeping tablet, all night I kept thinking about Daryl telling me the story of being bullied and his mum ignoring him. At about 3.30am I decided there was only one course of action I could take: I had to call his mum and ask if it was true or not.

I've spent years hating that woman. Perhaps there was never a reason to. Perhaps she was so odd because she was trying to protect herself from the son she knew was evil. Then again, maybe he's strange because he takes after her… All I know is that throughout this Cynthia has been a total waste of space not just for him but me also. Every time I call her she tells me not to bother her any more. Yet she's the closest person I have to someone who will really understand what I'm going through.

It took a lot of self-control not to get up and call her right there and then. Even I could see it wasn't a great idea to ring in the small hours though, so instead I lay in bed, watching the clock's digital glow changing shape every minute in the darkness, willing it to move faster, faster, faster. Safe to say, I don't have telekinetic powers – unless maybe I made it go slower.

By 6am the internal argument had started. Was it still too early? Officially it was daylight; in fact the sun had been up for hours. No, Cynthia might still be asleep. 6.30am. Still too early. 7am: maybe I could get away with that? But no, I didn't want the conversation to get off to a bad start, needed things to go smoothly, so better to wait.

By 8am I couldn't stand it any more. I tied my hair back in a ponytail (as if somehow tidying my hair would help tidy my mind and make me think clearer) and dialled. As soon as Cynthia heard my voice she became defensive.

'My dear, if you're calling to persuade me that he's innocent or to go see him -,' she began. Clearly like me she never says his name any more, but it didn't take a genius to know who 'he' was.

'No, no,' I interrupted quickly. 'Even I'm not so blind that I can't see that he's guilty. I just…I suppose I want to work out why…'

'…And thought you'd blame me because it's always the mother's fault?'

'Not at all, I just…' Just what? Now I was talking to her I didn't really know what to say. I suppose I hoped that we'd talk and she'd tell me about some clear trigger in his childhood that had caused him to become so damaged that he'd wreaked terrible revenge on all women. Maybe it was this incident where he'd locked himself in his room, maybe it was more complicated than that, but there had to be something, some reason, surely.

'People don't just spontaneously become rapists and killers. Do they? And if they do, surely it's because they're evil through and through – and if they're evil like that then it means they have no loveable traits, and that just wasn't Daryl. He could be so wonderful…so why does someone wonderful do something so terrible?' My words tumbled out, eager to escape my brain, where they'd been going round and round all night.

Cynthia gave a sigh. 'I know you want to understand but there's nothing I can tell you. Some people are just born twisted. I'm afraid Daryl was never right.'

Despite myself I felt annoyed, leapt to his defence. 'How can you say that about your own son?' I demanded.

'Because it's true, my dear,' she said simply. 'He's always been a little charmer – and a little liar. I don't know where he got it from because I'm not like that and his dad, God rest his soul, certainly wasn't. But from the day he could speak, I couldn't trust a word that came out of his mouth.'

What I wanted to snap was: 'Which came first, Daryl's problems or your attitude? You thought he was a liar so maybe that's why he became one.' I didn't though; trembling with the effort of holding myself back, I instead described the event from his childhood that he'd revealed to me.

'He did get bullied by some girls, but it wasn't anything much and the school took care of it as soon as I alerted them,' Cynthia said, matter-of-fact. 'He certainly didn't lock himself away or anything like that. The fact is that Daryl has always been a strange boy, and as soon as I heard that he'd been arrested I knew he was guilty. I don't want to talk

about him any more. As far as I am concerned, I do not have a son. I don't want to talk to you again, I'm sorry.'
Before I could say another word I heard the click of the phone being put down. She keeps doing this to me!!
'Right…okay…thanks for your time,' I found myself telling the dialling tone, stunned.
I'm no closer to finding out why Daryl did these things. No closer to discovering why, if he's been born bad, he decided to set up home with me rather than kill me.

Thursday 16
I just want this to end. I wish I were dead.

Friday 17
I can't tell anyone the stuff going round in my head. I can't share it. Because as terrible as I feel, it's like I'm belittling what those women have been through.
'Think you're feeling bad? Well put yourself in their shoes!' that's what I feel people would say to me. Well, friends probably would say…if I had any.
I'm invisible. I'm the invisible victim, apologetic for my very existence. Everyone looking at me and wondering: 'did she know? She must have had a hint at least. She must be so stupid not to have realised.'
But I didn't! I didn't know, didn't realise. At least…thinking about it now, I did know something wasn't right…but who the hell would leap to that conclusion? 'Something's wrong in my marriage. I know! My hubby must be a rapist!' It's just not the thought process of a normal person.
Even if I had thought it, for even a second (which I never, ever did, despite priding myself on being a touch paranoid and having a very over-active imagination) I wouldn't have believed myself, would have told myself off, shocked that I could think such a terrible thing about the person I loved. I'd

have felt like I'd betrayed him somehow, thinking something like that. It's not what normal people do.

And that's the thing, that's the key phrase – it's not what normal people do. Because I am normal, and that's the frame of reference I use to judge people. Normal, everyday life. I don't think about rapists, killers, paedophiles…bad people, bad things, it's not in my world. Or, I didn't think it was…

Sunday 19

The bloody cow! The two-faced, conniving, vindictive, opportunistic, money-grabbing… I've run out of words! I'm too flabbergasted to even swear!!

The first thing I saw this morning when I went skulking around the supermarket trying to get food without being recognised? Emblazoned across one of the red tops, was 'My hell in the Port Pervert's lair' and beneath it a photo of Hannah. Hannah! She's sold her bloody story!

Stunned, I picked it up, my brain refusing to believe what it was seeing. Oh the irony that, even after everything that's happened, I can still be surprised by what people are capable of. I stood there looking at that load of trash, thinking: 'No, it's not what it seems. She'll be talking about how normal we were, trying to get people to realise we weren't some kind of weird monster couple.'

So I actually paid for a copy of the rag and took it home with me. Shoved it up my jumper before I left the shop, of course, didn't want the paps to get a shot of me with a newspaper. The security guard by the doors gave me a really funny look as I did it, given that it's more the sort of thing he'd see a shoplifter do; I expect not many people who've paid for something shove it up their jumper or down their trousers or something afterwards…

INVISIBLE

The minute I got back to the house I retrieved the paper, not caring that the black ink had smudged onto my white bra, and spread the pages out to read. It was about two seconds later that the truth hit and the swearing started.

'The way he looked at me was pure evil,' I read aloud. What?! 'I knew then, like some kind of protective instinct kicking in, that if I didn't get away there and then, my number was up.'

She was on about that day when she and Amy had come round and he'd made them feel uncomfortable. Now, fair enough, that did happen, and with hindsight, it must have been quite scary for them, but come on, ultimately all he actually did was give them a funny look. Why did she have to sell the tale to some tacky tabloid and make loads more of it than there actually was? Why profit from other people's misery? She didn't even have the decency to warn me beforehand.

Hannah, a busty brunette, trembles as she remembers that awful night when she came so very close to death, was another bit that really stuck out for me. So close to death? Come off it, you can't kill someone by giving them a nasty glare. And also, frankly, she isn't busty – more flat-chested and athletic.

The worst thing though, the absolute worst thing, was that she wasn't just talking about that night. That wouldn't have filled more than a quarter of the page, even with a heavy dose of over-dramatic padding. No, she was talking about our everyday life. Mine and Daryl's. She made us sound like freaks.

We'd held a barbecue the other year, and she'd been terrified, apparently, as Daryl and I had leered at her over the sausages (yes, that's really what the newspaper story said, I'm not making that up). Now I do remember her being really drunk and making suggestive comments herself about the various uses of bangers, in a bad Carry On film kind of way. I don't remember her looking even remotely 'terrified'. Although I was a bit scared when she stood on the table and gave a rousing rendition of 'I'm Too Sexy' by Right Said Fred, while waving a particularly long sausage about and miming an act that had made Kim cover Henry's eyes. That bit of the evening hadn't made it into the article.

To be honest, Daryl had looked a bit scary when Hannah had vomited all over our new rug...but I'd managed to clear it up quite quickly and smooth things over as I'd bundled her into a minicab I'd ordered for her (and paid for!) so she could go home and get some rest. Funnily enough though, none of that was reported in Hannah's version of events either.

There was absolutely and definitely no leering over the sausages on my part though.

I suppose on the plus side, at least she's finally made me feel angry. Well done her, because for the first time since the trial's revelations, I'm red-rage furious. How much did she get for her lies and exaggerations? It's one thing to want nothing more to do with me - as hurtful as that is, I do understand – but we've known each other since we were kids so I don't get how she could betray me like this. At least other friends who have dropped by the wayside haven't stooped to this level.

Yet.

Finally I understood Mum's rage when she'd kicked the bed apart. I wanted to punch someone, tear something to shreds, destroy the way I'd been destroyed. I tore the newspaper up into tiny pieces in the bin, but was still fuming. I wanted to rant to someone who'd be as outraged as me. I almost called Kim but remembered she'd mentioned she was going out;

she goes out so rarely that I didn't want to disturb her happiness with my crap.

Then I picked up the phone and dialled Hannah to give her a piece of my mind. It gave a single ring before I wimped out and quickly ended the call, remembering the mess I'd made that time I'd phoned a newspaper to complain about their coverage after Daryl's arrest. Knowing Hannah she'd probably sell this Sunday tabloid a follow up tale of how the Port Pervert's wife had stalked, threatened and harassed her.

See? I'm finally learning to play this game.

Monday 20

How could I have loved a rapist and not known?

Tuesday 21

I got the truck back today. The police had held it since they confiscated it after Daryl's arrest. Now the trial is over, they've released it. It's stuck outside my house now and every time I see its massive shadow my heart jumps and I feel sick because I automatically think it means he's coming home.

What the fuck am I going to do with his truck? I could sell it, I need the money, but who is going to want to buy it?

A sicko maybe, who wants it for some kind of twisted memorabilia. Well, I can't let someone like that have it. So I'll have to have it crushed or something. I don't even know how to organise that. I'll look into it another day...

When Kim called for her almost daily check up on me, I told her about it. 'I can have a look into that,' she offered. 'I'll get everything organised for you.'

'Thanks, that's really, really kind of you,' I sighed with relief. 'But are you sure you have time? What with work and Henry and...'

'It's okay, I can sort it tomorrow afternoon; Henry can be picked up from school by P-' She stopped short.

'By who?' I asked curious.

'Oh, nobody, it doesn't matter.'

A nasty suspicious formed. 'You're not back with Psycho Sam again?'

She gasped in shock at the idea. 'No! Oh, look I wasn't going to say anything because, well, it's just not important compared to what's going on with you, but, well, I've started seeing someone.'

Normally I'd have been alight with curiosity. I didn't so much as feel a glimmer though. Well, maybe a dying ember. Still, I forced myself to sound interested. 'Oh, great. Who?'

'It's, well, it's Peter. Simpson. The solicitor.'

Now I did smile. Only the slightest turning up of my lips, a movement that felt almost alien, but it was still definitely a smile. I'd honestly started to wonder if I'd ever do that again.

'That's great news. He seems like a really decent guy,' I said. And he does. He really, truly does.

But do you ever really know anyone?

'I've liked him since I first met him,' she revealed eagerly. 'He's really helped me with Sam too, getting me a restraining order and making sure it's being enforced correctly. I just feel safe with him. I'm not that crazy person Sam turned me into, I'm me again only...only a hundred times happier and nicer!'

Despite the thick layer of cynicism and despair that surrounds me, I was happy for her. If anyone deserves this it's her. Besides, it's good to know that there are some decent men out there.

'He's great with Henry too,' she added. 'It was ages before I introduced them because I was so wary after Sam, but Peter totally understood that. And the first time they met, Peter gave him a Ben 10 toy – I must have mentioned at some point that Henry loved Ben 10 and Peter had remembered; how lovely is that? They played together with it for ages, and Henry was totally sold on him after that. I...I honestly couldn't be happier.'

'Hey, you're not crying are you?' I asked.

'Yep, tears of happiness,' she sniffed merrily.

'So how long's this been going on?' I wondered.

'We got together just before the trial. We...we'd met up a couple of times for lunch, just as friends, when Peter suddenly made this little speech about how he really liked me and very much wanted to be more than friends but knew I was vulnerable and hoped I didn't think he was being unprofessional and using his job to take advantage of me, and that I must say immediately if I felt uncomfortable or never wanted to see him again...

'He was so nervous that it sounded really formal and it just made me laugh. I didn't even think, just threw my arms around him and gave him a kiss right there at the table!

'I wanted to tell you but it just seemed ridiculous and frivolous when you have so much going on in your life.'

'So that was your big secret? I knew there was something! And honestly, I don't think it's frivolous, I think it's great. I could do with some good news for once.'

And you know what? It did make me feel happier.

Wednesday 22

I'm going mad. The same stupid things keep going round my head. I can't stop them. I can't answer the questions. I don't know why Daryl did these things. Even replaying the conversation with his mum doesn't help, and her assertion that he was 'born bad'. It can't be that simple. If I'd been a bit more switched on could I have seen something was wrong with him and helped him? Could I have stopped this from happening? Could I have saved those women?

I can't do anything, because I'm paralysed by this fear that I should have stopped Daryl.

Thursday 23

Was I so unattractive that the only way he could get his jollies was by taking it by force from others?

Why did he stay with me for all those years and not hurt me?

Why did he stay with me after he was arrested? He must have known the truth would come out eventually…

Friday 24

Why? Why? Why? Why? Why? Why? Why? Why? Why?
Why? Why? Why? Why? Why? Why? Why? Why? Why?
Why? Why? Why? Why? Why? Why? Why? Why? Why?
Why? Why? Why? Why? Why? Why? Why? Why? Why?
Why? Why? Why? Why? Why? Why? Why? Why? Why?
Why? Why? Why? Why? Why? Why? Why? Why? Why?
Why? Why? Why? Why? Why? Why? Why? Why? Why?
Why? Why? Why? Why? Why? Why? Why? Why? Why?
Why? Why? Why? Why? Why? Why? Why? Why? Why?
Why? Why? Why? Why? Why? Why? Why? Why? Why?
Why? Why? Why? Why? Why? Why? Why? Why? Why?
Why? Why? Why? Why? Why? Why? Why? Why? Why?
Why? Why? Why? Why? Why? Why? Why? Why? Why?
Why? Why? Why? Why? Why? Why? Why? Why? Why?
Why? Why? Why? Why? Why? Why? Why? Why? Why?
Why? Why? Why? Why? Why? Why? Why? Why? Why?

INVISIBLE

Why? Why?

It took a long time to write all those. I still don't have the answer.

Saturday 25

I'm at the end of my tether.

I had a call from the mortgage lender today; I've missed a payment. After a lot of negotiation, they've let me reduce the payments for a couple of months but it's been made very clear to me that this is a short term fix and that I have to find a better solution, fast, or my home will be repossessed.

The fact is, my savings are totally wiped out, and Daryl's too. It took everything we'd built up over our entire marriage to keep the house going and pay all the bills while Daryl was on remand – that and sending him £500 a month so he could basically have any luxury he could lay his hands on whilst in prison, the jammy bugger. It had been a huge struggle but what kept me going was the fact that there was light at the end of the tunnel. I'd kept telling myself that once the trial was over and Daryl was found not guilty, he'd not only be freed but probably get compensation for wrongful imprisonment or something; that would replenish all our savings and we'd be back on track again.

The flaw in that plan, of course, was that Daryl is guilty as sin.

Now I have no savings to fall back on, and I've no income either, now I've lost my job. How the hell am I going to get out of this mess?

I feel like I've died. I feel like this is the end of my life. Daryl's in prison, but I'm the one serving a life sentence.

Sunday 26

There's some kind of petition going round about me, I've discovered. It's ostensibly about the lorry, people want it off the street, they say it's causing an obstruction. But there's also a whole bit about how they want me out of the neighbourhood too! I've brought the area into disrepute and lowered house prices, or something.

Maybe I should do them all a favour and die. I just want this unending hell to stop, I want the peace of oblivion. If I got hit by a bus tomorrow, I honestly wouldn't care. What can I offer the world? Nothing, absolutely nothing.

No wonder the neighbourhood want rid of me.

Well, if I don't keep up with my mortgage payments they'll get their wish and I'll be out of here. I'll call an estate agent tomorrow and get the house valued, start the ball rolling with selling it. It won't be a huge wrench to downsize; I used to love this house but even though his stuff has been thrown away, everywhere I look I see Daryl and his filthy lies.

Anyway, in preparation for a visit from the estate agent, I've actually managed to clean up. Hoovering and dusting seemed to take forever and sap me of what little energy I have, but if I can be free from this place it will be worth it. Maybe living somewhere else will help me get better again. Be human once more.

Monday 27
So much for me and my big plan. I got up today, actually showered and washed my hair, then called the estate agent who Daryl and I had bought the house through. I'd figured that would be easier than going with someone new, as they'd be more familiar with the property.
That was problem number one, of course: that they *were* familiar with the property…and the owners.
The woman on the end of the phone was lovely and chatty, right up until the moment I gave my name and address. Suddenly she went very quiet.
'Hello? Are you still there?' I checked.
'Yes…'
'Sorry, thought we'd been cut off for a moment there.'
'Umm, the thing is, the market is quite depressed currently, what with the recession, so we probably won't be able to get you a good price. Perhaps you should hang onto the house for now or maybe try another company,' she said.
I laughed, thinking she was joking. 'I hope you're more enthusiastic when you come to selling it,' I joked.
Silence. Cold enough to give me frostbite. Only then did I get it. 'Are you saying you don't want my custom?' I checked.
An awkward clearing of the throat, another silence, then…
'We have to be realistic, we can't work miracles here, you know,' she replied. 'Your house has been plastered all over the news, people will see a picture of it and instantly know who has lived there. I'll be honest…'

'Oh, please do, I'm used to people giving me their bald opinions these days.'

'...no one is going to want to pay top dollar for a house a murderer has lived in. I doubt we could even get you a low offer. We really wouldn't want to represent you, sorry.' Then she put the phone down.

Well, at least she'd said sorry, most people don't give me that courtesy these days. Still, I was upset. I knew that the instant I called other agents I'd get the same response. Gutted, I called Mum and cried down the phone to her.

'Oh sweetheart, don't cry,' she said sadly. 'Anyway, you couldn't sell up right now really, could you?'

'Why not? I thought you wanted me to move on from Daryl, isn't this the perfect way?' I asked, amazed.

'Well, of course, sweetheart, but you've got to get his permission first, haven't you? Because he owns half the house too.'

Crap, how could I have forgotten about that?

'Get the divorce started, that way you can sort out all the financial mess at the same time,' Mum advised.

She's right. That's got to be my next move.

Tuesday 28

Okay, I'm a wimp. I could have used the visiting order Daryl's sent to me to go and tell him that I plan to divorce him and need his permission to sell the house immediately. I could have used the time to confront him too about what he's done and try to find out what the hell triggered this nightmare.

I could have but I didn't.

Instead I wrote him a letter. It wasn't a long-winded love note, instead it was short and to the point.

INVISIBLE

The thought of seeing him is too much, it makes me feel weird. Panicky, painfully heart-racy, and as if my stomach has turned into a washing machine churning round, and I'm horrified to admit it but there is also a tiny bit of me that gets excited too. Like, looking forward to it kind of excited. Oh God, I still love him. I do. I don't want to, wish with all my heart I didn't, but you can't turn those kind of emotions off like a tap. So instead I'm stuck in a heart-rending limbo where I love the man I loathe.

That's why I wrote the letter; better that than he see me and realise how I feel.

Dear Daryl,

I want no contact with you other than to discuss the business of wrapping up our marriage. We need to sell the house as I can no longer afford to run it single-handed, but I need your permission to do so. If you are agreeable I will get the ball rolling and send the relevant paperwork to you to be signed as and when. I also intend to start divorce proceedings.

I'm trying to be business-like and hold it together, and I really hope that comes across, but it's hard. As I wrote the words all I could think about was what he's done. I try and try to imagine what it must have been like for them. The victims. Their fear, their pain. His face over them, twisted as he inflicts himself on them. But I can't. All I can manage is some kind of B-rated movie-style of what he did. I know the facts, of course, relive those words from court, see again his victims' faces as they gave evidence, and it's...every word I can think of fails to do it justice. Horrific, evil, twisted, whatever, it doesn't sum it up.

How do you write to someone who is guilty of such things? The hardest part was actually signing off. I almost automatically put 'love', then tried 'regards' but didn't even want to seem that friendly so in the end I settled simply for signing my name.

JUNE

Saturday 1
I feel like I should be fighting to get back to normal but…fight what? There's nothing to fight. It'd be like thumping mist.
This time last year I was in Turkey.

Tuesday 4
Well, it took a week, but Daryl's reply arrived today. My hands shook as I stood by the front door and picked at the edge of the envelope, trying to open it but unable to winkle a finger in to get it started. Losing patience I gutted it, ripping it wide open and two pieces of paper fluttered out.
My heart dropped as I stooped to pick them up from the welcome mat, because I instantly recognised one of them as a visiting order. For a moment I just stood there, gathering myself. Squeezed my eyes shut in frustration, counted to ten, then opened them and started to read Daryl's note. It was as to-the-point as mine had been.
Babe,
I won't be agreeing to the house sale or divorce. You still are and always will be my Gorgeous. Come and see me and we can discuss it.
Forever
Daryl.
I sank to the floor where I stood, curled up like a baby and sobbed, hand over my head to somehow protect me. As I rocked gently, despair crashed over me and took my breath away. He is never going to let me be free, he will never leave

me alone. His love is like the sticky clay mud of a First World War battlefield, and I can't break free, I am slowly being sucked down and the more I struggle the faster my demise comes. I surrender, you win Daryl.

Wednesday 5
I'm lonely, I'm so desperately lonely, and I need a hug, to feel someone's arms around me, the human comfort of knowing someone cares and is there for me and only me, and yes, I know my parents are, but it's not the same as a partner, is it, it just isn't the same, and so the terrible fact is…I miss Daryl. And I hate myself for it.
I want a hug from the very person who has hurt me and put me in this terrible position. What a sicko I must be, what a sado-masochist. I know it's not really Daryl I miss, of course. It's the idealised version. I miss the myth that was my husband, my partner. I miss having someone to call and talk rubbish to. I miss knowing I have another person's love. I miss the stability and solidity that having a loved one gives you, the smug knowledge that you are not alone.
I hate myself.

Tuesday 11
I'm so sick of feeling crap. I feel so guilty about it; I shouldn't feel like this. What do I have to complain about really? In comparison to what Daryl's victims have been through?
Every time I feel sorry for myself I am eaten up with guilt. It's the same old story of comparing my horror with theirs, the same feeling of being in competition against those poor women, and losing miserably every time.

Thursday 13

Since discovering Daryl's secret I've changed physically almost beyond recognition. I look in the mirror and don't recognise the person looking back at me. Which is just as well, because I don't think I could look the old me in the eye, stupid, blind cow that I was. I've lost a stone and a half. Dropped 4 inches from my bum, five from my belly, three from my waist…
Nothing fits me. I need new clothes, but what's the point? Kim has given me some of her clothes. She's tiny – and I was amazed to discover they fit me (well, apart from the trousers are way too long for me because she's tall enough to be a model, while I am titchy).
'Can't have you looking like a homeless person, love,' she smiled gently when she gave me them. Bless her for standing by me.
Sometimes I find myself just staring in the mirror and talking. I hate myself. But I'm also the only one who understands how I'm feeling because there's not exactly a support group for women who discover they are married a monster. I'm all alone with only me to rely on, so I stare in the mirror and talk. Am I losing it? I'm scared.
I feel totally helpless. I have no control over my life now. I've been sacked, I can't imagine that anyone else will ever want to employ me, I'm hated by everyone in the world (apart from Mum, Dad, and one friend) and still regularly get death threats, I'm about to lose my home which is the only solid thing in my life right now, I've huge debts that I'll never pay off, oh, and my murdering rapist husband wants me to go see him.
I am punch drunk, barely feeling each individual blow now, just reeling and stumbling around as I fight to stay on my feet. Well you know what? I'm throwing in the towel. I am

sinking to my knees and refusing to get up any more, because if I do something else will just smack me one.

That's why I'm lying on the sofa, duvet pulled over me, crying and watching bad telly. Mobile and home phone are switched off, I want nothing to do with anyone or anything any more. The world can bugger off because I want no part of it.

Still, I can feel the two visiting orders lying on the hallway table. Their presence seems to thrum. They accuse me. Pulling the duvet closer doesn't shut them out. Throwing them away is something I don't seem to have the will for.

I wish I were dead.

Friday 14

It's a really blustery day outside. The wind is making the leaves in the trees sound like a hundred rattle snakes outside my window. And I can't stop crying.

Tears are streaming down my face but I don't bother wiping them away. I simply sit, and stare out of the window.

Saturday 15

I'm at a crossroads. Do I turn right or left? Do I live or die?

Actually, I'm sitting on the sofa with every sleeping tablet and painkiller I could find in the house spread out on the coffee table. I've been staring at them for the last two hours, in between crying hysterically. I mean, really hysterically. Uncontrollable moans that seem to come from the depths of my body, shaking hands, face like a snotty pig, the lot. And every time I think I've finally run out of tears I seem to find more. I can't stop. I can barely see as I write, and big tear splashes wrinkle the paper here and there, but these days writing is the only thing that keeps me (barely) sane.

Am I sane? Does contemplating suicide mean I'm sane or insane, given everything I've been through?

I don't know what to do. There are only two choices and I cannot decide whether to swallow the pills and slide into oblivion or sweep them into the bin and decide once and for all that, since I'm alive, I might as well try to actually live.

This is my Alice in Wonderland moment. Eat me, drink me. Should I go down the rabbit hole or not?

I definitely wish I were dead. If I could be knocked over by a bus right now it would be a relief. I want to stop hurting. I want to stop the guilt. I want to stop feeling apologetic for my existence.

Once upon a time I used to laugh. Imagine that. Laughing until tears were in my eyes and my stomach ached. I can't even remember the last time I smiled – not the tight, worried smile I give strangers who are looking at me and wondering why they recognise me (I smile at them hoping they'll be fooled into believing that they've met me before. Anything to stop them actually putting two and two together). Not the fake smile that almost hurts my face when I give it to my parents to show them I'm fine and they shouldn't worry. No, I mean a proper, spontaneous, smile-because-I'm-happy smile.

Remembering being like that is like thinking of a different person, and I have no idea how to get back to being her, that woman from a year ago. Actually, I know I will never be her again. Part of me is really sad about that; she was a really nice, genuine person who saw the good in everyone and was never suspicious. Part of me is also glad though because I'm angry at her stupid naivety and never want to see her vacuous face again. I am harder now, more cynical, fuller of hatred than I ever thought possible, and that is reflected in the stare I see when I look in the mirror.

INVISIBLE

I am full of utter despair and nothingness – and I want the nothingness to swallow me whole, to envelope me and never let me go again.

Would people notice if I were gone? Would they care? Aside from my parents, obviously, there is no one who would shed a tear, I don't think. To be honest though, I don't think anyone would celebrate either. No one would even notice, which is sort of worse. Even the locals with their petition would simply shrug with relief at getting their own way then move on with their lives; continue mowing their lawns, washing their cars, cleaning their windows without a second thought for me.

Ah, there is one person who would miss me though, I'm sure. My twisted husband. He'd have no one to taunt from his prison cell any more. Then again, it must be a boring game that he's playing with me because I'm too easy to wind up. I think he likes more of a challenge than I can provide. So even he would barely notice my passing, and certainly wouldn't shed any tears.

When I think of it, I've spent my whole life being looked through. Mum and Dad virtually trained me to be that way from the second I was born: stoic and quiet and accepting, just like them; they are the loveliest, most un-complaining people I have ever come across. Then I met Daryl, who never called me by my real name but instead gave me pet names of Gorgeous and Babe, diminishing me further into a yes woman rather than a flesh and blood wife with actual feelings to be taken into consideration. And now? Now I don't have a name either. Now I am bitch, scum, colluder. I am a person of many faces, none of which are actually mine.

It will be good to disappear all together.

I pick up a pill and stare at its pink-hued, grainy texture. Pop it into my mouth and swallow a gulp of water. I pause for a second hoping that this edge towards a decision will finally make me feel better. It doesn't. I try another one pill, waiting, hoping.

Right or left. Life or death. Which way should I go?

This time I scoop up several pills at once and shove them impatiently into my mouth. Shuddering, I take a huge mouthful of water and swallow, but the tablets stick painfully in my throat. Still I take more and more, ignoring the choking feeling that's building.

Then I think of my parents.

Imagine them when they hear the news of my death. See them at my funeral. Realise that they will never, ever recover from the loss of their child. They've been so quietly strong for me all through this, never judging, never accusing, just being there for me without question.

I jump up, shaking my head, and run to the loo, stick my fingers down my throat. A violent heave and undigested tablets splatter into the toilet bowl. I make myself sick again and again until there's nothing left to come up, then curl up on the bath mat, sobbing.

I can't even get suicide right. What's wrong with me?!

Anger burns through the self-pity then. I was right, I AM at a crossroads. And if I decide to live I can't do it for someone else's sake. It has to be for me...but I don't have anything to live for.

Sighing, shaking my head, I stand up and walk away, making the best decision I can for now: I won't take an overdose. Not just yet. I'll turn right and try to live. If things don't improve I can always kill myself tomorrow instead.

Sunday 16

Maybe all that bollocks about hitting rock bottom so you can start bouncing back is actually true. I do feel a little better today, having decided to live. I'm still knackered, crying and have a shite life, but I did get out of bed at a decent hour, and showered, cleaned my teeth and brushed my hair like a proper human being, then got dress into something that doesn't have an elasticated waistband. The jeans felt oddly heavy after all that time in pyjamas or jogging bottoms.

I tidied the house too, and made myself a proper meal for the first time in…I can't actually remember how long. My parents have made meals for me, and sometimes Kim has brought something over, but I've not bothered eating them, and as for me bothering to cook…no, that hasn't happened since the start of the trial.

When I tidied I came across a list of counsellors and therapists that my doctor gave me. I'm going to go, I've decided. I can't actually afford to pay for private sessions but I think I kind of can't afford not to either, otherwise I'll go doolally or go through with Plan A to top myself.

Besides, I'm already in so much debt that I can't afford to pay it back, so what's a bit more?

So I'm feeling better. Not miraculously and suddenly jumping around the room singing with joy – I still spent quite a few hours crying. But I'm…willing to try to live again. How long this will last is anyone's guess, and as I said last night, if I get peed off again I can always kill myself tomorrow….but if I kill myself tomorrow there definitely won't be another chance to live, so I'd best be very certain before going down that route.

I even dug out a yoga dvd Kim bought me, thinking it might help to calm my nerves. I did a bit tonight before coming to bed and writing, and it has made me feel a little more relaxed.

Monday 17

I keep looking at that bloody visiting form for Wakefield Prison – that's where Daryl has moved to now he has been found guilty and is deemed a dangerous category A prisoner. It's where all the highest security sex offenders in England and Wales tend to wind up, and apparently its nickname is the Monster Mansion. Nice.

So why would my own personal monster want me to go there and have a cosy little chat? Why does he want to discuss things? I know what the discussion will consist of; him swapping between browbeating me and sweet-talking me until I would swear that up was down.

Thursday 20
I've been given a hell of a lot to think about. Today I had my first appointment with my therapist, Marsha; she actually shuffled her schedule round to accommodate me when she realised who I was. I'm not sure how I feel about that, but clearly she thought I was an urgent case.

I'm not sure what I expected when I reached her office; maybe something like in The Sopranos, a slightly imposing room; or the classic lying on a couch thing, while the therapist sits behind you and then sneaks from the room as you talk, bored.

Instead, I arrived at what turned out to be Marsha's rather lovely home, and was shown into a cosy sitting room with relaxing knick-knacks scattered around: dolphins jumping from water, that kind of thing. A large window overlooked a beautiful mature garden with a lawn, impressive trees and hedges, and a kitsch little water feature, and Marsha indicated that I should sit in one of two big, squashy armchairs right beside it.

INVISIBLE

'Please, make yourself comfortable. Take off your shoes even, if you want,' she smiled. A proper, real deal smile; my first for a long time. Mum, Dad and Kim always give me uncertain smiles, as if they're worried I might find cheerfulness painful and shatter. Maybe I will. But at that moment it felt wonderful and I found my mouth turning upwards too, hesitantly but genuinely.

There's something nice about Marsha. She has a good atmosphere about her, gives off a trustworthy vibe – you know what it is, she seems content; boy, do I envy that. She's a large lady, comfortable-looking, and wears mumsy clothes, which adds to the whole Mother Earth thing she's got going on. Her skin glows with good health and her frumpy, neck-length, mid-brown hair may not be in a cutting edge style but it is super glossy.

I can imagine giving her a hug.

So when she said 'make yourself comfortable' I took her at her word and kicked my shoes off, before plonking down on the super soft cushions of the chair and being enveloped by it, and folding my legs up beneath me.

'Firstly, let me explain a little about how this will work. You can say whatever you want in here and it will be treated in the utmost confidence.' I nodded at her, believing every word, so she continued. 'You're not going to feel better instantly, in fact some people feel worse with counselling before they get better because some very powerful emotions and memories can be stirred up.'

That scared me a bit. I fidgeted in my seat and tried to cover it with a cough.

'Think of yourself as carrying very heavy luggage on your back; your emotional luggage,' she added. 'Every time you come here you'll leave a little bit behind, hopefully, until you reach a point where you're fully unburdened.'

'I like the sound of that,' I blurted out.

I'll be honest, I hadn't thought it was going to be easy for me to speak about what's happened, or to trust someone enough to be open, but I surprised myself with how much I said. Alright, I did hold some stuff back, of course, but basically I laid it all on the line as I gave her a brief history of what had happened, pausing as I spoke only to take the occasional sip of water from the glass she'd thoughtfully put out on a side table beside my chair.

Only when I reached the bit about what the consultant psychologist said at the trial did my lips start to tremble.

'Oh God, was it my fault?' I gasped. 'Was I such a harridan that that he hurt those women as a reaction, as a coping mechanism rather than hurt me?'

Marsha seemed pretty annoyed with the psychologist. 'It was her job to explain his behaviour, but sadly instead she seems to have tried to shift the blame on you, which wasn't correct or professional of her,' she said calmly, trying to mask the irritated look on her face. Just seeing that made me feel better – one professional dissing another.

'The thing is,' I confessed, 'that psychologist did make me feel like I was to blame, like it was our rubbish relationship that sent him over the edge. And then Daryl even mouthed to me, "It's your fault." He took great pleasure in telling me that.'

'We're all responsible for our own decision and reactions,' Marsha replied, then paused for a moment to give me time to control the urge to cynically roll my eyes. 'Let me ask you something: do you blame any of those women for what happened to them?'

'Of course not,' I scoffed, horrified she'd even suggest it.

'And yet Daryl also told one of them that she'd asked for it, didn't he?'

'Yes…' I said slowly. 'But…that's different.'

'Is it? In what way?' She cocked her head, as if genuinely fascinated by my reply. I tried to marshal my thoughts so I could explain the complex emotional reasons behind why. Instead it felt like the answer was a great big tangle of wool in my heart and soul and I couldn't figure out how to unravel it. Where to start?

'I-I don't know, it just is,' I finally settled for. Marsha simply looked at me, the light reflecting on her glasses so that I couldn't see her eyes properly. For the first time in the session I felt tense.

'I should have known what he was doing. I'm his wife, I should have known,' I wailed suddenly. 'I should have stopped him and nothing anyone says will ever change that. It is my fault.'

'Did he ever tell you what he was doing?' she asked.

I shook my head, frowning. 'Of course not; I'd have gone straight to the police if he had.'

She nodded. 'Did you ever see him attack anyone?'

'No.' The reply came out sullen, like a child. I felt annoyed with her and her stubborn refusal to get what everyone else in the world understood: that I'm to blame.

'Hmm. Did you tell him to hurt women?'

'No!'

'Then I really don't see how this can be your fault. Daryl made his decisions on his own, he is the only person responsible for them. Not you.'

'Well, I…' I hesitated, trying to think of something to say to persuade her. I couldn't. Not one single logical argument could be put forward. It's not my fault. No matter how much I feel like it is.

My hands twisted anxiously as I repeated the phrase in my head, trying to get it to sink in.

It's not my fault.

'But everyone says it is,' I whispered. A final offering in desperation.

She smiled, shook her head, then glanced at the clock. 'It isn't. We can work some more on this next week, if you'd like to come again?'

Definitely. Definitely! I do think I've left just a tiny bit of my emotional baggage behind at Marsha's. I feel kind of confused, as if my world has been turned upside down, because there has been such a sudden shift in the way I'm seeing things. Maybe I'm finally seeing things right way up again, after it was turned upside down by Daryl. Whatever, I'm looking at things differently and it's strange but wonderful.

I still feel guilty and awful but now I have a new mantra that I could almost skip to, it gives me such a momentary buzz when I think of it.

It isn't my fault. Daryl's responsible for his own actions.

Friday 21

When I woke up today I looked round the house and decided I'd had enough of these four walls. The journalists outside the house have thinned out now, and only the odd stubborn one still remains (see how quickly they've forgotten me and moved on to the next victim) so I sneaked out the back and went jogging.

It felt good pounding the streets, even though I could only manage a couple of minutes before having to stop, puffed out. A bit of a walk, then I pushed on with the jogging, alternating between the two when I had to, and all the time I repeated in time to the pounding of my feet:

It's not my fault.

It's not my fault.

INVISIBLE

It's not my fault.

I repeat it again and again, trying to make myself believe in my core that it's true. I hope it's true. That's how far Marsha's brought me already, in just one session though; I have hope again.

Thursday 27

For the first time today I found myself looking forward to something: my therapy session. As soon as I got to Marsha's I kicked my shoes off and made myself comfy in the armchair by sitting cross-legged.

We talked some more about Daryl. The conviction I'd felt from the last session had quickly faded and I feel weighed down with guilt again.

'If I could just find out why it happened,' I said. Tears wobbled on the edge of my eyes and I looked up, blinking furiously, trying to keep them in.

'Would you understand if he explained to you?' Marsha asked patiently.

I didn't get what she meant by that. If someone explains the reasoning behind their actions then you understand. What isn't there to understand? There had to be a trigger for all this.

'Maybe I did put too much pressure on him to have a baby and it did send him over the edge…but there has to be a reason why it did, like something that happened in his own childhood that scarred him emotionally so much that the thought of being a parent made him lose control. God, I don't know, I'm not the expert here…' I babbled to the ceiling, still blinking.

Marsha seemed to consider what I'd said for a moment. 'Tell me a good memory from your relationship,' she asked.

What did that have to do with what we were talking about? Confusion made the tears disappear slowly as I spoke, describing the time Daryl arrived at the house as a surprise, only a few weeks before his arrest, and I pulled a sickie from work so we could spend the whole day together.

But as I told the story, instead of feeling happy at the memory, or sickened because I now know that he was in such a good mood because he'd raped someone the night before, I started to feel something else. Angry.

It was Marsha's clever questioning that did it. She didn't lead me to any conclusions, didn't put words in my mouth or thoughts in my head, but as I answered her, describing the day and emotions in greater detail I suddenly saw the whole thing from a different perspective, like looking at one of those posters that's all crazy coloured dots, and then something shifts and suddenly you can clearly see a picture.

Daryl totally manipulated and managed me that day. I'd thought it was really romantic the way he'd just turned up, but actually he'd just expected me to drop everything for him. The really annoying thing is I'd thought it myself for a fraction of a second that day, then dismissed it, thinking I was being silly.

I always did that, always told myself that any negative emotions I had were my problem. I never had the confidence to say them out loud or to say no to Daryl. Or anyone else for that matter, because now I'm home and still thinking about the session, I can see it's what I was like with friends too, especially Hannah.

All through school I followed her round like a sheep, doing things I didn't really want to do simply because to say no would cause an argument. It was never anything major, just silly things like which film we'd go see, which clothes to wear (if we both wanted to wear a red top for a night out, or something, she'd always be the one to wear it while I'd put something else on), even which boys to chat up. I've spent my whole life placating, smoothing things over, keeping the peace, making sure everyone around me is happy, while forgetting about my own happiness.

While at Marsha's though, the whole revelation took my breath away. I sat there, open-mouthed, trying to get my head around it.

'Oh my God, Daryl did stuff like that to me all the time,' I gasped, furious. 'He managed me. Even when Daryl was in a good mood, he'd make sure everything was done if and when he felt like it, in the way he felt like. Even that time he surprised me outside work.' Marsha had no idea what incident I was referring to but didn't interrupt me. 'I thought it was really romantic, but thinking about it now, it was totally controlling! He'd never, ever have given up time at work for me. In fact, he'd have kicked off about it.'

My eyes darted around the room, unseeing, as memories raced through my mind. 'Rows were always blamed on me, tension was always my fault, somehow it was always me who was manipulated into apologising even when I knew I'd done nothing wrong,' I added, conviction building now as my fists clenched and unclenched. 'Sometimes when I was with him I felt like I was going mad because he'd so often convince me that black was white. He had a hold over me like he was Rasputin or something!'

Suddenly I looked up at Marsha, triumphant. 'You're right. When he said "It's your fault" he just didn't want to take responsibility for his own actions. Part of his unique way of torturing people is to make them feel guilty. It's something he's always done to me, and he even did to the women he attacked too.'

It's one thing to be told something by someone and accept it, as I had done at the last session when Marsha had pretty much told me the same thing. It's a whole other feeling to

come to that same conclusion yourself. I could have screamed in frustration at my old self for not being able to see – but also felt overjoyed because now I can see, and one of the chains tying me to Daryl has been snapped. I can feel it like a physical lightening of my being.
'He's a high-functioning psychopath and sociopath,' Marsha explained. 'They are charming, manipulative, and lack any emotional empathy, which is why when they want something they go after it without concern for who might get hurt along the way.'
Yep, that sounds like my husband.
I'm going to get away from that bastard. It's going to take a while, but one day I'm going to be free of him once and for all.
'I just wish I could have seen it at the time,' I hissed, shaking my head furiously. 'I was so judgemental of my friend Kim's relationship and couldn't understand why she didn't realise how awful her boyfriend was. Yet there was I, with someone a hundred times worse, but I was blinded for some reason.'
'Did she realise something was wrong with your relationship?' asked Marsha, before taking a sip of water.
'She tried to subtly tell me once but I didn't listen. In fact I felt annoyed, hurt.'
'So she could see what was wrong in your relationship but not in her own,' Marsha said. 'Why do you think that was?'
I shrugged. 'I suppose she was just too close to her own relationship. Couldn't see the wood for the trees and all that. But she had the distance from my marriage to be able to see it clearly.'
Marsha nodded, and I waited expectantly for her to say more. She just looked on me. Then realisation dawned. Oh, I

get it now – that's exactly why I could see what a scumbag Psycho Sam was, but couldn't see Daryl for what he was.

'The other thing, I suppose,' I said slowly, thinking aloud, 'is that…well, if he'd been hitting me it would have been easier to see I was in an abusive relationship. Not easier to get out of, just easier to…comprehend. But…manipulation and psychological games are harder to identify somehow.'

'A lot of women would agree with that, definitely.'

Hmm, lots more for me to think about…

Friday 28

I actually slept a bit better last night. Between the therapy, and the exercising I'm forcing myself to do now, I'm feeling stronger. Not strong, definitely not strong; I am still broken and pathetic, but now I am at least trying to pull myself together.

The jogging is boring as hell but gives me time alone that somehow clears my head instead of filling it with more crap. And I'm doing yoga. So much yoga it's coming out of my ears. That dvd Kim bought me has been a real God-send. I tried it one night in desperation when I couldn't sleep and now I'm addicted. I mean literally addicted. I do it in the morning, in place of my missed sleep. I do it in the evenings, when I can't face watching more telly, and I can't sleep…

Why? Why? Why? That's the question that keeps me awake; yes, I'm still driving myself mad with that. It's whirling round and round my head and there doesn't seem to be any escape from it. I'm exhausted by it. I come up with theories and shoot them down just as quickly. I've got to know the reason, I've got to understand. It's fine to say that Daryl is responsible for his actions, and I do know it wasn't my fault but…What if there was something I could have done to stop it? What if I could have spotted it earlier?

But more than anything, I just need to understand why the man I loved was a violent manipulative monster.

Saturday 29
More red bills are landing on my doormat. I'm in big trouble. I've started scouring the local paper for jobs, even though I can't imagine anyone wanting to employ me round here, but really I need to get rid of this house.

Kim and Peter came over for dinner tonight. I know it sounds pathetic but I'm still not up to much; I get exhausted very quickly and have trouble concentrating on things, so I just did a huge vat of spag bol. They didn't seem to mind though, and even brought over some wine to share.

'Not for me, thanks,' I said, putting a hand over my glass when Peter poured for everyone. Kim pulled a face, amazed. 'Oh, I just don't like the thought of drinking since the trial. I'm too on edge all the time, and I'm scared I'll lose control and fall apart if I have any booze,' I explained.

She nodded, understanding immediately. Peter looked sympathetic too. 'How are you doing?' he asked gently.

'I'm okay,' I nodded, the lie tripping off my tongue lightly, because what else could I say? 'But I did have something I wanted to ask you. I know you're not a divorce lawyer, but I wondered if you knew...can I divorce Daryl even if he doesn't want me to?'

Peter frowned and bit his lip. Then ran over his hands through his black hair, which always seems to point in different directions. Clearly the answer wasn't going to be the straightforward 'of course!' I'd been hoping for. Kim gave him a look before taking another mouthful of food.

'You've had a conversation with Daryl about this, I take it?' he checked.

'Wrote to him,' I confirmed, nodding. 'He wrote back saying he'd never agree, basically. Though he did put some nonsense in about being willing to discuss it if I visit him.'
Peter looked thunderstruck for a second, then swallowed hard. 'Well, it might be worth considering...' Before Kim or I could argue he ploughed on. 'The only way you can get a divorce without your husband's consent is for you to have lived separately for five years or more. He won't be able to defend your divorce petition then, although he can ask the court not to grant the final decree because of major financial or other type of hardship – but I don't see how that could be applied in this case.'
I pushed my plate away and doubled over, leaning on the dining table, head in hands, suddenly weak. 'Five years?' I croaked into the glass surface. 'Are you sure there's no emergency rule for cases like this, you know, extenuating circumstances where you discover your spouse is a murdering psycho?'
I heard someone stand, a rustle of movement, then felt a hand rest on my shoulder. 'I'm really sorry,' Peter apologised.
'Is it worth you checking with someone? This isn't your area of expertise...' I said desperately, hauling myself upright to look him in the eye. His hand dropped uselessly to his side, and he stood awkwardly, clearly not knowing what to do with himself.
Finally he shrugged helplessly. 'I can check but I know you have to wait five years, unless he agrees to the divorce.'
Kim leaned over the table and grabbed my hand, squeezing it. Her brow furrowed into a frill and she sighed. 'Maybe it's worth talking to Daryl?'
I shook my head. 'After all that's come out about him, does he strike you as the reasonable type? No, he just wants me to visit so he can mess with my head and play his little mind

games. He's no intention of giving me what I want, I'm sure of it.'

She squeezed my hand once more and threw a worried look at Peter.

Bugger, bugger, bugger, there was no way I was letting that bastard ruin our evening. It's the first time I'd even attempted to cook for anyone for an eternity, so I gave myself a shake.

'Enough about depressing things,' I said, forcing myself to be bright. 'Tell me all about you two!' To show I was totally fine I even forced down a mouthful of spaghetti and sauce.

Kim and Peter looked at each other again, smiling shyly, almost apologetically, but they couldn't keep their happiness under wraps. Their faces positively glowed as they spoke about their relationship, their plans to move in together, and how wonderful Peter thought Henry was.

Everything seems to be moving apace, but they look so right together that it doesn't seem too fast.

Finally, I stood and started clearing the plates, with Peter hurrying to join me. As we went into the kitchen, he seemed anxious to say something and my heart fell a little; I hoped he wasn't going to say more on the divorce when I was trying so hard not to think of the next five years I faced being Mrs Port Pervert.

'I, err, I wondered if I could ask your advice on something,' he said nervously, setting the plates down carefully and licking his lips.

'Of course,' I replied, curious.

'Umm, well...' he sent a nervous glance in the direction of the living room where Kim was flicking through my old CDs. 'I'm thinking of...well, proposing to Kim, what do you think?'

This last sentence had come out in such a rush that I just stood there blinking for a second. Then went to squeal but managed to stifle it, realising Kim would hear and wonder why I was giving her fella a bear hug in the kitchen. Instead I settled for silently pumping my arms and jumping up and down, a huge grin on my face.

Peter smiled right back, clearly overjoyed by my reaction.

'Bloody brilliant, that's what I think,' I hissed gleefully. 'When? Where? What's the plan?'

'Really? You think she'll say yes?' he confirmed.

I rolled my eyes. 'I've never seen her happier. Now come on, spill!'

Suddenly Kim appeared in the doorway, waving a Stone Roses CD. 'God, I haven't heard this in years! Can I put it on?'

If she saw the way me and her fella froze guiltily, she didn't give anything away. Just goes to show how the innocent mind doesn't spot suspicious behaviour…

'Yeah, no problem,' I squeaked. 'Actually, that's a 'best of', but if you look in my bedroom, I might have their original album somewhere.' That bought us some time as she wandered from the kitchen.

'Quick, tell all,' I urged Peter.

'I'm going to take her and Henry on a surprise trip to Euro Disney – I thought Henry should be involved?' I nodded that his thinking was probably correct. 'Well, their favourite Disney film is Toy Story. So I was going to get Buzz Lightyear to ask her if she'd spend infinity and beyond with me. Too cheesy?'

Umm, yes, way too cheesy, but it's also the sort of thing Kim will adore, and that's what I told him. At this, if he'd have smiled any wider he'd have wound up with a flip top head!

I have to say, despite the bitter divorce blow, tonight's been one of the best I can remember – and one that I know won't be tainted with anything untoward in years to come.

Finally, there's some truly good news in my life. Without Kim and Peter's example I think I'd give up and decide all men were total shits and love is for suckers. How tragically ironic though that as I'm desperately trying to get rid of my husband, Kim is gaining one.

Five years. How can I be that man's wife for another five years? I keep rubbing the empty space where my wedding ring used to be; maybe I hope subconsciously that if I rub hard enough I'll magically erase the marriage. If only.

Sunday 30
So, I'm stuffed as far as divorce or selling the house or anything is concerned. But I've come up with a plan. I was lying in bed, trying to sleep as usual, but for once it was anger making me toss and turn rather than guilt and bad memories. Suddenly a flash of inspiration struck at 4am. I'm going to speak again with Peter and with Marsha too, and see what they think.

JULY

Sunday 7

I pick up the new visiting order Daryl has sent (he sends one every week now) and my stomach flips at the thought of seeing him, a rush of blood pounding in my ears and making my heart race.
I hope I'm ready for this.

Thursday 11

I've been given the go-ahead by Marsha and Peter, and I've booked myself in, so tomorrow I face Daryl for the first time since court. Seems sort of fitting somehow, as I've just realised that tomorrow is the anniversary of us getting arrested; I won't be celebrating that, but it did mark a…turning point in my life, shall I say, and hopefully tomorrow will too. The first day of the rest of my life, possibly.
I'm sick with nerves, can't think of tomorrow without my stomach feeling like it's trying to churn its way out of my body. As for my heart, I've been fascinated and fairly freaked out to discover that when it pounds hard enough I can actually see it against my chest.
Last night I found myself once again wishing I were dead. I stood talking to my reflection in the mirror, crying about how useless I am, worrying that Daryl will send me back to the pathetic specimen I used to be; I could already see it happening before my eyes.
Or worse, going to the prison and finding a man broken by the discovery of his two sides. Why worse? Because then I might feel sorry for him. Slide into that abyss again and I might as well be dead.

I opened the bathroom cabinet and took out the bottle of sleeping pills. Stared at it. Then put it back again. Because I have to try this. I have to speak with Daryl and put my plan into place. If it doesn't work, if things go really badly and I wind up a blubbering wreck then…well, I can always kill myself tomorrow.

Friday 12
The journey to Wakefield prison seemed to take both an incredibly long time but also to fly by. All too soon I found myself parking the car, going through the security checks of a rub down and walking through a metal detector, had my passport scrutinised and then I was led into a room full of low tables, each with four chairs. I sat down, swallowed nervously and waited.
I didn't have to wait long. Seconds later, the door opened and the prisoners filed in. As soon as I saw Daryl it felt like someone had punched my solar plexus and my heart leapt painfully. I clenched my hands together tightly to stop my urge to fidget, and forced myself to meet his eye.
Calm, I had to stay calm. I knew what I'd come to say, and I was going to take Marsha's advice and harness my anger and nerves to get me through this. I hate confrontations though, get so worked up that my heart pounds and the adrenaline just seems to make me want to cry. Still, I have improved a little lately, and I knew this time I couldn't afford to get like that so used the deep breathing techniques I'd learned in yoga.
Daryl gave me a predatory smile, the kind a cat gives a mouse, as he eased himself into the plastic chair opposite me then leaned back and assessed me.

'Hello, Gorgeous, you've lost more weight. Don't get too skinny, you'll look gaunt,' he greeted. 'How are you?'

'Fine…thanks,' I replied stiffly. My throat was really dry, so dry I could barely swallow. 'I just need the loo,' I announced suddenly, jumping up again.

As I stood, a guard came over and accompanied me to the ladies' toilets. I had a quick wee, washed my hands, saw they were trembling like crazy. I had to get myself together, couldn't let myself fall to pieces so quickly. I took a sip from the cold water pooled in my hand then splashed my face lightly with the remainder. Deep breath, a quick check in the mirror; I looked okay, no real outward signs of nerves. That gave me the courage to walk out of the loo again, get patted down, then march back over to Daryl.

'I want a divorce,' I announced before I'd even sat down again.

The pupils in Daryl's ice-blue eyes contracted. 'I'm trying to be civil to you. I wanted to see you and talk about things, and you can't even be bothered to ask me how I am before you start with your demands,' he said, voice dangerous and low.

'I didn't come here for a row,' I replied, voice steady, fidgety fingers plaited firmly in lap. 'But I didn't come here for a chat about old times either.'

He looked at my hands, eyes narrowing. 'You're not even wearing your wedding ring. We're still married you know – or are you out fucking other people already? I bet you've been doing that ever since I got arrested, haven't you?'

'Don't be ridiculous,' I snapped. I know I shouldn't have shown him he'd touched a nerve but I couldn't help it.

Instantly he leaned forward and we started a whispered argument, faces inches from one another.

'How could you?' he demanded.

'How…?' I was flabbergasted. 'How dare you accuse me of being unfaithful when you're in prison – or doesn't rape count as adultery?! You hypocritical, vile… How could you do those things? Why, Daryl? Why? I need to know.'

Instead of answering he reached out towards me. 'Don't touch me!' I hissed, and squirmed away as though he was poisonous.

The anger rose inside me, making me shake far more than the nerves had. I wanted to tell him exactly what I thought of him, but snapped my mouth shut and shook my head. Not like this. I needed to stay calm and in control. Right now I was playing into his hands; he wanted to rile me. I had to stick with my plan.

Frustration registered on his face as he realised I wasn't going to bite further. 'You're a cunt, you're a cunt. You're just a fucking cunt,' he sneered.

Those were the kind of words he'd thrown at his other victims too, when he'd been raping them. Thinking of them gave me strength.

'Well, that's charming,' I replied sarcastically. 'You'd think given the circumstances, of the two of us I'd be the one swearing and name calling, but I'm not.'

That was the moment I'd been waiting for. It was the tipping of the balance of power. Suddenly Daryl didn't seem to know what to do now I was the one being calm and he was floundering in rage.

'I think you should leave,' he snapped.

'I'll leave when I'm good and ready, when I've finished our talk.' I couldn't believe my own gall. It felt exhilarating rather than nerve-racking.

'You've really fucking blown it now,' he shook, spittle flying from his mouth, cheeks reddening. 'You'll never get what you want from me. How dare you?'

'That line again, Daryl? How dare I what? Speak my mind? Very easily. I've discovered I've got one since you've been locked away, and I'm rather enjoying using it,' I smiled sweetly.

'Yeah, well, you were so desperate to trust me. It was all your fault, everything was your fault. You kept nagging me about kids, I couldn't talk to you about anything; it's like that psychologist said, you're the reason why I was forced to hurt those women. And you couldn't even see what was in front of you, you just blindly kept on seeing what you wanted to see, kept on trusting me.'

It was the biggest metaphorical slap in the face he could give me. But I'd known it was coming and barely blinked. 'You're right,' I nodded. 'I did blindly trust you and that makes me sad. But then, trust and love are pretty normal behaviour within a marriage. As for nagging you about a family...yes, I was desperate for your child. And now, somewhere out there, one of your victims has a living breathing reminder of the vile things you've done to her. She has a beautiful baby created from hatred that should have been ours, created from love.'

For a second he looked stunned and there were tears in his eyes. He held my gaze for one, two, three heartbeats, perhaps thinking of the very different lives we could have had if only he were normal. Then he blinked and the tears were gone.

'You still haven't asked how I'm doing,' he said petulantly, changing the subject. 'It's not easy for me in here, you know. I'm victimised by staff and inmates. My cell is tiny and there's no separate loo, it's right there in the same room as I sleep in; have you any idea how disgusting that is? Then there's the mandatory drug testing, and you know how much I hate needles…'

Was the big bad killer really whinging for sympathy?

'I haven't even done anything wrong,' he added, folding his arms, shirt sleeves straining across his huge muscles.

I looked in his eyes and could see he believed it. I was a bit scared when I realised that.

'My God I'm so glad I came over today to have this out with you because you really believe your own lies,' I gasped, stunned. 'You have something broken inside you, there's some emotional circuitry that's gone wrong with you.'

I'd known that before, of course I had. But to stare into the eyes of someone and see close up that they aren't connected properly, aren't like other people, is a revelation. If you weren't looking for it you might miss it, but now it was blindingly obvious to me.

Daryl's smile was back as he lounged back in the plastic chair and it creaked in time to his gentle bouncing.

'You know why I kept in touch with you after the arrest?' he whispered conspiratorially. 'Because I though the jury would look at prim and proper you, with your neat clothes and your perfect hair, and your little girl walk, and it would colour the way they thought of me. I thought they'd think someone like you would never be with a nasty bogeyman.'

He sneered this last word, twisting his smile. 'You couldn't even get that right though, could you. Fucking useless bitch.'

Revulsion shuddered through me. Time to end this charade.

'Will you agree to the sale of the house, and to me divorcing you?' I asked calmly. 'I'm willing to visit again and talk about the details with you, if you agree now and sign this paperwork to allow me to put our home on the market.'

Even as I was speaking he was shaking his head, smirking, arms still folded, slumped in his seat like a teenager. 'Nope. I'm not going to let you go, Gorgeous. Never. I love you,' he snickered, shark eyes glinting with humour.

I held his gaze and nodded. Now was my moment. 'That's fine, I expected no less. I know you must be feeling impotent in your cell, unable to exert any power over women, so you're reduced to playing this game with me,' I said, leaning forward to be certain he caught every word.

'But know this: I will win in the end. All I have to do is wait for five years and then I can divorce you whether you like it or not. There's nothing you can do to stop me. And in the meantime I'll be out and about having fun, living my life without you in it, while you will be stuck in here.' I waved my hands around airily to take in the depressing brick and concrete that surrounded us.

There it was, that familiar, furious look that had always sent me back-tracking and apologising in the past. Daryl's face like thunder, the storm clouds had well and truly gathered. I swayed slightly but held my ground, still staring straight into his eyes as they bored into me.

His full lips were white with fury. Then he swallowed and smirked.

'Well there's nothing you can do about the house,' he replied, head bobbing arrogantly. 'I'll never agree to its sale. We'll be tied to it for the rest of our lives. You'll be tied to me.'

Still I held his gaze. 'You lose, Daryl,' I smiled. Then I stood and walked away.

He must have been too surprised to react, because it was only as the guard buzzed the door to let me out that I heard Daryl's voice calling out to me. 'Don't see how I can lose. Tell me what you mean.'

I felt the familiar pull of guilt and more that always made me do as Daryl said. The urge to spill the beans was almost overwhelming. Almost, but not quite. Marsha had prepared me for this and I carried on walking, even though my legs felt like they belonged to someone else and wouldn't seem to work properly.

I kept on walking until I reached my car and climbed inside. Put the keys in the ignition. Rested my hands on the steering wheel amazed at how very calm and in control I'd been...

...And then I fell apart.

How I cried. For the loss of the man I'd loved, for the children I'd imagined, for the future I'd thought was guaranteed. It's all gone, all dead, and I finally allowed myself to grieve.

But more than anything, I sobbed for the young woman who had wanted all those things. I've never allowed myself to really mourn her passing because it made me feel guilty, as if that was somehow detracting from what Daryl's victim's had suffered.

That girl was an innocent victim too though. She didn't deserve what happened to her.

Trembling, I pulled my phone out from the glove compartment where I'd had to leave it, and dialled my parents. They'd lost that girl too, and now I could suddenly see how hard it must have been for them to see her death and watch me shuffling around trying to be her lookalike replacement.

Dad answered.

'Th-thank you for everything you've done for me,' I stuttered through the shuddering breaths the tears were causing. 'I'm so sorry for what I've put you through.'

'Love, what's happened?' he panicked.

'I'm fine, d-don't worry,' I huffed between sobs. Then I laughed, because actually it was true. I'd just confronted Daryl and had survived, shattering nine years of control he'd had over me.

'I'm fine,' I repeated, 'for the first time in a long time.'

'I don't understand. Has something else happened?' he said, then I heard muffled conversation as he put his hand over the receiver, followed by a clearer, 'Here's your mother.'

'Sweetheart?' Mum's voice sounded high and worried. But as I explained everything I found myself laughing again through the tears and she was laughing too, with relief. Maybe I was hysterical. Whatever, it felt good. This morning I'd felt like I was weighed down with worry, now I was so light I could fly or run at 100 miles an hour or something.

'I'm so proud of you,' Mum said as we ended the conversation.

Yeah, I'm proud of me too. Part one of the plan went just how I thought it would. On Monday it's time for phase two. Daryl would do his nut if he realised what that involved...

SEPTEMBER

Sunday 8
Well, it's two months since I implemented phase two of the plan, and it all went really well.
Basically, I defaulted on the mortgage and handed in the keys of the house to the bank, and have declared myself bankrupt.
Everything Daryl and I owned has been sold off or given to charity, apart from a handful of things of sentimental value that I kept. Kim and Peter did the selling on my behalf as I didn't want people to know whose things they were buying. They even found a home for the truck – it's gone to a charity that a friend of Peter's is involved in, who just so happened to be fundraising for a lorry to distribute goods to orphanages in Romania. Apparently, the charity couldn't believe their luck when a 'mystery benefactor' donated one to them.
The proceeds from the sale were split fifty/fifty between Daryl and paying off my debts; I didn't get a penny. I don't care. All I wanted was to be free of Daryl. I'm sure he's furious that I've managed to escape being tied to the house, and him, forever.
I told him he'd lose his twisted game, but he just didn't believe me.
Now all he can do is wait helplessly in his prison cell as the days pass, knowing that all too soon five years will have gone by and I can divorce him whether he likes it or not.

INVISIBLE

While I wait for that glorious day, I've got to get on with life though. I feel so much better now I've moved to a different town on the other side of the country. Sometimes I catch someone looking at me as if they recognise me, but they can't seem to place me. So far so good.

This is a fresh start, in a tiny flat that's sparsely furnished with things from charity shops, but I love it because everything here is my taste. No impractical cream couch and carpets, no cold glass dining and coffee tables. Nothing pristine and perfect and sterile.

Instead I've painted the bedroom a deep, rich red, and the lounge a vibrant blue. To be honest it's a bit garish, but I don't care because I did it myself and they're colours I never would have been allowed to have when I was married.

I've even managed to get a job at my local clothes shop. It's not much money, but it isn't taxing either and at the moment I still need all my strength just to keep myself together. I'm getting stronger emotionally and physically, but it's still an effort a lot of the time. I feel a bit like a shattered teapot that's been stuck back together and looks fine but leaks when you try to use it. At least I have managed to patch myself up somehow though, and maybe one day some of those leaks will be dammed too.

Thursday 13

Just back from seeing Marsha. It's an exhausting trip, even though I stay overnight in a B&B, and really I should consider just finding a local therapist but...I trust Marsha and the thought of starting all over again with someone else is more than I can bear. Marsha keeps me sane.

As soon as I kick my shoes off and settle cross-legged onto the wide, comfy armchair, I start talking. And God it feels good to be able to say anything I want and know I won't be judged.

Today I finally confessed my two deepest, darkest secrets to her, the first being my jealousy of Miss E, my doppelganger victim who has now had Daryl's baby. Marsha listened patiently as I finally talked my way round to realising that I'm not a bitch for feeling that way. That I'm not some sicko who is jealous of what happened to her; I'm not even envious that the child is Daryl's. I simply long for a child, and am a little jealous of every woman who has one.

'It just seems more pronounced with Miss E because of the complexity and strength of emotions involved with all your memories of that time. That and the fact that she looks like you,' Marsha explained. I nodded; that made sense.

I told her about how sometimes I want to die and that I get through it by saying 'I can always kill myself tomorrow.' Her reply surprised me.

'That's actually a really good coping mechanism,' she said. 'You're not telling yourself you can't do it, which you're obviously not strong enough to do at the moment, but you're also not giving in to the feeling. You're simply telling yourself that you can't do it today. Good idea.'

Wow, and I'd thought she'd think I'd need institutionalising or something. I'd been so scared of confessing that to her.

But she also took the time to point out that apparently if I take all my sleeping tablets they won't kill me, just make me sleep for a really, really long time. Good job I never took them then, it would have been a right disappointment...

There's no miracle cure for my problems though. The counselling helps but I still constantly have trouble sleeping, still feel terrible, still drive myself mad with questions. All I can do though is keep my head down and plough through this, hoping that one day I might just feel normal again.

INVISIBLE

Monday 16

My emotions are like the ebb and flow of the tide. Sometimes I'm still so lost and angry and confused and hurt and…everything else negative that the world can chuck at me. It's hard, so hard, not to fall apart again then. Not to pull the duvet over my head and scream: 'I give up world!' Not to let myself be washed away by wave after wave of overwhelming feelings.

But there are also times when I'm together and fine. Fine-ish. There was a time when the bad days happened far more frequently than the good days. I think now the balance is tipping though. It's an even split probably currently. Hopefully it will eventually be more good than bad…. Although sometimes I worry that I'm broken for all time now.

Tuesday 17

As the counselling works its magic, I find I'm able to think clearly away from it too. Like, today I had a revelation…

Why did I hang on so hard to a marriage I hadn't even been happy with, one I'd been considering walking out on before the arrest? It's something I've asked myself again and again, and today I came up with an answer of sorts: it's a bit like being mugged.

Okay, here's my logic for that… When you're mugged, logically you know that your handbag is relatively worthless and its contents can easily be replaced, and so the right course of action is to let it go. Yet instinctively many people hold on. Clutch it tighter against them and pull for all they're worth, trying to keep hold of a £30 piece of pleather that contains a cheap phone and some even cheaper make up. Someone's trying to take it from them and so they'll do whatever it takes to stop that thief.

That was me with my marriage, I think. Logic said I should have walked away, but when the going got tough and he was arrested, and it felt like someone was trying to tear us apart, I instinctively clung to it instead, telling myself everything would be fine in the end. Idiot.

Saturday 21
Today was Kim and Peter's wedding. I'm lying in a hotel room, exhausted but happy. It was uplifting to be surrounded by so much joy.
It has though, stirred up a lot of old feelings and memories. As Kim and Peter exchanged vows I kept thinking of my own wedding day. I had so many hopes and dreams, and truly believed that that day was the start of them all coming true…
Theirs was a very small affair, but wonderful, and the looks on their faces as they exchange vows at the register office… It was exactly how two people in love should look at one another; as if no one else in the world exists but them and their happiness. They glowed.
Kim looked like a model in her cream, 1950s-style dress. When she threw her little posy of purple flowers though, I didn't bother joining the rush to try and catch it.
They'd asked me to do a reading too, but I gently refused. 'It makes my stomach squirm just thinking about standing in front of people and speaking,' I'd explained. 'And what if someone realises who I am? I want the day to be about you two, not about me and my dramas.'
'None of our friends or family would ever say anything bad to you,' Peter had said, and Kim had nodded fiercely, tears making her eyes sparkle.

'I know; I know they must be lovely people to be anything to do with you two, but...' Finally they'd accepted my decision.

To be honest I'd been in two minds about even attending the wedding, but I'm so glad I did. Kim has been my rock through all of this; I don't know what I'd do without her. And in taking on his role as Kim's protector and guardian angel, Peter seems to have adopted me too. She's got a good man there. Funny to think they wouldn't be together if it hadn't been for Daryl's crimes.

After the ceremony and photos (during which I smiled nervously and tried to hide behind other people) everyone nipped across the road to the pub where the small reception was being held. A gorgeous meal and all kinds of speeches later, I took a tiny sip of champagne to toast the bride and groom – my first taste of alcohol in a very long time. It seemed wonderfully fitting though that it should be such a celebratory drink.

Soon it was time for the obligatory disco. It was fun, actually. In the darkness that was only lifted by the rolling blue, green and red flashing lights, I even had a little dance. Then I sneaked away while no one was looking, trying to stay invisible so I could make my escape.

Now I'm in my hotel room and I'm having a little cry. Not a huge self-pitying sob-fest, just a scattering of tears because I'm so happy for Kim and the wonderful life she has ahead of her.

OCTOBER

Thursday 3
Since Kim and Peter's wedding I've been struggling with something. In the end I confessed all to Marsha, needing to know how to handle it, and if I was going completely insane.
'I keep thinking about the good times with Daryl,' I admitted guiltily. 'I used to hate thinking about those times, they made me feel sick – they still do, very much so, at one level, when I think about the terrible things he might have done first, to be in a good mood...'
I swallowed, eyes darting round the room as if trying to escape the words I was about to say.
'...But I'm so lonely that sometimes I...' I stopped, reluctant to go further.
'This sounds like a big confession,' probed Marsha gently. 'Something you don't even like admitting to yourself.'
I shook my head quickly to confirm she was right. She continued. 'Okay, think of it this way: if you don't recognise it and accept it, you won't be able to take the next step, which is to stop it.'
Ooh, clever. I thought about it for a few more moments, while Marsha waited patiently, and then ploughed on.
'Sometimes I miss Daryl so much it hurts. Physically hurts. It's weak, I know, and maybe that's why he was with me, because I'm weak and pathetic and being with me made him feel powerful in the same way that raping those women made him feel powerful. Maybe with me it was emotional

rape. I know our relationship was screwed up, abnormal. And I'm trying to come to terms with that,' I gabbled. 'But you're right, maybe part of that is acknowledging my 'addiction' like they do at Alcoholics Anonymous. My name is so and so and I'm a bastard-aholic.'

Marsha nodded. 'This is just another part of the grieving process, of letting go.' It is? Great, because I really want the letting go bit, and this harking back to 'the good old days' is worrying and confusing the hell out of me.

'You loved him,' she said simply. I did. I hate to admit it now, it feels dirty and wrong, but I did. 'You haven't allowed yourself to acknowledge that or say goodbye to him properly because you feel repelled when you think of him. But you have to allow yourself to say goodbye to the man you thought he was; the one you loved. Otherwise you'll never be free. Think of it this way: it's as if the man you loved died.'

'I wish he had died. It would be so much easier then,' I nodded.

I drew my knees up in front of me and hugged them, pushing myself further into the squidgy back of the large armchair. Turned and stared out of the window as I spoke, unable to meet Marsha's eye.

'The thing is, it's like there are two different people when I think of Daryl now. When we were together all I saw was my amazing husband, who had some control and anger issues, which I swept under the carpet. Then when I realised the monster he really was, that was all I could see; the Port Pervert. Now though...now sometimes I find myself wanting him back...

'No,' I corrected quickly, 'not wanting him back as such... Ah, it's so hard to explain...' I sighed, still staring out across the lawn. 'I don't want him back, not the reality of him. I want the fantasy. I want to go back to feeling loved and having a normal, boring life with a normal, boring bloke.'

Another deep sigh that made my whole body shudder. 'Then I get annoyed with myself, because it's like saying I want the Port Pervert to be my husband, and I honestly, truly don't want that. I don't want mardy, controlling, murderous Daryl back, I want… This doesn't make any sense, does it…?'

'It does. You have to acknowledge the man you thought existed, acknowledge the love you had for him, then you can finally start the process of letting go and moving on from him. You've reached a really big moment in your healing process.'

'Really, because it feels like I'm going backwards…'

'You're not. Trust me.'

'It's just easier to think of him as a monster than a man,' I said, finally turning my head to face Marsha. 'Because if I think of him as a person then I wonder why he became the way he did. I even start wondering stupid things like, well, maybe he did really love me. Is someone like that truly capable of love? I doubt it, yet he fooled me for so long. I don't know. I don't know him. I'm not even sure I know me any more.'

I hugged my knees tighter then let them go. 'I suppose I just thought that once I'd confronted him and symbolically won his stupid power game, that would be it. I'd be free from him, you know? That's how it always is in films: there's a big confrontation scene, and then the winner instantly gets to walk away and live happily ever after, all their problems solved.'

The light shifted across Marsha's glasses momentarily as she adjusted them on her face. She took a moment then replied.

INVISIBLE

'What do you think you have to do to get your happy ending then?'

God knows. But finally, we thrashed out a way for me to face my feelings. I'm going to write a letter to Daryl, one that will never be sent, of course; and hopefully I'll pour all my feelings out and leave them on the page.

Friday 4

So, here's the letter I have written not to the monster, not the Port Pervert, but instead to the fantasy man (who did on occasion truly exist) that was my husband. I'm sort of surprised by the tone of it; it almost felt like it wrote itself.

Dear Daryl

I know I'll never send this letter – and I wouldn't want to – and for that reason I know I can put down all kinds of things I'd never admit to your face.

I miss you. I really do. Insane, isn't it? It's been almost seven months now since I found out the truth at the trial. My life had changed utterly. Aside from the obvious, I've a new car – the cauliflower car had been beaten up one too many times; a new flat, and lots of new furniture. You'd be blown away by the way I've started a new life – I can see your face now. You'd come inside the flat and be so proud of what I've achieved.

'Wow, my babe did all this on her own?!' you'd gasp. And you'd give me a big hug. Your face all lit up, and your head thrown back with laughter. You wouldn't have chosen the colours yourself – the dark red in the bedroom, and the knobs painted yellow in the kitchen especially – but you'd be so impressed. Your approval always meant the world to me. It still does. Just imagining your reaction makes me smile and feel better. But you'd tut at the red paint splashes on the carpet!

I'm not writing this to have a go at you. I've tried to be angry - and sometimes I still am – but on the whole I'm not very good at

it. It just eats away and grows and ends up making me feel worse. So instead I'm taking a different tack...
I forgive you.
Not for what you did to others, that isn't my place. This is about me and you only. I forgive you for what you did to me.
It's hard. But I'd rather let it go and forgive you, because it's better for both of us. Being angry and bitter will kill me. And won't make any difference to you at all because you can't see it or feel it. But love and forgiveness are far more powerful emotions. They will heal me.
Perhaps on some deep, cosmic level you'll feel that love and forgiveness and it will help effect your actions in the future and the way you feel about yourself. I think your low self-esteem has an awful lot to do with your actions — ironic as most people think only someone with a vast ego could do what you did. You're all front though, that's why you need to 'prove' yourself by overpowering others. Emotionally, physically...
Perhaps you really did love me, and in some way you were fighting against that badness in you and that's why you didn't hurt me like the other women. Well, that makes as much sense as anything else...that is to say, no explanation will ever really make sense to me. It's all insane.
There's a distinct possibility that I'm just kidding myself, but what's the harm? You've already inflicted all the damage you could on me and others; there's nothing left for you to do. That's why I have to accept the way I feel, embrace it, then open my arms up again and let it drift away. I do this not for you, but for me, so that one day, a day that grows closer all the time, I'll be free completely.
Sometimes I imagine you coming round. When I'm walking home at night I imagine you're waiting outside for me, standing by the wall, one arm up on the pillar, one leg resting up on a step, looking

all confident and at ease. But you never are. And then I have to remind myself of where you really are, and why.

I still ache for you, Daryl. I still long to put my head in that funny hollow in your chest that seems made for my head, and I can almost feel you breathing on my head — you know that funny habit you've got, like you're trying to heat up the top of my head? Feel your arms wrap all the way round me. Sometimes, to help me go to sleep at night, I pretend you're spooned up behind me. We fitted together so perfectly.

But I'm not daft, I know we were far from happy together. That we argued, snapped, sniped. That you were selfish, controlling, manipulative… I often wonder what there is to love about someone with so few loveable traits. Don't know. But I managed it anyway…until I discovered your absolute true nature.

So again I say, I forgive you. With that, I give myself the gift of a blank piece of paper on which to write my life. A true fresh start free from emotional baggage.

Goodbye.

Thursday 10

As soon as I'd settled, cross-legged in the chair and made myself comfy for my counselling session, Marsha asked if I'd written the letter. I smiled, feeling relaxed.

'I did, and it's really helped,' I nodded. 'I'm feeling much more at ease somehow.'

Saturday 12

Kim has come to stay for the weekend. As soon as she arrived though I noticed she seemed edgy and uptight, as though she had something to tell me but was dreading it.

I poured a glass of wine for each of us, feeling confident that I could handle a small glass without it triggering a meltdown.

'Everything okay?' I checked as I handed over her goblet. 'Something you want to tell me?'
She bought herself some time by taking a sip. 'You know me too well,' she said, face halfway between a smile and grimace. 'Well…it's really exciting, but it's also really sad…'
Hmm, well that ruled pregnancy out then. What on earth could it be, I wondered.
'Peter, Henry and I are…we're moving to Australia!' she announced apologetically.
That I hadn't expected. Now it was my turn to take a gulp of wine as I tried to rearrange my face into surprised delight. I think I managed it. Then I laughed, the news sinking in and genuine pleasure replacing the fake act.
'Bloody hell! This is huge…it's massive…' I said slowly, shaking my head. 'But it's also a brilliant opportunity. So…how come? When did all this happen? When are you leaving?'
'One question at a time!' she laughed, clearly relieved by my reaction.
Peter had apparently decided to emigrate and had put in the paperwork before he and Kim had even met. When they'd got together they'd found themselves talking about it more and more and decided to go for it together, but hadn't wanted to say anything until it was sorted. They figured that that way, if their application wasn't successful it didn't matter.
'But it was successful, and Peter's got a fantastic job lined up in Sydney. He's got an aunt and uncle, and some cousins over there too, so we'll know people when we arrive,' Kim explained, flushed with excitement. 'The only problem is leaving you. I'll miss you so much!'

'I'll miss you too, believe me,' I replied, pulling a pained face. 'Think of the lifestyle you'll have over there though, enjoying the great outdoors in all that lovely sunshine. It'll be wonderful for Henry.'

'He can't wait,' she smiled shyly.

I'm so pleased for her. I'll miss her like crazy though, she's my best friend, and has kept me going through the worst time of my life. I'll never forget what she's done for me.

DECEMBER

Saturday 16
Last night I had a dream. I was in the arms of a man who gently ran a finger along my jaw then said: 'I love you.' Then I woke up. I'd forgotten how transforming the human touch can be, how warming and floaty it is to know someone loves you. Even though it was only a dream, it felt so real that I was in a good mood for the rest of the day.
Sad isn't it? But I don't care. It made a nice change, and now I'm starting to wonder…could I one day have that feeling for real? It's as though somehow the dream has melted part of me. I feel…excited almost about the possibility of a future at some point.

Friday 22
Kim and Peter came over for the last time tonight before they jet off to their new life in Oz. I can hear them in the living room, whispering excitedly to one another as they lie on the pull out sofa bed. They're like a couple of kids. As for Henry, he can't sleep at all either and instead has spent the evening bouncing round the room as if he's eaten way too much sugar and E numbers.
'I'm a bit worried he thinks the streets are paved with sweeties or something, he's looking forward to Sydney so much,' Kim confessed with a laugh earlier.
They've got their proper leaving do tomorrow, so it's a real flying visit, but I'm just grateful they made the effort to

come and see me – especially as I had decided not to go to their official drinks.

'Too many people...' I'd explained apologetically, wrinkling my nose.

They'd accepted it, because they know I never go out. The thought makes me nervous, I'm scared someone will recognise me, and then there is the thought of getting home...I know it's stupid but I worry a lot about bumping into someone like Daryl.

Peter and Kim though accept me for who I am, no questions, and it's one of the many things I love about them. I can't imagine them not being here for me, especially Kim.

Tonight though, she did at one point put her hands on my shoulders and given me a stern look. 'I understand why you won't come to our drinks, but you know at some point you're going to have to stop apologising for your existence and really join the world again. Hell, maybe even have some fun.'

'Fun?' I gasped in mock horror, my eyebrows shooting up. 'Never heard of it.'

But as I lie in bed, hearing the gentle rustle of their excited conversation, I think maybe she has a point. It's taken me a long time to pull myself out of the quagmire of misery and reach a point of neutrality in my life, and I'm loving the peace of it. Perhaps though, there is more I can expect than simple steadiness. Perhaps I should take a look at how to be, dare I say it, happy.

Perhaps that should be my new year's resolution.

JANUARY

Thursday 11
I marched into the counselling session as usual and settled down for a good chat. Marsha looked at me and smiled.
'I love the way you walk into the room all confident, kick off your shoes, and make yourself comfortable,' she said. 'They are the actions of someone who is really at ease with themselves. And you've done it since the very first time you've come here.'
I have? I thought about it and nodded. 'Yes, yes, I suppose I have,' I laughed, not quite sure of the point she was making.
She leaned her arm on the left armrest of her chair and surveyed me for a moment. 'You're happy, relaxed and at ease with yourself. Really, you always have been. I think our work here is done…unless you can think of anything else we need to cover.'
Flummoxed, I opened my mouth to argue but couldn't think of a single reason why I should continue seeing her.
'You really think I'm ready? That I'm okay, I'm not crazy and I'm not going to fall apart?' I checked.
'You're as sane and fixed as the next person,' she said with a smile.
'Blimey, that's a scary thought for everyone else out there,' I joked. Then suddenly became serious. 'I'm still driving myself mad with "why"; why did Daryl do those things.'
'But you have coping mechanisms in place now,' Marsha replied.

'Yes, I've found a way of blocking it now, when the thoughts whirl around my head like a tornado threatening to uproot my sanity and smash it on the ground,' I nodded, mock-philosophically.

'Sometimes there is no "why"' that's what I tell myself. Now I'm aware that it's simplistic, maybe even a bit trite. But frankly I don't give a toss because it's helping keep the madness at bay.

Sometimes there is no 'why'. What I mean by that really is that I'll never get it. I'll never understand. Even if Daryl were ever to sit me down and explain his thought process and feelings in mind-numbing detail I still wouldn't comprehend why because I'm, well, normal for want of a better word. And he isn't, he's got something in him that's broken, something that stops him being like other people.

Maybe he was born with it, maybe it got broken at some point in his life, but I think it was too late for him by the time he met me. I couldn't have fixed him even if I'd realised he needed fixing.

So yes, back to the why (it's always back to that). I'll never understand it even if I'm told it, because what explanation can there be for hunting women down, raping them, even killing them. What could he tell me that will then make me have a light bulb moment where I think: 'Oh yeah, that makes sense. I can totally see it from his point of view now.'

There may be reasons for it – maybe he was abused him or something, I don't know – but there are no excuses for it. So when the whirling 'why' comes along and threatens to take control of me, that's my new mantra. Sometimes, there is no 'why'.

I've taken another massive step towards freedom. I feel…tranquil.

Sunday 28

One of the few things I decided to keep when I left the house was my diaries. It might seem like an odd decision; I'm sure most people wouldn't want to revisit a terrible past like mine. Me neither, really. But avoiding it won't change the fact it's happened, and maybe I can learn some lessons from sometimes reading entries from when I lived in a fool's world of denial and blindness. I've had to forgive him so that I can move on, and it's worked a treat…but forgiving is not the same as forgetting. I will never allow myself to be that person again.

This excerpt from five years ago is a prime example. We'd had some kind of row and I was tying myself up in knots about it.

I'm struggling not to text Daryl. Wondered about 'Are you ready to talk yet?' That's quite neutral. Shows the door's open, that I'm willing to forgive him his tantrum if he apologises.

I hate being in limbo like this, I can't stand it when he disappears off the face of the earth just to punish me. What if this time he doesn't come back? Decides he's had enough of the rows and wants a fresh start. After all, sometimes he says 'having a relationship shouldn't be this hard.' I can't imagine my life without him.

But if that's what's going to happen then he needs to tell me, not keep me dangling. I'm a 'rip the plaster off' kind of girl – if something's got to be done and is going to hurt, just get on with it, because prolonging it will only make it worse. I'd rather be told the no holds barred, no shit truth than be messed around and left dangling. And he knows it. Which is why he does it…

In the end of course, I had made Daryl a grovelling apology. It makes me sad to think of that young woman being played; allowing herself to be played. But it also makes me happy, oddly, because I know now that I can spot a manipulator from a mile away, and I am stronger than that woman ever was.

At the start of the diary I was keeping the year of the arrest, when life started to cave in, I wrote something quite profound. *If you're not happy with something, change it; if it won't change, get rid of it.*

When I wrote it I'd claimed I was going to try to live my life by that line. I wish I had, it might have saved me a little heartache...but hindsight is a wonderful thing, and all I can do about the past is vow to learn from it. So now I'm taking that piece of wisdom from two years ago and this time I WILL live my life that way.

I'll do it on my own too. I've realised I rely on others too much. Growing up, all I wanted to do was keep my parents happy because they are so lovely; when I became a teenager I became friends with Hannah and I did my best to keep up with her, following her around like a puppy, taking her lead; then came Daryl, who controlled me completely, manipulating me so blatantly, yet it never occurred to me to mind, not really. Even after him, I relied on Kim so much, leaning on her instead of standing on my own two feet.

Now I'm learning how to live for me and no one else, and to keep myself going rather than hand that responsibility over to others.

I am not helpless. I just act like I am.

That's not to say I asked for what happened to me. Good grief, how could anyone ask for that? A whole lifetime of lies and horrific revelations... But I have to take responsibility for my part in it. Not for the attacks because only with hindsight can I see now what was going on there, but for what I allowed Daryl to do to me.

I knew something was wrong in my marriage and I said nothing. I was unhappy and I did nothing to change it. I realised I was being lied to and my strings pulled by a master puppeteer, yet I told myself it was all in my head because that was easier than facing reality. I told myself it was my fault and desperately tried to change my own behaviour, instead of confronting Daryl for his failings.

I will never accept behaviour like that again. I have to draw a line in the sand right here and now and say 'no more'. I refuse to accept crappy friends like Hannah (who I now realise I never actually liked much, so what the hell was I doing trying to please her and make her like me?!). I refuse to be in a relationship that makes me contort everything that is me in order to make it work. I have to have the confidence to say to people: 'this is me, like it or lump it', instead of doing whatever it takes to be liked by people who aren't actually likeable themselves.

I never do that, incidentally. I've realised I've never decided in the past whether or not I like someone, instead I worry about making them like me. Ridiculous. No more making myself invisible to help others.

No more feeling guilty, either, for my own suffering. I know what I've been through can never compare with Daryl's victims' traumas, but it isn't a suffering contest - if it were, they'd win hands down. But I need to stop comparing myself, finding myself lacking, and apologising for my existence,

Finally, I'm starting to immerge, I think. I'm finding myself. I won't be invisible any more. I'll never let myself disappear again.

MARCH

Monday 5
As the shop is quietest on a Monday, I've taken today and tomorrow off to visit my parents. They seem happy in their new home too. At the time, I think they both felt like moving away was something that was being foisted on them, because of everything that had happened with Daryl. The silent phone calls had persisted, the odd threat, and in the end they, like me, had recognised the need for a fresh start.
It's the best thing they've ever done. It's given Mum an excuse to buy all kinds of new knick knacks, rugs, cushion covers, and so on, while Dad has stoically agreed to everything she's requested because, bless him, all he really wants is for her to be happy again.
She's definitely that. To hear her talking, the old house was a real dump (it wasn't, it was lovely) and had all sorts wrong with it. 'Oooh, the oven was in totally the wrong place', 'the stairs were so steep, they hurt my knees, and so awkward if you wanted to take any furniture up and down them', 'there was a terrible draught coming from somewhere if you sat in the wrong place in the lounge', and so on...
Luckily, the new place seems to have no such problems. Well, for starters it's a bungalow, so she definitely can't complain about the stairs. She's barely recognisable as the avenging angel who kicked a bed apart in anger; so typical of her though that she didn't get that angry for herself, only for me. That's how we are in this family though; we love with all our hearts and always put the other person first.

Now though, my fierce protector has been replaced by my good old mum again, never happier than discussing which curtains would best suit the conservatory. Although there was one interesting little result of Mum getting in touch with her anger – before she moved she told her grumpy neighbour, who was always complaining about leaves from Mum's hanging baskets blowing into his garden, that he really ought to get a life. Nice one, Mum! Seems neither of us is as scared of confrontation as we used to be.

Dad gazes at Mum with adoration as she talks about whether or not to have nets or muslin in the conservatory windows. Funny, I never used to notice how in love they still are; I never used to notice them as people somehow, I don't think. After everything we've been through together though we are more than simply daughter and parents, we are friends too.

Still, for all Dad loves her, too much soft furnishings talk will send him off to the garden, which he is passionate about. He spent ages today walking me round it, telling me in minute detail all his plans for the beds and borders; he has all the time in the world to perfect it now that he has retired.

Geraniums and buddleia here, fuchsia there, a vegetable plot to grow their own tomatoes, carrots, lettuce... As he talked a squirrel bounded quickly over the lawn to the big tree at the bottom of the garden, and suddenly I remembered that weird obsession I'd had before with the squirrel at their old place, longing for its simplicity of life. I've come a long way since then.

At the end of Dad's gardening monologue, I flung my arms round his neck and gave him a big hug. 'Love you,' I said into his neck.

INVISIBLE

I could feel him smiling as he hugged me back and patted me awkwardly.

'Love you too. What's brought this on?' he laughed.

'I'm just happy,' I replied.

I'm just happy.

APRIL

Sunday 8

Argh! I'm so bloody nervous! Tomorrow I start my diploma course to train as a legal secretary. What the hell am I doing? What if I can't hack it?

Oh, sod it, I've tackled worse things than this and got through it. That's one good thing about what's happened to me; I feel like I can tackle anything now, because I know I am far stronger than I think.

This is it, the start of an exciting new future for me. I'd had the idea growing for a while, and had wound up having a chat to Peter about retraining and launching myself into a proper career. He'd thought I'd be great at it, after all I'm organised, can type, and well, I have a knowledge of how barristers and the legal system work, thanks to my past. Might as well put it to good use!

Peter's even put in a good word for me at a friend's firm of solicitors, so I've got a job lined up while I train that could turn into something even better once I've got my qualification. Who knows, I might even progress to become a solicitor myself at some point.

Get me, making exciting plans for the future! Not bad for someone whose husband consistently called her an air head...

Mum and Dad are really proud of me too. Mum reckons legal secretary sounds so much more impressive than my old job – and she's right. She called me earlier to wish me

good luck for tomorrow, and as soon as I'd put the phone down it rang again. This time it was Kim.
'Good luck! We're thinking of you!' she sang.
'Thanks! I need all the luck I can get!' I laughed.
'You should have more faith in yourself,' tutted Kim. 'That man destroyed all your confidence…'
There was a time when just that mention of Daryl would have made my blood pressure soar and my shoulders shoot up to under my ears. Instead I just brushed the comment away with a 'well, I'm fine now.'
I really feel like Daryl's old news now though. Which is great. Believe me, I know how lucky I am to be able to say that because I'm sure it will take his rape victims a lot longer to feel like that. Will they ever?
But as for me, I think I've come a long way. I've shied away from the memories, then finally forced myself to examine exactly the depth of the pain, betrayal, hopelessness. To revisit the world of lies he built around us.
Now though, I've stepped away from it. I've done what I hadn't truly thought was possible: I've moved on. Will I sometimes still think of what happened and get upset, and be influenced by it? Maybe. I've learned never to say never. No one can second guess the future – after all, I thought I had a future that was all mapped out but it was built on nothing at all.
So now I take one day at a time, and tomorrow is looking pretty darn exciting.
'Anyway, how are you doing?' I asked Kim, taking the subject away from me.
'Oh, I'm fine! Peter's at work and Henry's just playing around in the pool. And…guess what? I'm pregnant!'
I screamed down the phone then, probably bursting her eardrums, but that's okay because she joined right in and burst mine back! After that we chatted animatedly about

why tiny socks are so cute, whether she felt like she was having a boy or a girl (girl, but she changes her mind daily), how excited Henry and Peter were… She promised to email me her scan picture too; she'd had it done that day, and had been desperate to tell me her news now she knew the pregnancy was going well.

'Come and visit soon,' she begged as we said our goodbyes. 'I know you're really busy now being high-powered…'

'Yeah, right!' I laughed.

'…But visit soon!' she finished.

Hmm, maybe I will.

DECEMBER

Sunday 9

Noon - Well here I am at the start of a trip of a lifetime. Going to Australia, to visit Kim, Peter, Henry and their new addition, little Eve. I've never been on a trip like this – in fact I've never gone anywhere alone, so I'm drinking it all in and making the most of every moment.

I'm currently sat next to a woman who has been filing her nails for 45 mins. I'm amazed she's got anything left. Eventually, by the time we reach Singapore to re-fuel, presumably all that will be left will be bloody stumps.

How bizarre, the Captain's just made an announcement. No sleeping on the floor is allowed. Who on earth would?!

The file's still out…

Anyway, I booked this holiday in November as soon as Eve was born, and it felt like it would never arrive, but suddenly here I am, flying for 24 hours solid, on my own, to Sydney. Boy, am I looking forward to this holiday. It's my first since the Daryl incident (as I now call it. Well, God knows it needed some kind of shorthand title and nothing was going to do it justice) and I reckon I really deserve it after everything.

Funny, people think it's brave of me to get on a flight alone and fly to Oz, but I don't feel it. All I'm doing is getting on a plane one end and getting off at the other, where Kim is meeting me. It's a picnic compared to everything else that's happened to me.

This holiday isn't the only good bit of news I've had lately. My training is going really well, and my employers are so impressed with me that I'm already in line for a promotion.

Seems I'm a natural legal secretary! And last Friday I went out with some women from work and I met a guy called George; we're going to meet up, hopefully, when I get back in a month's time. That's helping with the old positivity!

He's not going to be The One, I know that. But he'll be a step towards finding The One. Time to dip my toe in the water again, but I'll be looking out for sharks. Of course, I worry that basically every man is a shark of some form or other, or that I've got truly bad taste in men and will somehow, in a room packed with hundreds of normal blokes manage to pick the only twisted, perverted weirdo in it…but I can't hide away from life forever. I won't let myself.

Seriously, does that woman have nails made of steel? Ooh, blimey, I think she's finally finished filing!

Anyway, I'm 34,000 feet up in the air and feel like I can see my future laid out below me. Maybe I'll train to be a solicitor, maybe I'll fall in love and have oodles of babies, maybe I'll even move to Oz myself, who can say. Whatever happens, life is just waiting for me to grab it, and from now on I'm only going to accept good things.

I'm free. Totally free.

EPILOGUE

WAKEFIELD PRISON

Tuesday
Every day is the same, a numbing grind of boredom divided by work, exercise time, and staring at the four walls of my little cell. At least I don't have to share with anyone, so it gives me plenty of time to think about everything.
My past. The mistakes I've made. How I'd put them right in a flash if I could go back in time. I can't of course, all I can do is learn from it, and my God have I.
Yes, I won't make the same mistakes again. I won't get caught.
The divorce came through today. Which means that fucking whore is out there somewhere celebrating, thinking that she has won. But that's okay, let her have her time of triumph, it'll make it all the sweeter when I show her how to really play the game.
I'm being a good boy, I'm never in trouble in here, and in twelve years I'll charm the parole board like I can always charm anyone I want to. Then I'll be free to go after that little bitch and make her pay for what she's done to me.
I win.

THE END

BARBARA COPPERTHWAITE

INVISIBLE

ACKNOWLEDGEMENTS

I OWE HUGE thanks to so many people for listening to me as I became increasingly caught up in the writing of this book, so apologies if I miss anyone out.

Firstly, I have to thank Paul Humphreys. Invisible may have happened eventually without him, but his support made it easier, faster, and far more pleasant! The difference he made can't be underestimated. What's more, he created the amazing book cover for me – talented, eh?

I was given great insight into how the police worked by Lindsay Baxter, who has also been a good and true friend to me. As if that weren't enough, she even introduced me to Richard Graham, a legal eagle who was so patient when replying to my many and varied random queries about court process, etc. Any factual innacuracies are my own, either through misunderstanding or for the sake of the story.

Thanks to my guinea pigs, who not only had to listen to me describing plots and plans in great detail (your patience and stellar friendship in not telling me to just shut up will be forever appreciated!) but also read the first draft of my novel and made positive, constructive comments. My wonderful mother, Eileen (a true inspiration!), my sister, Ellen, Jean Jollands (official nagger for constantly telling me to keep writing – thank you), Fiona Ford, Mary Hykel Hunt, and Kerry Harden: all take a bow, please.

I'm so very grateful to you all.

Printed in Great Britain
by Amazon.co.uk, Ltd.,
Marston Gate.